fresh powder

Susanne O'Leary was born in Stockholm, Sweden. After graduating from the French lyceé in Stockholm, she married an Irish diplomat. She has spent most of her adult life either on diplomatic postings with her husband or in Dublin. They now live in County Tipperary. Susanne trained as a fitness teacher and has published two books on health: *Look Great, Feel Great for Life* (Gill & Macmillan 1999) and *The Life in Your Years* (Gill & Macmillan 2000). Her first novel, *Diplomatic Incidents* (Blackstaff Press), was published in 2001; *European Affairs* (also Blackstaff Press) followed in 2003. *Fresh Powder* marks a further milestone in Susanne's writing career. www.susanne-oleary.com

FRESH POWDER

SUSANNE O'LEARY

NEW
ISLAND

Fresh Powder
First published 2006
by New Island
2 Brookside
Dundrum Road
Dublin 14

www.newisland.ie

isbn 1 904301 97 5

British Library Cataloguing in Publication Data.
A CIP catalogue record for this book is available
from the British Library.

Typeset by New Island
Cover design by New Island
Printed in the UK by Cox and Wyman

10 9 8 7 6 5 4 3 2 1

For Marianne

prologue

'Lucy?' Claire called as she walked into the hall of the small flat near the college campus. 'Lucy, are you there?' There was no reply. Then she remembered that Lucy was at her yoga class, or was it step aerobics? Something sweaty and tiring in any case. Claire took off her jacket and kicked off her boots, leaving both in a heap on the hall floor, and walked into the living room. It was empty, the sofa cushions plumped up, the magazines Claire had left strewn on the floor the night before stacked tidily on the leather trunk that served as a coffee table and the tea mugs cleared away into the tiny kitchen. She walked to the door of Lucy's bedroom and listened for a moment. There was not a sound but, just to make sure, Claire opened the door slightly and peered in. The room was deserted, the bed neatly made and Lucy's slippers side by side under it. Her notes were stacked in tidy piles on the small desk, a row of pens arranged with military precision beside them.

1

Claire knew that Lucy's few items of clothing hung in the wardrobe, colour coded, beautifully pressed and ironed. Like a bloody hospital, Claire thought. Her own room always looked as if she had just been broken into. She closed the door and walked back into the living room.

With a contented sigh she settled on the sofa, opened the small paper bag she had brought home and carefully took out a cinnamon Danish pastry. She took a big bite and closed her eyes as she chewed. Oh, yes, this was just what she needed, especially when the day had turned out so depressing which, combined with the dreary weather and Dublin traffic, would make even the most strong-willed fall off the wagon. Claire lay back, put up her feet, settled the paper bag on her stomach and put the bun on top. She felt under the sofa. Where was it? Had Lucy found it and tidied it away? No, there it was. Good. Claire pulled out the bulky novel she had been reading surreptitiously and opened it. This would be a welcome break from the heavy reading of her French literature course. She settled back and, eating the still-warm cinnamon Danish, was soon lost in the story.

As the hero carried the heroine into the bedroom, Claire became aware of a brooding presence in the living room. Still chewing, she looked up. Shit. Lucy.

'Hi,' Claire said and sat up guiltily, quickly stuffing the novel back under the sofa.

Lucy didn't return Claire's smile, but just stood there in the doorway, looking angry. Her red hair, usually pulled back in a tight knot, was coming undone and her face was pale. 'What are you doing?' she asked, her voice deceptively gentle.

'Nuffing,' Claire mumbled through her mouthful. 'Whaddayamean?'

'I don't mean eating a huge sticky bun, even though you're supposed to lose a stone by next Friday, so don't bother hiding it,' Lucy said, glaring at Claire. 'I don't give a shit about your weight.'

'What?' Claire swallowed so quickly she nearly choked.

'I mean, what are you doing with Gary?'

Claire dropped her Danish. 'Gary?'

'Yeah. Gary. Tall dark guy. Fourth-year Law student.'

'I know who he is.'

'Of course you do.' Lucy's tone was scathing. 'I mean you wouldn't be snogging a complete stranger in your car in the dead of night, now would you? You wouldn't do whatever you were doing in the back seat with someone you had just bumped into.'

'What?' Clare stammered, her face suddenly crimson. 'How …'

'How do I know, even though I was away for the weekend? Oh, a little bird told me. I had a very interesting conversation with someone who had nothing better to do than to peek into a car that was parked in the bushes behind the college bar.'

3

'Who?' Clare demanded.

'Marie-Terese Hannigan.'

'Oh shit.'

'Yeah.' Lucy walked into the room and stood hovering above Claire like a bird of prey ready to strike.

'The nosy bitch,' Claire said. 'When did this happen?'

'You know. It was last weekend.'

'No,' Claire said, 'I mean when did you find out?'

'Just now. Tonight.'

'At your yoga class?'

'I didn't go to yoga. Marie-Terese invited me for a drink. She said she had something very interesting to tell me.' Lucy paused. 'God, you're such a tart.'

'It was Gary's fault. I was drunk, and he …'

'– took advantage of poor innocent Claire? Rape, was it? Maybe you should report him to the police.' Lucy slowly shook her head. 'But I'm afraid that won't wash. No, not at all.'

'OK,' Claire said, recovering the half-eaten bun from the floor and wiping her fingers on her skirt. 'It was just a little fling. But so what? It's none of her business, or yours for that matter.'

Lucy glared at Claire, her green eyes like hard pebbles. 'Are you really that dim, or are you just pretending? You must have known that Gary and I … that we …'

'You what?' Claire sat up straighter. 'You went out with him twice about three months ago and

4

then said you didn't want to get serious. You said you would just be friends …'

'For now, yes. But I thought …' Lucy sank down on the chair by the sofa.

'– that he would live like a monk until you decided you were ready?' Claire asked. 'And when would that be? In a year's time when you had your degree? I don't think he really grasped what you meant. He seemed very much on the prowl and completely unaware that he was supposed to wear a chastity belt for the next year.'

'Men don't wear chastity belts.'

'Whatever.'

Lucy was silent. She sat there, looking at Claire as if she was struggling with her feelings. Then she sighed and shrugged. 'I suppose you're right. I should have known he wouldn't understand what I meant. He's not the kind who would be prepared to hang around until I felt ready to make a commitment.' She smiled bitterly.

'I don't think he could even spell "commitment",' Claire said, 'let alone know what it meant.' She looked at Lucy pleadingly. 'Ah, come on, Luce, let's forget about him. He's a sleazebag. Not worth fighting about.'

Lucy looked thoughtfully at Claire. 'Yeah. You're right. It doesn't matter now, in any case.'

'What do you mean?'

'I'm not really interested in him any more,' Lucy said. 'Or anyone else for that matter.'

'Then why did you behave as if I had broken

up the romance of the century?' Claire asked, puzzled by the sudden change in Lucy's voice.

'I just got so mad when I found out what you'd been up to, that's all. It was the principle of the thing, the idea that you would do a thing like that behind my back, can't you see that? It was a pretty rotten thing to do, you know.'

'For God's sake, will you listen to yourself,' Claire snapped. 'A pretty rotten thing,' she mimicked in a squeaky voice. 'Just because I had a bit of a snog with a guy you used to fancy. You can't have him so neither should anyone else? Is that it?'

'Well, no, but …'

'But what? Oh, shit, Lucy, will you get over it! And, OK, I'm sorry. Next time I'll apply for your permission in writing.' Claire drew breath.

'Yeah, right.'

'So, come on, tell me what's going on with you,' Claire urged, anxious to move on to something else. 'I know there's something on your mind. You're making that face.'

'What face?' Lucy asked, looking at Claire with an odd expression.

'That I've-decided-to-do-something-you'll-hate-but-it's-for-the-best face. Go on, spit it out. What is it this time?'

Lucy took a deep breath. 'I'm leaving.'

Claire stared at her. 'What?'

'I'm going to London.'

'I beg your pardon?' Claire shook her head and

laughed. 'Sorry, I thought you just said you were going to London.'

'I did. I am, I mean. Going to London.'

'For a holiday, you mean?'

'No. For good. Well, for a few years anyway.'

'What?' Claire knew she sounded stupid but she couldn't take it all in. 'Is it because of … Gary and me? I mean, have you just decided this right now?'

'No.' Lucy looked away, as if she didn't want to meet Claire's eyes. 'I've been thinking about this for a long time.'

'I don't understand. You have been thinking about what for a long time?'

'The situation.'

'What bloody situation?' Claire demanded.

There was a guarded look in Lucy's eyes as she looked at Claire again. 'It's not working.'

'What's not working?'

'Us.'

'Us? What's that suppose to –'

'Living here in this flat,' Lucy said. 'I can't stand it any more. You must have realised we don't really … we're not very compatible.'

'Well, yes,' Claire had to admit, 'it has been getting a little irritating, I have to say. I mean you're so bloody … I don't know … uptight. Yeah, that was the word I was looking for. And so bloody driven.'

'Uptight?' Lucy demanded. 'Driven? Well you're a lazy slob, if you must know. I'm fed up having to pick up after you. We're living here two years, and you haven't hoovered the living room once, or even done the washing up.'

'Oh, shut up,' Claire snapped. 'And here's another thing – you're such a prude. You watch me like a hawk, always complaining when I bring a guy home and we have a bit of a cuddle on the sofa.'

'I don't know what you mean.'

'You never know what I mean when you can't face the truth,' Claire remarked. 'It's always me who's in the wrong, isn't it? You think you're so perfect.'

'There you are, then,' Lucy said. 'We can't live together.'

Claire felt a stab of dread, like a cramp in the pit of her stomach. 'But …' she stammered, 'I mean we could work it out, couldn't we? We could talk about this and maybe come to some kind of agreement. We've known each other all these years. We've had rows before and always worked it out.' She looked pleadingly at Lucy. 'Ah, come on, Luce, you weren't really serious, were you?'

'Yes, I was. I am, I mean.' Lucy twisted her hands in her lap, as if trying to keep them from shaking. 'I've been dreading telling you but now, when there are only two weeks to go, I just …'

'Two weeks to go to what, exactly?' Claire demanded.

Lucy started to speak very fast, as if she was afraid she would lose her nerve if she didn't get it

8

off her chest at once. 'I'm going to do a degree in marketing. In London. I didn't tell you when I applied because I wasn't sure I'd be accepted, but then I was, so I went ahead and made all the arrangements. And last weekend, I went to London and put down a deposit on a flat. I'm leaving at the end of the month.' She drew breath and looked at Claire.

'What?' Claire shook her head, trying to clear her mind. 'Let's take it from the beginning. A degree in marketing? It's the middle of October now. You'll have a Commerce degree in less than a year. Are you going to throw away two years of hard work?'

'I have never felt really happy with Commerce,' Lucy explained, 'and I have been thinking of doing marketing for a long time, and maybe getting into advertising eventually.'

'What? But you have never told me any of this. I had no *idea* you had the remotest interest in marketing. And I thought we always discussed everything with each other.'

'I didn't think you'd approve. I thought you would think it was silly. But I've been talking to Maire-Terese about it, and she really understood. She thought it was a great idea.'

'She did, did she?' Claire suddenly felt very hurt. 'And you didn't bother to ask what I thought?'

'I didn't think you'd be interested.'

'What do you mean?' Claire protested. 'I

wouldn't be *interested*? I can't *believe* you didn't talk to me about such an important decision.'

'You would have tried to talk me out of it. And you wouldn't have wanted me to leave.'

'Well, no, but … Why can't you do marketing and advertising and whatever it was you wanted to do right here? In Dublin?'

'The best courses are in London and I would have a better chance of getting a job if I did this particular course. And then …'

'Yes?'

'After working in London, I might go abroad. New York, LA, who knows?'

'New York? LA?' Claire repeated, her head spinning. 'Jesus, Lucy, what is all this? And what am I going to do? I can't afford the rent on my own.'

'You'll get someone else to share this flat,' Lucy said. 'It's in such a great location, so close to college and everything, you'll have a new flatmate in no time at all.'

'No time at all,' Clare repeated bleakly. Lucy was right of course: accommodation was so scarce. She would have a new flatmate very soon. But that wasn't the point. Lucy was leaving and Claire didn't know if she could bear even the thought of saying goodbye. They had been inseparable since their very first day at school and she couldn't imagine an existence without Lucy.

'You might get someone from your own course,' Lucy said.

'Yeah but …' Something suddenly occurred to Claire. 'That flat in London – you said you made a deposit?'

Lucy looked slightly uncomfortable. 'Eh, yes, it was two months' rent in advance. And I also had to pay the university fee.'

'Can't have been cheap. Where did you get the money? Your mother? That must have made a big dent in her savings account.'

'Of course not. I couldn't ask my mother to give me all that money. No, I … I'm afraid I had to borrow from …' She paused, seeming oddly out of breath. 'Please, Claire, I had no choice. Don't get mad, but …'

'Oh no!' Claire exclaimed, appalled. 'Our money! Our waitressing money! You took the money we *slaved* for. We had nearly three thousand pounds. Oh, I can't believe it. Please tell me it isn't true.'

'It was my money too,' Lucy said. 'Half of it, anyway.'

'So you only took out half, then?' Claire asked.

Lucy looked down at her hands. 'No,' she muttered. 'I had to cash all of it. Well, nearly.'

'How much is there left?'

'Thirty-four pounds and fifteen pence.' Lucy looked pleadingly at Claire. 'I'll pay you back. I promise. As soon as I can.'

'But we were going to have that money for Paris,' Claire whispered. 'We were going to have such a great time when we graduated. Oh, Lucy …'

'You go,' Lucy said. 'Why can't you go to Paris anyway?'

'On my own? With thirty-four pounds and fifteen pence?' Claire laughed sardonically. 'My God, I'll really have a blast!'

'But, by then, I might have paid you back. If I send you something every month …'

'And that will take care of it, you think?' Claire's voice shook and her eyes filled with tears. 'It's not the money, don't you realise that? It's the fact that …' She stopped. 'Why didn't you talk to me about this? Don't you know I would have given you the money if you had only asked?'

'No, you wouldn't. You would have said I should stay and finish my degree.'

'OK, maybe I would, but …' Claire stopped, hurt replaced by anger, as she thought of the argument they had just had. 'You stormed in here just now, guns blazing, accusing me of stealing your boyfriend, of doing something *really* low, when what you did was a hundred times worse! I was supposed to be the bad guy, when …'

'I didn't mean to put it that way.'

'I don't give a shit what you meant,' Claire snapped. 'I suppose you thought it would be clever to attack me first, before you made your big announcement?'

'No, that's not what I …'

Claire didn't say anything. She leaned her head against the back of the sofa and stared at the ceiling, her face white. 'I can't believe it,' she whispered. 'I can't *believe* you did this.'

'I'm sorry,' Lucy whispered, 'but you have no idea how much I want to go to London.'

'God, yes,' Claire said bitterly. 'Enough to turn you into a liar and a thief.'

'Oh, Claire, please,' Lucy pleaded. 'Please, try to …' Her voice trailed away.

Silent tears rolled down Claire's cheeks but she made no effort to wipe them away.

'Claire?' Lucy said, her voice trembling with emotion. 'What can I do to make you forgive me? Please tell me how I can …'

'You can fuck off,' Claire mumbled, 'that's what you can do. Just fuck off and never come back. I don't ever want to see you again.'

1

Ten years later

It was hot, hotter than Lucy had imagined New York in April could be. It must be nearly a hundred degrees, she thought as she came out of the subway. Just my luck. Now I'll look flustered and sweaty at the interview. But, oh, please God, let me get this job. It's my last chance. I just have to succeed. She clutched her briefcase, straightened her skirt and walked into the building.

Lucy had been in New York for nearly a year, during which she had gone from one dead-end job to another, working in cocktail bars, hamburger joints and department stores while she looked for the perfect position, the first step on the ladder of a brilliant New York career. She had even spent three weeks as 'personal assistant' to the wife of a business tycoon, but had left when she realised she was no more than a glorified cleaning lady. She hadn't come to New York to wash cashmere sweaters by hand and run errands for some snooty bitch with a bad attitude. She was thirty-two and a professional woman, not an eighteen-year-old just out of school. If she didn't get a proper job soon she would have to go back to Ireland. This call from the agency had come in the nick of time.

She looked at the list of names on the big brass plate in the foyer. Then she found it: Freeman & Schwartz. Eighteenth floor.

There was only one other person in the lift, a tall man who glanced at her briefly as she pressed the button for her floor. Lucy darted a glance at him. He was good-looking, she thought, a man you'd notice in a crowd. She looked at him again as the lift started to rise. His looks were unusual: dark blond hair, cut-glass cheekbones and brown eyes. He seemed determined and powerful, not someone you would mess with. She stepped further away from him. He glanced at her with an amused little smile. Lucy looked straight ahead. Then, suddenly, the lift stopped.

'Oh God,' Lucy said in a small, frightened voice.

'I beg your pardon?'

'The lift. I mean, the elevator. It stopped.'

'Well yes. I noticed.'

'What are we going to do?' Lucy stared at him as if he had the power to make it start again.

'Not much *to* do. Except wait.'

'Wait?' Lucy's briefcase dropped out of her suddenly clammy hands on to the floor. She could feel beads of sweat break out on her forehead and her mouth was dry. She hated being locked into small spaces: it always made her panic.

'Oh no, I can't wait. I can't stay here. I'll be late. Please,' she begged, 'oh please get us out of here. I can't breathe.' She tried to prise the doors apart, nearly breaking her nails in the process. Then she kicked the doors. 'Shit!'

The man caught her by the shoulders. 'Calm down,' he ordered. 'Don't get hysterical. That won't help one little bit.' He spoke very slowly, as if she were a child. 'I'm going to press the alarm button,' he continued, 'and I'm sure someone will get us out of here very soon.' He pressed the button. 'There. Let's see what happens now.'

They waited more than ten minutes while Lucy continued to wring her hands and her unwilling companion tried to calm her down.

'Nothing is happening,' she whispered. 'I can't stand this much longer.'

'I'm beginning to agree with you,' the man said, taking a mobile phone from his pocket. He punched in a number. 'This is Patrick Delacy,' he barked. 'I'm stuck in a lift in this building … What do you think I want?' His voice was cold. 'I want to get out of here as fast as possible … Yes, that's right.' Delacy paused for a moment and glanced at Lucy. 'There is a young woman with me who is very late for an appointment,' he said into his phone. 'She has an appointment with … who?'

'The advertising agency,' Lucy said. 'Freeman & Schwartz. Job interview.'

'Freeman & Schwartz,' he repeated into the phone. 'Tell them Miss … what's your name?'

'Lucy Mulcahy.'

'Miss Lucy Mulcahy is a little late for her appointment and will be there as soon as possible.' He shoved the phone back in his pocket. 'Shouldn't be long now. My secretary will take care of it.'

'Your office is in this building?' Lucy asked, momentarily forgetting her panic.

'That's right. Nineteenth floor. Delacy, Delahunty and King.'

'Oh.'

'So, you're looking for a job with Al Freeman?'

'You know him?'

'Yes. I'm his lawyer. I recently represented him in a legal case. Got him half a million in compensation.'

'I see,' Lucy muttered. She liked him less and less. Full of himself, she thought, and picked up her briefcase, feeling sure the lift would start moving any minute. She was a little annoyed at herself for losing her cool. She would just breathe deeply and try to relax the way her yoga teacher had shown her. She took a deep breath. Then the lights went out. Lucy screamed. She screamed for a full minute, unable to stop.

Patrick Delacy grabbed her shoulders again. 'Stop it,' he ordered. 'Stop screaming at once, or I'll hit you. Come on. Take a deep breath.' Lucy tried to do as he said. 'Lean on me,' he ordered. 'It's going to be all right.'

But Lucy was still in a panic. 'No!' she shouted grabbing him by the lapels of his linen suit. 'This is the end. We're going to die!'

'We're not going to die, you little fool,' he snapped. 'The elevator has not moved since it stopped.' He started to stroke her hair. 'Try to calm down, now. I'm sure it's just a short circuit somewhere,' he said in a more gentle voice.

'You think so?' Lucy sobbed. 'Do you really think so?'

'Of course.'

The lift moved slightly, then stopped again. Lucy was gripped by a new wave of panic. She pressed her face against Patrick's chest and closed her eyes. 'Holy shit, this is it. We're going to die,' she whispered into his incredibly soft shirt. Patrick muttered something soothing and put a big warm hand on the back of her neck. 'There,' he murmured, 'there, there. Shhh …'

Suddenly, the lights came on and the lift started to move again. Lucy and Patrick froze, staring at each other as if in a daze. The lift kept going up.

'I think it's working,' Lucy said, stepping away from him, smoothing down her skirt.

'It seems to be, yes,' Patrick replied and straightened his jacket. He cleared his throat.

'We're nearly there,' Lucy said, picking up her briefcase.

The lift rose smoothly and came to a stop at the eighteenth floor. The doors slid open.

'Well, eh, this is where I …' Lucy started.

Patrick held the door with his hand, looking at her with a strange expression. 'Good luck,' he said.

'Thanks.' Lucy walked out of the lift and turned to look at him, but the doors were already closing. Feeling a little wobbly, she walked down the corridor toward the big double doors with 'Freeman & Schwartz' in large black letters. She stopped and stared at the name for a minute. The letters seemed to glow with a kind of supernatural force; powerful, forbidding and intimidating. Lucy's knees started to shake as she thought of the interview. Then she spotted a door with the word 'Restroom'. Great. The loo. I'll go in and touch up my make up. I must look a fright after … Oh God what a nightmare.

She walked through the restroom door into a shimmering glass and chrome interior, noticing with relief that she was alone. A white face, huge, frightened eyes and tousled hair met her gaze in the big mirror. Get a grip, she ordered herself. Don't blow this chance. She breathed deeply and tried to relax her shoulders while she pushed her shirt back into the waistband of her skirt. Feeling a little calmer, she smoothed back her hair and re-touched her lipstick. Look sharp, Lucy told herself, look professional and confident. She brushed a little blusher onto her pale cheeks while she continued to give herself a lecture. 'You *will* get this job,' she muttered, 'you will …'

*

The man was naked and very beautiful. Claire stood in the darkness admiring the straight shoulders, muscular chest and arms, flat stomach and rippling muscles of the thighs and calves. The rich red velvet curtain behind him and the soft light gave his skin a warm glow and his body a sensuous quality not normally associated with the male nude.

'*C'est beau, n'est-ce-pas?*'

Startled, Claire whipped around from the painting and stared at the man who had appeared out of the shadows. '*Eh, oui …*'

'Like, how you say … perfect? A little like Michel-Ange, I think.' His accent was so strong, Claire found it hard to grasp he had switched to speaking English. 'The light is good here in this *galerie*,' he continued. 'They know this … art … must have the soft *lumière*.'

'I know.' Claire nodded, her eyes still on the painting that glowed like a jewel on the white wall. 'That light makes it kind of magic,' she said in French.

'*Absolument.*' He turned to look at her again. 'You speak very good French for an English-woman.'

'And you speak terrible English for a Frenchman. And I'm not English.'

'No?' He smiled, his teeth white against the dark stubble on his chin.

'I'm Irish.'

'Oh? I've never met an Irish woman before. Only *des petites Anglaises.*'

Claire studied him more closely. He was tall, with a head of dark wavy hair. He was dressed in a leather jacket and tight jeans and smelled of French cigarettes and some kind of exotic aftershave. When he moved into the light of the next painting, she saw that he was very young.

'But I'm curious now,' he said. 'How come you speak such good French?'

'I have been in Paris for over four years,' Claire replied without thinking.

'You are a student, then? What do you study? And do you live alone? Near here?'

Claire suddenly felt irritated. 'What is this, some kind of interrogation? Are you with the police?' she snapped.

'No, of course not. Why are you so defensive?'

'How would you feel if a complete stranger started grilling you about your personal life?'

'If it was a very beautiful woman, I wouldn't mind at all.'

Claire felt her face turn red. She moved away from the painting. The young man followed. She tightened the belt of her trench coat and stepped sideways again, beginning to regret coming into the gallery this late in the evening. She had wanted to catch the exhibition before it ended and had just managed to get in after work. This sudden intrusion was ruining her enjoyment and preventing her from concentrating on the exhibition, she told herself.

'But I am disturbing you,' he said, echoing her thoughts. 'I have already seen the whole exhibition. I will leave you to look at the paintings alone.'

'Oh … Thank you.' Claire felt a tiny pang of disappointment.

'I will wait for you at the bistro on the corner, yes?'

'Oh, but … I don't know … I have to …' Claire didn't know what to say. A little voice whispered, don't do this, he might be dangerous. He might be a rapist, a murderer. And in any case, you promised yourself – no more picking up young men like this. You're old enough to know better.

'*A toute á l'heure.*' The stranger turned on his heel and walked out into the spring evening.

*

'Yes?' the receptionist said as Lucy approached the desk. 'What can I do for you?'

'I have an appointment … I mean I *had* an appointment with Mr Freeman. I'm Lucy Mulcahy. I'm sorry if I'm late, but …'

'Oh yes,' the girl replied, looking a lot more friendly. 'Lucy Mulcahy, that's right. Mr Delacy's secretary phoned just a minute ago explaining what happened. Mr Freeman is waiting for you in his office. You can go straight in.'

Lucy grasped her briefcase and nervously entered the huge oak-panelled office. A big man with black hair, seated in an enormous leather chair, was smoking a cigar and looking out the window. He swivelled around as Lucy came in, blew out a cloud of smoke and looked at her through narrowing dark eyes. 'Lucy Mulcahy?' he said.

'That's right.'

'Sit down, then. I can't talk to you if you cower by the door.' He indicated a chair opposite him.

Lucy sat. Freeman stared at her. 'So,' he finally said after a long silence, 'you're Lucy …'

'Mulcahy, yes.'

'Right. And you're looking for a job here?'

'That's right. I sent you my CV, I mean my résumé. And I brought a sample of some of the advertising campaigns I've been working on.' Lucy opened her briefcase, extracted a pile of papers and laid them before him on his huge desk. He glanced at the papers. 'Hmm,' he muttered. 'It said in your résumé you have a degree in marketing. That's good. And a diploma in design? OK. And these campaigns were … ?'

'In London. I worked there for a few years before I came to New York a year ago,' Lucy explained. 'I didn't manage to get a job in advertising here straight away, so I worked in a couple of restaurants, but that was quite good, because I got to know the city and I think it's not a bad experience actually, and …'

Al held up a hand to stop her nervous babbling, then pulled out a drawer and took something out of it. Lucy jumped as he threw it into her lap. She looked down. It was a sweet wrapped in gold paper.

'What do have to say about that then?' he demanded.

Lucy looked at the sweet. 'Well, thanks, but I don't really eat chocolate.'

'I don't want you to eat it – I want you to sell it. To them out there.' He jerked his thumb over his shoulder at the window behind him. 'To all of New York. All of America. The world. How would you do that?'

Lucy looked down at the sweet again, realising her answer would decide whether she got the job or not. She thought for a moment. 'Children,' she said.

'What?'

'I would target children. Aim an advertising campaign at children under seven. They are most receptive at that age. I would change the wrapper to something with the latest cartoon character. Then I would flood supermarkets with these sweets, try to have them displayed at checkouts and …' Lucy stopped, thinking she had blown it. What a terrible, clichéd idea, she thought, I might as well just … She started to get up.

'I get the picture,' Freeman interrupted. 'A really underhand and unprincipled campaign, I have to say.' He looked at her intently for a moment. 'You're hired,' he said.

*

Claire stood in the door of the small bistro and hesitated for just a moment before walking in. This is mad, she thought, and decided to walk right out again. But he had seen her and waved to her from his seat at a table near the bar. His smile was so wide and his eyes so warm that she simply sank down on the chair he pulled out.

'I'm a teacher,' she blurted out, as if to warn him she wasn't to be trifled with.

'I knew it,' he said, 'I just knew it.'

'Why?'

'Oh, you looked so prim in there, when you snapped at me. I felt like a little boy again.'

'Can't have been such a long time ago.'

'Maybe not. So, tell me, my dear *prof*, what is your name?'

'Claire,' she said. 'Claire Dillon.'

'Lovely name.'

'Thank you.'

'I ordered you a drink,' he said and pushed a glass toward her. 'Pastis.'

'Aren't you the little optimist,' Claire said, knocking back the pale grey liquid in one gulp.

2

My best frend by Emilie Marchand, Claire read. *She is called Anabel and lives next dor. She has red hair and lovely brown eyes and very long legs. She waits at the door when I come home and then we go for a wak. Then we have dinner togedder and she helps me wit my homework. Anabel is very kind and lisens to me when I am sad. She never says I'm silly if I cry and she lovs to play. She can run reely fast because she is grown up and not little like me. My daddy liks Anabel too and he says she is very bjottiful. I lov Anabel and she lovs me. She will always be my best frend.*

Claire put down the essay. What a strange neighbour, she thought idly. But Emilie would have to work harder on her spelling. Her writing was much better now, though. She had really improved since the beginning of the school year. It was nice to see that at least one of the children in her class was making an effort. But it was difficult to manage a class of thirty children of different nationalities, all from homes with different attitudes, cultures and traditions. Not to mention the parents. Dealing with them was at best difficult, at worst a nightmare, which was most of the time. She wondered what Emilie's parents were like. She had never met them, only spotted a young au pair girl picking Emilie up from school. Claire felt suddenly envious of people like that, who seemed to have everything without much effort. She sighed and looked out the window. It was raining again, a cold mean rain that seemed more like January than June. Early summer in Paris is not what it's cracked up to be, she thought, gathering up the essays. It was getting late and she had a staff meeting before she could go home. She would finish correcting later.

*

'What are you wearing?' Becky asked one Friday evening in June, as Lucy was coming out of the bathroom, a towel wrapped around her hair. Becky was one of Lucy's friends from London, who had been working in New York for over five years. She had invited Lucy to share her tiny flat and the exorbitant rent until something better turned up.

'I don't know,' Lucy replied. 'I'll have a look in my wardrobe later. I have to dry my hair and do my make-up and …' Lucy didn't want Becky's advice about what to wear tonight, even if she was PA to the fashion editor of *Glamour* magazine. Lucy was going to a working dinner at Al Freeman's apartment. 'It's the washing machine campaign,' he had said. 'I thought you had a few ideas?'

'Yes, I do. I was going to work on my presentation over the weekend.'

'Great. But I thought, if I could get a few of the best brains together, we could come up with something really sensational. We have to come up with a killer idea fast or the client will go to another firm. And this way, we can all pull together and thrash out the whole thing. There will be a lawyer as well to go through the contract. That way, we'll have the whole deal together much more quickly. I thought it might be a good idea for you to see how we work under pressure here.'

'I see.'

'OK. See you then. Eight o'clock Friday. My place.'

Work under pressure, Lucy said to herself. I thought that was what we were already doing. She had been working at the agency for three months and was still trying to get used to the fast pace and cut-throat edge of American advertising.

'Have a look at your clothes now,' Becky insisted. 'I want to see what you have.'

Lucy sighed. 'Oh, OK then. But remember,

it's not some kind of date.' A few minutes later, she came out of her bedroom with a selection of dresses.

'How about this?' she asked and held up a grey wool dress.

'Boring.'

'But it was very expensive. It's from a designer collection. I know it's a bit plain, but I can accessorise it.'

'With what? Rosary beads and sensible shoes?'

'Oh, all right. This one?' The navy long-sleeved dress with a white collar also got the thumbs-down from Becky.

'But it's a working dinner,' Lucy protested. 'I have to wear something businesslike. Look, this navy suit, wouldn't that be perfect?'

'Not to a dinner in Central Park West. That's a really posh address. Only rich people live there.'

'I don't think Al is exactly what you'd call rich,' Lucy remarked.

'No? What would you call him then? Just stunningly well-to-do? Maybe he had to really scratch to get those millions together.'

'I don't know. But I do know tonight is just work. Everyone else will be in a power suit.'

'How dull. I think this is a perfect opportunity to show off your assets. You never know who'll be there. You might catch yourself a really wealthy man. What is that at the bottom of the pile?'

'The black and white two-piece?'

'No, the black lace thing. Looks like a nightie.'

'Oh that. It's just something I bought by mistake. It's a Donna Karan dress from last year's collection. I was going to bring it back but they wouldn't take it because it was a sale item.'

'Show it to me,' Becky ordered.

Lucy held up an exquisite black lace dress. It had a short tight skirt and a low-necked bodice held up by thin straps, plunging to the waist at the back.

'Perfect.'

'But it does look like a nightie. I'll feel naked in it.'

'Haven't you followed the latest fashion news? Naked is so now. In fact,' Becky stated, 'naked is the new black. Go on, wear it. You'll look stunning. I bet all those New York bitches will be showing off all they've got.'

'Don't be silly. They are all professional women, just like me. Nobody is going to be remotely sexy. I'm wearing the navy suit.'

'At least put on a bra with a bit of lace underneath and undo the top button, just to show you're a woman,' Becky suggested. 'And high heels. A pair of fantastic legs are not a disadvantage on your way up the career ladder, are they?'

'It's a business meeting, not the Miss Universe contest,' Lucy said sternly.

'But men are men, wherever they are,' Becky said.

*

Claire walked up the dark street toward her apartment building. Even though it had stopped raining, it was still cold and windy. She was tired after a long day and the staff meeting had been very long-winded. She pulled the collar of her coat tighter around her neck. God, it was freezing. Would summer never arrive? It was getting dark and she had the uneasy feeling someone was following her. She looked over her shoulder but saw no one. The lights from the little bistro on the corner shone invitingly through the stained-glass windows. It looked so safe and cosy in there and there was a wonderful smell of something simmering in herbs, garlic and wine. Oh, I would love a glass of wine, a plate of beef stew and some fresh bread and cheese, Claire thought. Her stomach rumbled in reply. Why not? There was nobody waiting for her and there wasn't much in the fridge, as she hadn't had the time to stock up. She turned around, pushed the door open and stepped into the warm restaurant.

'Mademoiselle Claire!' The owner of the bistro beamed from behind the counter. 'How lovely to see you. Are you alone?'

'All alone tonight, Monsieur Renaud,' Claire replied with a smile. 'Is there a table free? I'm starving and I just couldn't resist the lovely smell.'

'Over here by the window,' M. Renaud replied and rushed over to a small table. He pulled out a chair. 'Please, sit down. I'll get you a menu.'

'No need.' Claire sighed happily and sank down on the chair. 'I know what I want. Some of your lovely paté, then a plate of that'– she sniffed – 'divine *Boeuf Bourguignon* and half a carafe of your house wine.'

'*Toute de suite, Mademoiselle.*'

Claire unbuttoned her coat and took off her scarf. She glanced out the window and saw a dark figure. She looked again. Could it be … ? Was someone really following her? But the window was all steamed up and she couldn't see clearly. No, it was impossible. Don't let your imagination run away with you, she ordered herself.

'*Voilà*,' Monsieur Renaud's voice interrupted her thoughts as he came back to her table with a plate of paté, a little basket of bread and the wine.

Claire sipped her wine and felt a little more relaxed. The bistro was her second home: a place to eat good simple food when she got tired of take-aways; someone to talk to, as Monsieur Renaud and his wife were very happy to do at any time of the day or night; and a window on the world, or in any case the street and the people who walked past. Funny how I never feel lonely in Paris, Claire thought as she tucked into the plate of paté and salad. It's as if I've lived here all my life. I mustn't begin to get nervous.

'*Ça vous a plu?*' Monsieur Renaud cleared away her plate and topped up her wine glass.

'It was delicious.'

*

'Al's place' was a penthouse apartment in a big, elegant building on Central Park West with not one, but two uniformed doormen who saluted as Lucy entered the lobby. The lift was bigger than Lucy's entire flat, and the apartment ... It was incredible. Amazing. Enormous. Beautiful. She was still trying to find the right words as she followed the maid down the endless corridors and vast rooms. She finally walked through the door to the living room where about a dozen people were standing at the huge picture window, drinking champagne and admiring the breath-taking view of Manhattan. The men were tall, the women slim and they all wore black. Lucy recognised a few people from the office, but the majority were unknown to her. She felt the navy suit was almost garish compared to the funereal garb of her fellow guests.

'Lucy!' Al walked across the floor. 'Wow! You look great! Doesn't she, honey?' he said over his shoulder as a slim woman, her blonde hair scraped back in a simple knot, walked in carrying a tray of canapés. 'My wife, Penny,' Al said.

'Hi, Lucy,' Penny said. Her black dress was the epitome of understatement and the single strand of perfect pearls around her elegant neck whispered class. 'You look lovely.' Her voice was slightly hoarse and her accent hinted of finishing school and horseback riding.

'Thanks,' Lucy replied. 'So do you. I mean ... It's nice to meet you.'

'Come and have a drink,' Penny said. 'And look at the view. It's really spectacular.'

'It's wonderful,' Lucy agreed, momentarily forgetting her nervousness as she looked at the glittering lights of thousands of windows and the dark square of Central Park below. 'Really beautiful.'

'I know. It's a fantastic sight. I'm still not used to Manhattan by night even after all these years.'

'You're not from New York, then?'

'No, Texas. I grew up in Houston. My father is in the oil business.'

'Oh,' was all Lucy could think of saying. She had had no idea that Al had such a glamorous wife. So he didn't have to scratch for the millions, she thought, he just married them.

'Here's our last guest,' Al announced. 'Patrick! Great, you made it.'

Lucy felt like a deer caught in the headlights of a car as she stared across the room at the man who had just arrived. Their eyes met for a split second. My God, she thought. It's him. He didn't seem to have noticed her, but laughed and chatted and drank champagne until Al tapped him on the shoulder.

'You haven't said hello to Lucy.'

He turned around. 'Hi Lucy,' he said with an easy smile. 'Get stuck in any lifts lately?'

*

Cheered by the food and wine, Claire hurried home. She let herself into the dark apartment,

34

took off her wet coat, hung it on the mahogany stand in the hall and sighed happily. She loved this place; it was so cosy and welcoming, even if it was a little scruffy and not exactly in the chicest part of town.

She switched on the light and her image sprang into view in the tall mirror. She looked a little pale and her dark curly hair was still wet. She pulled the shirt out of her skirt, thinking she had to lose a little weight. All her skirts were beginning to feel really tight. But the long day had come to an end, and now she was just looking forward to a bath and then bed. She yawned and walked slowly down the dark corridor to her bedroom, stripping off her scarf and cardigan, dropping them on the floor in a long trail. I'll tidy up at the weekend, she thought, kicking off her shoes. I might even sort out my whole wardrobe.

She was undoing the button in her skirt when, suddenly, she froze to the spot. What was that? No, probably nothing. These old buildings always creaked and groaned. Something to do with the plumbing. I must stop watching those late-night horror movies, she said to herself, they make you very jum- Oh, God! Her heart nearly stopped as the door of the huge wardrobe at the end of the corridor slowly creaked open. She could hear someone breathe inside. Jesus Christ, she thought, someone did follow me. He managed to get into the apartment and now he's going to …

'Please,' she begged in French, backing away,

'please don't …' But it was no good. A figure emerged from within the wardrobe and took her arms in an iron grip.

'At last, *mon amour*,' a voice whispered hoarsely into her ear. Claire tried to prise herself loose. She knew that voice, knew it so well …

'Please don't,' she pleaded. 'Please, no …' But it had no effect. The man dragged her into the bedroom and threw her on the bed.

'Now, my lovely,' he panted, keeping a tight grip on her wrists with one of his strong hands. 'I have waited long enough for this.' He ripped open her shirt and started to pull up her skirt. Claire tried to fight him off, but she was so tired.

'Oh, God,' she sobbed, 'go on then, do what you like. I just wish …'

'What?' the man demanded.

'I wish you would tell me when you were going to be back. I haven't done the shopping and there's no bread.'

3

'If you have finished your lemon soufflé, I think we have to start to thrash out some ideas here, before you get sleepy.' Al called the working dinner to order. 'Anyone want to start? Bill? How about you?'

'Well, I think we should let the ladies start,' Bill, a tall man with crew-cut black hair, said from across the table. 'How about your new protégé, Lucy?'

'Good idea,' Al agreed. 'So how about it, Lucy?'

Lucy looked at Al, trying to pull her thoughts together. 'Well,' she started, 'I really haven't finished my presentation. My idea should ideally be illustrated with a collage of pictures I'm putting together …'

'Ah, come on, Luce,' someone called. 'Give it a shot. Don't be so bloody precious!'

'Yeah,' Al agreed. 'Let's hear it, honey. Don't be shy.'

'OK,' Lucy said, 'but, please, it is just a rough draft and it needs a lot of work.'

'Of course,' another voice assured her. 'We just want some ideas we can work on. So do go on, Miss Mulcahy.'

'All right.' Lucy cleared her throat.

'Could you stand up, please,' a woman asked. 'It's easier if we can all see you.'

'Right.' Lucy stood up, her hands sweaty on the white tablecloth. She felt their eyes on her as she smoothed her skirt and straightened her shoulders. Patrick Delacy seemed to stare at her and Lucy felt her cheeks redden. Why does he have to be here, she thought, why does he have to look at me as if he thought I was ridiculous? She swallowed nervously.

'My idea,' she started, 'is for a television commercial. There would be a wedding …'

'Gee, that's so cute,' a woman's voice jeered.

'Now, shut up,' Al ordered. 'Let her continue. A wedding, you said?'

'Yes, and you would see this really pretty girl walk up the aisle on her father's arm, her gorgeous dress billowing behind her and lovely music and people wiping their eyes …'

'Sob, sob,' someone whispered.

'Big hats, flowers everywhere, the whole wedding thing,' Lucy pressed on. 'The girl walks up to her groom, who is …'

'– really gorgeous, and they are married and live happily ever after, just like in Cinderella,' the mocking voice suggested. 'Then he gives her a washing machine and she …'

'Shut the fuck up,' Al growled. 'Don't be such a bitch, Liz. Let Lucy finish. Then let's hear *your* idea, OK? Lucy?' Al urged. 'Try not to pay attention to her. Just let's hear what you had in mind.'

'Well …' Oh God, where was I? Lucy tried to block Liz and her jeering, the cold stares from her colleagues and Patrick's amused eyes from her mind.

'The wedding,' Al reminded her.

'Yes, anyway, the groom turns around and smiles at the young bride, and that would be a really wonderful moment, only he is about a hundred years old and has no teeth or hair. The groom, I mean.' Shit, Lucy thought, I'll never be able to explain. This seemed so brilliant yesterday.

'Oh,' Al said, staring blankly at Lucy. 'And the point would be … ?'

'Well,' Lucy babbled on, 'the voiceover would say: "Some girls will do anything for a Deep Clean washing machine." Or something like that.' She sat down suddenly, feeling her shaking knees no longer keeping her upright. There was a long silence. Then someone giggled softly. Lucy looked at her plate, wishing she could sink through the floor and disappear.

'Well,' Al said. 'Interesting idea. Mmm. Yes. Anyone else? Another idea?'

There was a murmur as everyone started to talk at once. Lucy slowly got up from her chair. 'Excuse me,' she mumbled. 'I have to …' But no one seemed to notice her.

I'll just slip away before they start taking me apart, she thought. I'll get my bag and leave. They might forget all about it by Monday. She walked softly out of the room and into the living room where she found her handbag, then out through the door. She turned left and walked down the long corridor, then left again. Where is the entrance hall? she thought. I'm sure this is the way I came in. That door there. Yes. That must be the way. She pushed open the door and walked into a big room full of clothes. Was this the hall? The hall closet? The light was dim. Lucy found a switch. The spotlights in the ceiling came on and she looked around. This was no hall closet. It was a huge dressing room. She stared in awe at the Aladdin's cave of designer clothes, shoes and accessories.

It was like a very luxurious department store. The clothes were hung in groups according to the seasons. 'Fall' it said on a card over rows of suits, skirts and slacks in hues of brown, dark green and beige. 'Winter' was all blacks and greys, 'spring' white, pink and light blue and 'summer' an array of vivid colours. The designers seemed to be split between Lauren and Armani for day and Gucci, Chanel and Prada for evening wear. There were stacks of cashmere sweaters and cardigans in plastic containers, silk shirts in special see-through drawers and rows and rows of shoes, handbags and belts.

'My God,' Lucy murmured, 'I bet she never says she has nothing to wear.' She took a red evening dress from its hanger and held it up in front of her, looking into the floor-to-ceiling mirror. It was gorgeous. Lucy was tempted to try it on.

She suddenly remembered Claire and how they had dressed up in her mother's dresses when they were small. Oh, Claire, she thought, how you would laugh if you saw me now. And, of course, Claire would have tried on a few dresses here, swished around in front of the mirror, not caring if she was caught, just enjoying herself. God, I miss her, Lucy thought, I miss the fun we had and the belly laughs, all those times when … But we grew up and realised we didn't really get on. And I … well …

Lucy sighed and hung the dress back in its place. She walked along the rows of clothes, mar-velling at the luxury of such a wardrobe. The back wall was taken up with wool and fur coats of all kinds. Lucy touched a mink jacket, soft as a whisper against her hand. Something glinted between a chinchilla wrap and a white fox cape. Lucy pushed the coats apart. She laughed out loud. My God, sequins. Some people have the strangest sexual fantasies, she thought, giggling at the image of cool, elegant Penny decked out in such an outfit. Al is obviously turned on by that kind of thing.

Still smiling, Lucy turned away and walked to the door. I better get out of here fast, she thought. Penny would probably shoot me and ask questions later if she found me. She opened the door and walked straight into someone coming down the corridor.

'Oops, sorry.' Lucy tried to catch her breath as she looked into Patrick's startled face. Slowly, a smile lit up his face. 'Hi,' he said. 'We seem to meet in the strangest places. What are you doing here?'

Lucy backed away, feeling at the same time self-conscious and annoyed at the teasing smile and amused look in his eyes. 'I might ask you the same question,' she retorted, trying to sound aloof.

'Al asked me to get some papers for him from his study.' He looked past her through the half-opened door. 'Jesus Christ, what a wardrobe.' He stepped in and looked around him. 'And everything according to the seasons. Saks Fifth Avenue is nothing compared to this. My, my, there must be at least a hundred thousand bucks in clothes and shoes here. Penny must be a serious shopaholic. No wonder Al has to work so hard for a living.'

'But she is from a very wealthy family,' Lucy remarked. 'Not that it's any of our business.'

Patrick turned around and studied Lucy. 'But you must have been a little surprised all the same?

I mean this,' he gestured at the clothes, 'is not the wardrobe of the average woman, is it?'

'I wouldn't know,' Lucy said, feeling oddly trapped there with him so close, surrounded by clothes, shoes and underwear.

'I mean,' Patrick continued, picking up a silk slip from a shelf, 'this must have cost a couple of hundred at least. Pure silk. And just look at the lace …' He held it up in front of her and tilted his head. 'You would look fantastic in this…'

Lucy backed away and stepped out into the corridor. 'I'm sure Penny wouldn't like to find us snooping in her wardrobe,' she said primly.

'Is that what you were doing?' Patrick laughed, putting out the light and closing the door.

'Of course not. I had to go home early and I just took a wrong turn. I thought this was the hall closet.'

'I don't blame you. Easy to get lost in this place. Why are you going home now?'

'Oh, I …' Lucy tried to think of a reason. 'I got a call on my cell phone from the super in my building. There is a leaking tap in my bathroom and …'

'I see. Very responsible.' He looked at her with mock seriousness. 'And I thought you might be running away because you were afraid nobody liked your idea.'

'Of course not.' Lucy said. 'And the campaign has nothing to do with you, anyway.'

'No, it hasn't. Nothing at all. But I couldn't help listening to their comments all the same.'

'And?' Lucy said, in spite of herself.

'Of course, Liz thought it was a load of sexist crap …'

'Good night,' Lucy said with all the hauteur she could muster. She walked quickly down the corridor, her high heels clicking on the polished parquet.

'But,' Patrick called after her, 'I just wanted to tell you …'

She stopped. 'Yes?'

'Everyone else loved it.'

*

'So how was your field trip?' Claire asked, pulling out of Michel's arms.

'It was all right,' he replied, smiling at her and putting his hands behind his head. He looked happy and relaxed lying there in the bed, his dark hair tousled and his brown eyes half-closed. 'Very interesting. And Nîmes is such a fascinating town. What about you? How was the staff meeting?'

'Magic. Everyone listened to me with bated breath and the headmaster wants to make me his deputy.'

'*Mais c'est magnifique, ca.*'

'No it's not.' Claire sighed. He never understood irony. 'It was the usual. Like wading through treacle.'

44

'Oh. I'm sorry my darling.'

'Yeah,' Claire said flatly.

'Why can't you just ignore them?' Michel said.

'Because I have to work with them and it would be easier if they at least took me seriously.'

'The P.E. teacher pinched your bottom again?'

'That too.'

'English moron.'

'He's from Denmark.'

'OK, Danish moron.'

'And the fourth-grade maths teacher kept leering at me all through the meeting.'

'*He's* English?' Michel asked, as if he was dying for a chance to say something really scathing about the English.'

'Dutch. Oh, forget it. I'll just have to accept that none of them will ever be professional enough to take me seriously as a teacher.'

'You're too sexy, my darling,' Michel said and put his arms around her. 'No man could possibly look at you and have serious thoughts at the same time.'

'You're as bad as them. Have they not heard that sexual harassment is a crime? I have a good mind to ...'

'I don't think it is a crime in France,' Michel said. 'If it was, half the male population would be in prison. No, sexual harassment is more like a ... a sport here.'

'Oh, please,' Claire said, pulling away. 'Let's forget the whole thing.' Why do I bother, she thought, he'll never understand. 'I'm glad you had a good trip,' she said, changing the subject.

'But I missed you, *chérie*, couldn't you tell?'

'How long were you waiting in that wardrobe? I came home later than usual.'

'I heard the lift and thought I'd give you a little surprise.'

'You gave me an awful fright.'

'You should be used to my little attacks by now.' Michel put his arms around her again. 'Admit it's fun.'

Clare leaned her head against his bare chest. 'Mmm,' she muttered. But she felt a rising irritation. They had been living together for two months now and she was still trying to get used to his strange ways. He loved pouncing on her when she least expected it and he always wanted to make love frantically, fast and often. She had found him so exciting when they met; so sexy, clever and sweet. But these constant surprise attacks were not exactly romantic and they didn't make her laugh any more. She had tried to explain how she felt, but there was no stopping him. Once he had even hidden behind the coats in the hall, stark naked, when her mother had just arrived for a visit. It had taken the whole evening and half a bottle of their best brandy to calm her down. I know he's a few years younger than me, she thought, but does he have to be so bloody childish? She jumped as he switched on the light.

'Where is that packet of Gauloises?' he muttered.

'Do you have to?' Claire asked as he struck a match. 'Can't you …'

'Go out on the balcony? But I'm too tired tonight and it's so cold. Don't be a boring little schoolteacher, *chérie*, I find that so tedious.'

'You used to find it exciting when we first met, remember?'

'And you used to find the smell of French cigarettes so sexy, remember that?' He lit his cigarette with his lighter and drew in the smoke with an expression of great satisfaction.

Claire didn't reply, but pulled out of his arms. She stared up at the ceiling and tried not to notice the acrid smell of the Gauloises. It had started raining again. Hard drops smattered against the window and the curtains billowed in a sudden, cold draught. Claire got out of bed to close the window, throwing her dressing gown around her shoulders. After closing the window, she stood for a moment looking out into the street. It was deserted, except for a man walking a small dog and a car pulling into the curb. The black tarmac glistened in the streetlight and a paper bag blew across the pavement. It could be any street, in any town, Claire thought, suddenly feeling bleak. And I could be any woman in any bedroom. Oh, I wish …

'*Chérie?* What are you doing?'

'Just looking out at the street.'

'What for? It's late. Come back to bed.'

Claire slowly crossed the room and lay down beside him.

'What is the matter?' Michel asked, taking her hand. 'You seem a little sad.'

'Just tired,' she replied. 'It's been a long day.'

'Then sleep,' he whispered.

She closed her eyes and went to sleep.

4

'Is Al in?' Lucy asked his secretary. It was coming up to Thanksgiving and she wanted to catch him before he left for the holiday weekend.

'No, he's gone to lunch with a client. Can I help?'

'I was just going to give him my presentation. But I can give it to him later.' Lucy put the folder she was holding back in her briefcase.

'Is that the Wax and Shine stuff? The floor cleaning product?'

'Yes.'

'He was really anxious to see it as soon as possible. Why don't you go in and put it on his desk? I'm going to lunch now, but write him a note and put it on top of the portfolio. Then he'll get it as soon as he's back.'

'Well … if you're sure it's OK.'

'Of course.'

'Great. Thanks.'

The girl rose and took her handbag. 'I'm off. See you later.'

'Bye.'

Lucy opened the heavy door to Al's office. It was eerily quiet without Al and the sound of his booming voice. She put the portfolio on the desk and looked for a pen. Then she sat down in the big leather chair and swivelled around to look at the view. So this is what it's like to be the boss, she thought. Very nice. She gazed out at the Manhattan skyline and the East River far below and then, giggling to herself, swivelled back to face the desk, took one of Al's cigars, put her feet up and picked up the phone. 'Get me the president,' she barked. 'I don't care who he's playing golf with.' She put the cigar in her mouth and pretended to smoke. 'Fire that bitch, Liz,' she ordered into the phone, 'and promote Miss Mulcahy at once. Give her a raise while you're at it, and tell her to take five weeks off. She can use my pad in Florida.'

'Very impressive,' said a voice.

Startled, Lucy straightened up and looked at Patrick Delacy standing in the door. 'Oh,' she stammered, her face red. 'I was just …' She awkwardly swung her legs down and replaced the receiver.

'Want me to light your cigar?'

'No thanks,' Lucy snapped. She got up from Al's chair and straightened her skirt. 'I was just fooling around. I came in to put my portfolio on Al's desk and then ...'

'You got carried away?' Patrick walked across the carpet towards her. 'You looked really cute playing the boss.'

'OK, fine. Have your little joke.' Lucy had found a pen and scribbled a few words on a note. 'Al's out. Lunch with a client.'

'I know.'

'What are you doing here, then? Everyone else must be gone to lunch too.'

'They are. The whole floor is deserted.' He came closer, too close. 'I was hoping to bump into you. I haven't seen you in weeks but here you are. And we're all alone.'

Lucy looked up at him, trying to appear cool.

'How about lunch?' he suggested.

'I was going to have a sandwich at my desk. I don't have time to go out.'

'We could have lunch here.'

'Here? In Al's office?'

'Yes, of course. He has all sorts of delicious stuff in his fridge.' Patrick walked over to a mahogany cupboard. 'I bet you didn't even know this was a fridge.' He opened the door to reveal rows of champagne bottles on the top shelf and all sorts of little jars on the lower ones. 'Just as I thought. Caviar. Shrimps. Pâté. And look, even quail's eggs.' He proceeded to take out a bottle of champagne and some of the jars and, before Lucy knew what was going on, the coffee table in front of the leather Chesterfield sofa had become an improvised picnic table.

'Sit down,' Patrick ordered and opened the champagne with a loud pop. 'Help yourself. I think there are some crackers in that basket over there.'

Lucy hesitated.

'Oh, come on,' Patrick said. 'Don't be such a stick in the mud. Sit down, I said.'

Lucy sat uneasily on the edge of the sofa. Patrick handed her a brimming glass and poured one for himself. He held it out to Lucy. 'To us,' he said.

Lucy sipped the champagne, looking at Patrick over the rim of her glass, feeling a little awkward. She looked at the food, not knowing quite where to start.

'Here,' he said, and popped a tiny quail's egg into her mouth. 'Good, isn't it?'

'Mmm …' She swallowed.

'How about some of this? Beluga, only the very best for our Al.' Patrick handed her a cracker covered in shiny black caviar.

'Lovely,' Lucy mumbled. She nibbled on the cracker, feeling the caviar burst in her mouth with a delicious taste of salt and sea. 'I've never had the real stuff before.'

'No?' he looked at her quizzically. 'I could have sworn you were the caviar sort of girl.'

'More like sausages and chips,' she muttered through a mouthful.

'And beer?'

'Oh yes, beer. Goes very well with sausages and chips.'

'Ah, but champagne is much more glamorous. And sexy. I couldn't imagine Marilyn Monroe or Mae West making whoopee after a big slug of beer, could you?'

'No, I suppose not,' Lucy laughed.

'So,' he said, filling up her glass again, 'how are you getting on in the big bad world of advertising?'

'I don't know. I find it a bit hectic, to tell you the truth. I hardly have a chance to catch my breath after finishing one job, before I have to start on another. And sometimes I even have to work on two different campaigns at the same time.'

'But I hear you're very talented. Al told me you're shaping up very well.'

'He did?'

'Uh-huh. Very well indeed.' Patrick smiled broadly at Lucy.

'Oh, that's … nice.' The champagne made her feel elated and at the same time relaxed. She was also beginning to feel a growing attraction to him. The way he touched her hand as if by accident, brushed against her as he refilled her glass and smiled at her in that cheeky way made her feel oddly dizzy.

'I have to say I admire the way you have settled in here,' Patrick remarked, looking earnest. 'It's not every girl that could do what you've done. New York is a tough city. Most young women find it really daunting. But you seem to be going from strength to strength.'

'Well, from Deep Clean to Wax and Shine in this case.'

'Whatever. You've really done well.'

'But I believe you're very successful yourself,' Lucy said, feeling a little self-conscious.

'Me?' He laughed modestly. 'I just took over from my father.'

'But law is so complex and so fascinating. What type of cases do you handle?'

'Our firm handles everything except criminal law,' Patrick replied. 'And my speciality is corporate law. Contracts and litigations mostly.'

'What about divorce cases?' Lucy licked some caviar off her fingers.

'Not if I can help it,' Patrick declared. 'That's one thing I try to avoid.'

'Why is that?'

'It's so depressing. Makes you wonder why people bother to get married. I mean, one minute they're standing there in front of the priest promising to love each other until death do them part, and the next they're splitting up and their lawyers are arguing about who should get the Barry Manilow CD collection.'

'But I'm sure that takes a lot of skill,' Lucy remarked with a little laugh.

Patrick shrugged. 'Very tedious work, though, even if it does bring in a lot of money. Do you want the last cracker?'

'What is Al going to say when he finds all his food gone?' Lucy asked, feeling a sudden stab of anxiety.

'He'll probably say, "Someone's been sitting in my chair,"' Patrick suggested. 'And, "Someone has eaten my food and now it's all gone."' He held up the nearly empty bottle. 'Do you want some more champagne, Goldilocks?'

Lucy giggled. 'No thanks. Oh, God, I shouldn't have drunk any champagne at all in the middle of the day.' She put her glass on the table and brushed the crumbs off the front of her white shirt. 'I better go. Lunch hour will be over soon and …'

'Plenty of time. There's a good half hour before they are all back. And Al will probably just go home after his big lunch meeting.' Patrick moved closer. 'I would really like to get to know you a little better, you know,' he mumbled into her ear, his warm breath on her neck. 'You're a very beautiful girl. I love those green eyes …' He sat back and studied her. 'No, they're not green, they're turquoise. Like the eyes of a Siamese cat.' He leaned closer again. 'Hi, gorgeous,' he whispered, his lips brushing her neck. Then, before Lucy had a chance to protest, he was kissing her mouth. Without thinking, she returned his kiss. What am I doing? she asked herself, but then forgot time and place, Al's office, Wax and Shine, even her career. Nothing seemed real, except Patrick's strong embrace, his lean body and the smell of his aftershave. He kissed her mouth, her neck. They slid off the sofa and down onto the soft carpet.

'This is mad,' she said, trying to pull away. 'The door …'

'I locked it.'

'You're a sneaky bastard.'

'I know.' He began to unbutton her shirt.

'Stop.' She put her hands over his. 'We have to stop this.'

'Are you kidding? It's far too late.' He had managed to undo all the buttons and slid his hands inside her shirt. Lucy closed her eyes and sighed.

'Oh, honey,' he whispered, 'you're so sweet, so very, very …'

'Oh God,' Lucy gasped, 'what's that?'

'Relax. It's just my knee.'

'Oh.'

'Shhh.'

'Mmmm …'

'Can I …'

'Oh yes … please … yes …'

*

'Mademoiselle Dillon?' The voice was hesitant.

Claire looked up. *'Oui?'*

The man held out his hand. 'Bernard Marchand.' He was tall, with aquiline features, light brown curly hair and hazel eyes.

Claire shook his hand. 'Emilie's father?' she enquired in English.

'That's right. I hope I am not interrupting?'

'No, I was just tidying up the classroom. How is she? Emilie, I mean.'

'Much better.' He smiled. 'Dying to get back to school.' His English was nearly perfect, with just a hint of an accent.

'Oh, that's good.' Claire smiled back.

'But of course, she's very tired. She was *so* ill.'

'I know. We were all worried about her. And I really missed her. When is she coming back?'

'Well, that's why I'm here.' He frowned and there was a worried look in his eyes. 'She is still not well enough to go back to school. She probably won't be back until after Christmas. She has to rest for a while longer. But the air in Paris is not exactly ideal for someone recovering from such a serious chest infection. Her doctor has recommended two weeks' recuperation in the mountains when she's a little stronger, so she'll be going to the Alps in about a month or so.'

'Sounds like a very good idea.' Claire went back to stacking the copybooks on her desk.

'Oh yes, it is. I hope I'll be able to organise it. But the problem is, I can't take two weeks off at that time.' There was an apologetic look in his eyes. 'That's why I'm here. You see, I was thinking ... I mean I was wondering ... The school ski break in February ...'

'Yes?' Claire looked at him, wondering what was coming next.

'Well, I know this is a little unusual, but …' He paused, took a deep breath, then started again. 'Emilie is very fond of you, you know. She is always talking about you and how kind you are to her.'

'She's a lovely little girl. And, of course, speaks wonderful English. Her written work is exceptional for a girl of six.'

'Well, we are a bilingual family. And, of course, she has a very good teacher,' Bernard Marchand replied.

'You're very kind.'

'Anyway,' he continued briskly, 'what I was going to ask you was: would you be able to take Emilie to our chalet in Courchevel in February?'

'What?' Claire said, taken aback. 'Where?'

'Courchevel. It's a ski station in the Alps.'

'I know that. I was just a little surprised.'

'I have a chalet there. Emilie loves it. Two weeks there would be perfect for her. I'm sure it would speed up her recovery immensely and, if you went with her, she could catch up on her school work at the same time.'

'Yes, but …'

'You wouldn't be on your own, of course,' Marchand assured her. 'Some American friends of mine are going to be there as well. The chalet is very big and there are plenty of staff to look after everybody.'

'Well yes,' Claire stammered. 'Sounds great. But, I mean …' She didn't quite know what to say.

'Emilie's nanny has just left, you see, and I haven't had the time to hire another one and there isn't much time left before Christmas ...'

Claire was still stuck for words. 'I don't know ...'

'I see. You have plans for the February holidays? I understand, of course ...'

'No,' Claire said. 'It's not that.' She looked into his eyes, trying to find the right words, to politely refuse with some kind of excuse that would sound plausible and get her off the hook. But what she saw there made her decide to try to be honest and tell him exactly how she felt. 'I hope you don't think I'm being rude,' she continued, 'but how can you just give your daughter away to a stranger like that? You know nothing at all about me. I could be an axe murderer for all you know. Or a drug addict, or a schizophrenic or ...' She tried to think of something really awful. 'Or a chain smoker,' she ended feebly.

'Are you?'

'What?'

'A chain smoker.'

'No, I don't smoke at all.'

'Good. That's perfect.' He laughed suddenly. 'I mean an axe murderer I could take, but smoking ...'

Claire didn't return his smile. But the way he looked at her made her feel suddenly awkward and she lowered her eyes and pretended to study

59

the papers on the desk. Typical, she thought, how these upper class people never put their children at the top of their list of priorities. She looked at him again. 'What about your wife?' she asked. 'Couldn't she take Emilie? But I take it she would be too busy as well?' she added with heavy irony.

'No … that is …' He looked suddenly very uncomfortable.

'Oh, I see. I suppose she'll be going to the Caribbean or something?' Claire snapped. She knew she was being cheeky, but she felt sorry for the little girl.

'My wife passed away two years ago.' His voice was expressionless.

Claire stared at him in shock. 'Oh, God, I am so sorry. I had no idea.'

'I understand. You couldn't have known.' He paused and they were both silent for a while until Claire felt forced to say something to break the awkwardness. 'I suppose this holiday will do Emilie a lot of good,' she mumbled.

'It will.' He looked suddenly a little brighter, more hopeful. 'Does this mean … ?'

'No, it doesn't,' Claire protested. 'It's a huge responsibility, you know, taking care of someone else's child like that.'

'But you do that here at the school. You have twenty children in your care every day.'

'That's different. It's called teaching.'

'So you're saying no, then?'

'I'm afraid so.'

'But I'm willing to pay a good salary.'

'I'm sure you are, Monsieur Marchand,' Claire said, feeling a flash of anger at the insinuation that the mere mention of money would make her change her mind. 'I have no doubt you would pay me a lot of money to solve your problem. But you can't just come in here and snap your fingers and expect everything to work out to your satisfaction in this way. Think of Emilie. How does she feel about this? Have you even bothered to ask her?'

'But, of course,' he said, now sounding annoyed. 'The whole thing was her idea. She asked me to do my best to persuade you. Now she'll be very disappointed, of course.'

'Oh.' Claire stared at him blankly.

'But let's not argue about it.' He took a card from his wallet. 'I've explained the situation. Think about it, at least. There's plenty of time to make up your mind. Here's my number. Call me when you've decided.' And, without saying goodbye, he walked out of the classroom.

*

'My God,' Patrick sighed, his mouth in Lucy's hair. 'Oh my God, you're fantastic.'

'Oh.' Lucy suddenly came to her senses. What have I done, she thought, I can't believe I'm lying half naked in Al's office with his lawyer on this very expensive carpet. She stared at Patrick, who was looking at her with half-closed eyes and a little smile on his lips.

'That was lovely,' he said. 'Can't think of a nicer way to spend my lunch hour.' He got up and started to put his trousers back on. 'Hope you enjoyed it as much as I did.' All of a sudden his voice was businesslike, as if all they had done was shake hands.

Lucy didn't know what to say. She slowly pulled herself together and straightened her clothes. 'Yes, well … Of course, it was great.'

'I'm sorry,' he said with an apologetic little laugh. 'It was a bit sudden, I know. It just kind of happened. Didn't mean to, really. Don't worry, I'll tidy up here. You just go on. I'm sure you want to get on with your campaign.'

'Yes, well …'

He looked at her as if he was trying to assess her thoughts. 'It was just a little fling, right? I mean you're not one of those girls who would expect some kind of commitment after just one … well, you know.'

'Of course not.' Lucy smiled at him, trying to look cool. 'I *have* been in New York a little longer than five minutes. Don't worry,' she added, 'your Barry Manilow collection is safe.'

He laughed, looking relieved. 'Thank God for that. OK, kid, see you around.'

'Yeah. Right. See you.' Her face burning, Lucy walked to the door, unlocked it and walked out. She crept down the corridor to the ladies' toilet, got into one of the cubicles, sank down on the seat and burst into tears.

5

Claire knocked discreetly on the door of the headmaster's office. It was the end of January, the beginning of the spring term, and there was not really anything she could think of that the headmaster could wish to discuss at the moment. Why had he asked her to come to his room for 'a little talk'?

'Come in,' a voice ordered and Claire opened the door and walked in.

'Take a seat. I'll be with you in a moment,' the headmaster grunted, without looking up from the piece of paper he was reading.

Claire sat on the edge of a chair on the other side of the desk, feeling increasingly apprehensive, but grateful that she had put on a clean shirt, her long grey skirt and new boots this morning. At least she looked neat and tidy. Except for the rustling of pages and the distant sound of traffic, the room was eerily quiet. Claire looked across the desk at the headmaster. He would be quite good looking, she thought idly, if it wasn't for the thin hair and the mole on the side of his nose. Why doesn't he have it removed, she wondered to herself, and why does he dress like that, in a brown suit and beige shirt and yellow tie? Is he colour-blind, or does he just have appalling taste? She jumped as the headmaster raised his head and looked at her with his sharp little eyes. 'Did you say something?' he asked in his Boston twang.

'No.'

'Could have sworn … Never mind.' He put down his papers, folded his hands in front of him and looked squarely at Claire. 'You're probably wondering why I asked you to come here today.'

'Well, yes, I was actually,' Claire said, fiddling with the collar of her shirt.

He cleared his throat. 'Well, Miss Dillon, I'm afraid I have to tell you I have some bad news.'

'Bad news?' Claire stopped playing with her shirt. 'Oh no. You mean I'm not going to get the new material I asked for? But those books are excellent. It's a new reading programme, you see, specifically aimed at children who live in a multi-lingual environment. I thought I explained all that in my letter …'

'It's not about the books,' he said, his voice stern. 'It's about you.'

'I'm sorry?' She stared at him with a feeling of impending doom.

'I'm afraid there have been some complaints.' He took a piece of paper from his desk and peered at it.

'Complaints?' Claire asked, taken aback. 'About what, exactly? I can't imagine there could possibly be anything to complain about. Most of the children have improved enormously since the start of the school year. And we get on very well. I really like them: they're a nice bunch. And I think they like me.'

'But the parents don't,' the headmaster stated.

'What? The parents? But what do they have to do with the children …' her voice trailed away.

'They do have them, you know; parents I mean.'

'Yes. But,' Claire stammered, 'what do they have to complain about?'

'Well, to put it bluntly, there seems to be a whole series of things.' The headmaster looked at the paper he was holding. 'For example, you told one of the girls she was fat and should go on a diet.'

'What? No, I didn't. I couldn't have. I would never dream of … Oh God,' Claire said as it dawned on her. 'I know what you mean. There is one girl in the class who seems to be heading for obesity with alarming speed. Pretty little girl. But I would never say such a thing. I think I just made a suggestion about her lunch box. I think I said she should ask her mother to give her fruit instead of that huge packet of crisps and that she might join the other children in their games in the playground instead of sitting on the steps watching them. That's all.'

'Well, you must have put it the wrong way. In any case, Miss Dillon, the children's eating habits are hardly your business.'

'I don't agree,' Claire said. 'I think weight problems in a child are always caused by the wrong diet. If you can get children to understand that at an early age, you're doing them a huge favour. In my opinion, giving children fattening unhealthy food is a kind of child abuse.'

'You have a lot of opinions, don't you, Miss Dillon?' the headmaster said.

Claire looked at him, trying to work out why he was being so hostile. 'And what's wrong with that?'

'Hmmm. But let's continue.' He glanced at the paper again. 'Here it says you told one of the boys not to be "smart". And another time you told him to stop being "bold".' He looked at her, his eyes even smaller than before. 'We *want* the children to be smart. Smart is good. And to be bold is to be brave. I looked it up. Brave or daring, it said. And that is good too. So why …'

'Hold on a moment,' Claire said. 'I think there is a slight misunderstanding here.'

'I'll say.'

'Smart in Ireland means cheeky, you see. I told him not to be cheeky. And bold means naughty.'

Claire laughed, relieved that the problem was only a minor one of language.

'Which brings me to another comment from the parents. Your accent.'

'What's wrong with it?'

'It's Irish. We don't really approve of ethnic accents here. I though I made that clear when you started. The parents have told me that some of the children are developing a brogue.' The headmaster looked at her coldly. 'You came here with such excellent references and qualifications. But I have to say that, apart from your accent, I don't like your attitude, Miss Dillon. This school has a very good reputation among the expatriate community. We try our best to provide a good Anglo-Saxon education for children who are either resident here permanently or are going back to schools in the United States or England. We have to keep up very good standards so that the students can go back to their own country and fit in at the best schools there.'

'Of course. I know that.'

'In that case, why have you not made more of an effort to keep up a strict discipline and to stick to the curriculum? You seem to teach in your own way, without the slightest thought about …'

'But it's working, isn't it?' Claire said, trying her best to sound positive. 'I wish you would come and see for yourself. Some of those kids have a reading age well above their actual age.

Their written work is excellent and they are all so ... so *happy!*'

'I'm afraid this brings me to what I was going to tell you,' the headmaster said, ignoring her last comment. 'Your contract comes up for renewal at the end of this school year.'

'And?' Claire whispered. She clasped ice-cold hands in her lap.

'And I'm afraid we are unable to renew, Miss Dillon.'

Claire felt the colour drain from her face. 'What? I don't understand. Just because ... I think that's *so* unfair,' she blurted out.

'On the contrary. I think it's very fair. You will be teaching here until the end of June. That gives you a full five months to make other arrangements. I will, of course, give you a good reference. I don't think it will take you long to find a similar position. There are other international schools in Paris, and most of them do not have our very high standards.'

Claire sat there staring at him while it all sank in. You miserable bastard, she thought.

'So there we are,' he said, sounding satisfied. 'Is there anything you'd like to ask, or ...'

Claire suddenly felt a strong urge to lunge across the desk and strangle him with his yellow tie. She stood up, her knees strangely weak.

'No, Mr Funkhouser,' she said and walked out of the room.

*

'There. I think that's it,' Lucy said and lowered the lid of her suitcase. 'I don't think I've forgotten anything.'

'You're so lucky,' Becky remarked. 'A fortnight in the French Alps. Your job sure came with some fantastic perks.'

'It wasn't really a perk as such. Al always goes to the Alps in February. He invited me because this way he'll be able to work on that new account. And I will be expected to put in a lot of hours preparing this campaign. It's a huge one.'

'Pet food,' Becky said and wrinkled her nose. 'Not particularly glamorous, is it?'

'Advertising is not just about luxury goods, you know,' Lucy replied primly. 'Most things have to be carefully marketed. And I think this particular brand will do very well. It's all organic, you see, and sold in these recyclable containers.'

'How terribly responsible. Aren't pets so lucky?'

'They sure are. But it's not only that. I'm also supposed to think of a really different idea to market a new type of yoghurt drink. And I have to come up with something really good.'

'You have really raced up the career ladder since you started in that firm,' Becky said. 'I mean, from junior copywriter to Mr Freeman's assistant in less than a year, that's amazing. You only started to work there last April and here we are in February and you're a top executive. Makes my head spin just thinking about it.'

'It was the washing-machine campaign,' Lucy said, 'and the fact that Liz was stupid enough to get pregnant and go on maternity leave. Then she had twins and asked for leave of absence for a year. Didn't take much to step into her shoes.'

'What is she going to say when she gets back?' Becky asked.

'Oh,' Lucy shrugged. 'She'll be lucky to get my old office if she ever makes it back.'

'That's really tough.'

'Well, that's advertising. You have to keep your knees together if you want to get ahead.'

'Is that what you're doing?'

'You bet,' Lucy replied, colouring slightly. 'Anyway', she continued breezily, 'we'll have to work hard to get these two campaigns going.'

'Doesn't look as if you'll have much time for skiing,' Becky remarked.

'Oh, I'll make sure I do plenty of skiing. I can work in the evenings. I'm not going to miss those lovely slopes.' And, she thought, I'm not going to let the fact that Patrick Delacy is going to be there affect me. I'm not going to allow him to spoil the fun. And I'm certainly not going to let him treat me the way he did again. He conned me once, he's not going to con me again.

But, despite his behaviour, she had expected … What? She didn't really know what she had expected. A bunch of red roses the next day? A dinner date at an expensive restaurant? A promise of eternal love and an engagement ring? But he hadn't even called her or dropped in to say hello. Maybe he thought she was just a country bumpkin? Some little innocent from the auld sod that he could screw, then forget? I'll show the bastard, she had thought. I'll change my image and make him really sorry.

It had taken her less than two months. Her dark red hair was cut short and slicked back from her face, her eyebrows were shaped to a perfect arch and her skin, with the help of a new skin-care routine, became flawless. She lost fifteen pounds and her body was made even trimmer by daily work-out sessions with the personal trainer Becky had recommended. He was called Tony and he put Lucy through an agonising work-out every morning at 6.30 a.m. Becky, who had joined in the exercises from time to time and sporadically dieted in sympathy, had been seriously impressed.

'You look amazing,' she had whispered one morning as Lucy, in a tight-fitting black business suit and stiletto heels, was getting ready for work. 'It's scary how quickly you've changed. And that attitude. You're such a bitch. It's awesome.'

'Thank you,' Lucy said. 'It was hard work but I did it.'

'You certainly did.'

Lucy found that looking like a top executive made her think like one, and her brain started to work on overdrive. The ideas kept popping into her head: detergent, soap, toys, sportswear, there didn't seem to be anything she couldn't sell. But, even though her new look, her bitchy attitude and new confidence seemed to earn her both respect from her colleagues and clients and invitations to power lunches, dinners and chic events like book launches and gallery openings, it had no impact on Patrick. She hardly ever saw him. They had met briefly in the lobby of the building one day and he looked at her with a strange expression in his eyes. 'Hi, Lucy,' he had said. 'It's been a while. I was going to call you.'

'Really?' she replied. 'Lucky I didn't hold my breath. I would have been dead by now.'

He looked at her for a moment. 'You've changed,' he said. 'You really do look the part now.' Then he had turned on his heel and disappeared into the busy street. Lucy tightened her jaw as she locked her suitcase. Creep, she thought.

'Work and skiing,' she said to Becky. 'That's all I'm interested in.'

'You're a real ski junkie,' Becky remarked. 'I don't know anyone who gets such a kick out of sliding down mountains like you do. A bit unusual for someone from Ireland, though.'

'I learned in London.'

'What?' Becky stared at her. 'You learned to ski in London?'

'No, I mean I went on a lot of ski trips when I was working there. I went on those cheap package tours to the Alps.'

'Oh, you went with a group then? That must have been fun.'

'Not really. The people I went with spent most of the time in the bars getting drunk. I was the only one who did any serious skiing.'

'You must be really good.'

'I'm average, I suppose. I never tried the really dangerous slopes. But maybe this time I will. Skiing is such a wonderful sport.' She looked dreamily at Becky. 'It's more than a sport, actually. It's the most exhilarating thing in the world. It's better than – '

'Sex?'

'No.' Lucy looked down at her suitcase, then looked up again. 'Yes,' she said, 'you know, in a way it is. And it lasts a lot longer.'

*

Claire ducked out of the rain and walked into the metro station. When the train arrived at the platform, she pushed through the crowd and eventually managed to find a seat. She put her briefcase on her lap, folded her hands on the clasp and rested her chin on them. It was three weeks since her conversation with the headmaster and she had not done anything yet to find another job. She hadn't even told Michel. It had been such a huge shock and she still found it hard to believe it had happened.

As the train jerked forward and gathered speed, Claire stared at the colourful advertisements on the carriage wall. What am I going to do, she thought as she looked at an ad for face cream and the lovely smooth face of the model. *A little bit of magic*, the blurb said. That's what I need, Claire thought, a little bit of magic to find a job I like as much as this one, and then some more magic to stop my heart from breaking when I have to say goodbye to my class. They're such a lovely bunch of kids. But I really have to pull myself together soon and look up some schools. She sighed and shifted in her seat as the train pulled in at another station and more people got on. Maybe I should go back home? she said to herself. Do some kind of course and change career? But she couldn't think of anything she liked better than teaching and she couldn't bear the thought leaving Paris, her cosy flat and all her friends. And Michel ... But she suddenly realised that she could possibly put up with not seeing him again.

As the train started again, Claire moved her eyes to the next poster; a winter scene. Somebody beside her lit a cigarette and she glared at him. Didn't he know smoking in the metro was against the law? She was going to say something, but the man gave her such a dirty look that she didn't dare, just coughed ostentatiously and briefly waved her hand in the air to dissipate the smoke. She turned her attention to the poster again and looked dreamily at the snow-covered mountains, the blue sky and the skiers with their tanned, happy faces. *For a week in paradise, contact your travel agent*, she read.

6

There was no sign of Al in the VIP lounge. The only people there were Patrick and a girl who was engrossed in the latest issue of *Vanity Fair*.

'Hi,' Lucy said as coolly as she could.

'Hello, Lucy,' Patrick said.

'Where's Al?' Lucy asked.

'Not here yet. This is Tiffany, my ...' he paused.

'I see,' Lucy said, glancing at the girl. She looked as if she hadn't finished high-school. She was very pretty but had made desperate attempts to hide it. Her hair was dyed purple and stood up in little spikes all over her head, her ears were festooned with rings and there was a stud in her nose. Her short nails were painted the same shade as her hair; she was dressed in a pair of torn jeans that hung on her slim hips and a black T-shirt under a leather biker jacket of the same colour. So this is his latest girlfriend? What a creep, going out with a teenager, Lucy thought. She held out her hand. 'Hi, Tiffany, nice to meet you.'

Tiffany barely glanced up from her magazine. She was chewing gum and her eyes seemed weary. 'Yeah,' she muttered and continued reading. Then she sighed and made her chewing gum pop.

'Tiffany,' Patrick snapped. 'Say hello properly. And throw away the gum.'

'Jesus,' Tiffany sighed, 'this is going to be one hell of a trip.' But she stood up and limply shook Lucy's hand. 'Pleased, to meet you,' she mumbled, 'charmed to make your acquaintance and all that crap. That OK?' she asked Patrick. 'Or should I curtsy as well?'

They were interrupted by the arrival of Al with Penny in tow. 'Hi everybody,' he boomed. 'Great you're all here. Hope you're looking forward to this trip as much as I am.' He put his arm around Lucy and gave her a squeeze. 'I'm so glad you're coming. I know you'll love it. You've met Tiffany?'

'Oh, yes,' Lucy replied.

'Great. Sorry we're a little late, but Penny had so much luggage we had to pay for excess weight. Don't know why she has to bring enough clothes for an army, but that's women for you.'

Lucy smiled at Penny, who was looking quietly elegant in a black trouser suit and a white wool coat with a huge fur collar. Penny smiled back with more warmth than usual. 'He just doesn't understand style,' she mumbled in Lucy's ear. 'He thinks I could go on a skiing holiday in what I'm wearing and just a change of under-wear.'

Lucy laughed. 'I'm sure you'll look perfect on every occasion,' she said. 'And I bet you're a great skier as well.'

'She skis like a pro,' Al cut in. 'Leaves me for dead all the time. I just don't bother to try any more. Penny and Patrick will be doing the kamikaze stuff as usual. I'm just going to let them at it.'

'Don't you ski at all?' Lucy asked.

'Yes I do, but only a little bit. I usually do a couple of hours on the easier slopes. That's enough for me.'

'What about Tiffany?' Lucy enquired. 'Are you a good skier?'

'Nah, not really,' Tiffany drawled. 'I find it a big pain in the ass, if you want to know the truth.'

'Listen, gang, I think we're boarding,' Al interrupted.

Lucy smiled at the air hostess as she entered the plane and looked for her seat in the first-class section. She was beside Al and Penny, who were already sitting down studying the dinner menu.

'It's going to be hard to stick to a diet with all this lovely food on offer all the time,' Penny sighed.

'I know,' Lucy agreed.

'What are you on?'

'On?'

'Yes, which diet are you on? Zone, Atkins, Weight Watchers … Are you doing low carbs or low fat?'

'I just kind of watch everything,' Lucy replied, feeling slightly inadequate. 'No special diet, really.'

'Interesting,' Penny said, looking at Lucy curiously. 'But it seems to work for you in any case.'

'Thanks.'

'Patrick is going to have his hands full with Tiffany. She has been borderline anorexic since she was fifteen.' Penny shook her head. 'She is a real headache that girl. I think he's a saint to take her on.'

'Take her on?' Lucy asked. 'How do you mean? Aren't they …'

'That's right,' Penny nodded. 'They are. And they're really close, despite the age difference. She's only eighteen, you know.'

'What? I'm sorry, but I have to say that I think that's disgusting,' Lucy protested hotly. 'A man his age with such a young girl. And she has all those problems. Isn't it really horrible that he's taking advantage of her like that? Do her parents know? Shouldn't someone tell them?'

'Someone has,' Patrick's voice said in her ear. 'And they're delighted.'

Lucy stared at him.

'She's my little sister,' he said.

*

The bus wound its way up the mountain on a narrow road full of hairpin bends. There was a thick fog and Claire couldn't see much of the landscape through the grimy windows. Emilie was asleep, her head on Claire's shoulder, still tired after the train journey.

The fog cleared as they neared the ski resort. 'Look,' Claire said to Emilie, 'the mountains.'

'I know. We will be there very soon.'

'Are you all right? Not tired any more?' Claire asked.

'No. I'm fine,' Emilie said. 'I always sleep on the way up to the village.' She started to button up her jacket. 'It's funny to be here without my daddy.'

'You must miss him. I hope you won't be feeling too lonely.'

'Maybe a bit. But it will be fun to go skiing. Daddy said he booked me into the ski school for the whole two weeks we're here. I'm going to try to pass the test for the *deuxième étoile*.'

'The second star? What's that?'

'It's a ski medal, silly.' Emilie laughed. 'First, you do the teddy bear test, then the first star, then the second and then the third and then …' She thought for a moment. 'After that, it's the *chamois*, but that's *really* hard. Haven't you done any of those?'

'I have never skied in my life. But I'll have a go.'

'You'll have to start with the teddy bear test,' Emilie declared. 'I did that one when I was four. You'll have to stay on the green slopes for a few days. Daddy says children are much better at skiing than adults.'

'He's probably right. It would be easier for me if I was six like you.'

'Are you very old?' Emilie asked.

'God, yes, I'm ancient.' Claire smiled at Emilie, then looked out the window again. Not ancient, but getting on a bit, she thought. Old enough to know better. It's time to cut loose and move on.

'Come on, we have to get off the bus now,' Emilie ordered as the bus came to a stop.

Claire put on her jacket and gloves and stood up. She followed Emilie into the winter wonderland that she had been attempting to glimpse through the grimy windows of the bus. The cold thin air, the dazzling white snow and the beauty of the mountains took her breath away. The snow-covered Alps rose majestically against the blue sky and Claire suddenly felt very small. It was as if she had been transported to another planet. She lifted her face to the mountains. 'Wow,' she whispered. 'This is fantastic.'

'*Allez, mademoiselle,*' exclaimed an impatient voice, '*vous bloquez tout le monde!*'

'Sorry,' Claire muttered to the bad-tempered Frenchman, who was trying to get past their luggage that the bus driver had unceremoniously dumped in the snow.

'Claire Dillon?' A tall young man with short black hair dressed in a ski jacket and jeans was standing in front of her.

'That's right,' she replied.

'Welcome to Courchevel. I'm Dave. The chalet girl,' he added with a little laugh. 'I'm here to take you up to the house.' He spoke with a heavy Liverpool accent.

'Oh, thanks. This is Emilie Marchand.'

'Oh, of course. We have met before. You're very welcome too, Miss Marchand.'

Emilie giggled and hid behind Claire.

'Is this all your luggage?' Dave asked.

'That's it. And Emilie's case is over there.'

Dave grabbed their suitcases and loaded them into a small Renault that was parked nearby. 'The chalet is further up the hill. Right in the middle of the nursery slope. Very handy for beginners.'

Claire looked out the car window as they made their way through the village. The houses were built mostly in the traditional mountain-chalet style. The roofs had at least a foot of snow on top and there were icicles hanging from every balcony. The streets were full of people in ski clothes, some carrying skis on their shoulders. Further up the slope, Claire could see chair lifts loaded with skiers on their way up the mountain. There was a carnival atmosphere about the whole station.

Dave filled Claire in on the chalet party while he drove. 'There's Mr Marchand's friend and American associate, Al Freeman, and his wife Penny. Then there's Patrick Delacy, a New York lawyer, and his half-sister Tiffany. Actually, Mr

Delacy had an accident on the slopes earlier today. He's still at the clinic.'

'How awful. Was it serious?'

'No, not really. He twisted his knee. He has to take it easy for a few days.'

'I see. So that's the chalet party?'

'Except for Mr Freeman's assistant. She's Irish like you. She was supposed to collect you but she got held up with Mr Delacy and his knee. She happened to be skiing on the same piste so she helped the rescue team get him down and into the clinic.'

'Irish? What's she like?' Claire asked, delighted with the prospect of meeting a compatriot. They might have some fun together.

'A real career woman,' Dave replied. 'Really sharp. Anyway, that's the party. They have all been here since Saturday.'

'So what do you do in the chalet?'

'I do the cooking and shopping and generally make sure everything is clean and tidy.'

'You must be very busy,' Claire said. 'I mean the cleaning alone …'

'There's a cleaning woman, a lovely girl from Senegal. She comes in every day. She also does the laundry. Everything has to run like clockwork. This is a top-class chalet.'

'It must be,' Claire replied, impressed.

The chalet was more like a huge villa, built of wood on cement foundations in a style that could only be described as 'Gingerbread', with a veranda wrapped around the middle. It had three storeys and, as it was built on a steep slope, like every home in the village, even the basement had a view of the mountains on the other side. On the ground floor there was the garage, laundry room and other utility rooms. There was an impressive hall and a huge winding staircase.

'Wow,' Claire whispered, glancing into the living room as they climbed the stairs. It was enormous, with oak-panelled walls, a high vaulted ceiling and big windows with breathtaking views of the mountains on one side and the village and valley on the other. Two huge comfortable sofas faced each other in front of the fireplace and there were big armchairs by the windows and beside the bookcases that lined the walls. There were Persian rugs in beautiful colours on the floor and a real bearskin in front of the fireplace. The room was both luxurious and inviting.

'What a fantastic room,' Claire said.

'It's not bad,' Dave replied. 'If opulence is your bag. I'm a bit of a minimalist myself.'

The bedrooms were on the top floor. Claire peered into one, a huge room with a queen-size double bed. They walked down a long corridor, past bedroom doors and into a big sunny room with pictures of cartoon characters on the walls.

'This is my room,' Emilie announced. 'Look, there's Bambi. And Mickey Mouse and Donald Duck and Pluto. Aren't they cute?' She bounced on the bed. 'I love this bed. It's a lot softer than my bed in Paris. And I have my own bathroom.'

'It's a beautiful room, darling,' Claire said.

'Your room is next door,' Emilie said. 'It used to be the nanny's room but I don't have a nanny any more so now you can sleep there. Is that OK?'

'Of course.'

'I'll show you,' Dave said.

'I'll be back in a minute to help you unpack,' Claire promised.

'You don't have to. I can do it myself.'

'Good girl.' Claire smiled at Emilie and followed Dave out.

'*Voilà*,' Dave declared and threw another door open. 'This is your room. Not bad for the servants' quarters.' He placed her suitcases in the middle of the floor. 'I'll be in the kitchen. It's beside the dining room. Whistle if you need me. You know how to whistle, don't you?'

'Just put your lips together and blow?' Claire laughed.

'Right on, babe. Drinks in the living room at seven thirty. Dinner at eight. See you later.' Dave gave her a wink and left.

The room was spacious and bright. It was furnished in the French-farmhouse style, with oak furniture and *Provençal* print fabrics. The bed was big and looked comfortable, and there were two easy chairs in front of the television set. The bathroom was of the five-star variety: pink marble, with a huge bathtub, a separate shower, lots of fluffy towels and shelves stacked with toiletries. But the best thing about the room was the spectacular view of the snow-capped mountains. Claire padded across the thick carpet to the window. She could see far into the valley below. She turned away reluctantly. Time to unpack and get organised. There would be plenty of time to admire the scenery later.

*

At 7:35 p.m. Claire walked into the big living room of the chalet, feeling a little apprehensive. Emilie was already in bed, exhausted after the long trip. She had eaten her supper in front of the fire in the small study. 'I'll have dinner with the big people tomorrow,' she said, 'but today I'm too tired.' Claire left her tucked up with a storybook and her teddy bear.

Three people were standing in front of the fireplace, drinking champagne and talking softly. A stocky man turned around and smiled at her. 'Ah,' he said, 'you must be Claire.' He squeezed her hand in a crushing handshake. 'I'm Al. Great to meet you. How the hell are you?'

'Fine, thanks.'

'Come and meet everyone. This is Penny, my wife.'

'Hi, Claire,' Penny said. Claire guessed her to be in her mid-forties. She had the smooth skin, wide eyes and tight chin of a woman with either fantastic genes or a very good plastic surgeon. She wore grey wool trousers, a white silk blouse and the pink cashmere cardigan around her shoulders was tied in the knot only people who go to expensive private schools know how to master.

'And Tiffany,' Al continued.

'Hello,' Claire said to a tall girl who looked as if she had escaped from a punk rock group. 'How nice to meet you.'

'Hi,' Tiffany replied flatly.

'And there's the invalid,' Al said, turning to one of the sofas, where a blond-haired man sat with one of his legs propped up on a stool. 'Patrick Delacy. Claire Dillon, Emilie's teacher.'

'Hello, there,' he said and held out his hand. 'Forgive me if I don't get up but …'

'No, please don't,' Claire said and shook his hand.

'But where's Luce?' Penny asked. 'She's late again.'

'Must be finishing that e-mail I asked her to send,' Al replied.

'Luce?' Claire asked.

'Yeah, she's my assistant,' Al said. 'Sharpest goddamned brain in my firm. Comes up with the best slogans every time.'

'I heard she's Irish,' Claire remarked.

'That's right.' Al nodded. 'She is. Looks it too. Red hair, green eyes. Hell of a good-looking girl. But she's more of a New Yorker than all of us put together. Toughest broad I've met in a long time.'

'Here she is now,' Penny announced. 'Hi, Luce.'

'Hi, honey,' Al said. 'Come and meet one of your countrywomen.'

Claire turned around and looked at the woman standing in the door, a woman with red hair and turquoise eyes, and her heart nearly stopped. She felt her face get hot and her breath catch in her throat. She wanted to say something, but couldn't. She suddenly felt as if everything was happening in slow motion and Al's voice sounded as if it came from a great distance.

'Lucy,' Claire mumbled. 'Oh, my God …'

7

'You two know each other?' Al asked, looking from Lucy to Claire as they stared at each other in shock.

Lucy was the first to speak. 'Claire,' she said, her voice hoarse. 'I don't believe it. How is this possible? What are *you* doing here?'

'I'm … I mean, I came with Emilie,' Claire said, the words tumbling out of her mouth. 'The little girl … I'm her teacher and I live in Paris and her father asked me to bring her …'

'A teacher?' Lucy said, still looking as if she didn't understand. 'In Paris? So you did go there after all?'

'Yes, I did,' Claire replied almost automatically.

'And *you're* Emilie's teacher then?' Lucy asked. 'That Irishwoman Dave told us about who will be looking after Emilie while she's here?'

'That's right.'

'Jesus,' Lucy said, shaking her head. 'That is *so* weird.'

'So you do know each other?' Al said again, looking at them with great interest.

'Yes we do ... did,' Lucy said. 'We used to be friends. In school. But we ... we lost touch. We sort of drifted apart.' She went up to Claire and gave her a peck on her suddenly very cold cheek. 'How amazing. How long has it been? Ten years? Yeah, it must be at least that.' She sounded nonchalant, almost as if she didn't really care. 'How are you?' she continued. 'You haven't changed a bit, you know. You look exactly the same.'

'Oh, Lucy,' Claire whispered, still in shock. 'You ... you cut your hair.'

'What? Yes. That was a long time ago.'

Lucy kept staring at Claire as if she was trying to take it all in and Claire stared back. Oh, God, she thought, this is unbelievable. Lucy. After all these years. We haven't seen each other since that day ten years ago, and all I can say is did you cut your hair?

I might look the same, but she has changed, and it's not the hair. She looks so thin and ... hard and ... Is this really happening? Claire thought. It's like the kind of dream you have after drinking too much. But I haven't drunk anything at all, yet.

As if she could read Claire's thoughts, Lucy walked to the drinks trolley, poured herself a large vodka and knocked it back in one go. 'Isn't life weird,' she said, 'last time I saw you I thought I'd never meet you again. And here you are.'

'A bit of a shock all right,' Claire said, still staring at Lucy as if she was a ghost.

'You're telling me.'

'But this is amazing,' Penny exclaimed. 'Here we are in the Alps in the middle of France and Lucy has come all the way from New York and Claire from Paris and, boom! The two of you turn out to be childhood friends. Isn't that just *incredible*?'

'Yeah,' Patrick agreed. 'It certainly is a small world.'

'A bit too small, if you ask me,' Lucy muttered.

Al looked from Lucy to Claire. 'This promises to be a *really* interesting holiday,' he remarked. 'But first, let's go eat.'

They slowly filed into the adjoining dining room, which was beautifully decorated with blue *toile de jouy* wallpaper, thick white silk curtains, carved oak furniture and beautiful paintings.

Claire sank down on the chair Al pulled out for her, grateful to sit down at the big oak table and steady her shaking knees. Dave served tomato salad with mozzarella and basil, and there was a clink of glasses and cutlery and a gentle murmur as everyone started to eat. Claire stole a glance at Lucy, still not believing she was there. But she was, and it felt like a knife in Claire's chest.

Ever since that day ten years ago, when she and Lucy had parted company, Claire had thought of her often, asking herself over and over again why Lucy had done what she did. Was it my fault, she had asked herself. Was I so awful to live with that Lucy had to run away? Claire had tried her best to cope with the sadness and loss and the feeling of having failed, somehow. Unable to understand and forgive, she had slowly put it at the back of her mind, trying to pretend to herself it had never happened. And, with time, the memories had softened and faded. She didn't even know what happened to Lucy and thought she would probably never see her again. But then, here she was, large as life, and all the hurt and disappointment flooded back into Claire's mind, the grief she felt at their parting as real as if it happened yesterday. And what about Lucy? How did she feel? It was impossible to tell. It would be difficult to see through that hard, glossy shell and discover her true feelings. Lucy suddenly looked up and met Claire's glance, her green eyes glittering like glass, and Claire looked away with an involuntary little shiver.

'Well,' Patrick said, looking at Claire with a smile. 'What a lovely surprise. Not one, but *two* Irish girls. How did that poem go again? "Both beautiful. One a gazelle." Something like that. Irish poem, actually.'

'Which one is the gazelle?' Penny asked.

'Oh,' Patrick said with a little smile in Claire's direction. 'That's a secret.'

'You know what?' Tiffany said, addressing

91

herself to Patrick as she lifted the cheese off her plate and poured vinaigrette on her tomato salad. 'I don't think you should drink like that. It's not good after all the painkillers and tranquillisers they pumped into you at the clinic.'

'That's right, honey,' Al replied. 'I do agree with you.'

'What do you mean?' Patrick laughed, re-filling his wine glass. 'I was just inspired by all this female beauty to quote some poetry. What's wrong with that?'

'It's weird, that's what,' Tiffany said. 'And it's not the way you usually talk.'

'Why this sudden concern?' Patrick asked, taking a sip of wine. 'I thought you didn't care what I did as long as I left you alone.'

Tiffany shrugged. 'I don't. I just wanted to make sure you don't freak out or anything.'

'How is your knee, Patrick?' Penny asked. 'Is it very sore?'

'Only when I laugh,' Patrick grunted. 'That doctor pumped me full of dope. It makes me feel really out of it.'

'Such bad luck,' Penny said. 'And just when I had booked some great off-piste skiing with a guide for tomorrow.' She sounded politely concerned, but there was an annoyed look in her eyes.

'You'll just have to cancel it,' Patrick said. 'Or bring Al.'

'Hey, hey,' Al exclaimed, 'leave me out of this. I'm not a champion skier like the two of you.'

'I'm sorry, Penny,' Patrick said. 'I know you were looking forward to it. But it really wasn't my fault.'

'It was nobody's fault,' Lucy said, cutting her chicken into tiny pieces. 'Just one of those silly things that just happen.'

'Silly?' Patrick demanded, his angry tone startling Claire. 'Just happened?' he continued. 'I was skiing at my own pace, minding my own business, when you careered into me and nearly killed me. If I wasn't so considerate, I would sue the pants off you.'

'Considerate?' Lucy spluttered. 'That's a joke. Go on, sue me then. I would like to see you laughed out of court. And, for the record, I did not "career" into you. You fell over all by yourself. I just said "hi", and you lost it completely. If you're so easily startled, why don't you stick to the nursery slopes?' She picked up her wine glass and drank deeply.

'You're the one who should try easier slopes,' Patrick retorted. 'What were you doing on the most difficult slope in the station? I suppose it was that half-wit of an Australian instructor who put you up to it.'

'How can you say that after all Warren did to help you? But I suppose we should have just let you lie there. You could at least have said thank you.'

'Warren,' Patrick snorted. 'What a name. Where's he from? Queensland?'

'What do you mean?' Lucy demanded. Her eyes narrowed. 'Oh, I *see*. You think he's *gay*?'

'He didn't look exactly straight,' Patrick replied. 'With that hair.'

'Just because he has a pony tail, he's supposed to be gay?' Lucy snorted. 'And, in any case, what would it matter if he was? You mean you only accept help from heterosexuals?' She laughed ironically. 'So I suppose if you were drowning and someone was trying to save you, you would ask them about their sexual preferences first?'

'Come on now, you guys,' Al pleaded. 'Cool it. No fighting at the table.'

'Well, I didn't start it,' Lucy muttered with a withering glance at Patrick.

'You mean I did?' Patrick demanded angrily. The drugs combined with alcohol seemed to have put him in a very bad mood. 'Don't talk a load of bullshit,' he snapped.

'See?' Tiffany said. 'I told him to stay off the booze.'

'Stop fussing. I'm all right.' Patrick turned to Claire. 'Tell me more about yourself,' he said, his sudden warm smile a sharp contrast to his earlier black mood. 'You live in Paris, right?'

'Yes. I do.' Claire smiled back at him, relieved that the hostilities seemed to have ceased for the moment. She was wondering why Lucy was so irritated with Patrick. Or was she like that to everyone? Had she become really bitchy, or was this the way they behaved in corporate America?

Suddenly needing the comfort of food, Claire took another helping of roast chicken and garlic potatoes from the dish Dave was offering her.

'Fantastic city, Paris,' Patrick remarked.

'It's wonderful,' Claire agreed. 'I love living there.'

'Did it take you long to get here?' Tiffany enquired.

'It was rather a long trip, actually,' Claire replied. 'Even with the TGV. And then that long journey by bus.'

'It doesn't seem to have affected your appetite,' Lucy remarked. She pushed away her half-eaten chicken. 'But you always liked your food, as far as I can remember.'

'I like to see a woman eat,' Al stated, mopping up the remains of his sauce with a piece of bread. 'There's nothing sexier than a girl who likes her food. Right, Patrick?'

'Absolutely,' Patrick said with feeling, looking at Claire.

*

'*Alors, mademoiselle.* We're going to try a snow-plough turn. *C'est très facile.*'

'Right,' Claire replied, her knees shaking a little. She looked down the slope. It was the nursery slope, but it seemed very steep to her. But at least this time she had finally managed to stay on the button lift all the way to the top of the slope. She looked at Antoine, her ski instructor, while he slowly demonstrated the turn.

'You see, you start by skiing in a plough *comme ça*, with the tips of your skis together, straight down the hill. Then you bend the knees and put your weight on the left ski, if you want to turn left. See, I'm turning left. Keep the left ski edged against the snow and the right one flat.' Antoine turned slowly. 'Now you do the same.' Claire tried to do exactly as Antoine had shown her, and she nearly succeeded. But at the last moment the skis went from under her and she fell in a tangle of skis and poles.

'Shit,' she complained. 'I'll never get the hang of this!'

'You will. You just have to keep trying,' Antoine reassured her as he helped her up. 'But you must really *want* to ski. You do want to, *non*?' Antoine looked at her, his handsome face concerned. Claire looked back at him. It's true what they say, she thought, French ski instructors *are* divine. This one was a prime example: blond, blue-eyed and bronzed. He was also rather short, not very bright and newly married to the receptionist at the ski school, who kept a jaundiced eye on all his female pupils. 'Antoine does not have lunch with his students,' she had said, as she eyed Claire in her brand new black ski suit, which made her hips look especially shapely. 'And he *never* gives private lessons.'

Claire was sharing Antoine with a German couple, two Dutch girls and a Japanese businessman, all of whom were much quicker to learn than she was. But, what the hell, the sun was shining in a clear blue sky, and the snow was perfect. Claire was having fun. She found that learning to ski made her forget everything: time and place, struggling to get to know Emilie and even the tension between herself and Lucy.

Claire found it very difficult to cope with the fact that Lucy was there, under the same roof. They spoke to each other in polite, bland sentences and avoided each other as much as possible but, sometimes, Claire found the air nearly crackle with tension and she wondered if they would be able to go through the next two weeks without some kind of confrontation.

Then there was Emilie and the discovery that she was not the sweet little girl Claire had imagined. The first morning had started so well, with Emilie happily putting on her brand new ski suit and chatting about the ski school and the fun she would have there. She would spend the whole day with her group, leaving Claire free until five o'clock.

'I want to ski down to the school,' Emilie announced as they were collecting their skis and poles in the garage of the chalet. 'I want to whiz down really fast.'

'But you forget that I can't ski, darling,' Claire protested. 'We have to take the bubble lift down. I'll carry your skis, if you want.'

'But I want to ski.' Emilie glared at Claire.

'You take the boring bubble. You car g abou e at the bottom of the slope.'   happened

Claire stared back at th   onishment. She didn't know sv   ie could be this awkward.

'But darling …'

'No. I'm *not* going down in the lift like a stupid baby.'

'But,' Claire tried, 'I think I should stay with you until you get to your group. Just for today. When I have had a few lessons, we can …'

'NO!' Emilie shouted. 'I WANT TO SKI!'

'But darling, listen to me,' Claire pleaded, feeling as if she was suddenly in a scene from *The Omen*.

'I don't want to listen to you. You're stupid.' Emilie sat down on the floor and stuck out her bottom lip. 'I'm going to tell my daddy about you. He's going to be so angry.'

'Please, Emilie, get up and put on your hat and gloves,' Claire said. She tried to pull her up, but Emilie seemed to have suddenly put on about a hundred pounds and Claire couldn't get her off the floor.

'No.' Emilie wrapped her arms around herself and stuck her chin into her chest. Claire stared helplessly at her, feeling very hot in her ski suit and boots. 'Are you going to sit here all day?'

'Yes.'

'OK.' Claire sighed and put on her ski hat and gloves. 'In that case, have a great day. I'm going to

ge_ _ _le down to the ski school and start
my le_ _ _ _ your teacher you didn't want to
come a_ _ _ _ ly don't want to try to get
the seco_ _ _ _ _ _ ust have to be happy with
the first _ _ _ _ _ _ n next year all the other
children wil ...

Emilie looked up at Claire. 'You're just trying
to trick me, aren't you? You're pretending not to
care. But I know you do. You can't just leave me
here. You have to look after me. It's your job.'

Suddenly something snapped in Claire. She
leaned down and grabbed Emilie's arm. 'You
listen to me, you little brat,' she whispered. 'You
get up right now, put on the rest of your clothes
and get your ass in gear. You're coming with me
on the bubble, and that's final.'

They stared at each other. Emilie was first to
look away. 'All right,' she muttered. 'There's no
need to lose your temper.'

'Lose my temper? I'm just a little annoyed.
You wouldn't want to see me *really* angry, darling,
believe me.'

'I'm not scared of you.'

'And I'm not scared of *you*.'

'You pinched me.'

'I was just trying to pull you up. Let's not
waste any more time. We'll have to hurry down to
join your ski group, or they'll go off without you.'

'Oh, all right.' Emilie was suddenly more
willing. They travelled down to the bottom of the
nursery slope in the bubble lift, Claire in

thoughtful silence and Emilie prattling ~~~~ this and that, as if nothing at all had ~~~~

*

'Miss Dillon?' Bernard Marchand's ~~~~ voice sounded hurried.

'Yes?'

'Just calling to check that everything is all right.'

'Everything is fine.'

'Really? You're getting on with Emilie all right?'

'Of course. Why wouldn't I?' Claire made a face at herself in the mirror over the fireplace in the study.

'So there are no problems? Emilie can be a little bit stubborn at times.'

You're telling me, Claire thought, recalling the power struggle in the late afternoon about not eating a huge hamburger before going back to the chalet and the ensuing sulking that was still taking place as Emilie pretended to watch a Disney cartoon instead of an episode of a truly vulgar teenage sitcom that was her own choice.

'Stubborn?' Claire said. 'I don't know what you mean. She has been a little rebellious but I'm well able to handle that sort of thing.'

'You are?'

'Absolutely.' He could have told me about this, she thought, feeling suddenly very annoyed. Then she remembered the *faux pas* she had made about his wife and felt both embarrassed and guilty. He probably didn't have it so easy.

'Are you sure?' he said. 'You have been there three days already.'

'Mr Marchand,' Claire interrupted, 'If you don't trust me to take care of your daughter, why don't you come down and do it yourself?'

'No, no,' he protested. 'I do believe you. It's just … I mean nobody has been able to …'

'What?'

'Never mind. I don't have the time to discuss this right now. I have to go to a working dinner …'

'But it was you who rang me,' Claire said.

'Are you in a bad mood?'

'I wasn't until just this minute.'

He sighed. 'Look,' he continued, sounding suddenly brisk, 'I just called to see if Emilie was all right. I didn't want to have a bad-tempered discussion with you.'

'Emilie's fine. Do you want to talk to her?'

'No, I haven't time. I'll call tomorrow, if that's all right.'

'Of course.'

'But, before I go … Could I ask you something?'

'About what?'

'When we talked about this trip and I asked you to accompany Emilie, you said no immediately. I didn't think there was any way I could persuade you. Then, a month later, you called and said … well, you know what you said.'

'Yes, I said I would be delighted to take you up on the offer.'

'That's right. So what I wanted to ask you was, why?'

'Well,' Claire started, wondering what he would say if she told him the truth. What is the truth, she asked herself. Unexpected thoughts flashed through her mind. I'm fed up with my life. What life? Pretending to have this romantic relationship with a student half my age, living in a grotty apartment in the wrong part of Paris and never having enough money? Having been fired from my job and having to say goodbye to those children I've become so fond of? Or maybe I should tell him that, since the day he walked into my classroom, I can't stop thinking about him, that I have never felt so attracted to a man in my whole life. She cleared her throat. 'I needed a break,' she said.

'Oh. I see. You needed to get away for a bit?'

'Something like that.'

'I understand. Well, I have to go now, I'm afraid. Goodbye then, Miss Dillon, I wish you a very good night.'

'You too,' Claire said, feeling a little awkward. 'I mean have a good one too. Night, I mean … Oh, damn. Good night.' She could hear him laughing as she hung up.

*

'Look,' Tiffany said at breakfast the next morning. 'It's still snowing.'

102

'Isn't that great?' Lucy poured coffee into her cup and reached for an apple.

'There'll be a couple of inches of fresh powder on the slopes,' Penny said happily. 'Fantastic.'

'And it is just about five degrees below freezing and no wind,' Dave filled in, coming in from the kitchen with a jug of hot milk. 'And I just heard on Radio Courchevel that *ze wezzer is going to cheer up and sunshine will be provided.* And last night they said that *zere was a lot of snow falling even on ze bottom, and we can expect a big risk of avarice on all pistes.*'

Emilie giggled.

'If the weather stays this good, Warren and I are doing The Three Valleys tomorrow,' Lucy announced. 'We'll be gone all day. Do you want to come with us, Penny?'

'That's a lot of skiing in one day,' Penny remarked. 'All the way across the next two valleys and back. I don't know if I'll be up to it.'

'But you're a much better skier than any of us,' Lucy said. 'I wouldn't go down some of those black slopes you seem to love.'

'I'm just a little older,' Penny sighed. 'I don't mind the odd swift, steep run. It's the long haul all day I find a bit too much to cope with. But I'm sure you'll love it, Lucy.'

'Are you going with them, Claire?' Al asked, taking out a cigar, but putting it back in his pocket just as quickly when Penny frowned at him.

'God, no,' Claire laughed. 'I'm staying in the

kindergarten class with Antoine. I don't seem to be a very fast learner. Most of my group are whizzing down the red slopes by now, but …'

'You'll get the hang of it,' Patrick said. 'Some people take a little longer, that's all.'

'Maybe I don't try hard enough,' Claire replied. 'I've never been good at lessons. Remember what a klutz I was at ballet, Lucy?' For a moment, she forgot the bitterness and was transported back to those days when they were ten-year-old girls and best friends, those happy days, when they had been convinced that nothing could ever come between them.

But there was anger in Lucy's eyes. 'No, I don't,' she snapped. 'Don't remember much about that at all.'

'Maybe you don't want to remember,' Emilie piped in. 'I try to forget horrible things too. Because if you don't think about them, they don't make you sad.'

Claire looked thoughtfully at Emilie. Then she put a hand on Emilie's shoulder and gave it a little squeeze. 'Oh, darling,' she whispered, 'how right you are.'

'More orange juice, Emilie?' Dave asked.

'No thanks.'

'If you've finished your breakfast, why don't you go and put on your ski clothes?' Claire suggested. 'And, if you're really quick, I'll put a chocolate bar in your lunch box.'

'Two!' Emilie demanded.

'No, just one,' Claire said in a calm but firm tone.

'Two.'

'One.'

'But I want two chocolate bars,' Emilie insisted. 'If you don't put two bars in my lunch, I won't go to ski school at all. So there.'

'If there is any more arguing, there'll be no chocolate at all and a smack on your bottom,' Claire retorted. 'The choice is up to you.'

Claire and Emilie looked at each other in a silent battle of wills.

'Oh, OK.' Emilie slunk out of the dining room. 'Meanie,' she muttered as she left.

There was a brief silence.

'You sure don't take any prisoners,' Patrick said.

'Is it really necessary to be so strict?' Lucy asked. 'I mean, she is such a sweet little girl.'

'She is about as sweet as the Wicked Witch of the West,' Claire replied. 'And you have to be one step ahead all the time, or she'll eat you alive.'

Lucy suddenly laughed. 'It's so strange seeing you being the authoritarian, Claire, considering what you were like as a child. You were oddly like Emilie, if I remember correctly; always arguing and scheming to get your own way.'

'I'm *so* relieved your memory has come back,' Claire shot back. 'And maybe you're right. I might have been a bit of a handful when I was that age. But that's why I know how to cope with her. It takes one to know one, I always say. I know what goes on in that little head before she knows it herself. Besides, that kind of child is a lot more honest than the Goody-Two-Shoes you were.'

Lucy returned Claire's smile with a cold stare.

'What does her father think of threats and physical abuse?' Penny enquired.

'I suspect he knows exactly what she's like,' Claire said. 'Dave told me she has had six nannies.'

'Well, that might just be staff problems,' Penny suggested. 'It is difficult to get any kind of domestic staff these days. It is in New York, in any case. I'm sure it's the same over here.'

'It must be such a drag to be rich,' Lucy murmured into her mug of coffee.

'What?' Al asked. 'I didn't catch that.'

'Oh, nothing.'

'Well, I'm ready to head off,' Patrick said, getting up from the table.

'Are you really well enough to ski?' Penny wanted to know.

'Yes, I am. But this is the first time since my slight accident, so I'm just going to do the slopes around here with Tiffany. I'll stay on the blues this morning and then maybe a couple of reds this afternoon. Are you coming, little sister?'

'Do I have to?'

'Yes, you do,' Patrick said, his voice stern. 'It will do you good. Fresh air and exercise. Just what you need. Either you come with me or go for a walk in the village.'

'OK then.' Tiffany sighed as she rose. 'I'll come with you.'

*

'*Bonjour*,' the lift operator said as Lucy showed him her ski pass. She smiled back and followed the queue of skiers as they slowly shuffled forward toward the chair lifts. When she was finally seated beside Warren, the chair lift rose swiftly up the steep hill and Lucy looked down at the beautiful scenery below as she travelled to the top.

It had turned into a perfect day. The sun shone from a cloudless sky on the white slopes, snow-covered trees and skiers far below in their vividly coloured clothes. There was a competition on one of the pistes and Lucy could see little puffs of snow each time the skiers went around the slalom poles. The sound of music in the distance and the faint smell of garlic and chips from one of the restaurants added to the holiday mood.

Lucy had never felt so intensely alive, so content and carefree. There was something about the air, the light and the whole atmosphere that made her forget everything and just think of this moment, this place and the challenge ahead. It was such a welcome break from the frustration she felt about Patrick, constantly fighting the attraction she felt for him and the hurt of his behaviour towards her.

'It's the c__. God, it had been such a shock to ___ __ their __ Lucy didn't quite know how to deal with __ __ __ should she pretend nothing had ever happened and hope Claire had forgotten all about it? Wasn't it time to move on, Lucy thought, nobody can hold a grudge that long. It's not as if it was a major crime … Why couldn't Claire understand why I needed that money? She never really listened to me when I talked about what I wanted to do. If she had, she wouldn't have been so shocked … But things will work out eventually, Lucy thought. I'm earning enough now: I can pay her back and all will be forgiven. I might even give her a thousand extra as a thank you. That should make her happy. Lucy smiled and closed her eyes to the sun and breathed in the clear, cold air. 'Oh,' she sighed, 'isn't it strange how it all makes you feel you can do anything?'

'You get a kind of high on a day like this,' Warren agreed. 'But it is deceptive. The mountains are dangerous. You can never trust them.'

Lucy looked up at the jagged peaks outlined against the blue sky. They loomed above, majestic, mysterious and proud. 'I can't imagine that there would be any danger now,' she replied. 'It's such a gorgeous day. There isn't a cloud in sight, not even down in the valley.'

'Look.' Warren pointed into the valley below. 'See the haze down there?'

'Yes?' Lucy said, as she looked. 'I can see just a hint of mist.'

'Means a change in tempera⸻
explained. 'But not just yet. By ⸻
afternoon, there'll be low clouds. ⸻ they
come up this far, we'll have thick fog. ⸻

'Really?'

'Yes, there's a big risk of that happening. But
don't worry about that now. Let's just enjoy the
skiing. We'll be back before the weather changes.'

*

'Isn't this such a *fancy* place?' Emilie said, looking
around the tea rooms as they were waiting for her
teacher to join them.

'I know what you mean,' Claire agreed. 'It
must be the most glamorous *salon de thé* in the
Alps.'

'All the ladies are wearing fur coats,' Emilie
remarked. 'And look,' she whispered, 'there is
even a man in a mink jacket over there. A bit
girlie, don't you think?'

'I know.'

'I don't think my daddy would put on clothes
like that,' Emilie giggled. 'Or wear jewellery.'

'I suppose not.' Claire smiled as she imagined
the macho-looking Bernard Marchand in a mink
jacket and a heavy gold chain and bracelets.

'He thinks you're *really* pretty,' Emilie said,
tilting her head and studying Claire critically.

'Does he?'

'Mmm. He told me. He said you have royal
blue eyes. What is royal blue?'

olour of a kind of ink people used to put i... ...e fountain pens years ago.'

'In th...olden days?'

'The olden days,' Claire corrected.

'Do you remember them?' Emilie wanted to know. 'Those *olden* days?'

'I suppose I do.'

'So does my daddy. He talks about them a lot. He says you remind him of a girl in a book he had when he was a little boy. A girl with dark curls and royal blue eyes. Do you have a fur coat?'

'No. I don't really like them.'

'Good. Because I really *hate* fur coats,' Emilie stated. 'Small animals have to be killed to make them. Did you know that? I think it's *awful* to be killed and end up on the back of some rich old bitch.'

'What?' Claire stared at Emilie. 'Where did you hear language like that?'

'Tiffany. I heard her say that to the other lady last night.'

'Penny?'

'Yes, that's her name. They were talking in the living room. But Penny got *really* cross and said did you mean me, and Tiffany said if the shoe fits. And then Penny got even crosser and walked out of the room.' Emilie looked at Claire, her eyes wide. 'Is Penny a rich old bitch?'

'You shouldn't listen to other people's conversations.'

'But I couldn't help it. It's not my fault they didn't see me. I was right *there*. But you didn't tell me. Is Penny –'

'Mrs Freeman,' Claire corrected. 'You shouldn't really call her by her first name.'

'Mrs Freeman. But is she really a ...'

'Never mind that now.'

'Then can I have another cup of chocolate? They're very small cups and it's hours till dinnertime and could I have one of those little chocolate croissants as well, they're so light, I promise I'll eat everything all up at dinner and *jump* into my pyjamas.'

'Slow down.' Claire could not help but laugh. 'Yes, you can. I know you worked very hard at your skiing today, your teacher told me. And I will have more of everything too. Skiing sure makes you hungry.' She sat back in the comfortable chair. This was such a warm, cosy place after the icy winds outside. A fire flickered in the grate, there was a murmur of conversation, classical music was playing softly and the smell of chocolate and freshly baked pastries wafting through the air would make even the most disciplined slimmers succumb.

'You're very nice today, Claire,' Emilie said, taking a huge slug of her chocolate.

'I'm nice, because you're so very good,' Claire smiled. 'So I hope you'll be like this all the time from now on.'

'Look at that funny shop across the street,'

Emilie said, changing the subject. 'Why do they have a shop like that in a ski village? Wouldn't you freeze if you wore things like that under your ski suit?'

'Well maybe the, uh, ladies who wear those kind of things don't do much skiing.'

'Oh. But what do they do instead?'

'Oh look,' Claire said, 'here's your teacher now. She looks really cold.'

'Let's order some hot chocolate for her too,' Emilie suggested.

*

'I can't,' Lucy protested. 'It's too dangerous. I'll break my neck, and it will be all your fault.'

'Of course not,' Warren argued. 'You'll be fine. You're becoming a really good skier, you know.'

'I was only pretending.' Lucy looked down the mountain, her knees shaking. A black slope. The most difficult of all. And Warren was trying to make her go down this virtually perpendicular drop. The icy wind made her shiver even more. Oh, God, I'll never come out of this alive, she thought.

It was half past three in the afternoon and they were on their way back to the resort. They had enjoyed the spectacular scenery and the warm sun on their faces while they slowly travelled up. But, when Lucy stood at the top of this steep slope on what was now the shaded side of the mountain, she was beginning to change her mind. The mountain top loomed above her, casting a dark shadow on the snow, and a cold wind had started to blow. She looked up and could see grey clouds approaching.

A group of about ten children had just arrived at the top of the piste with their instructor. Lucy looked at them. They were about six years old and all wore helmets. How irresponsible of their instructor to bring them to a black slope, she thought. How are they going to get down? But the children went over the edge and swooped straight down the nearly vertical mountainside at break-neck speed like a flock of birds.

'See?' Warren said. 'Small children can do this easily.'

'They don't have the sense to be scared,' Lucy replied. 'And children never really look down the slope. They only see what's right in front of them. And, in any case, those French kids were born on skis.' She stared down the slope again, the sheer drop making her stomach lurch. This was going to be hard.

Warren looked up at the gathering clouds. 'We better get started if we don't want to get caught in the fog and low cloud,' he urged. 'I'm sorry, but the only way back is down.'

'I know,' Lucy whispered.

'We'll take the bubble at the bottom of this one,' Warren said. 'That's the last lift, then we just have a few more slopes and we're home. You'll be sipping *vin chaud* before you know it.'

'If we're still alive.'

'Come on, it's not that bad,' Warren laughed. 'Just ski down to that marker over there and turn. I'll be right behind you.'

'OK.' Lucy pushed off. It wasn't too hard at first and the sound of Warren's skis behind her was reassuring. She skied around an outcrop and stopped with a gasp. Shit, she thought as she looked at the sweep of the slope straight down the mountain. This is impossible. But I better keep going, or I'll panic, she said to herself, and made a deal with God to be very, very good if only he would help her get down the piste in one piece. She slid down carefully to a place where she could turn. She turned again, listening to Warren's skis behind her. Another turn. She was so nervous her muscles felt like spaghetti.

'We're nearly there,' Warren shouted as he skied past her. 'Hurry up now, or we'll miss the last lift.'

Lucy stood for a moment, the freezing, damp cold making her whole body feel stiff. She tried to spot Warren and, as she squinted through the whirling mist, she saw him disappear into the fog.

*

Startled by a sound somewhere in the house, Penny had woken up not knowing where she was. She sat up in the bath, looked around her, confused, and slowly recognised her surround-

114

ings. She suddenly felt cold and turned on the hot water tap. She must have been asleep for quite a while. She took the tumbler of bourbon from the edge of the bathtub and drank deeply as the water became warm again. She drained the last drops from the glass and lay back, lifted a leg and pointed her toes. Still good, she thought, my legs are still as good as ever. Rich old bitch? Is that what she called me? But I'm still young, still in my prime. I – She froze. What was that? Another sound. Someone in the kitchen. Dave must be back from the shops. She lowered her leg back into the water. Better get up or I'll go to sleep again. Is that old age? Getting sleepy in the bath? No, she reassured herself, it was just the effects of skiing combined with the bourbon and the warm water. Another shot won't do any harm.

Half an hour later, Penny, still in her bathrobe, drifted into the kitchen, feeling deliciously relaxed. She was going to ask Dave to make her some tea, and she would even, just this once, have one of those lovely scones she had refused yesterday. Just one wouldn't cause that much damage after all that skiing. And just a tiny speck of strawberry jam … She stopped dead and stared at the young man sitting at the kitchen table. She giggled suddenly, thinking if this was still a dream, it was rather a nice one.

He looked up from his plate of bread and cheese.

'*Bonjour Madame.*'

'Eh, *bonjour*,' Penny replied. 'I'm sorry, I don't speak very good French.'

'Oh.' He rose politely. 'But I speak a leetle English. I am Michel.'

'Of course you are. But do sit down.'

Michel resumed his seat. 'And you?' he asked.

'And I what?'

'Who are you?'

'Who am I?' Penny sank down on a chair opposite Michel. 'That's a good question.' She propped her chin in her hand and looked deep into his eyes. 'You want to know who I *really* am?'

'Of course.'

'OK. I'll tell you. My name …' Penny smiled conspiratorially, 'is Peggy-Sue Kowalski.'

8

Lucy was beginning to feel dizzy. It's like being trapped in a carton of milk, she thought. I don't know up from down. She had somehow managed to catch the last bubble lift, hoping she would catch up with Warren. But, when she got out of the lift at the top of the next slope, she found herself alone. She looked up, trying to see the sky, then ahead. Nothing, just swirling whiteness. She looked down at her skis, trying to figure out how steep the slope was, and pushed forward. She suddenly slid nearly straight down and had to do a sharp turn to stop herself falling. OK, she thought, her heart pounding, I'll just traverse for a bit then … what's that? A marker. Great. 'Follow the markers,' Warren had said, before he disappeared. The bastard. Wouldn't you think he'd stick around? Probably sitting in the bar of his hotel having a laugh about it right now. No, he wouldn't. He must have gone for help. Everyone must be frantic worrying about me. OK. Keep going. Next marker. And the next. Lucy was beginning to get the hang of it, adjusting to the gradient of the slope. It was colder now, a numbing, damp cold that seeped into her bones. Don't stop, she ordered herself, don't sit down in the snow even for a moment. Then you'll never get up again. Keep going.

Slowly, slowly, Lucy managed to get down to the bottom of the first slope. She saw the shape of a house ahead of her. The restaurant just before the next piste. She knew it well: they had lunched there the day before. Omelette and salad, she remembered, her stomach rumbling, followed by a slice of sinful chocolate cake. Maybe there's someone there who could … But the building was dark, the shutters closed. Lucy sighed and pressed on, down the next piste. Two reds and a blue, then I'll be there, she told herself. Hurry up now, the daylight's beginning to fade. Must get home and tell everyone I'm alive. They'll be so worried, some of them crying, maybe even praying. It's not fair to frighten them like this. Lucy struggled on in the gathering gloom, fighting to stay upright, down the steep slope.

*

Penny hitched up the bathrobe that was threatening to fall off her shoulder. 'Tea?' she asked, holding the teapot aloft.

'*Non, merci,*' Michel replied. 'I like wine with ze cheese.'

'Of course. How about one of these, then?' She indicated the plate of scones.

'No, thank you.'

'Never mind,' Penny said, helping herself to another and putting a big blob of strawberry jam on top. 'This is my third one. I shouldn't really, but they are so delicious. Sure you won't have one?'

'*Non,*' Michel shook his head with a little laugh. 'I don't like – how you say – scanns?'

'S-C-O-N-E-S,' Penny mouthed. 'They are divine. But soooo bad for my figure. Ooops, a blob of jam down my ...' She peered at her cleavage and fished up the jam with her finger. 'But you don't seem to give in to temptations. I suppose that's how you keep that lovely shape?' She sucked her finger.

'What?' Michel was looking at Penny's chest. 'Shape? What is ... ?' His eyes travelled up to her face.

'It means your ...' Penny ran her hands down her body, 'figure.'

'Oh. You mean *silhouette*?'

'Yeah,' Penny said, slowly eating her scone. 'That's what I meant.'

'You have a very bjottifol *silhouette, Madame.*'

'Not Madame. Penny.'

'Penny?' Michel looked at her, confused. 'But you said your name was ... Peggy ... eh ...'

'Did I? Oh, shit. No, no, that is just my ...'

'*Nom de jeune fille?*'

'What's that?'

'It is the name of the woman before the ... eh ... *mariage*.'

'Yeah, yeah, that's it. But,' Penny put her finger in front of her mouth, 'it's a secret. Shhh ...'

'Shhh.' Michel echoed, copying her gesture. Then he grinned. 'You are a very interesting woman. *Une femme très interessante.*'

'Oh, thank you,' Penny beamed. Nobody had called her interesting before. 'But do have a bite.' She held out the last of her scone, dripping with jam. 'Go on, try it,' she urged.

Michel leaned forward and bit delicately into the scone.

'Good?' she asked.

'Mmm,' he murmured, his mouth touching the tips of her fingers. He started to lick the jam off them.

'Thought you'd like it,' Penny purred.

*

'Hi, Dave,' Claire said as she and Emilie reached the front door of the chalet. 'Can we help you carry all that shopping?'

'Oh, thanks,' he replied. 'I had to go out for some milk and stuff. Then I realised we were out of a whole lot of other things so I got rather weighed down.'

Claire held the door open for him as they walked into the garage.

'We've been to the tea salon,' Emilie said, taking off her anorak. 'We drank lots of hot chocolate and we had cakes and buns and …'

'Stop,' Claire said, 'Dave will think we had some kind of pig-out. He'll think we won't have any room for dinner.' She bent down and helped Emilie take off her boots.

'But we do,' Emilie said. 'We have lots of room. I have skied all day and I just know I'll be hungry again very soon.'

'Isn't it great to be young,' Claire said wistfully, taking off her own boots, 'and not have to worry about calories.'

'But you don't worry about them,' Emilie said. 'You never say no to food.'

'Shhh,' Claire said. 'There's no need to make me sound like a hungry hippo. Here, give me that bag, Dave, and Emilie will take the bread.'

'But I forgot,' Dave suddenly exclaimed as they were walking up the stairs. 'You have a visitor, Claire.'

'Me?' Claire asked, mystified. 'Who?'

'He didn't tell me his name. But he did say he was one of your students. Funny, he seems a little old to be in primary school …'

Claire didn't wait to hear the rest. She ran up the last steps, down the corridor to the kitchen and pushed the door open. The scene that met her eyes made her gasp. 'Michel!' she snapped, suddenly losing her grip on the bag she was carrying.

Michel whipped his head around. '*Chérie!*' He let go of Penny's hand, shot up from his seat and tried to put his arms around Claire. 'Are you not pleased to see me?' He kissed her on both cheeks, but she glared angrily at him.

'What are you doing here?' she snapped in French. 'Why did you just arrive like this out of the blue without telling me you were coming? And *what* are you doing with that jam?'

'I missed you so much. I just hopped on the train from Paris this morning. Thought I'd come and spend a couple of days with you. I explained this to that nice chef who works here and he said I could wait for you here in the kitchen and he even gave me something to eat. Then this lovely lady offered me some …'

'You hate jam,' Claire interrupted. 'And here you are licking it off that …'

'Emilie,' Dave said, taking the bread from her, 'why don't you go into the living room and watch TV? The children's programmes are just starting.'

'No,' Emilie said, 'I want to stay here. This is much more interesting.'

'And I'll bring you some of those chocolate biscuits you like?' Dave continued.

'And Coca-Cola?'

'And Coke,' Dave sighed.

'Oh, all right.' Dave disappeared with Emilie in tow.

Claire didn't notice Emilie and Dave leave. She continued her tirade for a full five minutes, only stopping for breath when Michel snapped at her to shut up for just a moment.

'Listen, darlings,' Penny interrupted their arguing. 'Would you mind speaking English? My French is a bit rusty and I'm having a little trouble following what you're saying.'

'This is a private conversation,' Claire snapped.

'Yes, but I saw him first,' Penny replied. 'I don't know where he came from, or what he's doing here …'

'I came from Paris,' Michel said, 'and I come here to … to *rendezvous* with Claire …'

'Oh?' Penny said. 'I see.' She looked from Claire to Michel. 'I get it now.'

'No, you don't,' Claire said. 'Michel is one of my students.'

'What?' Penny said, looking confused. 'He's very tall for a …'

Claire sighed. 'I teach English to adults in the evenings,' she explained. 'And Michel is one of those, that's all. He happens to be here for some reason and just popped in to say hello, and now he's popping right out again. OK?'

'*Non*,' Michel argued. 'It is not. I am going to stay. I have a room in ze village for one week.'

'You what?' Claire exclaimed.

'But that's wonderful,' Penny beamed. 'Then we can see *lots* of each other.'

'He seems to have seen rather a lot of you already,' Claire remarked, eyeing Penny's bath-

123

robe. 'Al was coming back shortly after us, you know. He was asking for you.'

'Oh God,' Penny muttered, pulling her robe together and getting up from her chair. 'I better go. Bye, bye,' she chanted and waggled her fingers at Michel. 'See you around?'

'*A bientôt*,' Michel smiled as she sauntered out of the kitchen. '*Une très belle femme*,' he said to Claire as the door swung shut behind Penny.

'Stunning,' Claire said in a flat tone. 'Listen,' she continued, 'you can't stay here. I'm working, you know. I'm looking after that little girl. And, if you stay, you'll just get in the way. Why don't you go back to Paris? I think there's a train this evening. I'll be back in ten days or so …'

'No.' Michel shook his head. 'I want to stay here and do a bit of skiing. Two of my friends from university are here.'

'Oh, God,' Claire sighed. 'What am I going to do with you? I just want to do this job and then go back to Paris. I can't have you hanging around.' She looked at him sternly. 'Stay then. But, please leave me alone. Try to pretend you don't know me. Do you think you could do that for me?'

'But why, *chérie*?' Michel asked.

'Please. Don't ask. Just do it.'

*

'Put another log on, Patrick,' Al suggested. 'I'm still feeling a bit cold.'

'It's the damp,' Patrick said, stirring the embers with a brass poker and placing a big log on top. 'The fog creates this terrible damp cold.'

'How's your knee, Patrick?' Penny asked, wrapping her hands around a glass of hot whisky.

'Not too bad. I managed to ski without feeling too much pain.'

'It's getting late. Is everybody home?' Al asked.

'Everyone except Lucy,' Patrick said.

'Probably gone for a drink with her coach,' Penny said. 'I thought that's what she said she would do. And then they probably went on somewhere. She'll be home later.' She looked out the window. 'It's very foggy out there, though.'

'A bit like that dark forest in my storybook,' Emilie said. 'We could pretend we're in the wilderness and cut off from silverisation.'

'Civilisation,' Claire corrected automatically.

'And we have only stale bread and mouldy cheese to eat,' Emilie continued.

'What a bloody nightmare,' Tiffany muttered.

'No,' Emilie said, 'not a nightmare, silly. An adventure. And we can pretend Dave is a friendly woodsman who is bringing us meat to eat and that boy who was licking jam off Penny can be ...'

'Emilie!' Claire chided.

'Oh, sorry. Mrs Freeman, I mean. He was licking jam off Mrs Freeman.'

'What?' Al asked. 'What are you talking about?'

125

'Come on, darling,' Claire said, 'let's go and see if Dave's all right in the kitchen, will we? We'll take this lovely candleholder that looks like a reindeer. You can hold it if you're really careful.'

'OK,' Emilie agreed, taking the candlestick. 'Let's go and say boo to him.' The candle flickered, casting huge shadows on the wall as they made their way down the corridor to the kitchen.

*

Lucy couldn't tell what colour the markers were. It was becoming even darker and she felt like just lying down in the snow and going to sleep. But the thought of the calamity it would cause if she … Oh God, don't even think about it. Got to get back. Al and Penny will be sick with fright by now, Claire so upset. Little Emilie frightened, Tiffany … No, forget her. Patrick … Oh God, Patrick … What if I never see him again? The thought of Patrick made her feel a little more alive and gave her a reason to keep going. She struggled on, his face shimmering before her eyes like a mirage. The fog was still whirling around her. She saw a shadow ahead. Thank God. One of those little huts. She shuffled forward and grabbed the edge of something, the corner of the hut, probably. There was a light right above her and she lifted her face, trying to figure out what it was. It looked strangely like a … No, it couldn't be. And that noise … is that a car? My mind is playing tricks. I'm hallucinating like those people who got lost in the Andes. Lucy closed her eyes and hung onto the side of the hut, trying to clear her head. Claire, she suddenly thought, I have to talk to her. I don't want her to hate me. If I survive this, I'm going to do my best to make it up to her. Lucy's knees gave way and she sank down in the snow. Don't lie down, she told herself. Never lie down. Get up, stand up straight …'One, two, three,' she muttered. 'Just like at ballet, and lift, two, three … Oh, Claire …'

*

The ballet teacher's voice echoed in the big, cold hall. The pianist looked bored as he played the tune over and over again. 'One, two, three and lift, two, three, *Demi plié,*' the teacher called. 'Arms round and soft, and hands … Claire, where's your hand?'

'It flew out the window,' Claire muttered under her breath. Lucy giggled while she tried to keep her feet in position and her back straight. Claire blew on the back of her neck, making her wobble. Lucy lost her balance and nearly fell on Claire and the whole line of girls collapsed in laughter.

The ballet teacher clapped her hands. 'Please, behave now, girls, you know the exam is next week. We want to be ab-so-lu-tely … What do we want to be? Class?'

'Absolutely perfect,' the class chanted.

'Exactly.' The teacher nodded. 'That wasn't bad, but Claire, you have to try to concentrate, and Lucy, you must learn to straighten your back. What do I always say?' She looked questioningly at Lucy.

'Pull up your breastbone,' Lucy replied.

'And …?'

'Tuck in your bum,' Claire whispered.

'Tuck in my derrière,' Lucy said, trying not to look at Claire.

'That's right.' The teacher clapped her hands again. 'All right, girls, floor work. Places, please!'

Twenty ten-year-old girls dressed in pink leotards and ballet shoes took their places in the middle of the worn parquet floor.

'Prepare,' the teacher said. Twenty pairs of feet adopted the second position. 'And …' Twenty pairs of arms went up in the air. The music started again. 'One, two, three …'

'Why do you try so hard?' Claire whispered to Lucy. 'You look as if you're going to explode.'

'But I want to get my exam. Don't you?' Lucy whispered back.

'I don't care,' Claire mumbled. 'Do you want to have dinner at my house tonight? My mum said to ask you. You can call your mum from home.'

'I don't have to.' Lucy lifted her arms again and did a half-turn. 'My mother isn't home.'

Claire went up on her toes in a wobbly *elevée*. 'Then we'll go to your place,' she suggested in a low mutter, trying to keep her balance. 'We can order pizza like the last time and watch videos and dress up in your mother's clothes. Please, Lucy?'

'Oh, OK. But only if we can go to your house next time.'

Claire landed back on her heels with a thump. 'Deal.'

*

Lucy wrapped her arms around herself where she lay in the snow, the memories flooding into her mind like pictures in a storybook from long ago. Although her face was stiff with cold, she smiled as she remembered. Then she frowned. 'But I broke it,' she mumbled, 'I broke the deal.' I broke it for money and success, she thought. And it worked, boy, did it ever. But why do I feel so miserable sometimes, then? Why am I so lonely? Suddenly a big lump of snow landed on her forehead, waking her out of her daze. Snow, she thought, I seem to be lying in snow. She turned, got up on her knees and tried to stand, but was too numb to move further. She grabbed the side of the hut and heaved herself up again. She tried to find her skis, but her legs did not seem to want to obey her. As she stood there, frozen to the spot, she heard that faint sound again ...

9

'And they lived happily ever after,' Claire said.

'Did they?' Emilie wondered. 'How do we know? Maybe they discovered they didn't like each other when they got back to the castle? Maybe Cinderella didn't want to be queen? Maybe she wanted to get a job in a bank?'

'Of course she didn't.'

'How do you know?' Emilie insisted. 'Did anyone bother to ask her?'

'Well, I mean ...' Claire looked at Emilie's troubled face. 'She seemed so happy, didn't she?'

'You should never take anyone for granted, my daddy always says. Or that they want what *you* think they want.'

'Does he?' Claire asked softly, thinking Emilie was very young to be so philosophical.

'Yes, he does. So I hope the prince asked

Cinderella if she was *really* sure she wanted to be queen.'

'I'm sure he did and she was very happy.' Claire showed Emilie the picture at the end of the book. 'Just look at how handsome the prince is.'

'He looks a little bit stupid,' Emilie remarked. 'I mean the way he carried on after she had run off. And another thing …'

'Yes?' Claire asked, tucking the duvet around Emilie.

'You know when the clock struck twelve and everything turned back into what it was before?'

'Mmmm?' Claire put the book away.

'Well, how come the glass slipper didn't disappear?'

'Eh … well … Yes, you're right. That was a bit strange all right. But, if it had, there wouldn't have been much of a story, of course.'

'And Cinderella would have gone home and that would have been it. She would have carried on being the maid and those awful step-girls would have kept pestering her.'

'Just like in real life,' Claire said. 'But that's why we need fairy tales. We need a little bit of magic to cheer us up.'

'Yes,' Emilie sighed and snuggled deeper under the bedclothes. 'Magic is nice. You could get in here beside me if you're cold. There's plenty of room.'

'Good idea. Move over then.'

Emilie made room for Claire and she got in beside the warm little body. 'Thanks, sweetheart, this is much warmer.'

'It's so cosy being here together in my bed.'

'Being cold is not very nice, is it?'

There was no reply from the small bundle. Emilie was fast asleep. Claire turned on her back and looked at the window. The moon appeared behind the clouds and cast an eerie glow in the room. Good, she thought the weather has cleared. Everything will be back to normal tomorrow. I'll be able to sort out the situation with Michel. I'll have to tell him it's all over. I can't go on like this. She sighed. The room was quiet, except for the Mickey Mouse clock ticking on the wall and Emilie's light breathing. The rest of the world seemed far away.

I wonder if Lucy's back, Claire thought. That's another problem I'll have to sort out. We have to talk. We can't just go on behaving like strangers: it's becoming unbearable. We were so close once, as if joined by an invisible bond. When did it all go wrong? Was it happening slowly and I didn't notice? Claire's thoughts went back to that time that felt so long ago now but she couldn't really get a grip on her memories. She snuggled closer to Emilie and nearly dozed off, but then decided to go back downstairs. Maybe Lucy was back. They might even get a chance to talk tonight after everyone else had gone to bed.

*

'I'm finished in the kitchen,' Dave announced, looking into the living room, 'but Lucy's still not back.'

'But I heard the door open and close downstairs about half an hour ago,' Claire said and put her teacup on the small table beside the sofa. 'I thought it was Lucy arriving back.'

'That was me putting out the garbage,' Dave said.

'Where could she be?' Penny said, looking up from her copy of *Vogue*. 'If she was having a drink with her coach, wouldn't she be back by now? Maybe they went on somewhere after dinner?'

'But then she would have called, wouldn't she?' Al said. 'Did she have her cell phone?'

Claire shrugged. 'Don't know.'

'No, she didn't,' Penny said, waving a mobile phone in the air. 'This was lying on the coffee table. It's hers, isn't it?'

'Yes, it is,' Al nodded.

'It's late,' Patrick said, getting up from his chair by the fireplace. 'Are you sure she was having dinner in the village?' He glanced out the window. 'She can't still be up there, can she?'

'Hope not,' Dave replied. 'There was bad fog on the upper slopes all afternoon. But she was with Warren, her ski instructor. He's very experienced.'

'At what?' Patrick said, sounding annoyed. He looked from one to the other. 'Don't you think we should tell someone? Shouldn't we at least alert the mountain rescue centre and tell them she's missing?' He looked at Claire as if willing her to agree with him, and she was surprised by the fear in his eyes.

'Hold on now, pal,' Al soothed, looking very reluctant to do anything but stay in his comfortable chair and finish his brandy. 'No reason to panic yet. Let's wait another hour.'

'But it might be too late,' Patrick insisted. 'She might be in real trouble up there – lost, hurt, what do we know?'

'It's pitch black,' Penny said. 'Even if they went out now, they wouldn't find her. I mean if she really is missing,' she added. 'Which I doubt. I think she's gone out with her instructor and I don't blame her. Nice-looking man.'

'I've left some of the beef casserole in the fridge, in case Lucy is hungry when she comes back,' Dave said. 'I'll be in my room if anyone needs me. And try not to worry. I'm sure she's with Warren.' He walked out of the room and closed the door softly behind him.

'Yes,' Claire said, more to reassure herself than anybody else. 'That must be what happened. She's with Warren. They're down in the village having dinner right now. She probably just forgot to tell us.'

'What do you mean?' Patrick demanded. 'Are you suggesting she would just take off like that without telling us? That's not like Lucy, is it?'

No, it isn't, Claire thought. Not like Lucy at all. All of a sudden, she felt a cold finger of fear creep up her spine. She looked at Patrick and she saw her own dread mirrored in his eyes.

'Easy to forget if you're attracted,' Al said. 'I mean if a girl really likes a guy, she might just get carried away, know what I mean?'

'No, I don't,' Patrick snapped. 'And I suggest we take this seriously, instead of making snide comments like this.' The door opened and he turned around, his face flooded with relief. 'Oh, here she –'

But it was Dave. 'There's a phone call.'

'Lucy?' Patrick asked.

'No, it's Monsieur Marchand,' Dave said apologetically. 'For Claire.'

Patrick's shoulders slumped. Then he grabbed Lucy's mobile. 'I'm going to raise the alarm,' he declared. 'Something has to be done.'

'Yes,' Claire said. 'I think you're right. You call them and I'll go and speak to Mr Marchand. He might have an idea about what to do next.'

Her legs oddly weak, Claire walked up the stairs and into the study. She picked up the receiver. 'Hello?'

'*Bonsoir*, Mademoiselle Dillon.'

'*Bonsoir*,' Claire replied flatly.

'You sound a little strange. No problems with Emilie, I hope?'

'No, no, she's in bed, fast asleep.'

'Good.' His voice sounded so warm and reassuring, Claire's eyes filled with tears. She suddenly sobbed.

'I sense something is wrong. Can you tell me what it is?'

'Oh, Mr Marchand, it's terrible,' Claire exclaimed, the words tumbling out of her mouth. 'Lucy hasn't come back from her ski trip and we're so worried. There's been bad fog up there and she didn't call to say she'd be late. It's not like Lucy not to come back without telling anyone and –'

'Slow down,' Bernard Marchand said. 'Tell me exactly what has happened.'

Tears coursed down Claire's cheeks as she explained the situation.

'When did she leave?' Marchand asked.

'This morning. She was going to do The Three Valleys with Warren. That's her ski instructor. We were expecting her back around six, but there's still no sign of her. And this really bad fog came down onto the upper slopes around three o'clock.'

'I see. Is she a good skier?'

'Very good.'

'And this Warren? Her instructor. Is he experienced? Does he know this area well?'

'I … I don't know. I suppose so.'

'Right.' There was a long pause. 'Have you called the mountain rescue people?'

'Yes, Patrick's doing that right now, but I don't see how they can possibly do anything in the dark.'

'Has the fog cleared?'

'Yes.'

'Then they might, if she had the sense to stay on the slopes. They can go up with snow scooters that have really strong headlights. She is a sensible young woman, would you say?'

'Oh, yes. Very.'

'Good. I'm sure she is all right. Probably just stuck somewhere and has decided to wait till morning. There are plenty of little huts up there where you can take shelter. That's what I would do. And if her instructor is experienced he will have done just that. Try not to worry.'

'If something happens to her, I'll never forgive myself,' Claire whispered as if to herself.

'Why? I don't see how this would be your fault in any way.'

'No, but she is my closest friend. Was, I mean. Years ago.'

'Years ago? And now?'

'We had a silly row and I was so stupid I didn't understand, wouldn't forgive her, and now … Oh, God, now, if she is …' Claire couldn't say the word. She started to cry in earnest, violent sobs racking her body and her hand shook so much she could hardly hold the receiver to her ear.

'Mademoiselle Dillon,' Marchand said sharply. 'Claire!'

'Yes?' Claire stammered.

'Try to calm down.'

'Calm down? How can I, when …'

'Take a deep breath.' The warmth and

sympathy in Marchand's voice was suddenly gone and he sounded angry. 'Go, on, do as I say. Try to pull yourself together.'

Claire drew a shuddering breath. 'All right,' she said. 'OK. I'll try.'

'Good girl. I understand you must be very worried, but going to pieces will not help you or the others.'

'I suppose,' Claire mumbled. His voice was so reassuring, even when annoyed, that she didn't want him to stop talking. She hung onto the receiver with both hands as if her life depended on it. 'Don't go,' she whispered.

'I'm here.'

'Thank you.'

The door to the study suddenly opened and Patrick stood there, his face white. The receiver dropped out of Claire's hands. 'What's happened?' she asked. 'Have they found her?'

'Yes,' Patrick said. 'They have.'

*

Lucy woke up. God, I'm stiff and sore, she thought. Why … Oh, the exam. Claire and I must have been at ballet practice. I'll never get the hang of the steps for the floor work. And I'll *never* do the splits like that again.

'Oh, sorry, didn't know if you had woken up,' Dave said.

'What?' Lucy opened her eyes fully and looked around the living room, then at Claire on the other sofa, asleep, her hair tousled and her mouth slightly open the way she always slept. 'Oh … yes,' Lucy mumbled. 'I'm awake.'

'Feeling OK?'

'Yes … no … What time is it?'

'Nine o'clock or thereabouts.'

'In the morning?'

'Of course. I was just about to pull back the curtains. It's a lovely sunny day.' He looked at her again and frowned. 'Maybe you should try to go back to sleep?'

'No, I'm OK.'

'Sure? You look terrible.'

'No, I'm all right. Tired and stiff. But the fog … How did I get back?'

'It's a long story.' Dave sat down on the edge of the sofa. 'Warren was seriously worried, you know. He was up on the slalom slope with the *pisteurs* for hours trying to find you. Then, when he came down here to tell us, you were already back.'

'I was? How?' Lucy put her hand on her forehead, trying to remember.

'You were brought in by this guy who found you in the village. Outside the supermarket, he said.'

'What? I don't believe you.'

'It's true. You were hanging on to a sign saying "special offer, leg of lamb half price". You must have been seriously lost. But that's not the most amazing part of the story,' Dave said. 'This guy who found you turned out to be this tennis pro. Appears he has an apartment here.'

'Are you serious?' Lucy said, staring at Dave. 'Wow.'

'Oh yes. He carried you in here. It was like something out of a Tarzan movie. Tiffany was green with envy.'

'Oh, God. I can't remember anything at all from the time I sort of seized up on the mountain. Well, that's where I thought I was, in any case. But I must have made it all the way down without realising it. I just couldn't go on. I'm sorry to have caused so much trouble. I hope they weren't too worried.'

'No, I don't think so. Apart from Warren, the only two people who were really scared were Patrick and Claire. When that guy brought you in, they were both as white as sheets. Anyway, Patrick rang the doctor from the clinic and he came and had a look at you. But he said that there was nothing wrong, just to keep you warm. This room was the warmest. Claire had to keep putting logs on the fire all night to keep the temperature up.'

'Oh.' Lucy sat up, feeling a little dizzy. 'Did she?' She looked at Claire, who moved and gave a little snort in her sleep. 'She looks as if she could sleep for a while longer.'

'Yeah, I'm sure she could.'

'But I was going to ...' Lucy said. 'I wanted to tell her ...'

'I think that can wait until she's awake,' Dave said and got up. 'But I came in to ask if you wanted some breakfast. Are you hungry?'

'Starving. But I'd like to go and have a bath first.' She stood up, swaying slightly.

'Careful,' Dave said and grabbed her arm. 'You must be weak still. I'll help you to your room. Then I think you should get into bed and I'll bring you breakfast. OK?'

'Yeah, thanks. Let's go.' Lucy looked at Claire again. 'Tell her … Never mind. I'll tell her myself when she wakes up.'

*

Penny was lying on her bed late the following afternoon, her eyes closed, her face covered in green clay. She was trying to relax before dinner. It had been such a stressful day yesterday, with the fog and the drama with Lucy. The night had been worse, Penny thought; the room freezing cold, Al snoring beside her. He had forgotten to close the window so she had to get up and do it. When she was finally back in bed, it had been impossible to sleep, and she had been wide awake with her mind turning in circles. It had been too late to take sleeping pills, like she usually did during these sleepless nights that were becoming the norm rather than the exception. She had dozed off for an hour or so, but woke up still exhausted. And today there had been too big an avalanche risk to ski after a heavy snowfall during the night. She had tried to get out and go for a walk instead, but there was too much snow and she had ended up reading old issues of *Vogue* in the study of the chalet.

The face mask was beginning to dry, making her skin itchy. It felt a little like poison ivy, stinging and hot at the same time. Funny how you never forget sensations like that, Penny thought.

The door opened and she could hear footsteps on the carpet. The bed dipped. It was Al.

'Don't even think about it,' she snapped, her eyes still closed.

'What, honey?' Al asked.

'You know. Just leave me alone. And don't smoke that stinking cigar in here.'

'How did you know about that? I haven't even lit it yet.'

'I can smell it.'

'I won't smoke it in here.'

'Good. How is Lucy feeling?'

'Better. Looks a bit tired. But she's OK. We're going to work on the cat-food copy after dinner.'

'Isn't that a little hard on her?'

'She said it was all right. She knows this was not supposed to be just a skiing vacation for us. And she says she has some ideas she wants to go through.' Al put a hand on Penny's thigh. 'How about a hot tub? It's a long time till dinner.'

'No.'

'Oh, come on, baby. It'll do us good.'

'I'm not your baby. And I'm not in the mood.'

'What's the problem, honey? Are you not having a good time?'

'Not at the moment, no.' Penny opened her eyes and peered at Al, sitting there looking worried, his reading glasses on the top of his head and his unlit cigar in his mouth. He looked messy, with his shirt open, his hair sticking up and the five o'clock shadow beginning to show on his chin. And he suddenly looked old to Penny. He's only five years older than me, she thought. Do I look as old as that? She got up from the bed. 'Got to wash this thing off,' she muttered and went into the bathroom.

Al took his cigar out of his mouth and padded after her. 'What's the problem?' he insisted. 'Anything I can do?'

'No, forget it,' Penny mumbled into the face cloth. She patted her skin dry with a towel and studied her face in the mirror.

*

'You have to be careful,' Peggy-Sue's aunt had said when she was sixteen, 'with boys, I mean. They always take advantage of girls who are plain, because they know girls who are not particularly beautiful are desperate for attention.'

Peggy-Sue looked at Aunt Libby over her bowl of Cheerios. Ever since she had arrived at the house in Houston two years earlier, there had been nothing but criticism. 'Stand up straight, don't wiggle, walk like a lady, keep your knees together when you're sitting down, don't giggle, don't talk with your mouth full …' And the final insult: 'Don't *ever* mention your mother or that you grew up in a trailer park.'

Peggy-Sue hadn't see her mother since the day Aunt Libby had walked into the trailer to take Peggy-Sue to live in Houston with her and uncle Harry. 'It's for your own good,' her mother had said. 'You're going to a good school. This way you can get an education, maybe even go to one of those fancy colleges and catch a lawyer or even a doctor.'

'I think she's a real beauty,' Uncle Harry said as he walked into the kitchen, ready for the office. 'Won't it be fun to see her cause a stir at the country club this summer?'

'I don't think I would call that fun,' Aunt Libby said. 'And I have never seen her cause a stir.'

No, Peggy-Sue thought, you're too busy flirting with the lifeguards.

That summer, Peggy-Sue grew up. She stole her aunt's make-up. She smoked cigarettes behind the clubhouse. She won a beauty contest at the country club. She drank beer at teenage parties. She became a cheerleader. She dated Chuck Harris, who played in the high school football team. They necked in the woods and she got stung by poison ivy.

Early one morning, as she tip-toed up the stairs, her aunt blocked her way.

'What time do you call this?'

'Eh, four o'clock?' Peggy-Sue said, four beers and a couple of slugs of bourbon making her feel reckless.

'What have you been doing out until this hour? Weren't you told to be home before twelve?'

'Well, the party went on a little late.'

'You little tart. Just like your mother.'

'Don't talk about Mom like that.'

'Don't you take that tone with me, miss. You better do as you're told, or you'll go straight back to the dump you came from.'

'I don't care.'

'But your mother will,' Aunt Libby retorted. 'What would she say if she knew how you behave? She wanted you to go places, and she didn't mean in the back seat of a car.'

Peggy-Sue hadn't answered but had looked back at her aunt with blazing eyes. I'll show you, she thought, I'll go places. And then I'll spit in your eye.

I went places all right, Penny thought thirty-four years later as she looked at her own reflection in the bathroom mirror. Eat your heart out, Aunt Libby.

10

'Fabulous food for every feline,' Lucy muttered to herself while she typed on her laptop. 'Hmmm. Does that work? No. A bit pat. I have to think of something new.' She stretched her arms over her head, then rolled her shoulders. She had been in the study of the chalet for two hours, racking her brains. She was still feeling tired after her adventure two days earlier and had decided to take a break from skiing and work on the new account. There had been no opportunity to be alone with Claire and, as the memory of the incident faded, so did Lucy's desire for a confrontation. Humble pie was not exactly her favourite dish.

'Purrfect Cat Food,' Lucy said to herself. What a silly name. Oh, why can't I think of something really snappy? But I'll take a little break. Can't stay here all afternoon. She got up from the desk, walked out of the room and down the corridor. The house was quiet, except for the sound of Emilie's voice through the half-open door of her room. Lucy peered in. 'Hi. What are you doing?'

Emilie turned around from the pile of dolls on the floor. 'Oh, hello Lucy. Ooops, sorry!'

'Sorry for what?'

'I'm not supposed to call people by their first name without their permission, Claire said. It's not polite.'

'She's become so prissy,' Lucy remarked. 'Don't mind her, call me Lucy.' She squatted beside Emilie and looked down at the dolls. 'What are you doing?'

'I'm playing with my Barbies.' She held up two dolls. 'This is Barbie and this is Ken, her boyfriend.'

'Oh? And what are they doing?'

'They are going on a trip to the beach in Barbie's new car. Look, here it is. Isn't it nice, all pink and with this top you can take off. It's a Cadillac.'

'It's beautiful. Doesn't Ken have a car?'

'No, because he doesn't earn enough money. He's a lifeguard at the beach, you see. Barbie met him when she was on holiday in the Bahamas and she was wearing this bikini.' Emilie held up a tiny piece of material for Lucy to inspect. 'And then Ken fell in love with her and came back home with her and now they're dating.'

'And do you think they'll get married?'

'Not yet.'

'Because they don't know each other well enough?'

'No, because I haven't got the wedding outfit yet. I might get it for my birthday and then they can have a lovely wedding.'

'I'm sure that will be wonderful.'

'Yes, and then Ken is going to move into Barbie's house over there – look.' Emilie pointed to a doll's house in the corner. 'And Barbie will quit her job and have a baby.'

'But what will they live on, if she isn't working?'

Emilie looked thoughtfully at Lucy. 'It's just a game,' she said with great patience. 'They are just dolls, you know. They don't have to work or anything.'

'Of course. I knew that.'

Emilie was still looking at Lucy. 'Do you have a boyfriend?'

'No, not at the moment.'

'So you had to pay for your own holiday, then?'

'No, Al paid for it.'

'But he's not your boyfriend, is he?'

'He's my boss. And he's Penny's husband.'

'Patrick paid for Tiffany's trip.'

'Yes, I suppose he did.'

'Because she is very short of money?'

'No, because she's his sister,' Lucy said, her mind still on cat food. 'I don't think she's short of money.'

'She is. Patrick is always giving her money.'

'What do you mean?'

But Emilie had returned her attention to her dolls. 'I think this outfit will be very good,' she muttered, pulling a pair of bright green slacks up Barbie's legs, 'and Ken can wear jeans and this T-shirt.'

'Yeah, lovely,' Lucy said. 'But what was that about Tiffany?'

'And don't forget towels and sun-tan lotion,' Emilie ordered Barbie. 'The sun is very hot today.'

Lucy put her hand on Emilie's arm. 'What was that you said?'

Emilie pulled away. 'Not now. I want to play.'

'Oh, I'm sorry. But just tell me, what did you say about Tiffany?'

But Emilie had turned back to her game. 'But, if it rains, we'll get wet. We'll have to put the top back on.'

Lucy grabbed the Barbie and held it up. 'Hey, Ken,' she said in a squeaky voice, 'I heard something strange today. Tiffany is spending a lot of money.'

Emilie smiled at Lucy and picked Ken up. 'Yes,' she replied in a gruff voice. 'That's true. Patrick is getting sick of having to hand out lots of cash all the time.'

'How did you know that?'

'I heard it when I was doing cross-country skiing on the white carpet behind the sofa in the living room. They were having a drink by the window.'

'And what were they saying?' Lucy throat was beginning to ache from talking like a doll.

'Patrick asked why she needed money again when he had given her a thousand dollars only yesterday.'

'What did she say to that?'

'She said she needed a bit more and why couldn't he understand that it cost a lot of money to look the way she did. Then Patrick said he didn't believe it and that it all went up her nose.'

'Jesus. How did she reply?'

'You're not talking like Barbie,' Emilie complained.

'Sorry. What did Tiffany say then, Ken?' Lucy squeaked.

'She said she was sick of having to put up with all this – then she said a bad word.' Emilie looked at Lucy over Ken's head. 'Ken doesn't say bad words,' she explained.

'He's a perfect gentleman.'

'That's right, he is,' Emilie smiled.

'So what did Patrick say to that?' Lucy continued, waggling Barbie.

'He said he would very much like to know what Tiffany gets up to every day and she said it was none of his business and she was old enough to do what she liked.'

'Oh. Then what happened?'

'Nothing. Dave came in and asked if they wanted another drink and I stopped skiing on the carpet and waited for them to go out of the room.'

Lucy put the Barbie down and looked at Emilie. 'Have you told anyone else about this?'

'No, because it only just happened. I came up here then.'

'OK,' Lucy said and thought for a moment then held up Barbie again. 'Now, Ken, darling,' she croaked. 'We won't tell anyone about this, will we? It's a secret.'

'Why?'

'Because ... because ...' Lucy tried to think of a good answer. 'Ken isn't really a lifeguard. He works for the FBI.'

'You mean he's ...' Emilie stopped, '... undercover?' she whispered.

'That's it,' Lucy nodded. 'You don't think Barbie would fancy him if he were just a stupid old lifeguard, do you?'

'You're right. She wouldn't.'

'Of course not. Anyway, Tiffany is a spy, you see, and Ken is trying to figure out what she's up to. And, if we tell anyone, it will blow his cover. OK?'

'That's a really good idea,' Emilie beamed.

'So you won't tell anyone?' Lucy whispered in Barbie's voice.

'Not a soul,' Emilie whispered back behind Ken's head. 'Even under torture.'

'Excellent, Ken. You're a good agent. One of the best.' Lucy put Barbie down on the carpet, feeling suddenly exhausted. 'I have to go back to work now.'

'But will you come back and play with me again? You're *really* good at it.'

'I will,' Lucy promised. 'But remember our secret, won't you? If you happen to say anything by accident, just say you're playing a game or something.'

'OK.' Emilie turned back to her dolls and Lucy walked out of the room.

'But *chérie*,' Emilie said to Barbie in a deep voice with a French accent, 'what *is* your real name?'

Lucy stopped and turned around. 'What was that?'

Emilie smiled sweetly at Lucy. 'Just playing,' she said.

*

Later that night, as Claire was watching a late night movie in her bedroom, the phone on her bedside table rang. Who can that be? she asked herself. Michel? I asked him when he phoned this afternoon not to contact me again, but he never does what he's told. The phone rang again, the sound shrill in the quiet bedroom, breaking the spell of the film. Shit, why can't he leave me alone, she thought and lifted the receiver, her eyes still on the screen.

'Listen,' she snapped,' I thought I told you not to –'

'Mademoiselle Dillon?' a voice said that wasn't Michel's. 'I mean Claire. *Bonsoir*. Am I disturbing you?

'Not at all, Monsieur Marchand,' Claire said, feeling foolish. 'Good evening.'

'I was hoping you weren't gone to sleep.' His voice was warm and a little drowsy.

'What can I do for you?'

'Oh nothing, really. I just wanted to know how you were managing. How you are after the terrible fright you had.'

'I'm fine,' Claire said, feeling embarrassed as she remembered how she had behaved. 'And I should really say thank you for being so ...' She tried desperately to find the right words, to apologise for behaving like a child. 'For helping me,' she ended.

'You were upset. Quite understandable under the circumstances. I was deeply worried myself, you know.'

'You were?'

'Of course. I was afraid your friend would not come out of it alive, you see.'

'Really? Oh, my God. But you seemed so calm, so reassuring. I thought ... I felt such comfort talking to you and hearing you tell me not to worry.'

'Well, that's good.'

'Thank you again.'

'So are you and your friend ... Lucy? Was that her name?'

'Yes.'

'Are you getting on a bit better now? Have you been able to forget whatever it was you fell out about?'

'No, not really,' Claire said, feeling slightly ashamed. 'Well, we haven't had a chance to talk about it yet.'

'I hope you can very soon. It seemed to me …' He stopped. 'Sorry, none of my business, I suppose.'

'No, go on,' Claire said.

'Well, I was just going to say that when someone is in real danger, your true feelings for that person come out.' He paused again. 'What I'm trying to say, I suppose, is that it might be easier for you to forgive your friend for whatever it was she did to you after having been so worried about her. You might feel true friendship is about caring for each other and forgetting little upsets that hurt your pride. Or something like that.'

'Maybe,' Claire said, suddenly regretting having told him about Lucy the other day.

'But I sense you don't want to talk about that, am I right?'

'Yes. I'm sorry, but … No, not right now.'

'I understand. So,' he continued, 'you're all right, then?'

'Perfectly. Absolutely fine.'

'And not too cold, I hope?'

'Not at all. It has been very foggy, but the weather has improved, which is a great relief.'

'I'm sure it is. How is Emilie?'

'Very well.'

'Good. I hope you're getting on.'

'Oh, yes, we're getting on really well. How are you, anyway?'

'Oh fine. Tough day. Good though. I managed to get a very big account.' He sounded happy and rather proud of himself.

'Clever of you,' Claire said.

'Oh, I don't know. It's very much a question of luck too. What's that music I can hear?'

'It's a movie on television. *Un Homme et Une Femme*. I think it was a great hit years ago.'

'Oh yes, a real tear-jerker.'

'But nice.'

'Very nice. They don't really make films like that any more.'

'No. Pity.'

He was silent for a moment. 'I wonder,' he said, sounding a little hesitant, 'if you remember what you told me the last time we spoke?'

'About what?'

'About needing to get away from something?'

'Yes?'

'What was it you needed to get away from?'

'Oh, nothing really,' Claire said. 'Just the usual, you know, the daily grind.'

'I see. Well, the daily grind can be a bit trying sometimes.'

'It sure can.'

'So that *was* the reason you changed your mind about going?'

'Well, no, not really. It was mainly because …' she stopped.

'Because?'

'Well, Emilie. I didn't want to disappoint her.'

The words came out before Claire had a chance to think. It's true, she thought, it really is. I wanted to get away for a bit, but I also wanted to cheer her up and make sure she recovered properly from her illness. I wanted to …

'I'm glad,' he said, breaking the silence. 'You see, she misses her mother so.'

'I know.'

'You're a very caring person. I like that.'

'No … well, I …' Caring? She thought, nobody has ever said that. And I have never really cared like this before. God, am I really that selfish? Have I lived only for myself until now? 'You're very kind,' she croaked.

'I'm just grateful. It's nice to know Emilie is in good hands and that I don't need to worry about her. I know it was asking a lot to take her on this trip.'

'It's not as hard as I thought.'

'I'm glad. But I'm keeping you from your film.'

'No, it's all right. I wasn't really watching it.' Claire stifled a yawn.

'You sound sleepy. I won't disturb you any more.'

'You're not. It's nice to talk to you.'

'Is it?'

'Yes.'

'Good. So you wouldn't mind talking a bit longer then?' he asked. 'I don't really have any-body to chat to in the evenings. There's nobody I can …'

'Talk nonsense with?' Claire suggested.

He laughed. 'Mmm, yes. I seem to spend my days talking about business and my evenings watching the news and reading the papers and then just going to bed. I miss the kind of conversation where you say anything that comes into your head. You know what I mean? Where you exchange your thoughts and feelings, make little jokes and even have a good argument sometimes.'

'Oh yes, I know,' Claire replied softly. 'But I suppose your wife …' she stopped, afraid to step into forbidden territory. 'Sorry. I didn't mean to …' She stopped again, her heart beating.

He was silent for a moment but she could hear him breathe. 'No, it's all right,' he murmured. 'And you're right. Gwen, my wife … she was … we were …' He sighed. 'She was always here, you see. Always listening and … and making little comments and …' He paused. 'Well, you know.'

'Well, not exactly,' Claire said. 'I have no idea what you're going through. But I can imagine it must be very hard.'

'Yes, it is.'

They were silent for a moment. Claire desperately wanted to say something comforting, something that might cheer him up, but she also wanted to keep him talking, to hear his warm deep voice with that slight accent and the odd word in French. She could see him clearly in her mind the way he looked that day, standing in front of her in the classroom, his eyes so full of concern. He had looked tired and his strong chin had more than a hint of a five o'clock shadow. She could remember every detail: his grey wool overcoat with the slightly worn suede collar, the light blue of his shirt, even his navy silk tie with tiny white polka dots. She remembered looking at his hands, strong and lightly tanned and the wrists with black hairs, and the Hermès watch, its leather strap slightly frayed. His aftershave had been just a hint of a fragrance. Sandalwood? She had wanted to brush the lock of hair out of his eyes and rub away the smudges under his eyes, tell him he didn't have to be alone any more, that she would ... What? Well, she thought, do whatever it took to make him smile again. What's wrong with me, she thought, why do I want to take care of this man? He isn't really my type and he doesn't flatter me or admire me or tell me I'm sexy ...

'So you wouldn't mind, then?' he asked, his voice suddenly loud in her ear.

'What?' Claire laughed guiltily. 'I'm sorry? I was thinking of something else ...'

'You wouldn't mind if I called you from time to time? Just for an idle chat. To talk about ... I don't know, life, trivia, I suppose.'

'Of course not. I'm very good at that. Trivia, I mean.'

'And life?'

'I don't know about that. I'll do my best.'

'Thank you. You're very kind.'

'Not at all.' Kindness has nothing to do with it, Claire thought.

'But I'll let you go now. You must be sleepy. Talk to you soon?'

'Very soon. Good night, Monsieur Marchand.'

'*Bonne nuit*, Claire.'

Claire hung up with a smile and returned to her film. It was near the end, and the couple were getting into bed in a hotel room. As she switched off the television and snuggled under the duvet, Claire wondered what it would be like to go to bed with Bernard Marchand. He would be gentle and kind, she thought, undressing her slowly, kissing her each time he removed an item of clothing. She would unbutton his shirt and open it, revealing a lean, toned chest, slightly tanned, she was sure. They would sink into the big, soft bed and he would murmur lovely things in her ear while his hands stroked her naked body. '*Mon amour,*' he would say, 'my darling, you're so beautiful …' Then he would make love to her, slowly and sensuously, and it would seem like the most natural thing in the world. 'Bernard …' Claire murmured. She was still smiling as she fell asleep.

*

Penny was walking down the main street of the village, looking into shop windows. Having finished her skiing for the morning, she had parked her skis at the bottom of the slopes. She didn't felt like going back to the chalet for lunch and was planning to get a bite to eat in one of the small restaurants lining the main street. She looked at the clothes on sale, marvelling at the exquisite style of French fashion. Even here, in this ski resort miles away from Paris, the shops were selling the very latest in winter clothes. She was just thinking she didn't really need anything new, when she spotted it. A red jump suit. Simple, yet sexy, with that lovely French touch. I have to have it, she thought, and walked into the shop.

'Madame?' said the shop assistant, a beautiful young girl with a flawless complexion.

'The … eh, le … la …' Penny pointed at the suit in the window.

'The jump suit?' Her English was excellent.

'Yes, that's right.'

'Size?'

'Eight … I mean six.' For the first time in her life, Penny felt intimidated, which annoyed her. How did these French women always manage to make you feel old, fat and stupid? Penny wished she possessed this skill. It would come in very useful in New York.

'That would be a …' The girl eyed Penny's figure. 'Forty?'

'Thirty-four,' Penny corrected.

'Are you sure? Maybe Madame would feel more at ease in a bigger size?'

'Do you have a thirty-four or not?' Penny snapped.

'Yes, of course.' The girl took a suit from the rail. 'You can try it on over there.'

Alone in the tiny cubicle, Penny looked at herself in the suit. It was just a little tight over her hips. I shouldn't have had those scones, she thought. And maybe this red is a little young for me. The cubicle was stifling and Penny began to feel hot and sweaty. I'll ask if they have it in black and maybe just one size bigger.

'How are you getting on?' The girl poked her head through the curtain. 'Oh, well.' She paused. 'Maybe a size bigger? And a different colour. Or maybe something not quite so young?'

'Not quite so what?' Penny demanded. She stared at the girl. 'I'll take it,' she said.

'*Bien, Madame.*'

After paying the astronomical price, Penny snatched the bag from the girl and marched out of the shop. Full of buyer's remorse, she looked wildly around her. A drink, she thought, I really need a drink. She walked across the street, into the bar and sat down at a table. It was dark compared to the glare of the snow and afternoon sunshine outside, and she didn't recognise the man sitting nearby until he spoke.

'*Bonjour,*' he said. 'It's nice to meet again, *non?*'

Penny looked around. It was Michel.

'*Non,*' she replied. 'I mean, yes. Of course it's very nice to see you.'

'You look a leetle *triste.* Are you OK?'

'Yes, yes, fine. Just done some shopping. And now I'm going to have lunch,' she continued, changing her mind about the drink.

161

'Not just yet,' Michel said and put a hand on her arm. 'How about an apéritif to celebrate your shopping?'

'I don't know,' Penny said, thinking that paying a fortune for an outfit she would probably never wear was nothing to celebrate. 'I don't really drink a lot. Have to watch my – *silhouette*.'

Michel smiled. 'But just one drink. A *vin chaud*?'

'Oh, maybe just one, then,' Penny said, desperately needing something to cheer her up.

Michel called the waiter.

'This is lovely,' Penny said a few minutes later, sipping a glass of mulled wine. 'I feel better now.'

'Good. What did you buy? Something *très jolie*?'

'Oh, nothing really.' Penny finished her wine and put the glass on the table.

'Do you want one more drink? Or maybe some lunch?'

She pulled herself together and shook her head. 'No, I can't. And I think I'll skip lunch, actually. I really do have to be careful.'

'No more calories?'

'Exactly. Pity. Another drink would make me feel more relaxed.'

'Relaxed?' Michel looked at her thoughtfully. 'It means …'

'I know. What about something else? Something to smoke?'

'Smoke?' Penny exclaimed, shocked.

'Yes. Like this.' He put two fingers to his lips and pretended to blow.

'I know *that*. But how could you *possibly* think I would smoke?' she demanded angrily. 'You French are so irresponsible. I am appalled at the way everyone smokes here. I wouldn't be surprised if I saw a baby sitting up in his pram puffing away at a cigarette. Have you never heard of emphysema in this country? Or lung cancer? Or heart disease? Not to mention what it does to your skin!' Penny drew breath. 'And another thing: passive smoking. It's as dangerous as actual smoking.'

'Yes, yes, of course,' Michel cut in. 'I know what you are saying. You are right, of course.'

'You agree?'

'Yes. But you did not understand me. I meant something *completement different*.'

11

'Oooh,' Claire sighed, sinking into the sofa in front of the fire. 'I don't think I'll be able to get out of here again. I'll just have to stay here until someone hires a crane to haul me up.'

'Too much exercise?' Patrick enquired, putting down the *Wall Street Journal*.

'Too much of everything,' Claire agreed. 'Too much skiing, too much walking up the hill, too much food and drink. I feel utterly whacked.'

'It's probably because you're a beginner,' Patrick suggested, pulling a small embroidered stool in front of Claire. 'You overdid it today. Put your feet up there and relax. You'll feel better when you've had a bit of rest.'

'Thanks.' Claire put her feet on the stool. 'You're right about overdoing it, I suppose. I have been skiing every day since we came. A whole week. I can't believe it.'

'Are you making progress?'

'I think so. I'm doing blue slopes now and I can turn quite well, although to call them parallel turns would be exaggerating.' She looked around the room. 'Where is everybody?'

'I don't know. I suppose most of them are in the tub. And those who aren't are fast asleep. Except for Penny. She wanted to do one more slope. I saw her go up in the chairlift to the top of the "Saulire". She has great stamina, I have to say.'

'I know Emilie is watching TV so she'll be quiet for a while.' Claire put her head against the back of the sofa. 'It's great to have a moment's peace like this.'

'It sure is. This kind of holiday can be a bit trying.'

'I know what you mean,' Claire smiled. 'It's hard work sometimes, making conversation with everyone.'

'And you never get a chance to be on your own.'

'Maybe I'm disturbing you?' Claire started to get up. 'I'll go and lie on my bed instead.'

Patrick put his hand on her arm and smiled disarmingly. 'Don't move. I like talking to you. You're a very restful person, you know.'

Claire looked at him. 'Restful? Is that another word for boring?'

'No,' he protested. 'Not a bit. It's just that I don't feel the need to impress you, to pretend to be something I'm not.'

'Is that what you usually do with women?'

'Well, I suppose. A little bit. But with you I get the feeling I don't need to. And I guess it's because you'd see right through it.'

'That sounds scary.'

'It is. You *are* a little scary, actually. Just like my fourth-grade history teacher.'

'Gee, thanks a lot,' Claire laughed. 'You really know how to make a girl feel special.'

'But that's not what I meant at all,' he protested. 'She was such a warm, understanding woman. She had this lovely easy charm. You could always go to her with your problems. She was a real mother figure to me.'

'You didn't have a mother?'

'Oh, sure. I had a mother. But I didn't see a lot of her, to tell you the truth. She was always busy. Charity work. Fund-raising. She cared a lot about the poor and starving and was involved in big projects all the time. Then she and my dad split up when I was still very young.'

'That must have been hard.'

He shrugged. 'I don't know. Yes, I suppose. I didn't really miss my mother. She hadn't been around a lot in any case.'

'You stayed with your father?'

'That's right. Then I was sent away to school at twelve. But you don't want to listen to this, I'm sure.'

'Yes, I do. Go on.'

Patrick sighed and looked into the fire. 'My

father didn't remarry for a long time. He had a series of glamorous girlfriends. All my friends at school used to ask to come and stay with us in the summer, because there were always these beautiful women in skimpy bikinis around the pool. It wasn't easy for an impressionable young boy, I can tell you.'

'I can imagine.'

'Then, when I had just started Harvard law school, my father married again.'

'And Tiffany was born?'

He nodded. 'It was a very happy time, actually.' There was a faraway look in his eyes. 'I was away at college, but the vacations were wonderful. Tiffany was growing up and we were such a close family. Those were the best years of my life. But then …' Patrick's voice trailed off. 'Tiffany's mother left my father for another man. The family I had come to love broke up. A few years later, I got married …'

'You got married?' Claire asked incredulously.

'Yeah, but it didn't work.' He looked away.

'I'm sorry.'

'So that's it. The story of my life. I suppose it's a bit melodramatic.'

'Well, yes. Just like an episode of *Dallas*,' Claire said in an attempt to lighten the atmosphere.

He smiled. 'I didn't really mean to tell you all this. It was just that you're …'

'The spit of this elderly grey-haired history teacher?'

'That's it.' Patrick grinned. 'So now, tell me, teacher, what the *hell* am I going to do with Tiffany? She has been in trouble since she was fourteen: eating disorders, shoplifting, you name it. She has dropped out of some of the best schools in America. She's had therapy but that doesn't seem to have helped at all.'

'Therapy?' Claire asked. 'We don't really believe in that sort of thing in Ireland.'

'What do you believe in?'

'Oh, we think a good old boot up the arse is very effective in this sort of case.'

'A what?'

'A kick in the butt.'

'Good idea.' Patrick laughed and picked up the paper. 'Why don't you go and do that for me right now?'

'Do your own dirty work.' Claire threw a sofa cushion at him. He caught it and threw it back. Claire was going to hurl the cushion again, but Patrick moved closer and caught her hands. The were both laughing now, breathing hard, struggling with the cushion. Then, before Claire knew what had happened, their lips met and they were kissing. Patrick slipped his arms around her but Claire pulled back. 'What are we doing?' she panted.

'I don't know,' he murmured, 'but I like it.' He kissed her again and this time she kissed him back, closing her eyes and enjoying the feel of his arms around her and his lips on hers. He is one sexy guy, she thought. I wonder if kissing Bernard Marchand would be as good? The thought of Bernard made her stiffen and this time Patrick pulled away. 'What's the matter?' he asked. 'Something wrong?'

'Yes.' Claire lay back in his arms and looked at him through half-closed eyes. 'Nothing personal,' she said, 'but …'

'There's someone else?'

'No, not really …'

'OK,' he leaned over her again. 'In that case …'

Claire put her hand on his chest and pushed him away. 'I can't. Not now. Not here.'

'Why not? You're a lovely woman.'

'And you're out of your mind,' Claire filled in. She sat up. 'Listen, you're a hell of a sexy guy and I'd love to … I mean if … Oh, go away.'

Patrick lay back and put his hands behind his head. His wide grin and sleepy eyes made Claire nearly regret having rebuked him. 'You're right,' he mumbled. 'But maybe another time? Another place?'

'You never know,' Claire replied softly.

*

Penny could see practically the whole resort from where she stood: the jagged tops of the mountains, down the pistes and right into the valley far below. She could see smoke rising from the chimneys of some of the little huts on the slopes, the snow-covered trees and the cross-country tracks winding between them. There was hardly a sound, only the occasional cry from a bird, the swish of skis on the snow and sometimes a click from a ski pole striking a ski or a boot. Penny had come up on the last lift to do just one more slope before the evening, and she stood there for a moment, enjoying the near solitude and the peace. But it was time to go. She tightened the bindings on her boots another notch and, with a little whoop of pure joy, pushed off down the slope feeling not a flicker of fear, only exhilaration.

Penny had never felt afraid when skiing, not even when she was a beginner all those years ago in Aspen. She had taken a holiday there with Al because he was, as usual, trying to clinch a deal with a chain of sports shops. Penny, bored with business talk, had started taking skiing lessons and found her training as a dancer had made her a natural skier.

She stopped for a moment to catch her breath and assessed the slope. It was the steepest part of the piste, some of it very icy, where the skiers who had preceded her during the day had pushed the snow aside as they slalomed down. She told herself she would have to take this part more carefully, then she was annoyed at herself for feeling nervous. Don't be a wimp, she said to herself and pushed off. Then suddenly she lost her outer edge and felt herself slip sideways. She crashed painfully onto her hip. The wind knocked out of her and her heart beating like a drum, she realised how foolish she had been. I could have been killed, she thought. I could have broken my neck. Is that really what I was trying to do? Her hip was throbbing. She got slowly back on her feet and skied cautiously down the rest of the darkening slope.

*

'Where are you going?' Patrick asked Tiffany as she got up from the dinner table.

'Out,' she replied sulkily.

'Out where?' Patrick demanded. 'I thought I told you there would be no partying here.'

'Partying?' Tiffany snorted. 'In this hole?'

'I saw you talking to those boys outside the bar this afternoon,' Patrick said. 'I hope you're not planning to meet any of them tonight.'

'Those little French creeps?' Tiffany said. 'Give me a fucking break! No, I'm going to … to a see a movie, actually. The latest James Bond is on in the village.'

'Dubbed into French probably,' Lucy said.

'No, it said *version original*,' Tiffany replied. 'That means it's in English, right?'

'Yes, that's right,' Claire said.

'So that's where I'm going,' Tiffany continued, walking to the door. 'It's a long movie so don't wait up.'

'I think I'll go with you, actually,' Patrick said.

Tiffany's face hardened. 'I don't need a baby

sitter,' she snapped. 'I'm quite capable of going to the movies on my own, thank you.'

'I'm sure you are, sweetheart,' Patrick said silkily, 'but I wouldn't mind going out for a change. Anyone else want to come?'

'Yeah, sure, why not?' Al replied. 'And Penny too, right, babe?'

'No, I don't think I will,' Penny answered. 'I want to finish reading my novel and have an early night.'

'Claire?' Patrick asked. 'What about you?'

'Eh, no,' Claire replied, trying to think of an excuse. 'I'm expecting a phone … I mean I have to stay in case Emilie wakes up or something.'

'But Penny's here,' Patrick said. 'Won't she hear Emilie?'

'Of course I will. I don't mind.' Penny nodded.

'No,' Claire shook her head. 'I'll stay. James Bond is not really my thing anyway.'

'OK, honey,' Al soothed. 'There's no law against staying at home.' He pushed his plate away and rose from his seat. 'What time does it start?'

'I think it starts at nine,' Tiffany replied.

'Right, let's go,' Patrick said.

'Lucy,' Al said suddenly, 'why don't you come too?'

'Shit,' Tiffany muttered. 'This is turning into a kindergarten trip.'

'I don't know,' Lucy said. 'Maybe I should do a little more work on that copy.'

'Come on, honey,' Al urged. 'The cat food can wait till tomorrow. We're nearly there in any case. All we need is that slogan. It might do you good to do something else for a change.' He pulled out the chair for Lucy as she got up. 'Tell Dave we won't be having coffee, will you, Claire?'

'Dave's gone out,' Claire replied. 'He said he was going to a party. Told us not to clean up, he'll do the rest tomorrow.'

'OK. Come on then, Tiffany,' Patrick ordered. 'Let's go to the movies. Just like the good old days when we used to go to the matinées on Sundays, remember?'

'What are you talking about?' Tiffany demanded. 'Those must have been the *really* old days. I never went to any stupid matinée with you. You used to watch the football games on Sundays. And drink a lot of beer.'

'I bet he only wanted to look at the cheerleaders,' Al teased. 'Those cute girls in short skirts, right Patrick?'

'You could be right,' Patrick laughed. 'There's nothing cuter than the all-American cheerleader.'

*

'Claire?'

'Yes, Monsieur Marchand?' Claire said, sitting up straighter in the easy chair by the window.

'Bernard,' he corrected.

'Bernard.'

'Good. I feel I know you quite well by now.'

173

'Even though we've only met once?' Claire said, feeling herself blush as she thought of what she had been doing to him in her dreams.

'*Tout á fait*. So, how are you?' he asked. 'I hope I'm not disturbing you?'

'Oh no, not at all. We've just had dinner and everyone's gone out to the cinema.'

'You didn't go with them?'

'No, I was … not in the mood.'

'So you're all alone?'

'No. Penny's here. And Emilie.'

'Who?'

'Your daughter, remember her?'

He laughed. 'Of course. I was just thinking of something else. So,' he continued, 'it's all going well, then?'

'Very well.'

There was a brief silence, during which Claire wound the telephone wire around her fingers while she tried to think of something fascinating to say. 'It's snowing again,' she finally managed.

'Good.'

'Yes.' God, I'm boring, Claire thought, why can't I tell him something interesting; my opinion of world politics, or how to protect the environment or something? 'I saw a marmot today,' was all she could think of. 'It was running up this very steep slope in the snow. It was so cute.'

'A marmot?'

'Yes. A *marmotte* it's called in French.'

'I know.'

'Groundhog in America, I believe.' Shit, what a boring conversation, Claire said to herself. I sound like an old teacher and he sounds as if he's going to sleep. I'm going to have to wake him up. 'Knickers,' she said.

'What?' he exclaimed, sounding suddenly more alert.

'That's ladies' underwear in English. *Un slip* in French.'

'But I knew that,' he laughed.

'And a bra is *soutien gorge*,' Claire continued, getting carried away with her own audacity.

'I knew that too.'

'You're very well-educated, Monsieur Marchand.'

'Bernard.'

'Oh, no, I can't call you Bernard and talk about knickers at the same time. That would be far too familiar.'

'This is a very strange conversation.'

'I know. But not boring, I hope?'

'Far from it.'

'You sounded as if you were going to sleep, so I thought I'd say something to wake you up.'

'And you certainly did. Do you always talk about underwear with your admirers?'

'It's a great way to break the ice.'

'*Melt* the ice, you mean,' he laughed. 'And I'm sure you're very good at that.'

'I don't understand what you mean.'

'Oh, I don't know. You look quite demure at

first glance but then there's that fire just under the surface. I find that very interesting.'

'Hmm. Really?' Claire said, not knowing quite what to think. He had seemed so correct and reserved when they met, with a slightly military bearing. And here he was, flirting on the phone. It's my fault, she thought, I shouldn't have started talking about knickers. But he has been in my mind and my dreams for the past week. But he probably doesn't like women who talk dirty. His type of woman would be more strait-laced and well behaved ...

'Are you making any progress with your skiing lessons?' he asked, suddenly changing the subject.

'Not much, no,' Claire replied. 'I'm afraid I'm not the athletic type.'

'Well, some people just don't take to skiing, I suppose.'

'That's true. I wish I could be like Emilie. She's such a great little skier. And so brave.'

'Yes. She's a very courageous little girl. Not only about skiing. She is such a comfort to me, you know."

'Of course, she must be,' Claire said. 'I hope you don't mind if I ask you ...' she continued, feeling a pang of nervousness, but wanting to know how he felt, 'about your wife?'

'Of course not. What did you want to ask about her?'

'Oh, just what was she like? You told me a

little bit about her last night, but if you don't want to talk about her, I understand.'

'No, I don't mind,' he replied. 'I like talking about her life. It's her death I can't …' He stopped.

'Oh, God, I'm sorry,' Claire exclaimed. 'Let's forget about it. Maybe we should hang up now and …'

'No. Don't go.' His voice was a little hoarse now. 'I do want to tell you. There is no one else I can talk to like this. Gwen – that was her name …'

'Yes, I know.'

'Well, she was lovely.' He laughed softly. 'Of course I would say that, wouldn't I? But she was. She was small and blonde and very feminine. There was a dreamy quality about her. She loved books and music. She was not very practical and the house was always untidy and our bedroom was always in a mess, her clothes strewn every-where, her underwear and shoes …' He was silent for a moment. 'I used to complain about that. But now I miss it. I miss living with a woman and all those little feminine things … It's very tidy here. And quiet.' He sighed. 'I'm sorry. This has become a little too personal, perhaps. I didn't want to embarrass you.'

'I'm not a bit embarrassed.' Claire's voice was barely a whisper. 'And I'm so sorry.'

'Thank you. It was good to talk. To say those things. But it's getting late. I'm keeping you up. And I have to confess I'm a little tired.'

'Of course.'

'Good night, Claire.'

'Good night, Bernard.'

Claire hung up, feeling mortified. Why did I start talking about his wife, she thought, I really shouldn't have. Now I made him feel sad instead of cheering him up. And I made myself sad in the process. What am I doing? He's still grieving and I am not helping at all. I thought I might make him feel better, but that's really trite. How can you possibly 'cheer up' when you're trying to cope with such a loss? Claire leaned her head against the back of the chair. She felt totally drained, both emotionally and physically. She was still very stiff from the skiing and knew she wouldn't be able to sleep. She contemplated having a long hot bath, when she had an even better idea.

The hot tub, she said to herself. The hot tub on the terrace outside the study. Dave turns it on every evening. Maybe it's still on. It would be perfect for my aches and pains. And everyone's out except Penny, who's reading in her room. Claire quickly got undressed, wrapped a towel around her and slipped her feet into a pair of mules. She padded across the corridor, into the study and out onto the terrace. The fog had lifted and it had stopped snowing. It was freezing cold and completely still. She looked up at the night sky, where a full moon was just rising over the tree tops. Stars shimmered like tiny diamonds set in dark blue velvet and there wasn't a sound. She could see the village far below with its many lights like rows and rows of pearls. Up here, she felt as if she was on a distant planet, far removed from the troubles of the world.

Steam rose from the hot tub on the other side of the terrace and Claire picked her way through the snow, eager to slip into the hot water. There was an eerie light from candles set into the snow around the tub and, as Claire came closer, she realised there was someone already sitting in it, her head back, blowing out a thin stream of smoke through perfect lips. The woman slowly turned her head and smiled at Claire. 'Hi,' she drawled.

'Penny! Eh, hi.'

'Why don't you come in? The water's lovely and the whirlpool thing is fantastic for aches and pains. I had a bit of a fall today, banged my hip something awful, but the pain is already easing.'

'But … but you're smoking,' Claire stammered. 'I didn't know you smoked.'

'Don't worry,' Penny said, 'it's not tobacco.'

'You mean it's …' Claire couldn't believe it.

'Right,' Penny laughed. 'You guessed. You don't think I'd risk my health with tobacco, do you? But you're shivering. Get in, for God's sake!'

'Well …' Claire hesitated. 'Maybe you want to be on your own?' Her teeth were chattering and she pulled her towel tighter around her.

'Of course not. I'd love some company. This tub is huge. There's plenty of room for one more. I'll even let you have some of this lovely grass.

Excellent quality. Your friend certainly knows a thing or two.'

'My friend?' Claire asked, finally slipping into the tub. The hot water, combined with the massage of the underwater jets, were wonderfully soothing. 'Oh, this is soooo goood,' she sighed as she sat down. 'But what did you mean ...'

'Nothing,' Penny said. 'I don't know what I'm saying when I'm this tired.' She held out the joint to Claire. 'Here, have a drag.'

'No thanks, I don't really do drugs.'

'Drugs?' Penny laughed. 'Don't be so bloody tight-assed. This is not a drug. More like aromatherapy. Makes you feel fantastic. Doesn't make you fat and doesn't give you a hangover.' She pushed the joint at Claire. 'Come on, try it. It won't bite your nose off, you know.'

Claire looked at the joint. Why not, she thought. Live a little. See what all the fuss is about. She took the joint and pulled the smoke into her lungs. When she blew out, the smoke rose in the still dark air. She didn't feel much but Penny looked at her expectantly. 'Yeah,' Claire said. 'Oh yeah, this is great.'

'Didn't I tell you?' Penny beamed. She leaned her head back against the edge of the tub and looked dreamily up at the sky. 'Isn't this just magic?' she asked, her voice echoing in the still night. 'I could stay here all night looking at the stars.'

'I know. Me too.' Claire looked across the steaming, bubbling water at Penny. 'I love the way you speak,' she said. 'It's so soft and charming. So … kind of elegant with just a hint of a Texas accent. As a teacher I'm used to listening to people's accents. I can tell you're very well-educated. I suppose you went to finishing school?'

'Mmm, yes, in a way. The finishing school of life,' Penny said with an ironic little smile.

'How do you mean?'

'Hard to explain. Not something I feel like talking about. It feels like a hundred years ago, in any case.' Penny took the joint from Claire, pulled deeply and looked up at the night sky. A hundred years ago, she thought, and another life …

*

Penny walked across the cream carpet carrying a clipboard. She was wearing a Valentino dress and walking a customer around the first floor of the Fifth Avenue shop of Julio Scarpini, the famous shoe designer. It was early June and regular customers were invited to come in to look, touch and talk about the season's collection and place their orders. Penny had been working there over a month and was now a fully trained assistant with her sights set on becoming a manager – one of the women who knew the name of every customer, earned twice as much money as an assistant and received a free pair of Julio Scarpinis at Christmas along with a huge bonus.

At twenty-one, Penny had come a long way since she left her aunt's house. She had spent three years as a showgirl in Las Vegas, as a member of the famous 'Vegas Babes' dance troupe, which was not the career she envisaged when she had gone to that audition in Houston.

'But you'll get great training and experience,' the talent scout had argued, 'and, when your contract is finished, you'll be able to audition for one of the big dance companies in New York. Plus the pay is not bad, you have to admit.'

Having very little choice, Peggy-Sue had gone to Vegas. It was hard work: hours of practice every day, dancing on stage in the evenings, covered in layers of body make-up, wearing only a few sequins, dodging the men who wanted to 'buy her a drink and show her the view' from their suites.

When she had saved up enough to leave she moved to New York, but the dream of a place in one of those 'big dance companies' soon faded. Nobody wanted to hire her. She was either 'too short' or 'too tall' and, finally, 'too old'. The job at Julio Scarpini had been a stroke of luck. One of the 'Vegas Babes' who had come to New York at the same time had given Peggy-Sue the tip.

'They're just opening this store,' she had said. 'They need good-looking girls with a lot of class. Just like us, right? All you need to do is change your name, talk posh and walk like a fashion model.'

In two weeks, Peggy-Sue Kowalski had become Penelope Clark, who walked and talked with a cool elegance she had learned from old movies with Katharine Hepburn and Grace Kelly. 'Perfect,' the managing director said. 'I know you'll be an asset to our firm.'

Penny gestured to a waiter carrying a tray of champagne and microscopic sandwiches but the customer, a dark middle-age woman squashed into a Chanel suit, shook her head. 'No,' she said. 'Thank you, but I never eat between meals. I'd better finish my order. My son is picking me up in a few minutes.'

'All right,' Penny said and consulted the clip-board. 'I have written down the satin and leather evening shoe in blue, the leather pump in black and also dark green and the sandal with the purple ankle strap. Shall we go on?'

'Well I don't think there's anything else,' the woman said.

Penny lifted up a high-heeled flip-flop in hot pink. 'How about this? It's the most popular sandal this season.'

'But how do you walk in it?' the customer asked.

'Walk?' Penny said with a little smile. 'How do you mean?'

'Oh well.' The woman looked longingly at the sandal. 'I suppose that doesn't really come into it.'

'It would be fantastic with a Odabash bikini. You do wear one of those? And, of course, fuchsia is *the* colour in St Tropez this year.'

'How much?'

'$235.' Penny smiled. 'That's the cheapest shoe in our shop at the moment. Shall I put you down for a pair?'

'Oh, all right.'

'Anything else?'

'Not for now, no,' the woman had said. 'And here's my son, in any case. Al, honey,' she called, 'over here!'

12

'Men,' Claire said, sipping champagne, 'are very difficult to understand.'

'I know,' Penny agreed, lifting the bottle and peering at it through the gloom. 'Finished. Pity.' She put it back on the snow beside the tub.

'I think we've had quite enough, thank you,' Claire remarked with a giggle. 'Champagne and pot. My God. I think I'm having an out-of-body experience.'

'A what?'

'You know. When your mind is up there and you're down here. It's very nice,' she ended.

'Oh, yeah. Anyway, you were saying? About men?'

'They're tricky. Can't really get a grip on them.' Claire sighed and looked at Penny with a resigned expression. 'I seem to be attracted to the wrong men. Haven't yet dated a really decent guy, to be honest. What's wrong? Bad luck?'

'No, bad taste,' Penny stated. 'Some women just have appallingly bad taste in men. Something to do with sexual fantasies. You're probably attracted to very handsome men. The kind who are great in bed but hopeless anywhere else. Am I right?'

'Yes.' Claire sank deeper into the water. 'What can I do about it?' she asked.

'How do I know? I'm not a shrink.'

'Sorry. I thought, as you're so good at analysing what's wrong with people, you might know the solution as well.'

'Well, I don't. I do know when things are wrong, though. And, in this chalet, things are seriously wrong with everyone.'

'Everyone?'

'Yup. Take Patrick, for example.'

'Yeah?' Claire sat up. 'I'd love to.'

'No, hands off. Not for you. He has way too much baggage.'

'But I like that. And his baggage must be of that very elegant kind. Leather. With all the suitcases matching.'

'You don't want to know. Patrick is the product of screwed-up parents and a marriage that should never have happened. He needs a woman who is willing not only to commit, but also to sacrifice a great deal.'

'I might be prepared to do that for someone with those looks. What happened with his wife?'

'Sandra? That was her name. Awful bitch,' Penny muttered. 'She was stunning, of course. All Patrick's women are. But she was too ambitious. A lawyer like him. She hadn't graduated from law school when they got married. He had just started working for his father's firm. Then she qualified and was offered a job with this big firm in LA. She suggested they both go over and said Patrick was sure to find a job as well. But he said no. He wanted to start a family. He thought she should take a career break for a few years. Maybe work part-time. They had a row. "It's LA or me," he said. So she said "LA" and took off. He hasn't been the same since and that's eight years ago. Now he only dates girls who don't care about a career. Or marriage. Problem is, he needs a woman with brains. But he's afraid of them. Once bitten and so on.'

'Poor Patrick.'

'Patrick has to grow up,' Penny said. 'He's nearly forty but acts like a teenager sometimes. I know he had a very tough childhood and, deep inside him, there is a very sad little boy. But there's no need to take it out on every woman he meets. He'll never be happy if he doesn't learn to give a little.'

'But his wife was a bit of a bitch, wasn't she? I mean, to just take off like that …'

'It was his own fault,' Penny said. 'Why didn't he talk it through with her before they got married? But that's men for you. They think they are the masters of the universe.'

'Maybe that's why I'm having these problems?'

'Yeah, could be. But I think you should try a little harder to find a nice man.' Penny smiled at Claire. 'You deserve it.'

Claire sighed. 'But my problem is that I seem to end up with men a lot younger than me.'

'Well, younger men are great for the odd fling. But it never lasts. They eventually start looking at girls their own age.' Penny leaned forward in the tub and looked at Claire through the mist. 'You see, honey, a younger man always thinks that the older woman is safe, because he thinks she has decided what she wants and doesn't ask for commitments or babies. If she does, she's finished.'

'I know,' Claire said, remembering that day not so long ago, when she and Michel had been walking in the Jardin du Luxembourg and they spotted a family with four small children. The two older boys started to fight and the baby in the pram was crying. The parents looked so exhausted. Michel had laughed. 'I'm so lucky,' he said, 'to have a woman with a free spirit, who doesn't yearn for babies.' Claire asked him how he knew. 'But you're past the age when you're looking for that sort of thing,' he said, sounding as if wanting children was something you grew out of. Then he hugged her and didn't see the expression in her eyes.

'I keep promising myself not to get involved,' Claire said to Penny, 'but, then, I seem to fall in love and …'

'Hormones,' Penny snorted, 'that's all it is, not love.'

'How do you tell the difference?' Claire asked.

'Think about it,' Penny ordered. 'Just think about how you feel when you're with a man. What do you want from him?'

'Hmm, well, I want …' Claire thought for a moment. 'I want him to make me feel beautiful. I want him to make me feel loved and wanted and special.'

'Me, me, me,' Penny said. 'What about him, then?'

'How do you mean?'

'I mean how do you want to make him feel?'

'I don't know. I haven't really thought about it.'

'Typical,' Penny said. 'You don't seem to have thought about anyone else but yourself. Men are just there to make *you* feel good, aren't they?'

'Oh, come on, that's a bit harsh,' Claire protested. 'That makes me sound really selfish and horrible. As a matter of fact,' she continued, 'there is this man I met recently …'

'Yes?'

'Oh, I don't know, I'm just being silly. It's just that, well he's very sad about something and I feel so … I mean I want to make him feel better, happy again, you know?'

'Go on.'

'And I …' She stopped. 'Do you think you can fall in love with someone you have only met once?' she asked.

'I don't know,' Penny replied thoughtfully. 'I think you can feel strong attraction. True love comes from knowing someone really well. But tell me about this man. You only met him once? How come you know all this about him, then? About his sadness and how you want to make it better?'

'We talk on the phone,' Claire said. 'We have these lovely long conversations and I love talking to him. I love hearing his voice.' She shook her head. 'No, I'm just being silly. It's probably just some kind of infatuation and being up here in the mountains and all that. Puts your imagination into overdrive.'

'Real love is about forgetting yourself,' Penny said dreamily.

'I don't understand what you mean.'

'That's because you have probably never really loved anyone in an unselfish way. You know, the way you love a child. You'll do anything for them to be safe and well and you can't think about yourself until they are.'

'I don't have any children,' Claire said, trying to defend herself.

'Oh. Well, when you do, you'll know,' Penny said wisely.

'I'm sure I will. But men aren't like children, are they?'

Penny laughed. 'God, yes, they are; like you have no idea. A man, and we're talking mature men here, wants to be cared for by his woman. He wants her to put him first and herself second.'

'Ah come on, not all men are like that,' Claire protested. 'Not these days.'

'Oh yes, they are. All of them. And they will never be any different, no matter how much the modern girl protests about equality and all that crap. In a real relayon ... reelshun ...' Penny took a deep breath. 'When a man and a woman are together, I mean, first there is him, then there's "us" and then, much further down the list, there is you, I mean me, I mean her, the woman.'

'Oh.'

'But you see, honey,' Penny continued her analysis, 'it doesn't matter because, when you meet the right man, you won't mind. You'll be there for him and it will seem the most natural thing in the world.'

'How will I know? That he's the right one, I mean?'

'It's not something you can explain or describe, you just feel it.'

'Like when you met Al?'

Penny smiled. 'Mmm, that's right. When I met Al I knew he was the one. He knows how to treat a woman. He always did, right from the start.'

*

'I'm pregnant,' she had said.

'Jesus,' he exclaimed, his face white. 'How did that happen?' They were in Penny's bed in her tiny apartment one Sunday afternoon.

'How do you think?' Penny demanded. 'Do I have to paint a picture?'

'But we've been careful.'

'I know. But there was that one time you took me to that Italian restaurant and we drank too much wine and …'

'I had to carry you up the stairs. Yeah, I remember. Oh shit. What a bloody mess.'

'I know,' Penny said. She burst into tears and found she couldn't stop. I've ruined everything, she thought. How Aunt Libby would laugh if she saw me now. And Mom would be so disappointed. She cried bitterly, not only because of Al's horrified expression but also for her mother and, most of all, for herself, her hopes and dreams now shattered because of this baby. I'll never make manager now, she thought. There'll be no free Julio Scarpinis for me next Christmas. I won't even have a job.

'Oh, honey,' Al soothed, trying to take her in his arms. She pulled back.

'Don't worry,' she whispered, 'I won't make trouble.'

'There's only one thing to do,' he stated.

'No,' she protested. 'I'm going to have the baby.'

'Of course you are. That's why we've got to get married,' Al said, which made Penny cry even

192

harder. 'But what's the matter?' he asked, sounding frightened. 'Don't you want to marry me?'

'Yes,' she sobbed. 'Of course I do. But it's … I can't marry you.'

'Why not?'

'I'm not who you think.'

'What do you mean?'

'For a start, my real name is Peggy-Sue.'

'Oh? But that's cute. Peggy-Sue. I like that.'

'What about Kowalski? Is that cute too?' she wept. 'I'm Polish!'

'Well my name is Freeman and I'm Jewish!'

'I knew that, you idiot!'

'My second name is Mordechai,' he tried.

'So what? Oh, your mother will have a fit!'

'Yeah, she will,' Al nodded. 'You're right about that. She doesn't want me to get married at all. Never mind, honey, she'll come around. And she'll get used to your real name.'

'But my name's not the only thing I've been lying about.'

'You mean there's more?'

'I'm not the rich girl who only works for fun, like I told you. I grew up in a trailer park in Oklahoma.' Penny stared at Al through red eyes. 'What will your mother think about that?'

'Well, to tell you the truth, I grew up in a one-bedroom apartment in the Bronx. With no bathroom,' he added. 'And a couch covered in plastic. And we had cockroaches. That's some-thing my mother seems to have totally erased from her mind. My father made a lot of money in real estate about ten years ago but until then we were dirt poor.'

'That's why she'll hate me,' Penny said and started to cry again. 'She would want you to marry someone with money. Someone with real class.'

'But you *do* have real class,' Al protested.

'I was a Vegas show girl,' Penny said, wanting to reveal everything about herself while she was at it. 'I was one of the Vegas Babes.'

'No kidding?' Al said, awe-struck.

'It's true.' Penny got out of bed and started to rummage around in her wardrobe. 'I have the costume here, somewhere … Yes, here it is.' She held up the tiny pieces of material covered in sequins. 'This is my dance costume, look.'

Al stared at her, a strange look in his eyes. Oh, God I've really blown it now, Penny thought. Why did I have to tell him everything?

Al kept staring at her. 'Put it on,' he whispered.

*

'Yoo-hoo,' Claire called when Penny hadn't spoken for a long time. 'What planet are you on?'

'What? Oh,' Penny said dreamily, 'I was far away in another time.'

'Time to come back to Earth, then.'

'OK.' Penny stared into space for a moment, then she looked at Claire. 'Funny,' she said, 'that you and Lucy were friends when you were younger. You're so completely different.'

'Are we?' Claire said, surprised. 'Maybe. But we were very close once. Lucy must have spent more time in our house than in her own. Her father died when she was very small, and her mother had to work full-time. They lived in a small flat and Lucy was left on her own a lot.' Claire thought for a moment of those days so long ago. 'The strange thing was,' she explained, 'that we both liked each other's homes. I loved going to Lucy's flat because we could be on our own and play games and dress up without anyone seeing us. You don't have much privacy in a big family. But she liked my house because of all the noise and teasing and laughing. My brothers treated her like a younger sister.'

'It must have been a lot of fun for Lucy to be part of that big family,' Penny said.

'I suppose,' Claire mumbled, feeling a sudden pang of sadness.

'Then what happened?'

'Oh, I don't know.' Claire said. Lucy's ambition happened, she thought, greed and mistrust happened. 'We just grew up, I suppose.'

'Tough nut to crack,' Penny remarked.

'Our friendship?'

'No. Lucy. She's so uptight. Career, career, career, that's all she seems to care about. But I suppose her background explains a lot.'

'How do you mean?'

'I mean that someone from a poor background would be more determined to do well in a profession. Preferably one that brings in lot of money. If you grow up with nothing, then have the chance to have a better life, you'll grab it with both hands and never let go,' Penny said.

'You seem to know a lot about it,' Claire said, puzzled at the passion in Penny's voice. 'For someone who comes from such a wealthy family, I mean.'

'Oh,' Penny said in a lighter tone, 'I just imagined that it's how I would feel. But I think that's what Lucy came to New York for. To make it. Just like millions of other women.'

'Lucy has done exceptionally well,' Claire said. 'I always knew she would. She has been ambitious since she was in primary school.'

'How come you were such good friends?'

'Oh,' Claire said dreamily, slowly massaging her shoulder, 'we kind of complemented each other. Lucy was my anchor, really. I was a bit wild, I suppose. Lucy was very kind and helped me with my homework and generally stuck up for me when I was in trouble.'

'How admirable,' Penny said. 'But,' she added, 'I don't trust her.'

'What do you mean?' Claire exclaimed. 'Lucy's very …' Her voice trailed away. Honest, she was going to say, but that wasn't true. What Lucy had done was not what you'd call honest.

'I didn't mean she's dishonest,' Penny said, as if reading Claire's thoughts. 'Just that she's likely to get carried away with her success. That kind of woman will do anything to get ahead. If she keeps going this way, she'll leave Freeman & Schwartz and take half the clients with her. I've seen it happen before.'

'I don't think she would. She's very loyal.' Or used to be, Claire thought, wondering why she was sticking up for Lucy.

'Loyalty tends to fly out the window at the slightest whiff of success and money.' Penny smiled at Claire. 'But you wouldn't understand that way of thinking. You're not like Lucy. You're much more attractive, even though you don't seem to bother much.'

'What do you mean?' Claire demanded, and splashed water at Penny. 'Do I smell or something?'

'No, that's not what I meant. You just seem so laid-back. That carelessness is what makes you attractive. It's very restful.'

'I'm restful. Shit. You're the second person who's called me that.'

'Probably because it's true.'

'How wonderful,' Claire said.

'But there are lots of things you haven't told me. About your family, for instance.'

'Oh.' Claire shrugged. 'Noting much to tell.'

'No, no. I sense story here. You're hiding something. I can smell it.'

'It's the pot,' Clare said. 'It's making you smell things.'

'You can't get away with little jokes like that. Do tell me all.' Penny leaned forward and stared at Claire.

197

'All? About my family?' Claire sighed. 'They're all high flyers. My father is a solicitor. That's a lawyer in America. He has his own firm and two of my brothers are partners there. My sister Fionnuala is a doctor and my youngest brother is an architect. They're all married and have huge families. And all the children are geniuses. Even my sister's youngest child – he's only four – is a bloody genius. So there you are. Boring, don't you think?'

'What about your mother?'

'Oh, she's a genius too. Not only did she bring up five children, she has a doctorate in child psychology and has just written a thesis that has attracted huge attention in Ireland.' Claire smiled at Penny. 'Impressed?'

'Of course. But what about you? Where do you fit in?'

'I don't. I'm the big failure in the family. That's why I had to leave the country so I wouldn't embarrass them. Now they can just say their sister Claire is living on the Left Bank and writing a novel or something.'

'Are you writing a novel?'

'No, but I'm thinking about it.'

'Interesting,' Penny mumbled.

'Not really. But enough about me. Now it's your turn. I want to know everything about you.'

'There's nothing to tell. I'm just a boring old housewife.'

'But I'm sure you have a story too. Everyone

does,' Claire insisted. 'You and Al, for instance. Where did you two meet?'

'In New York. Long time ago. Not interesting and I don't really think I want to go there right now.'

'Oh, all right,' Claire said reluctantly, feeling cheated. 'Didn't mean to pry.' She was sure Penny's story was very interesting, but she didn't seem to want to talk about it. 'If we stay much longer, we'll turn into wrinkly old prunes,' Claire added. 'Maybe we should get out?'

'Too late. I'm a prune already,' Penny said with a little giggle.

'I don't know what you mean. I think you're very glamorous. I wish I could be like you,' Claire sighed. 'So slim and tall and classy. But that's impossible. You can't make a thoroughbred out of a draught horse like me.'

'You're more like a cute little pony. And I'm getting to the age when I should be put out to pasture,' Penny said, lying back in the tub, staring into space again. '*Some enchanted evening …*' she hummed, 'and … what comes next? *Something, something, hmm?* Can't remember. Do you? Funny about songs. They really take you back like nothing else …' She closed her eyes and seemed to drift off. Claire looked at Penny, wondering if she should wake her up. Was she more stoned than she seemed? Maybe that joint wasn't her first of the evening?

But Penny opened her eyes again and looked

around her vaguely. 'Where did she go …' she mumbled. 'Could have sworn there was someone here … Nope, must have been a dream.' The water suddenly stopped swirling and bubbling and it became eerily quiet on the terrace.

'What's the matter with the tub?' Penny mumbled. 'Must be the time-switch thing. Water is getting cold; got to get out of here,' she continued as if to herself, climbing out of the tub and quickly wrapping her robe around her. Without looking back, she started to walk to the door of the study.

'Hold on, I'm coming,' Claire called, following Penny's example. 'Oh, God, I feel so floppy,' she exclaimed as she climbed out. 'Where's my towel and where are my slippers?'

Penny didn't reply. She seemed to have forgotten Claire's existence. She wobbled across the terrace and in through the door. Slamming it shut, she left Claire, wet and cold, struggling with her towel.

'Wait,' Claire called, when she had finally managed to find her slippers. She walked with considerable difficulty across the snow, only to find the door locked. She shook it and called again, 'Penny! Open the door!' But there was no answer. Claire realised she was locked out on the terrace in the freezing cold dressed in only a very skimpy towel.

*

'Well, that was fun,' Al said as they came out of the cinema into the cold night. 'Let's walk back up the hill. I feel like some fresh air.'

'I think the bubble has stopped anyway,' Lucy announced. 'It's nearly midnight.'

'Look at the moon,' Tiffany said. 'It's huge.'

'Close enough to touch,' Lucy murmured as she looked up at the sky. There were puffs of steam from their breath, and the snow crunched under their feet. 'Minus twelve,' she said, pointing at the sign over the chemist's. That's pretty cold.' Not concentrating on where she was going, she bumped into Patrick. 'Sorry,' she mumbled.

'OK,' Patrick said, smiling down at her. He tried to take her hand, but she pulled away.

'What's the matter?' he mumbled in her ear. 'Don't you want to be friends?'

'Not with you.' Lucy walked further away from him.

'Let's speed up a bit,' Patrick suggested and started to walk so fast they had to run to keep up.

'Wait,' Tiffany panted. 'I'm out of breath. What's the hurry anyway?'

'Oh, come on, you little wimp,' Patrick laughed and grabbed her hand. 'You're half my age. You should be able to outrun us all.'

'I don't feel like running,' Tiffany snapped and snatched her hand away. 'It's too hard at this altitude.'

'I know,' Lucy agreed. 'I felt really weird the first few days. I was short of breath after only the slightest effort.'

'And my heart was beating like a hammer,' Al

cut in. 'Penny said it was because of all those cigars.'

'If you smoke, the altitude would affect you more,' Lucy agreed.

'I wonder if Penny's gone to bed,' Al muttered, changing the subject. 'She was very tired, she said.'

'But Claire will probably still be up,' Lucy said, 'she's such a night owl.'

'Lets have a night cap in the study,' Al suggested as the party arrived at the chalet. 'I'm really frozen.'

'Good idea,' Lucy agreed. 'That sure was a cold walk. I could feel it right through my jacket, even with the fur lining.'

When Al and Lucy came into the study, they found Penny, dressed in a bathrobe, fast asleep on the sofa in front of the dying embers of the fire.

'Penny?' Al said. 'I thought you were going to bed early.'

Penny slowly opened her eyes. She looked at them sleepily and smiled. 'Hi,' she mumbled. 'How nice to see you again.'

'Are you feeling OK?' Al asked, concerned.

'Oh yes, I'm feeling fine,' Penny replied. 'I'm feeling asolutlee … absolutely fantastic.'

'Where's Claire?' Lucy asked, looking curiously at Penny. She sounded really strange and there was a faint smell of something vaguely familiar in the room.

'Who's that?' Penny said. 'Oh, Claire!' She looked around the study. 'I think she was here only a little while ago. But then I think she went to bed.'

*

Claire had been knocking on the French window for what seemed like an eternity but the triple glazing deadened any sound from outside. She was shaking violently as she watched Penny snoozing by the fire. The bitch, Claire thought. She just walked in, shut the door and flopped down on the sofa. What am I going to do? Get back in the water? But there was no more steam rising from the tub and Claire realised that the water was rapidly turning from warm to ice cold. She walked to the edge of the balcony and looked down. Maybe I could jump? But it was too far. I'm going to die, she thought. I have the choice between breaking my neck or dying of cold. I just have to get inside soon. She went back to the window and peered in. She could see the door inside opening and Al and Lucy walking in. 'Lucy!' Claire shouted, knocking on the door again until her knuckles were raw. Someone else entered. Claire, her face pressed against the glass, watched as Patrick stood in front of Penny and said something.

Inside, Patrick spoke to Penny. 'Where's Claire?' he asked. 'I went past her bedroom door and it was open. She wasn't there. Have you seen her?'

'I'm here!' Claire shouted, but no one heard. She grabbed her towel with shaking hands, feeling the cold seeping into her bones. Her wet hair was frozen and she could feel the icy wisps against the back of her neck. 'Help,' she said weakly, 'please help me …' She sank to her knees, knowing this was the end. 'Lucy,' she whispered. 'Oh God …'

'Where could she be?' Lucy asked. 'When did you see her last, Penny?'

'I can't remember,' Penny said vaguely. 'We were having a chat and …'

'Where, honey?' Al asked. 'In here?'

'In the bath, I think,' Penny replied. 'I seem to remember a lot of steam … Out there.' She gestured limply toward the window, and they all turned around.

'Jesus Christ,' Patrick whispered. 'It's Claire, and she's …'

Claire stared dumbly, first at the silent gesticulating group, then at the towel lying crumpled at her feet on the icy decking.

13

They all stood as if paralysed, staring at Claire. Patrick was the first to move. He grabbed a wool throw from the sofa, ran to the sliding door and heaved it open. Claire grabbed the throw and fell into the room, no longer really caring that she was naked. The warm air of the room hit her like a blast from a giant hairdryer.

Al stepped forward and lifted her up as if she weighed nothing at all. 'Get some brandy,' he ordered. 'Quickly. Penny, move over, I have to put her in front of the fire. Patrick, put more wood on, and Lucy, go get her dressing gown and a duvet from her room.'

Claire huddled under the throw, shaking violently. She grabbed the glass of brandy Penny handed her and downed it in one go. The strong spirit burned her stomach but made her feel only a little better. She felt like crying, but no tears came. 'I th-th-thought,' she stammered. 'I th-th-thought ...' Her teeth were chattering so much she couldn't get the words out. She looked up at Penny, who was standing there in a daze.

'What happened?' Penny asked. 'How did you get locked out like that? I thought you had gone to bed.'

'Wh-what?' Claire said. 'B-b-b-but I w-was b-b-behind you. I c-c-called you b-but you d-didn't hear ...'

'Shh,' Al soothed. 'Don't try to talk. Here's Lucy with your dressing gown now. And your duvet. I'm going to down to the kitchen and make some mulled wine and you'll soon be warm again.'

'I got your pyjamas too,' Lucy said, 'and a pair of fleece socks. Sit up now, and I'll help you get them on.'

Penny seemed to wake up from her daze. 'Are you feeling a little better, Claire?' she asked, sitting down beside her. 'I'm really sorry. I don't know what happened.'

Al came in with a tray. 'Mulled wine,' he said, 'my own recipe. And after some of this stuff, you should begin to thaw out.' He put a steaming glass in Claire's outstretched hands.

'This is good, Al,' Lucy said, taking a careful sip. 'What's in it?'

'Wine, vodka and lots of cloves. A cinnamon stick and some lemon juice,' Al replied. 'It's hot, though, so be careful.'

'Lovely,' Claire mumbled, feeling the hot spicy drink going down her throat like velvet. She wrapped her cold hands around the glass and began at last to feel some warmth coming back into her body.

'What's going on?' Tiffany sauntered into the room, the earphones of her CD player stuck in her ears. She took the earphones out and sniffed. 'Funny,' she said. 'It smells exactly like Saturday night in college.'

'Sweaty feet, you mean?' Al said with a laugh.

'No, someone's been smoking.' Tiffany said. 'And I don't mean –'

'Oh that,' Penny interrupted. 'It's my aromatherapy candles on the terrace. I must have forgotten to blow them out.'

'Yes,' Al said. 'I know that smell.'

'I always light those candles when I'm having a bath,' Penny said. 'So relaxing.'

'Our bathroom always smells like a Moroccan souk,' Al said with a little smile in Tiffany's direction.

'You don't say.' Tiffany's face was expressionless

*

The next day, Lucy skied down the slope and stopped in a shower of snow only inches from the sun deck outside the restaurant. She took off her skis and looked around. She was meeting Penny and Al for lunch, but there was no sign of them among the guests enjoying the sunshine at the many tables. She undid the bindings on her boots and crunched slowly across the boards of the deck, the smell of food making her stomach rumble. Where were they? She put her hand up to shade her eyes and squinted at the deck chairs just below the restaurant. They were not among the sun-worshippers either. She consulted her watch. Half-past one. Had she missed them? She was also late, she felt, and sorely in need of food after the morning's strenuous skiing. A waiter came toward her. 'Mademoiselle Lucy?' he asked.

'Yes?'

'There's a message. From a Monsieur Freeman?'

'Oh?'

'Yes. He say he cannot make it. Please excuse and no worry. He say see you tonight.'

'Thank you,' Lucy said. 'How did you know it was me?'

The waiter, a handsome, somewhat slick young man, looked admiringly at Lucy. 'I get a very good, how you say, description?' He beamed at her, his white teeth dazzling in his brown face. 'Table for one?'

'What? Oh, OK.' Lucy followed the waiter to a small table beside the railing with a stunning view of the surrounding mountains. 'Great. Thanks.'

'Aperitif?'

'No. But bring me a Coca-Cola with ice. Then I'll look at the menu.'

'*Bien, Mademoiselle.*'

'I'll have the quiche,' Lucy said when the waiter came back, 'and a green salad.'

'A little wine perhaps?'

'No … yes, maybe just a glass of that rosé. And some water.'

'*Toute de suite,*' the waiter said and disappeared.

Lucy sat back in her chair, zipped open her jacket, sipped the Coke and closed her eyes. She felt content as the sun warmed her face and she could hear the murmur of the other customers. A dog barked somewhere far away, people called to each other on the ski slopes and there was the distant whirr of the ski lifts. It was lovely to relax like this, far away from the chalet. Lucy was curiously pleased that Al and Penny had cried off.

Last night had been really strange, with Claire, frozen and naked, falling into the room. She looked awful, her face white, her lips blue. And she had been shaking so violently she had trouble staying on the sofa. How horrible, Lucy thought, getting stuck out in the freezing cold like that. She could have frozen to death. She thought of how she had promised herself to try and talk to Claire, offer to pay her back that money and maybe rekindle their lost friendship. But when Lucy remembered the look in Patrick's eyes as he stared at Claire's cold, naked body, she felt a growing anger. How clever, she thought, flashing your boobs, even if they were blue, while pretending to be in danger. She changed her mind about making up with Claire, deciding that anyone who behaved like that deserved all the bad luck that hit her.

'Hi!'

Lucy opened her eyes and squinted against the sun. 'Oh, Emilie. It's you. What are you doing here?'

'I'm with my ski school,' Emilie said and gestured toward a table further away where about ten children and their teacher, dressed in the French ski school colours, were finishing their lunch. 'We've had a lovely lunch, *frites* and sausages and lots of Coca Cola, and now we're going to have some ice cream.'

'Sounds great,' Lucy smiled.

'Do you want to come and have some ice cream with us?'

'No, thanks. I'm waiting for my lunch.'

'Oh? What are you having?'

'Quiche and salad. Here it is now,' Lucy said as the waiter approached. 'Looks lovely.'

'Are you having dessert afterwards?' Emilie asked. 'There are some really yummy raspberry tarts.'

'No, I don't think so. But why don't you have your ice cream here with me?'

'OK. I'll go and get it.'

Carrying an enormous chocolate sundae, Emilie wobbled cautiously across to Lucy's table. 'Where's your teacher?' she demanded censorially of Lucy. 'Are you finished for the day or are you going up the mountain again?'

'You're full of questions today.'

'My teacher told us that it's going to snow later today, so we're finishing skiing early. It's going to snow and snow and snow, she said.' Emilie tucked into her ice cream. 'Claire is staying in bed today. She said she wasn't really sick. She got a chill so she wanted to stay indoors.'

'I know.'

'Maybe she forgot to put on her ski underwear?' Emilie suggested. 'You can get an *awful* chill if you don't put on your long johns. Isn't it funny she forgot, when she's always telling me not to?'

'Mmm. Very strange.' They continued to eat in companionable silence.

'You know,' Emilie said after a while, 'Penny is very kind. She gave him ...'

'Oh? That's nice,' Lucy said absentmindedly. She sipped her wine and let her thoughts drift while Emilie prattled on. If it starts snowing, I'll go back early too, she said to herself. I'll wash my hair and do a bit of work .

'... some money,' Emilie continued. 'Wasn't that very kind?'

'Eh, yes,' Lucy replied, planning the rest of the day in her mind. 'Who was kind?'

'Penny. I mean Mrs Freeman.'

'To who did she give money?'

'To whom,' Emilie corrected. 'That's what

Claire said, you can't give anything to a who, only to a whoooom.'

'Yeah, yeah, whom. Whom was it she gave money to?'

'Who,' Emilie said. 'You can't say whom was it. Don't you know how to talk?'

'Oh, God,' Lucy groaned. 'Are you sure you're not working for the CIA?'

'I don't work, I'm only a child.' Emilie glared at her.

'All right. Let's start at the beginning again,' Lucy said. 'Mrs Freeman is very kind. That's what you said, right?'

'Yes,' Emilie nodded.

'She gives money to people.'

'Not people. Just one. A man,' Emilie ended.

'Right. OK.' Lucy looked intently at Emilie. 'Which man?' she asked.

'Michel. He's that boy who was in the kitchen, you know that day. He knows Claire. And he knows Mrs Freeman. She gave him money at the café in the village yesterday. Then he gave her a present and she looked so happy.' Emilie paused. 'I have to go now. My teacher is calling me. Bye, Lucy. See you later.' And she was gone, leaving Lucy staring at her departing figure.

*

'Breakfast,' Dave chanted, bringing a huge tray into the dark bedroom.

'What?' Claire sat up in bed and stared at him

as he busied himself putting the tray on her bedside table and then went to open the curtains. She felt a sharp pain between her eyebrows as the sunlight streamed into the room. 'Please,' she croaked, shielding her eyes, 'don't.'

'Don't what?' Dave looked at her quizzically. 'Oh. Did we have a little too much to drink last night?' He let the curtain fall to let in just a thin beam of daylight. 'Better?'

'Yeah. Thanks.'

'I thought you might like breakfast in bed, even though it's nearly lunch time. I was told you got a chill last night.'

'Well, yes, that too.' Claire pulled the duvet up to her chin, still feeling a little cold.

'And Penny is still in bed,' Dave remarked, shaking his head. 'What did you get up to last night, I wonder?'

'Nothing really,' Claire muttered. 'We were just a bit silly.'

'I see. OK. Well, I brought you some coffee, toast, orange juice and that apricot jam you like. Is there anything else?'

'Aspirin,' Claire mumbled. 'In the bathroom.'

'Like that, is it?' Dave laughed and went to find the aspirin. 'There is a letter for you,' he said as Claire swallowed the pills with a mouthful of water.

'What? For me?'

'Yes. It was delivered by hand. It's there, on the tray.'

'Oh. OK.' Claire touched the envelope that was sticking out from under the cup. 'I'll read it in a minute. When I can focus my eyes.'

'Right. Well, enjoy your breakfast.'

'Thanks.' Claire flinched at the sound of the door slamming shut behind Dave. 'Oh, God,' she muttered to herself, 'never again.' Never champagne on top of pot and then brandy and mulled wine, she thought, lying motionless, waiting for the aspirin to kick in and give her some relief from the pounding in her head. God, what a weird evening, she thought, and what a really weird conversation. And it's even more peculiar that I remember every word. Even though Penny was sloshed, she made a lot of sense. She seems to know so much about people. And life. And men. Oh, yes, she is so right. Stay away from young men. I wish I'd never met Michel, never had a drink with him that day and then invited him to my flat and asked him to move in. Claire cringed as she thought about it. She felt a sense of shame to have been involved in such a relationship, based only on sex and her own selfish need for admiration. As Bernard Marchand suddenly came into her mind, his sad eyes and his deep, warm voice, she felt such a surge of compassion and tenderness it brought tears to her eyes. She felt a strange kind of pain, not in her head, but somewhere deep inside her chest. Suddenly thirsty, Claire sat up to drink some of the juice. She saw the letter, pulled the white envelope from under the cup and tore it open, the spidery writing dancing in front of her eyes. She gripped the page between her hands and tried to focus on the text.

Ma chère Claire, she read, noticing crazily that the words rhymed. *I am so sorry but I have to leave Courchevel in rather a hurry because I got a message from my professor at the university to go back to Paris for an urgent consultation …*

He (the professor) told me that I had to change my course and complement my studies with a technical diploma in Marseille. So, my darling, I'm afraid this is goodbye.

Claire looked up as she could hear a shout from somewhere in the house. What was that? she thought and listened for a moment. But the house was silent again. Maybe Penny was calling Dave for her breakfast, Claire thought, returning to her letter.

In any case, as you didn't seem very pleased to see me and you have not returned any of my calls, I was beginning to feel that our relationship was coming to an end. 'Oh, yes,' Claire whispered, feeling suddenly much better. *Also*, the letter continued, *with my new lifestyle, it would be very difficult for us to continue seeing each other. I will never forget you, my little Claire, or the wonderful times we had together. I will take my things from your apartment and push the key through the letterbox. I hope you will be very happy and that you one day will find a guy who is as great in bed as I am and as kind and loving. Be happy, my little one, and don't worry about me. I have great plans for a future business venture and I know I will be very successful. So, goodbye and thank you for the good times.*

With all my love,
Michel

*

'Did you make the call?' Penny asked, looking at Al from the bed. Her eyes were huge in her pale face.

'Yeah. I called the restaurant and told them to tell Lucy …'

'Not that call, you fool,' Penny snapped. 'The doctor. Did you call the doctor?'

'Yes, yes. Of course. He's on his way.' Al looked at Penny, trying to decide how ill she really was. She was still very tired that morning and wanted to stay in bed. Then, as he was reading the paper in the small sitting room next door, she had suddenly called out. 'Al, Al, I need you!'

'What's wrong?' he demanded, rushing in. Penny was as white as the sheet she was clutching and beads of sweat were running down her face. 'I think I'm having a heart attack,' she whispered. 'Please. Call a doctor.' Al sat down on the bed and stared at her. 'Are you sure?' he asked.

'Yes,' she insisted. 'I feel awful. I might need to go to hospital.'

He rang the clinic in the village and they promised to send someone straight away.

Al took Penny's hand. 'Honey,' he said, 'I just want you to know how much I love you. Don't worry about a thing. I'll look after you. If you're sick, we'll get the best doctors there are. I don't care how much it costs.'

'Thanks, sweetheart,' she whispered.

There was a knock on the door. 'The doctor's here,' Dave called.

'Show him in,' Al called back.

The door opened to admit a very tall and very thin man carrying a medical bag. 'Good morning,' he said stiffly. 'I'm the doctor on call today.'

'Thanks for coming so soon,' Al said and gestured to the bed. 'Penny, my wife. She's very ill.'

'All right,' the doctor said, pulling up a chair beside the bed. 'Let's have a look. *Bonjour Madame*. I'm Dr Luc Ligot.'

'Hi,' Penny said weakly.

'Maybe your husband could wait outside while I examine you? Do you mind?'

'No, that's all right. Al, go and wait in the study, will you?'

'But I want to be here in case she gets worse,' Al protested.

'The doctor's here now. He'll look after me. Go,' Penny ordered.

'Right. If that's what you want.' Al walked out of the room and back into the small sitting room, where he spent the next half hour pacing the floor, just like the day their daughter was born.

*

'It's a girl,' the nurse had said.

'I can see that.' Al looked at the bright red wrinkly creature that was his daughter. The nurse put the baby on the weighing scales. 'Nine pounds four ounces,' she said. 'A big baby.' She wrapped her in a pink blanket and handed her to Al, who took the baby awkwardly in his arms and looked into the angry little face.

'Hello,' he whispered. 'I'm your daddy. Welcome to the world.' The baby squinted at him, yawned and fell asleep. 'Oh darling,' he whispered, touching the wisp of blond hair on the tiny head with the tip of his finger.

'Sweetheart,' Penny mumbled from her bed. 'Give her to me.'

Al handed her the baby and together they looked at the sleeping infant.

'She's so beautiful,' Penny said.

'She looks like a smart kid,' Al announced. 'She'll go far.'

'She has your eyes.'

'And your cute little nose.'

'I want to call her Jenny after my mother.'

'You better call her Marjorie after mine or we can kiss that penthouse goodbye.'

'I suppose you're right,' Penny sighed. 'Marjorie it is. We'll slip Jennifer in as a second name. And she'll always be Jenny in my heart.'

The baby opened her eyes and looked crossly at them. She started to cry.

'What's wrong?' Al asked. 'Where's that nurse?'

'Don't worry,' Penny smiled. 'All babies cry. You better get used to it.'

Al got up from his chair. 'I'm going to call my mother and tell her about her first grandchild.'

'Don't forget to say she was six weeks premature.'

*

It was very quiet in the master bedroom of the chalet. Doctor Ligot was sitting on the chair beside the bed, his long arms wrapped around his bag. He looked at Penny questioningly. 'So, tell me,' he said, 'what's the problem?'

'I think I've had a heart attack. I'm sure of it, in fact.' Feeling exhausted, she lay back against the pillows.

'Tell me exactly what happened.'

'Well, it was a few hours ago. Just after I woke up. I felt so strange. I couldn't breathe. Then, suddenly, I was so hot, but the window was open and the room was quite cold. I started to … to perspire …'

'Perspire?'

'Yes. Sweat, I mean,' Penny said impatiently. 'I was sweating like … like a pig. My pyjamas were completely soaked. And the sheet too.'

'And … ?'

'That's it.' Isn't that enough? Penny thought. Do I have to have a seizure for him to show some interest?

The doctor opened his bag. 'I'm going to take

your blood pressure,' he said. 'Then I'll listen to your heart and your lungs.' He took out a stethoscope and leaned toward Penny. 'Could you lift up your nightgown?'

'Well?' Penny asked when he had finished his examination.

'Hmmm.' He looked thoughtfully at her. 'Tell me, Madame, how old are you?'

'What does that have to do with it, or you, for that matter?'

'Quite a lot.'

'In my country, it's considered very rude to ask a lady her age,' Penny said disapprovingly. 'I never tell anyone how old I am.'

'I'm afraid in this case you have no choice.'

'You speak very good English for a Frenchman.'

'I'm Belgian.'

'Oh? What part of Belgium are you from?'

'Liège. But I have to insist, Madame. Your age?'

'All right then. I'm …' She lowered her voice. 'Furry shhh …' she muttered.

'Sorry? I can't hear you.'

'Forty-six,' Penny whispered.

'Forty-six,' the doctor repeated, writing it down on his pad.

'There's no need to shout. Was that all you wanted to know?'

'No, there are just a few more questions …'

*

Doctor Ligot stuck his head in through the door of the study. 'You can go in now,' he said.

Al shot up from his chair. 'You've been in there for over an hour. Is she all right? I thought I could hear her scream.'

'She'll be fine. But she's very upset. I had to break some news to her about the state of her health.'

Al's face suddenly turned a sickly green. 'What?' he stammered. 'Her health? Is it serious?'

'I'll let her tell you herself. I had to give her a tranquilliser. She took it very badly.'

'What?' Al demanded. 'What did she take badly?'

But the doctor just put something on the table. 'That's my bill,' he said over his shoulder as he left. 'You can come down to the clinic and settle it later.'

Al didn't listen. He ran into the bedroom and took Penny, who was sobbing noisily, into his arms.

'Oh honey,' he gasped, 'is it very bad?'

She lifted her tear-stained face and stared at him with tragic eyes. 'My life is over,' she said. She started to cry again.

Al tightened his grip on Penny. 'Oh, my darling,' he mumbled. 'My poor, poor darling.' She put her head on his shoulder and kept weeping as if her heart was breaking.

'This is so unfair,' she cried. 'It's too …'

'Shhh,' he said, stroking her hair. 'I'm here. Don't talk.'

'But I was just thinking,' Penny wept, 'that I have never really done anything in my life. I've nothing to show, no achievements, no career, just a stupid high school diploma.'

'What does that matter? You're ill. We have to make you better. I'll do anything I can, I swear, honey.'

'You can't,' she sobbed. 'No one can.'

'You mean it's incurable?'

'Oh yeah, it's incurable all right,' Penny said bitterly.

'But there must be some kind of solution. We can get the best specialists. I'll get on to the Mayo clinic …'

Penny's sudden laugh was hollow. 'The Mayo clinic? Don't be ridiculous. Even they wouldn't be able to cure this.'

'But,' Al stammered, 'what disease is it?'

'It's not really a disease. More like a condition …'

'A condition? What's the prognosis?'

'Not good,' Penny sighed, wiping her eyes. 'You see it's the … Oh God.' She started to cry again.

Al grabbed her by the shoulders. 'The what?' he shouted. 'Tell me what it is for fuck's sake!'

'THE MENOPAUSE!' Penny yelled.

*

'Stop it!'

'Keep still.'

'But you're hurting me.'

222

'I'm just trying to get the tangles out of your hair,' Claire said.

'You have to do it gently,' Emilie instructed. 'Start from the bottom, then go slowly up to the top of my head. That's what my mummy used to do.'

'Oh?'

Emilie twisted her head and looked at Claire. 'Yes. Then she kissed the top of my head and said there you go my curly lamb. I only remembered that now, isn't that funny?'

'Yes, darling,' Claire said, carefully easing the comb through the silky curls. 'I suppose it was the combing that jolted your memory.'

'No, it was your hand on my head. And the smell of the shampoo. My mummy used the same one.'

'It's English,' Claire said. 'Crabtree & Evelyn, honey and lemon.'

'My mummy was English, you know. Her name was Gwen and she had blonde hair. It wasn't curly like mine; it was straight. And she could play the piano and sing really well and …' Emilie stopped.

'And … ?' Claire said.

'Nothing. Are you finished?'

'Nearly. There, I think that's it. Now you just get dressed and we're ready to go.'

'I don't want to go.'

'Why not?'

'It will be really boring. Why can't we stay

here, just you and me, and watch a video? We could grill sausages on the fire. It's going to snow a *lot* later on, my teacher said. It's going to snow and snow and …'

'But Al will be upset if we don't go. He has invited us all.'

'Why can't we stay here?' Emilie moaned. 'I hate going to restaurants with only grown-ups. I hate the food and I hate listening to people talking about all those politics and the cost of living and what will happen if the 'flation keeps going up and how old the wine is and …'

'Oh, sweetheart,' Claire mumbled and put her arms around Emilie, 'I do understand, I really do. You're quite right. It's not fair. You know what? I'll make a deal with you.'

'What's a deal?'

'It's when you promise something and really swear you'll keep it.'

'Oh? And what is that? The deal I mean.'

'If you come to dinner with us and are really, really good, I'll take you home early and I'll read three chapters of *Five Children and It* and stay with you until you go to sleep.'

'Four chapters.'

'They are really long chapters.'

'That's a really boring old restaurant.'

There was a brief silence.

'OK,' Claire sighed. 'You got yourself a deal. You're one tough negotiator.'

*

The night was still and cold. There were no stars and, as Claire looked up, one lone snowflake floated in the air. That snowstorm Emilie was telling us about didn't happen after all, she thought. She was walking behind the others up the street towards the big white building of the Chabichou, the most expensive restaurant in all of the French Alps. Floodlights illuminated the neo-gingerbread facade and the house looked as if it was made of icing sugar. A red carpet stretched across the snow to the pavement and a line of torches flickered all the way to the door.

'It's like the house of the Sugar Plum Fairy,' Emilie breathed.

'The house of some kind of fairy, anyway,' Al agreed. 'Fasten your chequebooks and let's go in.'

Half a dozen waiters took their coats and bowed them to a round table at the far side of the big dining room, overlooking the floodlit ski slopes and the woods beyond.

'Why are they bowing?' Emilie whispered.

'They're hoping someone has dropped money on the floor,' Al whispered back.

'Shut up, Al,' Penny muttered. She was looking especially stunning tonight, Claire thought, in a red jump suit that showed off her figure and made her blonde hair shine. She wore her hair down and more make up than usual, and the effect was both glamorous and sexy. Lucy looked elegant in white cashmere and beige Armani trousers and her face glowed with a light tan as a result of a full week of fresh air, sunshine and exercise. Claire felt rather plain in comparison. She had tied back her hair and put on a pink sweater with a low neckline and a pair of black trousers. A gold heart nestled in her ample cleavage and she had painted her generous mouth a deep red.

'Champagne.' Emilie beamed back at the waiter who appeared to materialise from nowhere. She looked deceptively angelic in a navy velvet dress with a white collar. She took a glass from the outstretched tray, brought it to her lips and managed a small sip before Claire snatched the glass away. 'But Claire,' Emilie complained, 'I want to have a taste. You said I had to behave like a big girl.'

'Not that big, darling,' Claire said and smiled at the waiter. 'Orange juice for the young lady, please.'

'Which one?' The waiter smiled warmly back at Claire.

'There's no need to suck up to her,' Al grunted. 'She's not paying the bill.'

'Al,' Penny said, looking sternly at him over the menu. 'I don't want to hear another word about money. It's very bad form.'

'All right, sweetheart,' Al said meekly. 'You're right. Sorry guys. I want you to have a good time. Forget I spoke.' He cleared his throat. 'Doesn't Penny look fantastic tonight? She's the most beautiful woman here, in my opinion.'

'Oh please,' Penny said, 'there's no need to overdo it.'

'OK.' Al looked down at the menu again. 'Let's order.'

'What's the matter with Al?' Claire whispered to Patrick, who was sitting between her and Penny. 'He's so demure. Penny is eating him alive.'

'They must have had a row. And it was his fault again.'

'She looks positively dangerous tonight. Did you see how she swept into the restaurant as if she owned it?'

'Maybe she does,' Patrick laughed. 'Al has bought a lot of property lately and he puts some of it in her name. Tax ploy, you know?'

'Caviar,' Emilie's voice said behind the huge menu. 'I want that. And lobster and oysters too. Then I could have the duck. Or the *filet mignon*. And look, they have *pommes alumettes*. And …'

'Slow down.' Claire could not help but laugh. 'You can't order everything on the menu. You'll get a terrible tummy ache if you eat all that. Let me order something nice for a starter. How about a tomato salad? It's not on the menu but I'm sure the chef will make it just for you. Then you could have half of the *filet mignon* and some of those potatoes. OK?'

'I suppose,' Emilie muttered. 'Why are there telephone numbers beside each dish? Do you have to order them by phone?'

'Those are the prices,' Claire whispered. 'I don't know why you got a menu like that. Usually, in these fancy restaurants, the men get the menu with prices and the women get one without.'

'That's not fair,' Emilie remarked. 'Why can't the women pay?'

'They usually do,' Penny said dryly, 'in one way or another.'

'Good evening, *messieurdames*,' said the head waiter, who had just arrived at their table, his pad at the ready. 'Do you want to order?'

'Well,' Al replied, studying the menu, 'it's a little hard to decide. The set menu looks good, but …'

'But?' the waiter said.

'The à la carte things look really delicious,' Penny cut in. 'I'll have a dozen oysters to start, then I think … Hmmm … *filet de chevreuil?*'

'That's venison,' the waiter said, 'in Madeira sauce.'

'Too rich,' Penny decided. 'I think I'll take the lobster instead. It's fresh, I suppose?'

'Of course,' the waiter nodded.

'Good. I'll have that then, but with no sauce. Just salad and a little vinaigrette.'

'*Bien, Madame.*' The waiter scribbled the order on his pad.

'Claire? Have you decided?' Al asked.

'Yes. I'll have the set menu. It looks great.'

'Good girl,' Al said.

'Make that two,' Lucy announced.

'Three,' Patrick said. 'Four with Tiffany.'

'But I …' Tiffany tried.

Patrick shot her a warning glance.

'That'll be five,' Al said, closing his menu. 'That's it then, except for the special order for the big and the little lady. And we'll have some wine, of course.'

'Champagne all round,' Penny said with a determined look in her eyes. 'All through the meal. Keep it coming.'

'*Absolument, Madame.*' The waiter beamed at her and closed his pad. He snapped his finger at another waiter. 'Veuve Clicquot,' he said, '*deux bouteilles toute de suite.*'

*

The meal was wonderful, Lucy thought. She had never eaten such delicious food and she would have had a really good time if only the circumstances had been different. But she had to endure looking at Patrick and Claire becoming increasingly friendly, talking softly, their heads together, laughing and teasing each other, Penny snapping at Al, flashing her eyes and smiling seductively at the waiters, Tiffany sulking on the other side and Emilie trying to keep her eyes open.

'Oh God,' Claire suddenly said, looking at the tired little girl. 'I think I'd better take Emilie home. She's beginning to fall asleep.'

'But I want ice cream,' Emilie protested, sitting up straighter. 'You said there would be ice cream with chocolate sauce.'

'There's something better than that,' Al beamed. 'Just hold on a second.' He gestured to the waiter. 'Now,' he said softly.

The waiter nodded and waved his hand at one of his colleagues. Suddenly, the lights in the restaurant dimmed and the door to the kitchens slowly opened to admit two waiters carrying an enormous cake bedecked with candles and sparklers. 'Happy Birthday to you,' Al sang. He waved his hands in the air. 'Everybody,' he shouted. 'Happy Birthday …' One by one, they joined in, until all the guests were singing. The cake was brought to their table and put in front of Penny. 'Happy Birthday, dear Penny,' everyone sang, 'happy birthday to you.'

Penny stared at the cake, at the sparklers and candles and, most of all, at the number 50 in red icing in the middle. 'Oh, God,' she mumbled, 'I don't believe this.'

'You thought I'd forgotten, didn't you?' Al laughed. He grabbed her face and planted a big kiss on her cheek. 'Happy birthday, my darling.'

Penny's smile was stiff. 'You shouldn't have,' she said. 'You *really* shouldn't.'

The waiter handed Penny a knife. 'Cut the cake, sweetheart,' Al urged.

The blade glinted in the candlelight as Penny held the knife aloft and there was a strange look in her eyes.

'Look out, Al,' Tiffany mumbled maliciously in Lucy's ear.

Penny plunged the knife into the middle of the cake. Al lifted his champagne glass. 'To Penny,' he declared. 'To the best little wife a man could ask for.'

'To Penny,' everyone murmured.

As Lucy drained her glass, she looked across the table where Claire whispered something in Patrick's ear that made him chuckle. Oh yeah, she thought, she's really going for it now. Well, she's welcome to the bastard.

'Claire,' Emilie complained, as she struggled with her piece of cake, 'I'm really tired. Can we go now?'

'OK, sweetheart.' Claire rose from her seat. 'I'm sorry, Al, but I think we have to go. Thanks for the lovely dinner, and happy birthday again, Penny.'

A few minutes later, Al stood up again, a little unsteadily. He raised his glass. 'To everyone,' he beamed. 'To all the lovely people here tonight. To Tiffany, you've really been very good. To Lucy, the best assistant I've ever had. And last, but not least, to Patrick. Thanks for all you've done for me.'

'I haven't done much,' Patrick protested.

'Sure you have,' Al argued. 'You're the greatest lawyer a man could ask for and also one of my best friends. And, if it wasn't for you, I wouldn't have hired Lucy. So *that* was ...'

'What?' Lucy exclaimed, nearly choking. 'What did you just say?'

'The best lawyer ...'

'No, about him telling you to hire me.' Lucy stared at Al, her eyes huge with shock.

'Yeah,' Al nodded, putting his glass down. 'He did. Just before you walked in that day. Best thing he ever did, I have to say.'

'But ...' Lucy stammered, 'I want to hear the whole story. You mean you wouldn't have hired me if ...'

'If Patrick hadn't called me just before you came into the office? That's right. I wouldn't.'

'And why not?' Lucy demanded.

'Because ...' Al sat down and thought for a moment. 'Can't remember why not, to tell you the truth.'

'Probably because you're a girl,' Penny suggested. 'Al said he wanted a man because he was sick of all the women gossiping and drinking coffee. I remember having an argument about it around that time. I said he was real macho pig and he ...'

'Yeah, right,' Al interrupted. 'I know. I'm sorry if I'm a little old-fashioned. I was brought up in the sixties. In those days, men went to work and women ... Women stayed at home and wore pointy bras.'

'I thought you had to move with the times in advertising,' Penny said. 'Keep up with the latest trends, you know?'

'Stop bitching for a moment,' Al said, 'and let me explain. I didn't know you were a woman. L. Mulcahy it said on the letter you sent. You had such a good résumé. Must be a guy, I thought.'

'But you called me …' Lucy started, looking confused. 'Oh, no, it was your secretary. She wouldn't have known.'

'I don't think I told her … I probably just said call this number and say I want an interview. Yeah, must have been. I was expecting a guy all the time.'

'Then Patrick rang you?' Lucy interjected.

'Told me to hire this really cute girl he had just met in the elevator. That's right. Said you had had a bit of a fright and needed cheering up. So I realised L. Mulcahy was a woman. Would have sent you on your way if it hadn't been for Patrick here.'

'I see,' Lucy nodded, glaring at Patrick.

'But I don't know why that should upset you,' Al continued. 'He was right. You *are* really cute, honey.'

'Oh please, Al,' Penny snapped. 'For once in your life, could you just be quiet?'

'What's the matter?' Al asked, looking from Penny to Lucy. 'I mean, apart from being good-looking, you've such a great talent for writing copy. And you got a very good job. It can't have been much fun waiting tables for a whole year. If it wasn't for Patrick …'

'You'd probably still be a waitress,' Patrick filled in with a dazzling smile. 'I think I did you both a huge favour, actually.'

'Well, thanks a lot,' Lucy said. She suddenly rose, knocking back her chair. 'I think I'll go back to the chalet. I'm very tired.'

'Yeah, you're looking a bit pale,' Al said. 'Are you feeling OK?'

'I'm fine,' Lucy said between her teeth.

Penny also got up from her chair. 'I think I'll go back with you. Tiffany? Why don't you come too. I think we've all had enough, actually.'

'Enough of what, honey?' Al asked, looking dazed.

'Men,' Penny replied.

14

'Look,' Emilie said as she and Claire climbed the last steep incline to the chalet. 'It's starting to snow.'

She was right. Huge snowflakes swirled in the air, first just a few, then more and more, until it was difficult to see where they were going.

'They look like feathers,' Claire said. 'It's as if a huge pillow burst in heaven and all the feathers are falling down to earth.'

'The angels are having a pillow fight.' Emilie laughed and tilted her face up. She stuck out her tongue. 'They don't taste of anything.'

'What did you expect, silly?'

'Wouldn't it be fun if they tasted of vanilla? Or strawberry? Then we could put them in a box and keep them in the freezer like ice cream.'

'And they would have no calories,' Claire said wistfully.

'Look. Dave put on the outside light and opened the door.'

'Let's get in quick, before we turn into snow-men.'

'Your dad called, Emilie,' Dave said as he helped them brush the snow off their clothes and boots.

'Oh?' Claire said, her cheeks turning pink. 'Did he want to talk to me?'

'No, he wanted to talk to Emilie.'

'Did you tell him I was having my dinner in a restaurant?' Emilie asked. 'And that I had a sip of champagne? And that I'm doing the slalom test tomorrow?'

'Yes, I told him about the restaurant. But I didn't know about the champagne or the slalom test.'

'Let's call him now,' Emilie suggested, kicking off her boots. 'It's not that late.'

'He said he was going out,' Dave replied, 'with someone called Annabel.'

'Oh, yes, I know,' Emilie nodded. 'He takes Annabel out every night.'

'Annabel?' Claire asked. 'Is that the friend you wrote about in your essay?'

'Yes. She lives in the apartment next door,' Emilie replied. 'They go to the park for a walk together nearly every evening. Daddy just likes her company, he says.'

'Oh, really?'

'Yes, he does. He says she is the best listener in the world. And she never argues with him.'

Claire stared at Emilie. 'But why …'

There was a sound at the door. Dave went to open it and Penny, Lucy and Tiffany nearly fell in, their clothes covered in wet snow. 'You look so funny,' Emilie squealed. 'You're all white.'

'My God,' Lucy panted, 'it's really coming down out there. I've never seen snow coming down in such buckets.'

'What did I tell you?' Emilie laughed. 'Didn't I say it was going to snow and snow and snow?'

*

'This is really a bit mad,' Penny complained as they waited in the lift queue the next day. 'It's still snowing like crazy. Why are we going up there only to have to feel our way down?'

'I'll be able to see perfectly even through this heavy snow,' Patrick said. 'I have these new goggles – they're supposed to be the best on the market.'

'You would,' Penny snorted. 'Oh, no, this is only a two-seat lift. One of us will have to go up alone.'

'Madame,' the man in front of her said, 'would you like to come with me?'

Penny looked at the handsome stranger and smiled broadly. 'Why not,' she said and sat down beside him as the chair lift arrived. 'See you up there,' she called over her shoulder to Patrick and Lucy as the chair lift disappeared up into the heavy snowfall.

'Isn't Penny such a daredevil these days?' Lucy remarked as she sat down on the next lift with Patrick. 'It's as if she wants to take every opportunity to have fun.'

'And what's wrong with that?' Patrick enquired. 'Look out, your ski poles are in the way.' He grabbed her poles and lifted them out of the way of the wires. 'There. Now you're OK.'

'Am I?' Lucy looked at him intently. He looked away. Their shoulders touched as they sat together on the narrow seat. It was curious how intimate you felt sharing a ski lift with someone, Lucy thought.

'These old-fashioned lifts are a bit cramped,' Patrick said, as if reading her thoughts. He shifted his shoulders, trying to get more comfortable. 'I suppose French people are smaller than the average American.'

'The new lifts are much more efficient. And they can take up to six people at a time. That's a lot quicker, of course.'

'And they're safer,' Patrick agreed. 'But they seem to have kept some of the older lifts on this side of the resort.'

'That's because the slopes over here are not as popular. Probably because the sun hits them very early and the snow is not normally very good.'

'Mmm. Probably.'

They were quiet, the whirring of the ski lift the only sound. Suddenly, the lifts stopped, and they were left dangling in the milky whiteness.

'This is also the kind of thing that happens with these old lifts,' Patrick said.

'I know.'

Neither of them spoke for a long time as they hung there, suspended in mid-air. The snow kept falling and soon they both had a layer of snow on their shoulders. Lucy felt awkward and tongue-tied as she tried to think of something to say. Claire would have said something funny now, she thought, something that would make us both feel more at ease. She glanced at him, sitting there staring ahead. What was going on in his mind? How could he just sit there so close, without feeling anything? Oh God … Lucy gripped the bar in front as hard as she could, trying to stop the tears from welling up. She looked down at the slope below. It looks quite close, she thought. Maybe I could jump? She looked ahead, trying to spot Penny and the stranger in the lift ahead, but it was impossible. Everything was lost in the falling snow. 'I hope Penny's all right,' she finally managed to say.

'She's about as all right as we are, I suppose.'

Suddenly laughter rang out from above. Then they could hear someone sing, then more laughter. 'I think Penny's making the best of the situation,' Patrick said with a little smile.

'I suppose.' Lucy shivered. 'It's getting very cold.'

'Yeah.' Patrick suddenly put his arm around her. 'We might as well try to keep warm,' he grunted.

'Yeah, sure.' It was strange to feel his arm around her like this. Comforting, somehow. She wanted to put her head on his shoulder, but didn't dare. He was only holding her to keep warm, after all.

Patrick squeezed her. 'Jesus, it's cold,' he said.

'I know,' Lucy replied.

'About ...' Patrick's voice trailed off.

'Yes?'

'Your job. You're very good at it you know.'

'And that was a big surprise?'

'Yes, no ... Those things Al told you. That's not what I said that day, really.'

'You mean what you *really* said was that you thought I was a bimbo but would be a good lay?'

'No ... I ... OK. If that's what you want to believe. Yes. Something like that.' Patrick stared straight ahead, into the falling snow. He cleared his throat. 'And that time ...'

'What?'

'Oh, you know. In Al's office.'

'Oh that,' Lucy replied, trying to shake off his arm without success.

'It wasn't such a big deal, was it? We just got a bit sloshed. A bit carried away, you know. I mean, nobody died or anything.'

'No. Nobody died,' Lucy replied in a flat voice. She shivered again, but not from the cold.

There was suddenly a whirring sound and the lift started to move. Patrick removed his arm. 'We're going up,' he said.

'Good.'

And the chair lift slowly brought them up to the top of the mountain.

*

Penny was really enjoying herself. The man who had invited her to share his chair lift, a good-looking Dutchman, was great fun. When the lift stopped, she had been really scared. But then he kept her laughing by telling jokes and singing dirty songs in Dutch, which he obligingly translated into faultless and idiomatic English. Penny was nearly sorry the lift started again. She could have stayed there all day.

'Look out, we're coming in to land,' the Dutchman exclaimed. He lifted up the bar in front of them. 'Nice to meet you. Maybe we'll meet again?'

'I hope so,' she said as she stood up and slowly slid down the small slope.

'*Tot later*,' he called as he took off down the piste and disappeared into the curtain of falling snow.

'Who was that?' Lucy asked as she skied down to join Penny.

'Oh, just a Dutchman. Very nice.'

'More than nice,' Lucy remarked. 'He was a bit of a hunk, I have to say.'

'Oh, yes,' Penny said with feeling. Then she laughed. 'He thinks I'm an artist.'

'Why?'

'Because that's what I told him.' Penny giggled mischievously. 'I said I live in a loft and I sell my nude paintings on the Internet. He was so cute. I wanted him to find me interesting.'

'I'm sure he did.' Lucy smiled. 'He probably thought you were one of those people who set up porn sites.'

'Shit, I never thought of that. But it doesn't matter. I'll never meet him again. He's going home tomorrow. Where's Patrick?'

'Over there. Struggling with those state-of-the-art goggles of his. I think the string just broke.'

'Don't laugh at him, whatever you do. He hates that. OK, Patrick?' she shouted back at the blurry figure.

'Fine,' came the muffled reply.

'Let's go, then,' Penny said and pulled her goggles over her eyes. 'Last one down is a rotten egg.'

*

'I couldn't see *anything*,' Emilie complained as they approached the reception of the ski school. 'But I did my very best and I didn't fall. I think I went around all the markers though and I even helped a girl up. She was just ahead of me and had fallen at the very last pole. She was crying because she knew she had failed the test.'

'Silly girl,' Claire said. 'It's just a test. Nothing to cry about. She can do the test again next year.'

'Yes,' Emilie nodded. 'But she is a bit of a cry-baby, that girl.'

'You wouldn't cry about a little thing like that, would you?' Claire asked.

'Of course not. But I know I passed. I'm so looking forward to having that medal. It's so nice. It will look lovely on the special board in my room with all the others. And Daddy said he would be so proud of me now that I have *two* stars.'

'We haven't seen the results yet,' Claire warned. 'You shouldn't count your chickens until they are hatched, my mother always said.'

'But I don't have any chickens,' Emilie said.

'It's a saying. It means not to be too sure of things before you know the facts.' Claire pushed open the heavy door and they went into the reception area. 'Now where is that bulletin board? Oh, over there on that pillar.' They walked over to the board, where a group of children and their parents were checking the lists of names. 'OK,' Claire muttered, scanning the pages, *trois étoiles*, no … Oh, here is your group, *deux étoiles*. Where's your name? I can't see it here.'

'What?' Emilie exclaimed. 'It must be. Look again. Emilie Marchand. My name is probably at the top.'

'No.' Claire shook her head with a feeling of dread. 'It's not here. Darling, I think there is a possibility that …'

'*What?*' Emilie shouted.

'That you didn't make it this time, sweetie.'

'It's a mistake,' Emilie stated, her eyes wild. 'They have made a stupid mistake. Go to the desk and tell them.'

'OK. Maybe you're right.' Claire walked over to the desk, where a young woman was talking to a couple.

'Ask her,' Emilie urged.

'Shhh, we have to wait our turn.'

'Oh nooooo. Come *onnnn*,' Emilie moaned.

At last, the couple departed and it was Claire's turn. 'Hello,' she said to the girl. 'I just wanted to ask ...'

'Yes?'

'About the test results over there?'

'What about them?'

'Well, we don't seem to be able to find Emilie's name ...'

'You've made a big mistake,' Emilie piped in.

The girl looked at them pityingly as if they were not quite right in the head. 'If the name's not there, it means the student has not passed,' she said very slowly.

'Could you look it up?' Claire asked, ignoring Emilie's glare.

'If the name's not there it means she has failed,' the girl repeated.

Claire beamed a fake smile at the receptionist. 'I do understand what you're saying. And, of course, I do not mean to criticise the French Ski School or any of its members but if you wouldn't mind, I would be enormously grateful if you would do me the *huge* favour of checking the list of pupils and their results?' Claire finally drew breath, feeling exhausted.

'You're not French,' the girl remarked. 'I can hear a distinct accent there.'

'No,' Claire agreed, trying to control her temper. 'I'm not French.'

'Claire,' Emilie moaned, 'make her look it up. I want my medal.'

'Shhh, sweetheart, I'm doing my best. Please, Mademoiselle,' she pleaded.

The girl sighed and rolled her eyes. 'All right.' She typed something into her computer. 'What was the name again?'

'EMILIE MARCHAND!' Emilie shouted. '*deux étoiles.*'

'Marchand …' the girl muttered. 'Ma … Oh yes, here it is. Four hundred and ninety points.'

'That's great!' Claire beamed.

'No.' The girl shook her head. 'It's not. You have to have five hundred points to pass.'

'Oh.' Claire looked at the girl, who now wore an expression of great satisfaction, then at Emilie, who stared back in shock. 'Darling, I'm so sorry,' Claire soothed, as big tears started to roll down Emilie's cheeks. 'Try to be brave, now. Better luck next time, eh?'

'It's not true,' Emilie whispered. 'It can't be.'

'I'm afraid it is,' Claire said. 'Please, Emilie, remember what we …'

'NO!' Emilie screamed and threw herself on the floor. 'NO, NO Nnn …' What followed was a scene Claire would never forget. Emilie lay on the floor screaming and kicking, while everyone turned to stare. Claire tried to lift her off the floor but Emilie kicked her hard on the shins.

'Stop it, Emilie,' Claire ordered. 'Everyone's looking at you.'

'WAAAA …' Emilie roared.

'What's going on here?' A male voice asked in French.

Claire looked up from the writhing, kicking, screaming child on the floor. 'Nothing really,' she shouted over the din. 'Just a little temper tantrum. We didn't get our medal, you see.'

'I know,' the man said. 'I was in charge of the slalom test …'

Claire moved away from Emilie. 'She's such a great little skier. What happened?'

'It was her time. She was too slow.'

'But the weather was so bad. She said she couldn't see a thing. Surely, you could make a slight adjustment?'

'That's not possible.'

'But she stopped to help another child. That wouldn't be taken into account?'

The man shrugged. 'Afraid not. This is the French Ski School, not some kind of playgroup. We teach the children to be tough. To become great skiers.'

'And not to care about others?'

'Not in a competition, no.'

'So, if she hadn't helped the other child, she would have passed?'

'Possibly.'

Claire stared at the man. 'She was exhausted,' she said. 'Couldn't you see that? She still is. That's why she's in such a state.'

'But what does that have to do with anything?'

Claire suddenly felt an urge to punch the man in the face, or at least twist his nose until he screamed. She took a deep breath. 'You're a moron,' she said loudly in English. She turned to the people in the hall who were watching them with great interest and pointed at the man. 'He's a moron,' she said. She hauled Emilie up from the floor, 'Come on, sweetheart. Let's go home.'

Still crying, Emilie got up. 'It's so unfair,' she wept as they went outside.

Claire looked at her tragic face and was suddenly very angry. 'Stop it,' she ordered. 'Stop feeling sorry for yourself like this. I'm ashamed of you. It was only a silly test. You still have a whole week to try again, remember?'

'But I'm so disappointed,' Emilie hiccupped. 'I would have passed if only I hadn't … It's all *her* fault, that girl I helped.'

'Oh Emilie,' Claire sighed. 'Don't you realise it was more important to help someone than to pass the test? I'm very proud of you for doing that.'

'I wish I hadn't,' Emilie muttered. 'And, in any

case, it was your fault as well. You and your stupid chickens.'

*

'Oh God,' Penny panted at the bottom of the last slope, 'that was not fun.'

'I know,' Lucy said. 'I had this awful feeling of *déjà vu*. I already got lost once. I don't want to go through that again, thank you very much.' She peered through the curtain of falling snow back up the piste, where a white figure was coming down very carefully. He doesn't look so dashing now, she thought. Not the champion skier we have all been forced to admire.

'Hi,' Penny said when Patrick was finally down. 'You looked a little awkward there. Those goggles not quite as good as you expected?'

Patrick pulled them off impatiently. 'They were bloody useless,' he grunted. 'I paid a fortune for them. And they're just shit.'

'That's advertising,' Lucy said, trying not to smile. 'Makes suckers even out of intellectuals like you.'

Patrick glared at her.

'Well, I've had it for today,' Penny said, taking off her skis. 'And that break in the weather they promised this morning didn't seem to happen at all.'

'I'm going for a drink,' Patrick muttered as he undid the bindings of his skis. Without another word, he put his skis on his shoulder and walked off in the direction of the village.

'Gee, thanks for inviting us to join you,' Penny said as she looked at his departing figure. 'What's biting him?' she asked Lucy.

Lucy shrugged. 'How should I know?'

Penny's eyes narrowed. 'What's going on between you two? Why are you always sniping at each other like that?'

'I really don't know what you mean.' Lucy picked up her skis and started to walk to the lift that would bring them up the hill to the chalet.

'Yes, you do,' Penny insisted, catching up with Lucy. 'I can feel it. There is some kind of ... oh look, isn't that Tiffany? On a snowboard?'

'Where?'

'Over there. Coming down off that piste.' Penny pointed at figure that could barely be seen through the falling snow.

'I doubt it very much. She doesn't even like skiing,' Lucy said, relieved at the interruption in Penny's inquisition. 'She's only been out once when Patrick forced her. The rest of the time she's been watching TV and moaning about how bored she is. I doubt if she'd start snowboarding all of a sudden.' Lucy squinted into the distance. 'Can't really see ... No, it can't be her. That's Warren right there. He gives private snowboard lessons in the afternoons. Charges a fortune for just one hour.'

'I could have sworn ...' Penny muttered. She shook her head. 'Strange.'

'Let's go,' Lucy urged. 'I'm getting so cold and

wet standing here. I'm dying to get into a bath and put on some dry clothes.'

'Sounds good,' Penny agreed. 'Then lunch. Do you think we might ask Dave to cook us something even though he isn't supposed to do lunch?'

'It's Friday. He's gone to the big supermarket in the valley because it would be quiet today. Most of the people who were skiing here last week are leaving tonight or early in the morning and next week's crowd will start arriving tomorrow afternoon. We'll have to either have lunch in the village or boil an egg or something ourselves in the chalet.'

'Friday already,' Penny said with a sigh. 'How time flies. But tomorrow will be a great day to ski. There'll be hardly anyone on the pistes.'

'Or in the restaurants,' Lucy added.

'Exactly. We'll have the place to ourselves. We'll have a wonderful day. Provided the weather improves, of course.'

'It will,' Lucy stated. 'It has to. It can't keep snowing like this for ever.'

*

The phone rang just as Claire and Emilie arrived in the door of the chalet. Claire ran up the flight of stairs to the hall and picked up the extension. 'Hello?' she panted.

'You sound strange.' Dave's voice seemed far away.

'I had to sprint up the stairs to get the phone,' Claire explained, trying to catch her breath. 'Where are you?'

'I'm still down here in the valley. I've done the bulk of the shopping but some of the fresh fruit and vegetables haven't come in yet because of the heavy snowfalls. And they're also waiting for a new delivery of meat and fish.'

'Yes? So?'

'Well, I thought that, rather than go all the way up to Courchevel and then back again, I'd spend the night here and do the rest tomorrow. The weather is supposed to clear and I won't have to drive back in this heavy snow ...'

'Sounds sensible. Are you staying in a hotel?'

'No, eh, I met a girl I used to know, you see. She has a flat in the town here. She works in one of the sport shops.'

'I get the picture,' Claire laughed.

'Do you think you'll be able to manage tonight? I was going to do roast chicken and it's all there in the fridge. Would you be able to take care of that?'

'Of course.'

'Sure?'

'Piece of cake.'

'There are two chickens and they are ready to go into the oven. It'll take about an hour at medium. The vegetables and potatoes are all prepared. You just have to cook them.'

'No starter tonight?'

'It was supposed to be cheese soufflé but I think we'll skip that.'

'I think that would be wise,' Claire agreed.

'I was going to make mushroom sauce to go with the chicken. Do you think you could manage that?'

'I'll do my best.'

'There's fresh bread in the bread bin and the wine is in the rack beside the cooker. I put a couple of Côtes du Rhône there last night, and …'

'Stop fussing, we'll manage. You have fun and we'll see you tomorrow.'

'The bread for breakfast is delivered to the kitchen door at about eight o'clock in the morning,' Dave continued, 'and I'll be back mid-morning with all the food for next week.'

'Great. Don't worry. We'll be fine.'

'Thanks a lot, Claire, you're a brick.'

'No problem,' Claire said and hung up. 'Except a tiny one,' she continued to herself, 'but, what the hell.'

15

'Medium oven,' Claire said, looking at the two chickens in the roasting pan. 'What does that mean? Come on, you tell me. It concerns you, after all.' But the chickens didn't reply. 'Don't just lie there, looking pale and interesting,' Claire ordered, prodding one with a fork, 'try to give me a little help here.' She poured herself another glass of wine. 'Mmm, lovely. Dave certainly knows his wine. I hope he's having a better time with his bird down the valley than I'm having with these.' She lifted one chicken leg and peered inside. 'Hmm, stuffed, eh? That's one advantage, I suppose. OK …'

'Who are you talking to?' Emilie asked as she came into the kitchen with an empty dish.

'Nobody. Did they like the hors d'oeuvres?'

'Yes, they did and they want more. And they

said they were starving and how long will dinner be?'

'One hour,' Claire replied. 'That's what Dave said. The cheese cubes are over there and the salami slices as well. Could you be an angel and put them on sticks?'

'I'll just pile them onto the plate,' Emilie replied. 'They're so hungry they won't be able to wait.'

'Great. By the way, darling, you don't happen to know what "medium oven" means? Do you think it means the middle of the oven?'

'No.' Emilie shook her head vigorously, making her curls bounce. 'I think it means the temperature. You know, you have to set the temperature before you cook anything.'

'Of course. You're a genius. So,' Claire mused, while she fiddled with the dials on the huge cooker, 'medium must mean something between hot and cold.'

'Yes, that's right,' Emilie agreed, putting cheese cubes and slices of salami on her dish. 'I like being in the kitchen with you,' she added. 'It's so cosy and fun. I bet you're a very good cook.'

'I do my best,' Claire replied.

'Need any help?' Patrick said, putting his head through the door.

'No, I'm fine. I've got everything under control. It'll be ready in an hour or so.'

'Great.' Patrick smiled at her. 'We're so lucky to have you. Nobody else seems to know how to cook. But that's New York women for you. Quite useless around the house. Thank goodness for real women like you.'

"Scuse me,' Emilie chanted. 'I'm coming through with the snacks.'

'I'll take those,' Patrick said and took the dish from Emilie. 'Do you want me to get you a drink from the living room? I've made a big jug of dry martinis.'

'No, thanks, I'm having some of this wine. It's excellent. But maybe you could help Emilie lay the table when she has finished serving the snacks?'

'OK. Anything else?'

'That's it. I'm just going to do the potatoes and vegetables and make that mushroom sauce.'

'Mmm,' Patrick said, 'I can't wait. This will be such a treat.' He beamed a dazzling smile at her as he left.

'Maybe you should have told him not to count his chickens?' Emilie piped up.

'Yeah, maybe,' Claire mumbled as she searched the kitchen for ingredients. 'Where are the mushrooms?'

'They're in that cupboard, there,' Emilie said and pointed. '*Cèpes* they're called. Dave fries them in butter and then he just pours some cream on them.'

'I see,' Claire said and stared at a packet she had just taken out. 'Oh God. These are dried *cèpes*. Shit.'

255

'What?'

'Nothing. Darling, why don't you go and see if Patrick's ready to lay the table now?'

'OK.' Emilie disappeared, leaving Claire still peering at the dried mushrooms.

*

'Dave would have had a terrible time trying to drive back up,' Penny remarked, looking at the weather report on television.

'He was right to stay,' Patrick agreed. 'Is Al back?'

'I didn't know he had gone out,' Penny said, looking startled.

'Yeah, he did,' Patrick replied. 'He went out about an hour ago. Said he was going somewhere a man could smoke a cigar in peace. I think he went to the bar across the road. It's impossible to get any further tonight.'

'Here he is now,' Lucy said as the door opened. But it was Tiffany, her hair covered in snow and her cheeks red from the cold.

'Where have you been?' Patrick asked in a voice that was both concerned and angry.

'Out.' Tiffany replied defiantly. 'There's no law against going for a walk, is there?'

'Not if that's all you did,' Patrick retorted. 'But I can't see how you could have been *walking* in this weather. You must have been in the village. How the hell did you manage to get back?'

'I got a lift with a snow scooter,' Tiffany

replied, sitting down on the floor in front of the television.

'A snow scooter?' Patrick demanded.

'Yeah. It's like a cross between a motorbike and a sled and it goes really fast.'

'I know what it is, you twit.' Patrick glared at her. 'Who was it? Who brought you back?'

'Oh, just a guy. Very nice,' Tiffany drawled, dreamily combing her hair with her fingers.

'But Al said you were in your room,' Penny interrupted. 'He said there wasn't a sound from you all day. I thought you were very tired and wanted to sleep.'

'Ah, well,' Tiffany said with a cheeky smile, 'he didn't actually notice when I left.'

'So you sneaked off and you've been gone all day?' Patrick asked.

'Most of it, yeah,' Tiffany replied.

'And what have you been doing all this time?'

'This and that.' Tiffany shrugged. 'I tried to ski for a bit but I gave up when I couldn't see, then I hung out with a couple of guys in that café by the ski jump. But it's late. When's dinner? I'm really hungry.'

'Aren't we all?' Penny remarked. 'I wonder if Claire's managing all right. There hasn't been a sound from the kitchen for some time.'

'I'll go and have a look,' Lucy offered, getting up from the sofa.

*

'*Kiss me once and kiss me twice and kiss me once again,*' Claire sang, '*oh la la la, c'est magnifique …*' She sighed happily and took another swig of wine. 'Lovely wine,' she said to herself. 'And these olives are just … mmm …'

'Dinner nearly ready?' Lucy asked as she came into the kitchen.

'No, not really.' Claire looked guiltily at Lucy. 'Oh, God, it's late. How time flies when you're drinking wine.'

'You mean you haven't even started?'

'I switched on the oven, but that's as far as I've …'

'Oh great. Jesus, you're priceless. Sitting here dreaming as usual. What the hell is your problem?'

'Just a small one,' Claire said. 'I don't know how to cook.' She smiled at Lucy over the rim of her wine glass.

Lucy stared at her. 'What are you talking about? You live in Paris, the capital of food. You must know how to cook.'

'The capital of restaurants, you mean. I never really cook. I eat out or get something from the *traiteur*. That's a kind of caterer,' Claire explained when Lucy looked confused.

'I see.' Lucy folded her arms and looked at Claire. 'But why didn't you say anything? Why did you make us think you could?'

'I don't know, really. I was going to have a go, but then I started tasting the wine. Just to see if it was OK, you know, and …'

'You're drunk.'

'No, I'm not. I just feel very relaxed. I just kind of forgot about the food.'

Lucy rolled her eyes. 'Wonderful. But I have to say I'm not surprised. You were always running away from responsibilities. Now I'll have to see if I can do something about dinner before we all starve to death.' She pushed up her sleeves and picked up a knife.

'What are you doing?' Claire's voice was just slightly slurred.

'Never mind.' Lucy had started cutting up the chicken. 'Just go out and tell them dinner will be a little late, and then come back here.'

Claire slipped out, glass in hand and made the announcement. 'There's been a slight problem with the oven, but dinner will be served in twenty minutes,' she said and went back into the kitchen without waiting for a reply.

'What did they say?' Lucy asked.

'Nothing. They were watching the news and drinking martinis.'

'Good. OK, don't just stand there looking stupid. Cut up these tomatoes.'

Twenty minutes later, a delicious smell filled the kitchen. Lucy had cut the chickens up into pieces and browned them in butter, and they were simmering in white wine and herbs in a pan. She had baked potatoes in the microwave and Claire had made a tomato salad following Lucy's instructions. They hadn't spoken much during the proceedings, except for Lucy snapping out orders like a sergeant major.

When everything was ready, Claire looked in awe at the beautifully arranged food on the serving dish. 'This looks great. Everyone's going to be so impressed. But where did you learn to cook?'

'Where do you think? In your house. I used to watch Mary, you know, the lovely housekeeper you had, when you were busy looking at MTV and talking to boys on the phone.'

'But when we shared a flat, you never cooked.'

'You were never there in the evenings, remember? But, yeah, I can cook. I had to do a lot of the cooking at home. *We* didn't have a maid, you see. *I* wasn't brought up to think the sun shines out of my arse.'

Lucy's scathing tone made Claire see red. 'All right, Little Miss Perfect,' she snapped. 'So you know how to cook? Big deal. There are a lot of other things you don't seem to be very good at.'

Lucy looked up from the food. 'Such as?' she demanded.

'Men. You haven't a clue about how to attract them.'

'And you do? I have to tell you that all that simpering and showing off your boobs is really pathetic.'

'What's that supposed to mean?' Claire demanded, fighting to stay calm.

'I mean that charade of getting locked out on the terrace stark naked. Was that supposed to be cute? "Oh Patrick,"' Lucy mimicked, "'I was so scared. I'm so cold, please put your arms around me and try not to get excited!"'

'It wasn't like that,' Claire protested, angry tears rolling down her cheeks. 'It was an accident. It was Penny's fault. She ...'

'Oh yeah, right. Blame someone else. Thought you were clever, did you? What a great excuse to show off your assets. But I'm afraid that all you managed to do was to look cheap. Oh, God, you really haven't changed a bit, have you? You're still such a slut. I remember how you used to flaunt yourself in front of the boys.'

'And you were such a prude,' Claire retorted. 'Did you know, in school, we used to call you Mother Superior behind your back? Frigid Bridget was another one.'

'I'm not even going to tell you what *you* were called,' Lucy interrupted. 'Only that it rhymed with –'

'SHUT UP!' Claire suddenly yelled. 'If you don't shut up, I'll ...'

'You'll what? Don't be so fucking pathetic.'

Beside herself with rage, Claire picked up a slice of tomato and threw it at Lucy. It landed on her cheek and slowly slid down her face, the juice clinging to her cheek. Lucy wiped it off. As if in slow motion, Claire saw Lucy take a fistful of tomato slices and ducked. The tomato splattered against the wall behind her. 'Ha!' she shouted. 'You missed!'

Lucy picked up another fistful.

'Stop,' Claire ordered. 'Just stop it!'

Lucy's arm fell. Breathing hard, they stared at each other across the table.

'This is mad,' Claire said, slowly coming to her senses. 'We have to bring in the meal.'

'You're right. Pity. I was beginning to really enjoy myself.'

'I could tell. You were just getting into the swing of it. Just like that time when ...' Claire stopped.

'What?'

'Forget it. Just something I remember from the time when we were friends. Before you turned into career bitch of the year. Before you thought that your own life was more important than us ... I mean me and you and ... But I suppose you have forgotten all about that.'

Lucy leaned across the table and stared at Claire. 'No, I haven't,' she said. 'I haven't forgotten anything. I have thought about it often all these years. Yes, I know I did something wrong. But have you ever stopped to think that, if you had acted a little differently, we might not have parted in such a bitter way?'

'I don't know what you mean. What you did was terrible.'

'Yeah, yeah, I know. But why did it come as such a surprise to you? Did you not *listen* when I told you what I wanted to do with my life? Did you never stop to think that I might feel I needed to do really well in my career, given that I didn't have your background and the security net of a well-off family?' Lucy shook her head. 'I can see by the surprised look on your face that you didn't have the slightest clue. And why? Because it was all about Claire, wasn't it? All about you and the fun you had and the guys you went out with and blah, blah, blah.'

Shocked, Claire stared at Lucy. There was such bitterness in her voice. Then her anger returned. 'That was a great speech,' she snorted. 'Poor little Lucy, was it? Poor misunderstood Lucy, who had to steal to get her way. Well, congratulations, darling, you seem to have got all you wanted. I hope you're happy.' Tears of anger and self-pity started to well up in Claire's eyes.

Lucy's expression softened. 'Oh, Claire,' she exclaimed, 'why can't we be friends again? Why can't you try to understand that ...' She paused. 'OK, so I shouldn't have helped myself to the money without asking. But I needed it in a hurry.'

Claire studied her nails without replying.

'I should have paid you back, I know,' Lucy continued, 'but I didn't have enough money to live on, let alone ...'

'My heart bleeds.'

'But now I do. I can pay you back with interest.' Lucy smiled at Claire. 'I'll even throw in a thousand extra. What do you say?'

Claire looked at Lucy, then down at the food, then back at Lucy. Without a word, she picked up the dish and carried it into the dining room. Lucy followed with the tomato salad.

'About bloody time,' Tiffany grunted.

'I'm starving,' Patrick said. 'Well done, Claire.'

Penny helped herself to the chicken. 'This smells divine,' she said. 'I didn't know you were such a fabulous cook.'

'It wasn't me,' Claire said. 'It was Lucy.'

'What?' Patrick looked confused. 'But I thought …'

'I can't cook for toffee,' Claire said. 'Thought I'd have a go, but it turned out to be harder than I thought. So Lucy stepped in and saved us all from starving to death.'

'Amazing,' Al said. 'I didn't know you were so talented in the kitchen, Luce.'

'Oh,' Claire smiled, putting an arm around Lucy's shoulders, 'there's a lot you don't know about Lucy.'

16

The explosion was so loud it nearly knocked Penny out of bed. She jumped up and raced to the window to look out. When she was halfway across the floor, another loud boom shook the windows. 'Jesus, what the hell was that?' she said, parting the curtains. She squinted in the bright morning light through the windows. There was another explosion, further away. Penny saw Patrick standing on his balcony and opened the window, letting in a blast of cold air.

'What's going on?' Penny called to Patrick.

'They're blasting away the snow from the slopes,' he replied, wrapping his thick wool dressing gown tighter around his tall frame. 'There must be a big avalanche risk with all that snow that fell yesterday.' Another boom drowned the rest of his words. He smiled and shrugged. 'They'll stop soon. Then we can go skiing. And the slopes are virtually empty at the moment. Most people are leaving. I've been hearing cars go down the road since about six o'clock. Talk about rats leaving the sinking ship.'

Penny shivered. 'God, it's cold.'

Patrick turned and walked to the open door of the balcony. 'I'm going down to breakfast. You better close the window or you'll freeze. How is Al?'

Penny turned to look at his sleeping form in the bed. 'Still out for the count. I think he had a little too much to drink last night. Thanks for taking him home.'

'No problem,' Patrick replied. 'And he wasn't really that drunk. He said he needed a little comfort, whatever that means.'

'No idea. Sorry. I have to go in. I'm beginning to turn blue.' Penny waved at Patrick and closed the window.

Another loud boom made Al stir in the bed. 'Penny? That you? What's the bloody noise?'

'They're blasting the snow off the mountain.'

'What for?' Al grunted and pulled the pillow over his head. 'Make them stop. It's giving me a headache.'

'They'll stop when they've done their job,' Penny said getting back into bed.

'Aren't you getting up?'

Penny pulled the duvet around her. 'In a minute. I just need to get warm again.'

'Sorry about last night,' Al said.

'Never mind. You missed a great meal though. Claire and Lucy did a good job.'

'Nice to see them getting on.'

'I don't think they are,' Penny said, plumping up her pillow. 'They were very strained last night. No, there's something not right between those two.'

'Just women's stuff,' Al grunted and turned his back to Penny. 'But I don't want to know. I'm sick of bloody women and their whingeing about their problems.'

Penny sat up. 'What do you mean?'

'If you're gonna start raving about hormones and all that menopausal crap again, leave me out of it. I just want to go back to sleep.'

'Charming,' Penny said and got out of bed again. 'I'm not staying here if you're going to be hostile. But, before I go, I'll have to tell you that you haven't the slightest idea about how women suffer, both physically and mentally. We have to go through having periods and being pregnant, then go through *agony* giving birth. And then the menopause and all the awful fear of growing old while you men just *sail* through life and expect us to want to have *sex* with you every five minutes …' She stopped when she realised her words were barely audible. Al's snoring was so loud it even blocked out the distant boom outside.

*

The blasting had stopped when Penny reached the bubble lift. She lifted her skis off her shoulder and stepped in. She was relieved to be alone in the bubble, as she didn't feel like making conversation with strangers. The doors of the lift slid together, the bubble swung into the air and started its ascent. Penny looked out through the grimy window and noticed the snow had stopped falling but the sky was still grey. The slopes were deserted, except for a group of children and their teacher. Penny tried to see if Emilie was among them.

Looking at the children, she suddenly felt a sense of desolation. Tears began to run down her cheeks. Never again, she thought. She wiped the tears absentmindedly away with her glove, but they kept streaming down her face. She wrapped her arms around herself, feeling suddenly chilled to the bone. The lift rose through the clouds, swinging gently. As a terrible sadness swept through her, Penny was oblivious to her surroundings. All her pent-up emotions bubbled up in her mind, all the frustrations and lost opportunities. The things she should have done, the babies that should have come, but never did. She lifted her face and stared blindly into space, while the tears kept running down her cheeks.

'Madame?'

Penny gave a start. The lift had stopped and the lift operator was staring at her through the open doors. She quickly wiped her face, grabbed her skis and shakily got off the lift.

*

'I better check Tiffany hasn't slipped into a coma,' Patrick said later that afternoon. He walked over to the far side of the living room, where Tiffany was slumped on the chaise-longue, eyes closed, earphones stuck in her ears.

'Tiff? Hello? Can you hear me?' When there was no reply, he turned up the volume on her Walkman, which resulted in a yelp of pain. 'What the fuck!' Tiffany shouted. 'Are you trying to make me deaf?'

'She's all right,' Patrick nodded.

'Just leave me alone, OK?' Tiffany grunted and resumed her position. 'I'm listening to music here.'

'If that's what you want to call it,' Patrick remarked and picked up the case of the CD. 'Oh, my! Opera?' He whistled, looking surprised. '*The Magic Flute?* Wow. What's going on?' He looked at Tiffany as she lay there as if in a trance. 'She has been behaving a bit oddly lately. Is she on something, I wonder?'

'Maybe she has just discovered she likes other kinds of music?' Lucy suggested. 'Oh, here's Penny. What's going on? You look upset.'

'It's snowing again,' Penny announced. 'And the roads are completely blocked. Nobody can get in or out of here. I just heard it from my … someone in the village. Most of the shops are closed. It's like a ghost town down there, except for the supermarket, the Ski Jump bar and one of the restaurants.' Penny paused for breath. 'Where's Dave? I'm dying for a cup of tea.'

'Oh, God, Dave,' Lucy said, her face pale. 'He should have been here by now with the shopping. There's very little food left.'

'Great,' Penny said. 'This is turning into a holiday in hell.'

'The lights are going out all over Europe,' Al said in a deep, gloomy voice.

*

'Hello, can you hear me?'

'Yes, Monsieur Marchand,' Claire said.

'Oh? You're suddenly very formal. I thought we were on first name terms.'

'And I thought I was the only person you could really talk to.'

'But you are.'

'Really? What about the lovely Annabel, then?' And how come you haven't called for several days, she thought angrily.

'Who?' His voice was suddenly full of laughter.

'That stunning woman who lives next door. The woman you take for a walk every evening, the woman you love to talk to, who is *such* a good listener and who never argues.'

'Oh. Emilie must have told you about her.'

'She certainly did,' Claire snapped. 'Which made me feel just a tiny bit foolish.'

'I don't see why.'

'Well, because …' she paused, trying to think of something cutting. 'Because you've been calling me every evening, and we have been having these rather personal conversations that have not been easy for me. But I thought … I mean …'

'Oh Claire,' he laughed, '*ma petite* Claire. You *are* the only person I can really talk to. Annabel is lovely but I couldn't begin to compare her with you.'

'You couldn't?' Claire asked, pressing the receiver even closer to her ear.

'Not at all. Forget about Annabel. She's not important.'

'She isn't?' Claire said, her voice suspicious.

'I swear. She's just a friend.'

'I see.'

'What were you doing when I called?'

'Nothing much. I was sitting up in bed, waiting … I mean listening to the radio. There's some lovely music playing. Can you hear it?'

'Yes. Cello is it? Dvorák, I think.'

'That's right. One of my favourites.'

'Really?' he said. 'Mine too. What else do you like? What are your favourite things?'

'Apart from whiskers on kittens, you mean?'

'Yes, Maria, that's right,' he laughed.

'Well, Captain von Trapp, if you really want to know, I like …' Claire paused. 'I like beautiful things. Nice music, lovely paintings. Especially paintings, I suppose. Really good books …'

'What sort of books?' he asked.

'I'm easy. Anything really … no, not anything,'

she corrected herself. 'I'm a little old-fashioned when it comes to reading. I like Jane Austen and the Brontës and also some of the French classics: Balzac, Stendhal … Not very original, I'm afraid.'

'I like those too.'

'You do?'

'Mmm. But go on …'

'Well, that's it really. I just like the things that gladden the heart. Lift my spirits. But what about you? What makes you happy?'

'At the moment, just sitting here talking to you.'

'Oh. Well, that's …' The line crackled. 'Hello? hello?' Claire shouted. 'The line is going. I'd better hang up.'

There was a brief silence but then she heard faintly: 'Claire? Don't hang up. I think the line is improving.'

'Yes, that's better. It's a bit windy, you see, so that must be why the phone lines are bad.'

'A bit windy? I just watched the late news and I believe there was a blizzard and you're completely cut off. I have to say I was really worried about you and Emilie.'

'No need. It's not as bad as they said. It's true there was a blizzard earlier. The police were even here to tell us not go out. But the wind has eased. It's still snowing like mad, but we're doing OK. Emilie is fast asleep.'

'No power cut?'

'No, thank goodness.'

'And you're not frightened?'

'Of what? I'm quite cosy here, under my duvet with the snow falling outside.'

'Sounds very nice. I wish I was there.'

'So do I … I mean …' Claire stopped.

'I know. I hope you're not cold,' he said.

'No, I'm very warm and comfortable.'

'In your cosy bed.'

'That's right.'

'And are you wearing …' he paused. 'What are you wearing? I'd like to know exactly what you look like at this moment.'

'What am I wearing?' Claire glanced down at her worn T-shirt and the old tracksuit bottoms she had put on for warmth. 'Nothing,' she said in a low voice.

'Nothing at all?'

'Mmm. That's right.' Let's see what he thinks of that, she thought mischievously.

He was silent for such a long while Claire thought they had been cut off again. She tried to imagine him there, in his apartment in Paris, maybe in his study. 'Hello?' she whispered. 'Are you still there?'

'Yes.' He was silent again. Then: 'Claire … I have been thinking a lot about you …'

'You have?'

'Yes …' He paused again and cleared his throat.

'Bernard? Are you still there?'

'Oh Claire,' he said. 'I can't help it … *je vous adore* …'

'What? You adore me? What's that supposed to …'

'You know very well, Claire, *mon amour*, my darling …' The line crackled again and died.

*

'What's the matter with you? Are you still asleep or something? Come on, I'm hungry. That porridge must be ready by now. And make me some cocoa.' Emilie tugged at Claire's dressing gown.

'What?' Claire blinked.

'Hello?' Emilie laughed. 'Wake up! I want my breakfast.'

'Oh!' Claire suddenly snapped to attention. 'Of course, you do. What do you want?'

'I just told you,' Emilie chided. 'Cocoa and porridge. And don't take that milk, it's gone all yucky.'

'Right. So it is.'

'Just put the milk out of *that* carton in the cup and put it in the microwave,' Emilie instructed.

'I know, I know, calm down.' Claire took the saucepan of porridge off the cooker and poured milk into Emilie's blue mug. 'Listen, sweetheart,' she said as she placed the mug in the microwave. 'Can I ask you a question?'

'What's the question?' Emilie looked up at Claire. 'Is it something important?'

'No, not really. I was just wondering,' Claire smiled into Emilie's hazel eyes, 'have you been talking to your father lately?'

'I talked to him ...' Emilie thought '... yesterday, I think.' She nodded, making her curls bounce. 'Yes it was yesterday. He called when we had just come back from ski school. I went into your room and talked to him on your phone.'

'And what did you talk about? Did he say anything about me?'

'Weeell ... kind of.' Emilie looked down and started to play with the fringe on the table cloth.

'What do you mean, kind of?'

'He asked me if we were getting on together, if we were good friends.'

'And you said?'

'That we are getting on fine and that you're a *very* good cook.'

'Oh God, you didn't! You know that's not true.'

'Well, I thought if he believed you were ... But then ...'

'What?'

'Oh.' Emilie sighed. 'I was still a little bit mad at you for shouting at me so I told him.'

'About what?'

'About telling me off for getting upset about the medal and that you won't let me stay up late and that I'm not allowed to eat *anything* after brushing my teeth and ...' Emilie stopped.

'Go on. What else did you tell him?'

'That you get really mad sometimes when I shout just a *little* bit and you never let me win when we play snakes and ladders or any other game.' Emilie looked mournfully at Claire. 'But he just laughed and said it was good for me and we're lucky to have you. Then I was mad at *him* for not being on my side and put down the phone.' Emilie hung her head and muttered something.

'What?' Claire asked and lifted Emilie's chin. 'I can't hear you.'

'I'm sorry,' she muttered. 'I do like you, really.'

'And I like you.' Claire laughed and hugged Emilie, feeling it wasn't really true. Her feelings for Emilie were growing much stronger than that and the thought of the holiday coming to an end made her feel suddenly very sad. 'Why don't you sit over there and have your breakfast,' Claire said. 'The others will be coming down looking for food in a minute so we might as well enjoy the peace while we can.'

'OK.' Emilie sat down and dug into her porridge with gusto, while Claire sank down on her chair again and resumed staring into space.

*

'Well,' Al said, wiping his mouth, 'that was … interesting. But thank you for sharing your porridge with me, Emilie, I was very hungry. It really filled me up.' He pushed back his plate and got up from the kitchen table. 'I'm going to have my coffee in the living room. Coming, Patrick?'

'I have a bit of work to do on the computer in the study,' Patrick replied.

'And I'm going to go and put my ten dollars

that auntie Penny gave me for helping in my purse,' Emilie piped up. 'I've never had dollars before. It's very nice, all green. Look.' She held up the note. 'What are you going to do, Claire?'

'What?' Claire said, lifting the receiver of the telephone extension to her ear. 'Still dead,' she muttered.

'Are you expecting a call?' Penny asked. 'You've been testing the phones all morning.'

'No, not really,' Claire protested. 'I just wanted to see if it was working or not.'

'Not,' Lucy said, clearing the dishes from the table as Al and Patrick left. 'All the lines are still down and even the mobiles are not working for some reason.'

Claire sat down at the kitchen table again. She was feeling very strange; elated and frustrated at the same time. And maybe a little frightened. What did he mean? How could he say a thing like that on the phone? She wanted to talk to him again, but didn't really know what to say. Was it really possible to fall in love with someone you had only met once? She loved his voice, she knew that. She also wanted to ease his pain and make him smile again. She loved talking to him, but he had ruined it. She would never feel at ease talking to him again. And maybe he had been joking? Or drunk? She couldn't really make up her mind what she felt about him. But she knew that there was one thing about him that was nearly irresistible …

*

277

'PASTRAMI.'

'That's not a word, Al,' Claire protested.

'What do you mean it's not a word?' Al demanded. 'Hot pastrami on rye. It's the best sandwich there is, and you say it's not a *word*?'

'I don't think it's in the *Oxford Dictionary*,' Claire stated. 'It's some kind of sausage.'

'So?' Al demanded. 'What does that prove?' He stabbed the board with his finger. 'It's a word, I say! And a bloody good sausage as well. The best. That word stays. Twenty points. Look it up if you don't believe me.'

'Oh, OK,' Claire muttered, studying the dictionary. 'Oh, yes, you're right, Al. It's mentioned here.'

'Knew it,' Al said, sounding satisfied.

'My turn,' Claire said. 'Hmm.'

'Oh please, hurry up,' Patrick ordered. 'We've been playing this stupid game for over an hour.'

'Can you think of anything else we might do?' Penny enquired. 'It's only nine o'clock. We've had dinner, if you can call cold ham and baked beans dinner. The TV's not working because the satellite dish blew off in the blizzard and it's too early to go to bed …'

'What's that noise?' Claire asked. They all stopped talking and listened intently to the sound of an engine outside.

'Snow scooter,' Penny said. 'It must be the police doing their evening rounds.'

'BRAT,' Claire said.

'What?' Patrick asked.

'That's my word,' Claire replied. 'Quite good, even if I say so myself. Your turn Patrick. Your last letters, I think?'

Patrick didn't reply but laid his letters on the board.

'SCREW,' Claire read. 'Lucy, it's your turn.'

'Oh, yes,' Lucy said with an expressionless voice. She carefully laid her letters on the board. 'There.'

'RAPED,' Penny read. 'Brilliant, Lucy.'

'OK,' Al said. 'I have a couple of letters left. I wasn't going to do this, but as everyone else has decided to be rude and there are no children present …' He put his letters down and leaned back.

'PIMP,' Claire read. 'Good word.' And you get double points on that square.

'I just happen to have those letters,' Al said, looking at Lucy, 'but it doesn't mean …'

'Lucy,' Claire said, looking at her scores, 'you're in the lead. But you were always so good at Scrabble.'

'And that's what I was trying to say,' Al interjected, pointing at Lucy. 'That's why I hired you. And for no other reason.'

'Because I'm good at Scrabble?' Lucy asked, lifting one eyebrow.

'No,' Al said, 'because you're bloody brilliant at selling. You were the best man for the job.'

Penny looked from Lucy to Al, a growing suspicion in her eyes, then down at the board.

'How about a drink?' Patrick said, standing up suddenly, tipping the board and scattering all the letters across the carpet.

17

'What was that?' Penny asked as she closed the bedroom door. 'That word?'

'What word, hon?' Al said sleepily and started to take off his shirt.

'You know,' Penny snapped. 'You know very well.'

'In the beginning was the word, and the word was …'

'Not that word. And don't try to be funny. I want an explanation.'

'Can we do this tomorrow? I'm tired and a bit tight, to tell you the truth. Patrick sure mixes a mean martini.'

'You didn't have to drink three of them, then start on the brandy.'

'I was feeling stressed. I needed something to relax me.'

'That's no excuse. There was no need to get drunk.'

'Why not? Everyone else was. I thought it was a great evening. I mean when we had finished that silly game. The girls were beginning to talk to each other and Patrick was looking very happy for a change.'

'The girls were snapping at each other like two terriers and Patrick was half asleep.' Penny kicked off her shoes and started to unbutton her silk shirt. 'But you're evading the issue. I want to know what that word meant. The word you put on the board when we were playing Scrabble.'

'Pastrami?'

'No the other word beginning with p: pimp.'

'Oh, *that* word.'

'Yeah, that word.' Penny sat on the bed and stared at Al. 'What's going on between you and Lucy? Are you beginning to look at younger women, is that it?'

'But all men look at younger women,' Al said. 'It doesn't mean anything. It's like window shopping. We look but we don't go into the shop to buy anything. Men love looking at women, you know. Especially women like Lucy. She's very cute, don't you think?' He started to take off his trousers.

'No, I don't,' Penny snapped, folding her arms across her chest and glaring at Al. 'I don't think she's a bit *cute!*'

'Oh, give me a break,' Al said. 'You don't think I fancy Lucy, do you? I think of her as a daughter, you must know that.'

'You already have a daughter, remember?'

'Yeah, but she's fat and looks like my mother,' Al replied, realising instantly it was the wrong answer. 'I mean … Ah honey, I'm tired and a bit drunk; the wrong words just seem to come out of my mouth.'

'You mean you wish Jennifer looked more like Lucy? Would you love her more then?'

'No, of course not. I love Jennifer. And I'm very proud of her and the fact that she has a PhD and is a professor at Harvard.'

'The youngest professor there,' Penny said proudly. 'So she's a little heavy. That's just puppy fat.'

'Puppy fat at twenty-eight? Isn't it time she lost it?'

'She will. She's a very attractive woman.'

'Yes, she's very, very beautiful. A lot more beautiful than Lucy or Claire or any of the younger women around here. Or anywhere. So are you. Can I go to bed now?'

'No. I want the truth right now.'

'The truth about what? I'll tell you anything you want to know if I can go to bed.'

'OK. I want to know what that word you put on the board was all about. And what you said to Lucy and the look on Patrick's face. What are you two up to?'

'Who?' Al stared at Penny. 'Lucy and me? Nothing, absolutely nothing, I swear.'

'No,' Penny snapped impatiently, 'you and Patrick.'

'Me and … what the hell are you raving about

now? And why do we always have to have our rows at bedtime?'

'For God's sake, try to listen.' Penny stopped. 'Oh, what's the use?' She got up and continued to undress. She looked at Al, standing there in his underpants with that worried look in his eyes. Like a little boy, she thought, just like when we were young and I was pregnant and he didn't understand all my mood swings and cravings. He was so sweet then, so understanding. He even rushed to the drugstore in the middle of the night to get me a strawberry milkshake or some pickled gherkins, whatever I wanted. And now he's a bit drunk and tired and just wants to go to bed.

'Why did I think I could get any sense out of you?' she sighed. 'And why did I think I could stop you admiring younger women?' She pulled her shirt out of the waistband of her slacks, took it off and threw it on the bed. 'I'm pretty tired myself,' she mumbled. 'Tired of this whole place, this holiday, them out there, you and the weather.'

'Well,' Al said, looking relieved, and climbed drunkenly into his pyjamas. 'There's only one thing to do and that is to go to sleep. You'll feel better tomorrow.'

'No, I won't.' Penny took off the rest of her clothes. 'Don't think you're off the hook. You're not going to sleep until I have an explanation.'

Al got into bed and pulled the covers up to his chin. 'It didn't mean anything. I just had those letters. It was a game. Just as you had the letters to make "cheat" and "flirt", remember? What if I asked you to explain that, huh? And what if I asked you to explain what you were doing with that young man Emilie was talking about a few days ago and jam?'

'Oh that,' Penny mumbled. 'That was just … well … nothing.'

'Oh? Didn't sound like nothing to me. But let's leave it for now.' He sighed and closed his eyes.

'Yeah, let's leave it.' Penny picked up her clothes and started to tidy them away. 'Just go to sleep.'

Al opened one sleepy eye.

'What are you looking at?' Penny demanded.

'You,' he murmured softly and closed his eyes again.

*

Lucy couldn't sleep. She had gone to bed, put out the light and closed her eyes, but sleep would not come. The weird game of Scrabble and the rest of the evening were still so vivid in her mind. Drinking dry martinis, then that arguing with Claire, while Patrick watched them through half-closed eyes, laughing to himself as Claire told Lucy her job was ridiculous. 'Selling cat food,' she had mocked, 'how stupid is that?' Lucy had tried not to retaliate with remarks of what a dead-end job teaching was. She didn't want to go near the can of worms she knew would explode if they started to tear strips off each other and bring up the inevitable subject of their break up. Fed up with Claire's sniping, she had walked out, leaving Claire and Patrick alone in the living room. They'll probably end up screwing anyway, Lucy had thought nastily, and good luck to them. They deserve each other. I can't wait for this awful holiday to be over and I'm back at the office again. She thought longingly of her desk, the view of Manhattan from her window, the sound of sirens far below, the buzz and excitement of starting a new campaign. She even missed the grey skies and the cold wind, the traffic and noise, the crush in the subway and the rudeness of New York cabdrivers. It just makes you feel so alive, she thought.

After an hour of twisting around in her bed, getting up to open the window, then closing it, reading a chapter of *Advertising: The Way Forward*, putting out the light again, turning her pillow around, throwing it on the floor and finally counting sheep, she gave up. She put on the light, sat up in bed and started to do her nails, a job she had neglected for the last few days. Her manicurist would not be impressed. Then she remembered all the other beauty routines she had forgotten to do ever since she had arrived, and went into the bathroom. Her legs were decidedly furry, her hair was flat, there was just a hint of a moustache re-growth on her upper lip and her skin looked dull and yellow in the merciless glare of the spotlights. I might as well do a total overhaul, she said to herself. And then I'll have a bath. I'm sure to go to sleep after all that grooming. Lucy went back into the bedroom, put some relaxing, slow jazz music into the CD player and got out her bag of toiletries.

Half an hour later, as she was sitting on her bed, curlers in her hair, a glob of hair remover on her upper lip, painting her toenails and softly singing 'Cry me a River', the door slowly opened. Lucy looked up, her hand with the nail polish brush frozen in mid-air. She stared at him. He was dressed in only a pair of light blue pyjama bottoms and his hair was messy. She wanted to say something cutting but she was so shocked nothing came out of her mouth.

'Hi,' he said. 'You look … lovely.'

'Get lost,' she croaked, putting the brush back in the bottle, snatching a tissue from her bedside table and wiping her mouth. She ripped the curlers from her hair and tugged her nightgown over her knees.

'Is that really necessary?' Patrick asked. 'I've already had a good look at your tush, remember?' He walked forward and sat on her bed.

Lucy moved further away, until her back was against the headboard. 'That's what I've been trying my best to forget,' she said, noticing against her will his lean chest covered in thick blond hair and his long dark eyelashes.

'You have a little …' he gestured with his finger to his upper lip.

'Oh, shit.' Lucy took another tissue and wiped her face again.

He put his hand on her knee. 'Lucy …' he started.

'No, go away.'

'I will, but just listen to me for a moment.'

'Take your hand off my knee.'

'OK,' he said and moved it onto her thigh. 'How's that? Better?'

'No.'

'It works for me.' He kept his hand there, just above her knee. 'I just wanted to talk to you for a while.'

'About what?'

'I don't know.' He shrugged in an exaggerated way. 'The weather?'

'It's snowing. Now leave.'

'Oh, no.' He shook his head. 'I'm not going to go away this time. What's that music?'

'Just some jazz.'

'It's lovely. Putting me in the mood.'

'For what?' she asked, even though she knew the answer.

'Don't pretend you don't know,' he chided. 'Don't pretend you don't have feelings for me.'

'Oh yes. I hate you.'

'Oh, no you don't.' He took both her hands in his and looked into her eyes. Then he pulled her forward until their lips were nearly touching. She could feel his hot breath on her face, smelling faintly of toothpaste. 'We have been really silly,' he murmured. 'And I'm sorry. But ...' He kissed her gently, barely touching her lips. 'It was your fault too.'

'Why?' she breathed.

He didn't answer, but leaned back on his elbow and studied her for a moment. 'I've been trying to figure you out,' he said, the conceit in his voice replaced by earnestness. 'Who are you, really?'

Lucy looked back at him without replying, suddenly at a loss for words.

'I mean,' he continued, 'you're so different from that girl I met in the lift. You've become so grown up, so confident and ...' he paused.

'And?' Lucy whispered.

'And scary.' Patrick ran his hand over his face. 'Oh, God, I don't know why I'm saying all these things.'

'Nor do I,' Lucy snapped. 'And I think you should get out of here right now.'

'I like you,' Patrick said suddenly. 'I really like you, Lucy Mulcahy. I like your sharp brain; I like your courage and your determination. In fact, you're a hell of an attractive package. But ...'

'Go on.'

'But you see, I can't ... I can't go through all that again.'

'All what again?'

'All the hurt and arguing and hate.'

'What are you going on about now?' Lucy

demanded, surprised by the sudden flash of pain in his eyes, gone as quickly as it had appeared, replaced by a sleepy, insolent smile.

'It's too late to fight, darling,' he murmured, drawing her closer again. 'Let's be friends. Let bygones be bygones. OK?'

His arms around her were oddly comforting. She leaned her head against his shoulder and closed her eyes. It was so nice to be held like this, not to be alone, but together, and she suddenly didn't care what he meant or what would happen next. 'I don't want to fight with you,' she mumbled. 'I didn't mean to ...'

'Never mind. I forgive you.'

'For what?' Lucy pulled back and stared at him. 'I don't think I have done anything that requires forgiveness.'

'What?' He looked at her with confusion in his eyes. Then he shook his head and pulled her close to him again. 'You're right. I should ask *you* to forgive *me*. Do you? Please say you do.'

'Of course,' she mumbled into his shoulder, feeling she'd agree to anything just to stay like this in his arms.

'Good.' He reached out his hand and put out the light. 'The elevator is going up,' he whispered. 'Right to the top floor ...'

*

Penny looked around the bedroom for her nightgown. Had she left it in the bathroom that morning when she had a shower? She padded

290

across the carpet and quietly slipped into the bathroom. She switched on the light and looked around. The nightgown was draped over the chair, where she had left it. As she reached out to pick it up, she caught sight of her naked body in the big mirror. She could see herself, head to toe, illuminated by the many lights in the huge bathroom. 'You're still attractive,' she said to herself. 'Oh yes you are.' She nodded at herself and smiled as she remembered how Al had looked at her just now. Normally, he would say, 'I just love that ass,' or something equally vulgar. But tonight, all he said was 'you', with such tenderness in his voice and such love in his sleepy eyes that it made her feel warm all over. He looked at her like that when they first fell in love. Did he still feel like that, she wondered. Was it possible he still found her beautiful? She turned to look at herself sideways. My bottom is still up there, she thought, my stomach is fairly flat and the boobs are quite firm. In fact, she said to herself, you're not such a bad looking old thing after all. She picked up her nightgown and started to put it on but changed her mind and let it fall to the floor. She walked out of the bathroom, across the bedroom and slipped into bed beside Al. She put her arms around his waist and snuggled closer to his big form. 'Darling,' she whispered.

'Yeah?' he grunted.

'Nothing. Just darling, darling …'

*

'DADDY!' Claire sat up in bed, yanked from a deep sleep. She jumped out and ran into the adjoining bedroom where Emilie, hiding under the bedclothes, was sobbing hysterically.

'What's the matter?' Claire panted, trying to unravel the sheets. 'Why are you screaming like that?'

'There's a … there's a …' Emilie wept.

'A what?'

'A monster,' Emilie sobbed.

Claire switched on the bedside light. 'Where?'

'Right there,' Emilie said and pointed a shaking finger.

'In the wardrobe?'

'Yes. That's where he's hiding.' Emilie grabbed Claire by the arm.

Claire wrapped her arms tightly around Emilie. 'Shh. Don't be afraid. There are no monsters here. Whatever gave you that idea?'

'Tiffany. She came into my room last night. We talked for a little bit, then she told me this story about a monster who likes to hide in wardrobes and eat clothes.'

'But that's silly,' Claire laughed.

'No, it's not. I saw him,' Emilie insisted. 'He had a green face and a big red nose with a wart on it and he had big ears and *huge* hands, and he was coming to get me.'

'There are no monsters here,' Claire repeated, giving Emilie little shake. 'It was only a bad dream. There are no such things as monsters, you know.'

'Oh yes there are,' Emilie hiccupped. 'There are lots of different kinds.'

'That stupid girl,' Claire muttered under her breath. 'I'm going to kill her.'

'Tiffany? But she's nice. And I asked her to tell me a story about monsters. Sometimes it's fun to listen to scary stories. We were scaring each other and we laughed a lot.' Emilie sighed deeply. 'But then I had this dream and, when I woke up, I was all alone and I wanted my mummy, and she wasn't there.'

'Poor little duck.'

'And I heard a noise and I thought this monster was in the wardrobe. And maybe ...' Emilie looked up at Claire. 'Maybe he's really there?' she whispered.

'OK.' Claire stood up. 'Do you know what? I'm going to put on the light and look in every cupboard. And if I find that monster, I'm going to tell him to leave and never come back.'

'Can you do that?' Emilie asked incredulously.

'Of course I can. I've done it before, you know. I've told the most awful creeps to pack their bags and leave.'

'You have?' Emilie wiped her face on the sheet.

'You bet. Just watch this.' Claire got up from the bed and switched on the light in the ceiling. Then, one by one, she opened all the cupboards until she had gone through the whole room. 'See?' She beamed at Emilie. 'No monsters.'

'What about the wardrobe?'

'I'm opening it now.'

Emilie put her hands over her eyes and whimpered as the double doors swung open.

'Nothing here,' Claire chanted. 'See?'

Emilie slid her hands from her eyes and peered at the wardrobe. 'Oh,' she breathed. 'It's just a lot of clothes.'

'Exactly.' Claire closed the doors, switched off the lights and sat down on the bed again. 'So now you can go to sleep.'

'OK.' Emilie lay down with a sigh of relief. 'But you have to tell me a story first. A nice one with no monsters in it. And a happily-ever-after ending.'

'All right.' Claire cleared her throat. 'Once upon a time,' she started, 'there was a princess who lived in a castle …'

Half an hour later, Claire tip-toed from the bedroom, with Emilie fast asleep. Just wait till I get my hands on that bitch Tiffany, she thought. I'll teach her to frighten little girls.

*

Lucy woke up, smiling into the darkness. Her whole body felt relaxed and warm. It had been so wonderful, making love like that, softly whispering to each other, touching, kissing, then … It felt such a natural thing to do, and they seemed so in tune, as if made for each other. Finally, she thought, we're together. He'll never leave me again, not after all the things he whispered and all the things we … She slid a hand along the sheet, wanting to feel his smooth skin under her hand, to touch his hair, his face. But her fingers only felt the empty pillow. Lucy sat up and put on the light. He was gone.

*

The blizzard gathered force during the night. At five o'clock the wind was so strong it made the chalet creak, tugging at the shutters, even making doors clatter in their frames. Claire woke up to the sound of the house groaning and the wind blowing through the half-open window, making the curtains flap. She got up slowly and closed the window, peering out into the white whirling mass outside. The snow was coming up to her windowsill, and she wondered if it would even be possible to open the front door. She shivered and got back into bed. She listened for a moment, trying to hear if there might be a noise from Emilie, but there wasn't a sound. I hope she'll sleep late, Claire thought, she was so tired, poor little thing. How she misses her mother ... Claire sighed and dozed off, to be woken, what seemed like only minutes later, by the window blowing open again. She peered at her alarm clock when she closed the window. Six o'clock. The wind was still howling outside, but there was no sound from Emilie. Good. She needs to sleep after the fright she got. That bloody bitch Tiffany. I'm really going to let her have it when she wakes up. I'm going to make her feel *really* bad!

Claire snuggled deeper under her duvet and nearly fell asleep again. But then she was suddenly wide awake. She just thought of a way to pay Tiffany back. What could possibly annoy her more than being woken up this early? She who likes to sleep till lunchtime shall have a rude awakening! Claire got out of bed, put on her dressing gown and slippers and marched down the corridor, rehearsing what she was going to say. 'You stupid little bitch,' she muttered. 'How could you be so cruel? Was it fun to scare a six-year-old like that? I'll scare you,' Claire promised. 'I'll teach you to …' She threw open the door and switched on the light.

'Wakey, wakey,' she chanted. 'Time to face the music and …' She stopped and stared at the empty bed. 'What the …' She looked around the room. She opened the bathroom door and looked inside. No Tiffany. The wind seemed to scream even louder as she stood there, looking around the deserted room.

18

'I don't know where she is,' Claire said to Patrick. 'Her bed has not been slept in so she must have gone out last night, when she left Emilie. Did you manage to get through to the police?'

'The lines are still down,' Patrick said, sitting down at the kitchen table, 'but I called the cell phone of the doctor in the village and it worked for some reason. He said he would go to the police station and ask them to come.'

'I hope he wasn't too annoyed at being woken up.' Claire poured water into the kettle.

'No, I think he's used to it. I don't care anyway. I just want Tiffany back safe and sound.' Patrick was very pale and his eyes were worried.

Penny walked into the kitchen. 'I've looked all over the house. There's no sign of her.'

'God, I hope nothing's happened,' Patrick

said, running his hand over his eyes. 'I can't imagine what it will do to my father if …'

'I'm sure she's all right,' Claire soothed. 'She's a tough girl. Here, have a cup of tea. It's good and strong.'

'Tea?' he snorted. 'Why do Irish people always pour tea into you when disasters happen? My grandmother was the same. The world is coming to an end, but have cup of tea, it'll make you feel a lot better.'

'But it does,' Claire said, 'try it. Here,' she pushed a cup in front of him. 'Drink that up now. What else are you going to do while you're waiting for the police? Do you want something to eat?'

'I couldn't eat anything,' Patrick said, 'even if there was something to eat.' He drank his tea.

'Nor could I,' Penny said, sitting down at the table. 'I feel somehow responsible.'

'You?' Claire asked. 'No, it was my fault. I should have checked on her and Emilie, but they seemed to get on so well. Little did I know …'

'Know what?' Patrick asked.

'It doesn't matter now.' Claire shook her head. 'I got annoyed at her, but, it was nothing really.'

'I know what you mean,' Patrick said glumly. 'She can be such a bitch, but she's had a lot of problems, you know. She seems so lost sometimes.'

'Poor kid,' Penny sighed. 'She needs help.'

*

'Look, Claire,' Emilie exclaimed an hour later, pointing out the window. 'Policemen.'

Claire opened the window.

'*Bonjour*,' the first policeman, a tall man with a craggy face and evidently the officer in charge, said to Claire. 'We're the police.'

'Of course you are,' Claire said, but was immediately contrite. This was no time to joke. 'Come in.' She moved aside to let the policemen into the kitchen. 'Sorry you had to climb in through the window but the snow is blocking the front door.'

The other policeman, who looked like a schoolboy, clambered over the window sill.

Patrick came into the kitchen. 'Oh, good morning.'

'*Bonjour*,' the first policeman said.

'Do you speak English?' Patrick asked.

'Yes, I do,' the first policeman replied in a heavy accent, 'but my colleague doesn't. What is going on here? What is the problem?'

'It's my sister. She's missing,' Patrick explained.

'And when did this happen?'

'We don't know,' Claire explained. 'We only discovered she was gone this morning.'

'But she was here last night,' Emilie piped in. 'She told me a story and gave me a big fright.'

'I see.' The officer took out a pad and a pen. 'Tell me what she looks like.'

'OK,' Patrick said. 'She's about five foot nine …'

'Five foot?' the policeman looked puzzled.

'One hundred and seventy five centimetres,' Claire explained. 'She has short purple hair ...'

'Purple ...' the officer muttered while he wrote.

'It stands up in points all over her head,' Emilie said. 'And she has purple nails as well and lots of earrings and this kind of little diamond in her nose.'

'Brown eyes,' Patrick continued.

'She's very pretty,' Emilie interrupted. 'Don't forget to put that in.'

'How was she dressed?'

'Jeans,' Claire said, 'and a thick white crocheted cardigan and a black top with thin straps underneath. That's what she had on the last time I saw her. And I think she had on a black leather jacket, but I'm not sure about that.'

'I can't find my anorak,' Lucy interrupted, coming into the kitchen.

'OK, she must be wearing a black anorak with a fur hood instead of the leather jacket,' Claire corrected herself. 'And a very long purple scarf, I forgot to mention that.'

The other policeman started to say something but was silenced by a glare from his boss.

'And I think she was wearing white snow boots,' Claire ended.

'I see,' the officer said, closing his notebook. 'So, when do you think she left?'

'Last night,' Patrick replied.

'Her bed wasn't slept in, you see,' Claire interjected.

'How do you know?' the policeman asked. 'That her bed was not slept in I mean?'

Claire sighed. 'Because it was not messy. It was made.'

'But maybe she made her bed before she left?'

'No, she didn't,' Claire said. 'She never makes her bed. Please, come and see her room. You'll understand what I mean.' She left Emilie and Lucy in the kitchen while she and Patrick led the two policemen up the stairs and down the long corridor. Claire threw open the door to Tiffany's room.

'*Mon Dieu*,' the officer exclaimed, staring into the room. 'There seems to have been a terrible struggle.'

'No, that's the way her room always looks,' Claire replied, 'but, as you can see, the bed is made. The cleaning lady makes it every morning. And yesterday was the last day she was here.'

'Mmm,' the officer muttered. 'I think we have to search the whole house.'

'We already did. She's not here.'

'Not to search for the girl. For clues.' He turned to his colleague. '*Fouillez la maison*,' he ordered.

'Is this really necessary?' Claire asked. 'I mean wouldn't it be better to search the village?'

'We search the house first. Then we search the village. That is normal police procedure.'

The policemen proceeded to search the house methodically, beginning with Tiffany's room.

'We better let them get on with it,' Patrick said, walking out of the room.

'Let's go down to the living room,' Claire suggested. 'This could take a while.'

Patrick put his hand on her arm as they walked down the corridor. 'What do you think happened?' he asked, his voice hoarse. 'I mean, you're a teacher. You must know better than anyone else what a girl that age would be like.'

'I'm a primary school teacher,' Claire said, turning to look at him. 'I wouldn't have a clue what goes on in the head of a modern teenager. When I was that age …' She thought for a moment. 'Seems like a hundred years ago. I was a bit wild too, you know, and it never occurred to me that anything bad could happen. To other people, yes, but never to me. I took risks, that's true, but I managed to stay out of trouble most of the time. I suspect Tiffany is quite streetwise, really. She seems quite bright as well.'

'I know she is,' Patrick said. 'I just wish she wouldn't be such a bloody handful. I'm sure it's all my fault, but God knows I've done my best. When her mother left, there didn't seem to be anyone but me who took any interest. But it's not easy to deal with a girl growing up, you know. I couldn't tell her about … well, all the stuff girls go through, if you know what I mean. Then my father retired and I had to take over the firm. And I had some problems of my own to sort out so …' He shrugged, looking a little embarrassed.

'I know,' Claire said. 'It can't have been easy for you. Teenage girls can be hell to deal with. I know I was. But listen, don't worry. I'm sure Tiffany is all right. And what can happen in this place anyway? I'm sure she'll waltz in the door at any moment and ask what all the fuss is about.'

'I hope you're right,' Patrick sighed. 'And then I'll wring her neck.'

'That's the spirit.' Claire patted his arm. 'Come on, let's have some tea in the living room while we wait for the cops to finish.'

'Oh no, not more tea,' Patrick groaned.

*

'What are they doing?' Penny asked an hour later. 'They must have been just about everywhere by now, including the attic.'

'They even looked at all my toys,' Emilie complained, 'and they didn't tidy up afterwards.'

'They nearly scared the pants off me,' Al complained. 'There I was, fast asleep, and then the door flew open and these goons burst into the room. I thought they were going to arrest me or something. They're still up there, going through the bathroom, if you don't mind. God knows what they think they'll find there.'

*

303

The sound of snow ploughs going up the hill woke Tiffany. Confused and sleepy, she looked around the room. Where am I? she thought. She threw the duvet aside and noticed she was wearing a shirt with 'Aussie Rules' in big letters on the front and nothing else. Her own clothes were lying in a heap on the floor. She stretched and yawned and then remembered. This was Warren's flat, right over the bar. What a fun night we had, she thought, and what a fun guy Warren turned out to be. And what a stroke of luck that he arrived at the chalet on his snow scooter just when I was beginning to believe that it was actually possible to die of boredom. And then we danced the night away …

*

'You're such a great dancer,' Tiffany had said as she sank down on a chair. 'For an Australian pansy, I mean.' She grinned at Warren and drank deeply from a bottle of beer. They were in the disco area of Le Ski Jump, the bar at the top of the village.

'What?' Warren shouted over the din of the music.

'Nothing. Just a little joke. My brother is convinced you're gay because you wear a pony tail. He's such a square.'

'Yes, he's a big pain in the neck, I have to say. Nearly bit my head off when he hurt his leg that day. Can't believe he's really your brother.'

'Half-brother.'

304

'Oh yeah? How come?'

'We have the same father but not the same mother. *His* mother was a stuck-up socialite who ran off with another woman. Mine is a former model who ended up leaving my dad as well. Another man in her case.'

'I see.' He looked at her with sympathy in his eyes. 'Can't have been easy.'

Tiffany shrugged, had another slug of beer and wiped her mouth with the back of her hand. 'It wasn't that bad. My dad brought me up. And Patrick. He was pretty cool when he was younger but now he's this really successful lawyer who lives for his work. Doesn't even have time to take a crap, if you know what I mean.'

'What about your mother? Why didn't she bring you up?'

'My mother? Oh, well, I don't think she was meant to have kids. I was a bit of a mistake, really. She is now on her fourth husband. I think she's been very clever actually. She just gets richer and richer with each husband. Talk about realising your assets.'

'Is that what you're going to do?'

'No way! I want to do something a bit more interesting than that. And I don't have that many assets.'

'I wouldn't say that.' Warren looked admiringly at Tiffany.

'Oh?' Tiffany said, thinking that she had been right to make a little bit of an effort tonight. She had put on skin-tight jeans, a black top under her white pullover and Lucy's black fur-lined anorak that she had found hanging in the cloak room. It was warm and snow-proof with a fur-trimmed hood that was both serviceable and pretty. She looked at Warren with huge kohl-rimmed eyes. 'Do you want to dance again?' she asked. 'It's a slow.'

'Sure,' Warren said and jumped to his feet. He wrapped his arms around her and, cheek to cheek, they danced without speaking until the end of the song.

'*Bon soir*,' a voice said as they pulled apart. 'You are dancing with *la plus belle*, Warren.'

'Hi Michel!' Tiffany exclaimed, letting go of Warren's hand and kissing Michel on both cheeks. 'Where have you been? I thought you had gone back to Paris.'

'*Non*, I tried, but it was impossible. No bus and no train.' He smiled and shrugged. '*Tant pis*, eh? I have fun here tonight. But where are the other ones? The people in your chalet? *La belle* Penny and *ma petite* Claire. Are they here?' He looked around the bar and disco area.

'No, I'm here on my own.'

'*Toute seule?*'

'That's right.' Her voice was drowned by the music that was starting up again. 'Oh I love this song!' she exclaimed. 'Do you want to dance?' She dragged Michel out onto the dance floor, leaving Warren behind, staring at them sourly.

'How did you get here?' Michel shouted as they danced to the fast music.

'Warren,' Tiffany yelled back. 'His snow scooter.'

Michel said something, but his words were lost in the din. Tiffany gave herself up to the music and the dancing despite the heat. She felt beads of sweat trickling between her breasts and down her back, but the beat was nearly hypnotic and she wanted to just keep dancing. When the song finally stopped, she looked at Michel, laughing at his red and sweaty face. 'You're not very fit,' she panted. 'You look as if you are about to collapse.'

'Just a little *coup de pompe*,' he replied, wiping his face. 'You're a very fast dancer.'

'How about a beer?' Tiffany suggested, walking away from the dance floor. 'Let's go back to Warren. And look, some of the other guys are there.' Warren had been joined by a group of young men; other ski instructors and lift operators who usually ended their evening in Le Ski Jump bar.

Tiffany laughed as they all kissed her on both cheeks and invited her to sit on their laps. 'I prefer to sit on my own behind, thanks,' she said. 'Get me another beer, though.'

Michel sat down beside her. 'So why are you here so alone?' he asked. 'Does your big brozzer know where you are?'

Tiffany laughed and drank some beer. 'No, he doesn't. I slipped out while they were all busy playing Scrabble.'

'What?' Warren exclaimed incredulously. 'Are you serious? Scrabble!'

'That's right. God, they're so boring. All of them. And they think they're so cool. Especially that Lucy. She has this great crush on Patrick and she thinks nobody's noticed. And he is interested in her but is too scared to start anything. Jesus!' Tiffany shook her head. 'They are perfect for each other. But they are too tight-arsed to do anything about it. I wish they would just give us all a break and go ahead and do it. But they never will. They're too scared.'

'Don't be so sure,' Warren said.

'Believe me,' Tiffany insisted. 'I'm the only one in that house who has a life. But enough about them.' She grabbed Warren's hand. 'Come on, just one more dance.'

'*A bientôt, mes amis,*' Michel called after them.

'Let's not go back to the others,' Warren said when the music stopped. 'I'd like us to be on our own for a change.'

'You just don't like Michel,' Tiffany said. 'I know he's a bit of a creep but I think he's kind of cute.' They pushed through the throng and joined the group at their table. Michel was smiling at one of the female ski instructors, whispering something in her ear. '*Petit con,*' she said, made as if to slap his face, stood up and walked off.

'What did she call you?' Tiffany asked as she sat down beside Michel.

He gave a Gallic shrug. 'Oh, you know, she thinks I am a stupid bastard.'

'That's not very kind,' Tiffany protested and put her hand on Michel's arm. 'I'm going to get a beer,' Warren announced, turned on his heel and walked toward the bar.

'Get me a Coke while you're there,' Tiffany called after him.

Michel put his hand on Tiffany's thigh. '*Ah, mon amour…*'

Tiffany removed his hand. 'I am not your *amour.*'

'But why not? You are *une tres belle fille* and I am …'

'*Un petit con?*'

Michel threw his head back and laughed. 'You're a very funny girl. I like you.' He took the thin cigarette proffered by the young man sitting on his other side and drew deeply, then offered it to Tiffany.

She pushed it away. 'I don't smoke.'

'But this is …'

'I know. I don't do drugs either.'

*

Tiffany snuggled into the duvet and enjoyed the warmth of the bed. Good idea, she thought, to stay here last night. Warren had been too tired to drive her home and, in any case, the blizzard was at its worst, so it would have been too much of a hassle, they had agreed. They had left the nearly empty disco and climbed the narrow staircase to the small flat above. It had taken a little while to sort out the sleeping arrangements and to explain her position on casual sex.

Warren was not amused. 'What do you mean?' he demanded angrily. 'You're some kind of religious nut or something?'

'No,' Tiffany said. 'It has nothing to do with religion. It's just that in the States it is not considered cool to have sex before you're committed to someone.'

'You're kidding.' Warren laughed. He tried to grab her but Tiffany moved away.

'I'm serious. I'm not going to have sex with you tonight so you'd better try not to get excited or anything.'

'So what do chicks like you do when guys like me want to hit the sack?'

'We just say no,' Tiffany said primly.

'I thought that was drugs.'

'It applies to sex as well. Casual sex is so sad, so soulless. It's just not worth it.'

'It never made *me* cry,' Warren muttered.

'You'll see. If you stop sleeping around and save yourself for the one person you're meant to spend the rest of your life with, you will have a much better chance of being happy.'

'That'll take a while. What am I supposed to do in the meantime?'

'Think of something else. Take up a hobby.'

'But sex *is* my hobby.' He moved a little closer.

'Ah, Tiff, come on, stop fooling around, let's go to bed.'

She pushed him away. 'No, I said. I mean it.'

'But,' Warren protested, 'I thought you liked me.'

'I do. I like you a lot. You're a very nice guy.'

'Nice?' Warren said. 'You think I'm *nice*? Is that all?'

'Yeah. I mean, no. You're great looking and everything, but …'

'Why did you come up here?' Warren tried to grab her again, but Tiffany moved to the other side of the sofa.

'I had no choice,' she said. 'I can't get back to the chalet and I thought your offer was strictly on a friendly basis.'

'I'm friendly now? *And* nice? Jesus. No girl has ever said things like that to me.'

'What's wrong with that?'

'Just about everything. I can't believe what you just said. And, if you're such a well behaved little girl, why do you walk around like that …' he made a vague gesture, 'showing off your tits?'

'What?' Tiffany glanced down at her clothes. 'But it's the fashion. Don't tell me you don't know about fashion?'

He sighed. 'I don't know what I know any more. I'm too tired to argue.'

'Good. Where's the bedroom?'

'Through there. And you can sleep on the couch. I'll get you a sleeping bag.'

But Tiffany sprinted across the room, into the small bedroom, banged the door shut and turned the key. 'Good night,' she called, ignoring Warren's protests, and quickly stripped off her clothes. She found a clean shirt in the wardrobe which she pulled on and got into bed. She was asleep before her head touched the pillow.

*

Tiffany laughed to herself as she got out of bed and crossed the floor to the window. Poor Warren, he had looked so disappointed. She knelt on the stool in front of the window and peered out. Two snow scooters, driven by men wearing dark ski clothes and policemen's caps, were slowly making their way up the hill. It had stopped snowing and weak sunlight tried to get through the grey clouds. Huge icicles hung from the roofs, and the snowdrifts came up to the first floor of most of the houses. The wind was still blowing, but not with the same strength as the night before. I better start thinking about getting back, Tiffany thought. But first, breakfast.

She had just finished making coffee and was laying the table in the tiny kitchen when Warren walked in, yawning and scratching his head. 'Oh Jesus, if it isn't Miss Chastity Belt,' he said. He pulled back his hair and secured it with a rubber band.

'Hi,' Tiffany replied, pouring orange juice.

'You look … different.'

312

'I took off the make up. But I can put it all back on if you want.'

'No, I like you like that, with your face all naked.'

'Breakfast is nearly ready. I didn't know what you normally have so I put out a selection. Sausages and bacon. I boiled some eggs too, they're nearly ready.'

'What a little treasure you are,' Warren muttered and sat down. 'What was that noise?'

'The police. Two of them went up the hill on snow scooters. I wonder if anything has happened?'

'Nothing happened here, in any case.'

'Don't start that again. I thought you understood.'

'Lucky for you I was well brought up. Get me some of that coffee.'

Tiffany poured the coffee and handed him the cup. 'I better get back to the chalet or Patrick will have a fit.'

'I'll take you back.'

'Great.' Tiffany sat down opposite Warren and knocked the top off an egg. 'But there's no rush. It's still early. They're probably still fast asleep up there. They won't even know I was gone.'

'Yeah, you're right. It's still early,' Warren agreed, draining the cup.

'More coffee?'

'Sure.' Warren held his cup toward her. 'You make a mean cup of coffee.'

'I know.'

'You really are a very talented girl.'

'That's true. Here's the sausage and bacon,' she said, putting a plate in front of him. 'I make the best breakfast in the world, you know.'

'And modest too.' Warren cut a piece of bacon and popped it into his mouth. 'This is great.' He looked at her across the table. 'Could I ask you a personal question?'

'Go ahead.' Tiffany sat down on the stool and propped her chin in her hands. 'I'm listening.'

'Well, if you found this ... person and felt you could commit to him, how long would it be before you would consider going to bed with him?'

'Depends.'

'On what?'

'On how quickly I could find out if we have something in common.'

'And I suppose that would take a long time?' Warren sighed, shook his head and picked up another piece of bacon with his fork. 'I don't really understand your whole approach here. Isn't it more important to find out if we ... I mean if someone is compatible sexually? Have you never had the hots for a guy?'

'Lots of times,' Tiffany replied, 'but they never turned out to be right for me.'

'So you drove him nuts and then dumped him? That must have made you really popular.'

'OK, listen.' Tiffany sat up straight. 'I'm going

to explain something to you. All my life, I've been around people who have messed up their lives. My parents and my brother just to mention a few. And those people up there ...' she made a gesture over her shoulder with her spoon, 'in the chalet. They're messed up big time.'

'Really? Why?'

'Because they don't know how to organise their lives.'

'And you do?'

'Not yet. They keep sending me to college but I don't think I'm the academic type. You see, that's my trouble. I don't really know what I'm good at. And, until I do, I can't really have a relationship with anyone.'

Warren frowned and thought for a moment while he chewed. Then he looked up, delighted. 'I've got it, Tiffany,' he exclaimed. 'You would make a brilliant bloody therapist.'

'Really?' Tiffany looked both surprised and pleased.

'Yeah.' Warren nodded, looking equally pleased. 'You know what's wrong with everybody and you seem to know what they should do about it. All you need is a degree in psychology, an office and a couch. There you are: problem solved. Can we go to bed now?'

Tiffany shook her head. 'No. I don't really know you and you don't really know me. We might be completely wrong for each other.'

'I know you're right for me. I just know it.'

Warren looked at Tiffany with longing. 'How am I going to convince you?'

Tiffany leaned across the table and kissed him gently on the lips. 'Tell me about yourself,' she said.

*

'No, it's not mine, whatever it is,' Al stated, looking at the small plastic sample bag containing what looked like withered leaves.

'No?' the policeman lifted one eyebrow. 'And what about this? It was also found in your bathroom.'

'Oh God,' Penny mumbled as the policeman held up another bag with a white powder inside.

'I will have to ask you,' the policeman said, 'not to leave this house until we return with Miss Tiffany.'

'You know where she is?' Patrick asked, startled.

'Yes. My colleague has just told me he saw her last night.'

Patrick rose. 'He knows her?'

'Yes.'

'But how?'

'That is police business.' He nodded to his young colleague and they left the room, banging the door shut behind them.

There was complete silence in the living room as the sound of the snow scooters died away.

'Jesus,' Al muttered. 'This is terrible. I can't believe it. Imagine little Tiffany putting that up her nose. This is really serious.'

'I suspected something like this,' Patrick mumbled, 'but I couldn't bring myself to believe it. I even accused her of it when she was going through all the money I gave her so quickly.'

'What, up her nose?' Emilie asked. 'How can you put money up your nose?'

'I think we'll go and tidy away those toys, now.' Claire quickly ushered Emilie out of the room.

'A bit of dope I could take. But coke …' Al said. 'I can't believe that kid could be involved in that.'

'This is *very* serious. If this comes out, it will damage my career, big time.' Patrick clenched and unclenched his fists. 'The little bitch. Well, she's finally done it. I'm not going to bail her out. She can sit there and stew and learn what happens when you break the law.'

'You mean you're not going to help her?' Lucy demanded.

'No.'

'Jesus,' Lucy exclaimed. 'You're a mean bastard. Have you no feelings? Is your bloody career more important to you than your sister?' And more important than me, she thought, the memory of his disappearance from her bed still making her blood boil.

'Yeah, it's a bit rough,' Al agreed. 'I understand how Patrick feels after all the trouble she has caused through the years. But she's just a kid.' He stopped, looking thoughtful. 'On the other hand,

317

we have to consider the implications of this for the business.'

'Are you serious?' Penny exclaimed. 'I don't believe what I just heard.'

'But it's true,' Al said. 'It could be very bad for the firm.'

'What do you mean?' Patrick stared at Al.

'Well …' Al mumbled.

The door opened. 'What are you arguing about?' Claire asked. 'Emilie is getting upset. This has been a frightening experience for her. First Tiffany going missing, then the police searching the house. She doesn't understand what's going on. And she heard you all shouting. Please try to keep your voices down. She needs to know things are getting back to normal.'

'I'll go and have a chat with her,' Lucy said. 'I'll play with her Barbies. She likes that.'

'Thanks,' Claire said. 'Now, how about doing something useful for a change instead of behaving like five-year-olds? I know the police told us not to leave the house but I think we should try to clear the snow. This is usually a job for a man, of course, if there happened to be one around, but …'

'OK,' Patrick said. 'I'll go.' He walked out of the door and down the stairs.

'Maybe you could give him a hand, Al,' Claire suggested.

'Right,' Al muttered. He walked down the stairs and joined Patrick in the garage.

*

'Go on,' Tiffany said. 'What happened when you told your parents you wanted a career in music instead going into business with your father? No, don't get up. Stay on the couch and tell me everything.'

'This is silly,' Warren said, putting his head back on the cushion. 'I can't see you.'

'But I need to practise. What was your father's business?'

'He has a sports shop. Tiffany, I ...'

'In Sydney?' Tiffany insisted.

'Yes. And at first he was pretty mad when I told him I wanted to be a musician. You see he took it for granted that I wanted to be in a rock band. Can we stop this now?'

'No. You're not? A rock musician, I mean.'

'No. What made you think I was?'

'Well, look at you. The pony tail, the earring, the designer stubble, those shades. I was convinced you were a drummer with some heavy metal rock group.'

'Look who's talking,' Warren mocked. 'You look like a refugee from the Addams family.'

'We're not discussing how I look at the moment. So you're not a rock musician, then?'

'No. I play the cello.'

'Wow! Pretty big instrument. How come your parents didn't notice? Are they blind?'

'I kept it at school. I told them I was in the school orchestra, but they thought I was just doing it for fun and that I was really more interested in rock. Then, when my music teacher told them he wanted me to go to the Academy of Music, my parents were stunned. But they went along with it, probably thinking I'd grow out of it or something, but when I was accepted into the Sydney Philharmonic, they were really annoyed that I didn't want to sell surfboards instead.'

'But what are you doing here if you're a cellist with this symphony orchestra?'

'Philharmonic,' Warren corrected.

'Same difference.'

'It's the summer break in Australia. And I love skiing so I always come here for a few weeks. And I can earn quite a lot giving lessons.'

'You're telling me. You've bled me dry, giving me those private snowboard lessons. My brother is getting really suspicious.'

'You didn't have to buy that snowboard. And you could have told him. I'm sure he wouldn't have minded.' Warren twisted his neck to stare at Tiffany. 'Why do you put on this act of being the problem child?'

'Because that's the best way to get attention,' Tiffany replied. 'But to get back to you …'

'No.' Warren sat up and swung his legs over the edge of the couch. 'I've told you everything. Even the colour of the wallpaper in my room at home, whatever significance that has on the state of my mental health.'

'I think that was a very important point,' Tiffany replied, nodding wisely. 'You grew up looking at daisies. That must have put a lot of thoughts into your subconscious.'

'I think you should wait until you have studied psychology for a few years before you continue analysing me.' Warren got up from the couch and walked across the room to where Tiffany was perched on a chair. 'But what about us?' He took her hands and pulled her up. 'Don't you think we have enough in common? I think we do. We're both pretty well-adjusted, bright, good-looking and young. I think we should …' He was interrupted by a loud knock on the door.

19

'Where are the shovels in this house?' Patrick asked. 'I have looked all over the place but I can't find anything.'

'Don't look at me,' Al grunted, pulling on his boots. 'I have never had to shovel snow here before.'

'They must be here somewhere,' Patrick muttered, walking over to the back of the garage where the wood was stored. 'Yes,' he called, 'I found one. A small one but it'll do. We can take turns.'

'Right,' Al said. 'But we have to open the door first.' He pulled open the heavy front door, only to be met with a wall of snow with just a chink of light above it. 'Christ,' he exclaimed, 'it'll take a week to clear this.'

'No, it won't. We'll have to get at it from the other side. We have to climb out the window.'

Once outside, Patrick started to clear the snow. 'This is one hell of a job,' he grunted.

'I know,' Al said, carefully lowering himself onto a pile of snow. 'Keep going. I'll take over when you get tired.'

'OK.' Patrick continued to shovel.

'About what I said in there,' Al started, resting his arms on his knees. 'I wasn't really serious. I just got a bit of a shock, you know.'

'Who didn't? I know Tiff has been acting up lately, but I had no idea it was this bad. But I don't see how it would have any effect on the business.'

'It might,' Al said. 'But we go back a long way. I don't want us to fall out over this. In any case, I could never find a lawyer who's as good as you.'

'It would take you a while.' Patrick threw a shovelful of snow over his shoulder.

'You're the king of small print.'

'I sure am.'

'What do you think she'll get?'

'Who? Tiffany? Don't know. I'm not familiar with French law. But they have no case, anyway.'

'Why?' Al asked.

'Because,' Patrick replied, as he lifted another load of snow, 'I have been thinking. How do we know the stuff was hers?'

'I thought it would be pretty obvious,' Al said.

'What do you mean?' Patrick turned to glare at Al.

'Well,' Al stammered, 'I mean look at how she's dressed and the way she talks.'

Patrick looked at Al, lifting one eyebrow. 'That makes her a drug addict? If you were in a jury selection, I would throw you out after ten minutes.'

'OK, I suppose that was a little judgemental. But she must have been up to something in the village. The police knew where to find her.'

'Yeah, but now that I think of it, the drugs were found in *your* bathroom.'

'So? You're not suggesting that either I or Penny ...'

'No, of course not. That's ridiculous.' Patrick leaned on the shovel, looking thoughtfully at Al. 'It could have been somebody who thought your bathroom was the perfect hiding place.'

'Claire or Lucy?' Al shook his head. 'No, I find that really hard to believe.' He took a cigar out of his pocket and stuck it in his mouth. 'But what about Dave? He just kind of disappeared and we haven't heard from him since.'

'Because he got stuck down the valley. But you're right. It could be him.'

'Yeah,' Al agreed. 'He looks more and more suspicious.' He counted on his fingers. 'He's English, speaks with a funny accent and he cooks. I've always thought there's something suspicious about a guy who cooks.'

'That's just circumstantial stuff,' Patrick protested. 'I might as well say you look like a gangster because you wear a camel's hair coat and drive a Mercedes.'

'What do you mean?' Al asked, sounding insulted.

'Forget it. It was just an example.' Patrick stuck the shovel into the snow again.

*

Claire looked at Penny.

'Shit,' Penny said.

'Yeah.'

'What are we going to do?'

'We?'

'Oh OK, it was all my fault,' Penny said. 'I brought the stuff into the house.'

'And I helped you smoke it.'

'There must be something we can do.'

Claire sat down on the sofa.

'What are you doing?' Penny asked.

'Thinking.' Claire sighed and stared into the empty grate of the fireplace. 'This is one hell of a mess.'

Penny sat down beside Claire. 'We have to think of something.'

'I know.'

'I just have to tell you I don't know anything about that other stuff.'

'The cocaine?'

Penny shivered. 'I can't even say it.'

Claire looked at Penny's white face. 'I believe you. The pot was just a bit of fun, really. I mean it's just light stuff, right?'

'Of course. And I don't really do it that regularly. It's just that I was feeling so low. I'm going through a bad patch right now, you see.

Mid-life crisis and all that garbage. It's not a big deal but it's not easy either. Then, the other day when I was in the dumps over that woman in the dress shop who treated me like … never mind.'

'Yes? Go on.'

'I met Michel. You know, that guy from Paris. You know him, don't you?'

'Slightly,' Claire said.

'Well, he said he had something that would make me feel really good. He had that stuff you saw. Just enough for a couple of joints. It wasn't cheap, but worth every cent. He buys it in Marseilles, he said, and sells it to his friends. Makes a bit of money to pay for his university course.'

'Shit, are you serious? Michel?'

'He looks so innocent. Like butter wouldn't melt, you know?'

'I know,' Claire muttered. 'The original choirboy.'

'So that's it.' Penny looked at Claire. 'Stupid, isn't it?'

'Mmm.'

'But I have to say pot is better than HRT. It relaxes you and makes you forget all your hang-ups. Just for a moment, of course. But I think it should be legalised for menopausal women.'

'That's as may be,' Claire said, 'but the problem right now is that it's very, very *illegal*.'

'I suppose the best thing to do is to wait and see,' Penny said after a while. 'See what happens, I mean. If Tiffany is found guilty of possession of cocaine, then that little bit of pot won't even be noticed. I'll feel awful, of course, but what good would it do for me to own up? Tiff would be in just as much trouble. Oh God, what am I going to do?'

'I don't know,' Claire replied. 'Why are you asking me? Why are people always asking me what to do?'

'But you seem so together. You seem to be so steady. Like a rock.'

Claire laughed ironically.

'What's so funny?'

'Oh, nothing.'

'It's just nerves,' Penny said. 'It's been such a strange day. I'm going to have a bath to calm my nerves. Pity the police took the dope. I could have done with a …'

'Stop,' Claire said. 'Don't even think about it.'

'Of course. Sorry.'

Claire shook her head and laughed again as Penny closed the door. 'Some rock,' she muttered to herself. 'If they only knew what I'm really like. If Bernard knew, he'd run a mile. Will I tell him and watch him do the sprint of a lifetime? Or will I just go on pretending to be this earth mother he thinks I am? Wait till he tastes my very own brand of home cooking!'

*

'Maybe you should take a break?' Patrick suggested. 'You look a little hot.'

'No, I've nearly managed to clear a path to the

327

door,' Al grunted, throwing another shovelful of snow over his shoulder. 'More like a tunnel, I suppose, but …' He leaned on the shovel, breathing hard.

'Come on, let me.' Patrick took the shovel from Al. 'We don't need you to have a heart attack on top of everything else.'

'No.' Al sat down in the snow again and rested his arms on his knees as he watched Patrick clear the rest of the snow. 'We have enough to worry about at the moment.'

He was silent for a moment. 'How are you getting on with Lucy?' he suddenly asked.

'Oh fine. Just fine.'

'That bad, eh?'

'No comment.'

'I'm sorry. When you asked me to hire her, I thought you and she would …'

'We're not.' Patrick leaned on the shovel, slightly out of breath. He looked at Al. 'I wouldn't normally talk about this. I mean I'm not the kind of guy who goes around talking about his love life …'

'And thank God for that,' Al muttered. 'Sorry pal, I didn't mean … Go on. If you need to talk to someone, I'll be glad to listen.'

'Well …' Patrick stuck the shovel into the snow. 'It's Lucy.'

'What is?'

'This whole thing. I know she has … eh, feelings for me and … so do I … For her, I mean.

I don't know who's fault it is but every time we get somewhere, something seems to go wrong. And we have such a good time, but then … I know it must be hard for her and … Shit, what am I going on about?' Patrick heaved what seemed like a truckload of snow over his shoulder.

'Take it easy,' Al said, getting up and taking Patrick's arm. 'Don't get yourself into a state. I can imagine what you're going through.'

'You can?'

'Yeah, sure. I know Lucy as well as you do. No, I mean not in that way, but …' Al cleared his throat, his face red. 'She is a great looking broad. Brainy too. But so intense. Reminds me of Sandy, your ex.'

'Tell me about it,' Patrick mumbled, leaning on the shovel again.

'You're scared shitless it will happen again, aren't you?'

'Well, yes,' Patrick said, relieved Al seemed to get the picture. 'So you understand that I can't … I don't want to get involved?'

'No,' Al said bluntly. 'I don't understand a goddamn thing.'

'What? But …'

'Just hold on a second, pal,' Al said. 'Listen to yourself. You sound like a real chicken shit. Women are a tough nut to crack, that's for sure. And you'll never understand 'em. No man on this earth does. But, if you're too scared to take a few risks, you'll end up sadder and lonelier than if you take the bull by the horn … I mean the woman by the … eh, whatever … Get it?'

Patrick looked at Al without replying.

'Did you get that?' Al almost shouted

'Yeah, yeah, I got it,' Patrick mumbled, struggling with another heap of snow.

'And another thing,' Al continued.

'Yes?'

'This conversation never took place.'

'Right.'

'Great. Want me to take over for a while?' Al asked.

'OK.' Patrick handed the shovel to Al and wiped his forehead.

'Women,' Al muttered as he worked. 'Bloody women.'

'Yeah,' Patrick said. 'Women.'

*

Claire threw open the door to Penny's bedroom.

'What?' Penny exclaimed and sat up in the bed.

'Were you asleep?'

'No, I was lying here trying to think.' Penny rubbed her forehead. She had been having a very strange conversation with herself, as if two people were arguing in her head. 'You can't tell Al about this, he'll leave you,' one voice had said. 'Of course you must tell him,' the other one protested. 'You've always told him everything. He is the only person on this earth who knows the true you.' 'But think of how angry he'll be,' the first voice insisted. 'He'll divorce you and cut you off without a cent. No more Chanel suits or Caribbean holidays for you, darling.'

'But there was no prenup,' Penny muttered.

'What?' Claire looked at Penny, confused.

'Nothing. What do you want?'

'I want to see if I can help you,' Claire replied, sinking down on the edge of the bed. 'I don't want you to have to deal with this on your own. So, let's talk about this again. But we have to be completely honest with each other this time, of course, or we'll never come to a solution.'

'I agree.' Penny nodded. 'Go ahead, then. Let's thrash this thing out.'

'First,' Claire started, 'you don't do cocaine, do you? No, I know you don't. Your nostrils are in such good shape. But if … I'll not judge you or anything, I just want to know if Michel … I mean where you stand.'

'I had nothing to do with the coke. Nor does Michel. He was only there a short time and I had my eye on him – I mean he never left my presence. He would have asked, anyway, when he sold me the marijuana. Which, I hasten to add, I only wanted for medicinal purposes, as I told you earlier. But, I have a feeling you know him a lot better than I do. I have a feeling there's a little something going on between you …'

'What? Me? And Michel?' Claire laughed. 'I just know him very slightly. He's one of my students. I teach English for adults, you see. He's in that course.'

'In that case,' Penny remarked, 'he must be at the bottom of the class.'

'He sure is. Oh, come on, Penny, You don't think I'd have anything to do with a little creep like that, do you?'

'Of course not,' Penny soothed. 'That would be so tacky. Not your style at all.'

'Not at all,' Claire agreed. 'So,' she continued, 'about you. All you know about Michel is that he sells some pot to his friends from time to time?'

'That's it.'

'OK. And I suppose you're worried that Al will find out.'

'Yes. His family are so old fashioned and strait-laced. The only thing *they* ever smoked is fish.'

Claire laughed. 'I know what you mean. But I was thinking; you're probably also worried about your family in Houston.'

'My family?' Penny asked.

'Yes. Didn't you tell me they were very well-connected? I mean, it would be so embarrassing for them socially, wouldn't it?'

'God, yes,' Penny said, 'very embarrassing.'

'So the best thing for you to do would be not to say anything.'

'You're absolutely right,' Penny replied. 'Even though I feel I should at least confess to Al.'

'Leave it for the moment,' Claire said. 'Go with the flow, that's what I always do.'

'OK, I will. What he doesn't know won't hurt him. It's none of his business anyway. And all of this is his fault,' Penny declared, suddenly feeling it was true. 'He stole my life.'

'He did?'

'Yes. He's one of those male chauvinist pigs who don't want women to … to … have a life. He wanted my whole existence to be only about looking after *him*.'

'Yes, but,' Claire said, a little puzzled, 'I thought that was the way it works. You know: first there's "him" and then "us" and then …'

'Who said that?' Penny interrupted.

'You did. You know, when we were in the tub.'

'What a load of crap.'

'Seemed very sensible to me,' Claire said.

Penny sighed. 'Yeah, well, I suppose it's true. No wonder we need a little pot now and then.'

'That's why you smoked pot? Because you were so frustrated?'

'That's right. Oh God, I feel so much better now,' Penny sighed. 'Now that I know whose fault all of this is.'

'Good. And I'm so glad we decided to be completely honest with each other.'

'Honesty is a very good policy.'

'The best,' Claire said.

20

'What are you doing?' Al asked as he came into the bedroom.

'What does it look like?' Penny walked from the wardrobe to the open suitcase on her bed.

'Packing,' Al said. 'It looks like you're packing.'

'Full marks. You're very smart when you put your mind to it.'

'But why?'

'Because, as soon as the roads are cleared, I'm out of here.'

'Why?' he asked again.

'I don't know. Maybe it's because I'm so bored I could scream? Or is it because I'm sharing a room and my life with someone who hasn't a clue about women? Or,' Penny continued, throwing a pair of shoes into the case, 'I need to go somewhere people talk about things that are more interesting than what they are going to have for dinner and how to sell *cat food*!'

'Why are you so mad? What have I done now?' Al looked at Penny, hurt and confused.

'What have you done? It's not about what you've done, really. It's your whole attitude. You just go through life in your own merry way, pre-occupied with your own concerns, and just take for granted that I will always be there, looking after your every need.'

'But honey,' he said. 'I don't understand. What started all this? The other night, you seemed so … I don't know … I thought we were getting close again.'

'You were wrong,' Penny replied, flicking through a stack of underwear. 'And all this inactivity has given me plenty of time to think.'

'About what?'

'About me,' Penny replied. 'For the first time in years, I have been able to analyse my situation, to take stock of my life.'

Al sank down on the bed. 'And … ?'

'Get up. You're sitting on my best cashmere sweater.'

'Sorry.' Al half-rose, handed Penny her sweater and sat down again. 'I don't understand what you're so upset about,' he said. 'I think we have a great life together.'

'*You* have a great life,' Penny snapped, 'thanks to me. But what about me? When have you ever stopped to think how I would like to spend the rest of my life? Or how it feels not to ever have had my own money? Or my own career? To have to start the day thinking about you and what *you'd* like me to do?'

Al got up from the bed. 'Well, isn't that tough?' he snapped. 'I really pity you. You've had such a hard time thinking about how to spend my money. And that you've been bloody good at! I don't know another woman in New York who's as good at spending money. I don't see what you have to complain about. You haven't had to do a day's work since we met. I even took care of your mother and got her out of the trailer park and into a condo in Florida. How many men would do that, huh?'

Penny didn't seem to be listening. She searched the dressing table, muttering to herself. 'Talcum powder, where is that box of talcum powder? Have you seen it?'

'What do you mean? Why should I give a fuck about your talcum powder?'

'It's that expensive kind. Chanel. I had a big box of it right here.'

'What's the matter with you? We're talking about our marriage here, what does your bloody talcum powder matter now?'

'Our marriage?' Penny asked, back in the swing again. 'Some marriage! I gave up a great career for you. And you have never uttered a word of thanks.'

'Oh, Jesus Christ, not that old argument again,' Al groaned. 'Not all that crap about how you gave me the best years of your life.'

'Well, I did. I was at the beginning of my career, when ...'

'Selling shoes? That's what you call a career?' Al started to walk around the room. 'I made you what you are today,' he said, stabbing a finger at her. 'I gave you status and class.'

'Class?' Penny sneered. 'Don't make me laugh. When we met, you were wearing snakeskin loafers and shiny suits. And your mother ...'

'My mother? We're going to bring my mother into it now?'

'You bet! I had to pretend to be something I wasn't. I hade to make up this fake background so she wouldn't look down on me.'

'That was your idea,' Al protested. 'I wanted to tell her everything, and to hell with what she thought, but you wanted to build up this image of yourself as the society girl.'

'But it didn't exactly hurt when you started to entertain clients, did it?' Penny retorted.

'Did I hear a word of protest? You were bloody good at keeping up the pretence. You played the part to perfection. Must be having been on the stage in Vegas all those years. You must have gotten plenty of practice faking it there.'

'In Vegas?' Penny said. 'What's that supposed to mean?'

'Well, I don't know what went on there,' Al replied. 'It's not exactly a boarding school for girls, is it?'

'What the hell do you mean?'

337

'I mean Vegas and you. You were one of the Vegas Babes. Glitz 'n' tits. The sexiest dance troupe in town. Makes a guy think.'

'Think what?' Penny demanded, putting down a coat hanger.

'I don't know what you were doing before you met me. You could have been doing all sorts of things.'

'Like what?'

'How do I know? Fraud? Sex? Drugs?'

Penny suddenly felt cold. 'What?' she whispered. 'You think I was involved in ...'

'No. Of course I don't.' Al sounded suddenly contrite. 'You couldn't have anything to do with that sort of thing.'

'No, I couldn't. I'm shocked you would even suggest it. You've never mentioned this before. How can you say a thing like that?'

'I know. OK, that was slightly unfair.'

'Slightly? And everything else you said was fair?'

'Yeah. I think it was all pretty fair.' Al's voice was bitter. 'And I don't think you have anyone to blame for your unhappiness but yourself.'

'You don't?'

'No. I've done my best to make you happy. But, if that's not enough, then ...'

'Then ... ?' Penny whispered.

'We're through,' Al said.

*

'The goldfish are in their bowl, swimming around,' Lucy said. 'Al? Are you listening?'

'Yeah.' Al was sitting on the sofa in the living room, staring straight in front of him.

'And they are looking at the cats, who are sleeping. OK?' Lucy looked at him impatiently from her seat by the small desk, trying to make him pay attention.

'OK.'

'And then one of the goldfish is saying: "It's really quiet around here since …" Al? Wake up! You said we had to finish this copy so we can start on the yoghurt commercial for that TV channel. I wanted to get started on it before we get back so … Al?'

'What's that?' Al looked vacantly at Lucy.

'Aren't you listening? I was telling you about the cat-food copy and my idea. I think it will really work.'

'I need a drink,' Al said and walked over to the drinks trolley. 'How about you? What will you have?'

'Oh, OK, I'll have a vodka and tonic.' Lucy sighed and stretched. 'I'm sorry. I'm sure you're as worried about poor Tiff as we all are. She's so young. And to have to go through being interrogated by the French police must be awful.'

'Mm,' Al said. 'What about you, Patrick? What will you have?'

'A beer,' Patrick replied, putting down his book. 'But at least it can't be as bad as the prisons in

Thailand,' Lucy continued. 'I saw a film about that once. This girl was caught smuggling drugs at the airport in Bangkok and she was thrown into jail at once without a trial or anything.'

'Please,' Claire said as she came into the room, 'do you have to? Isn't it bad enough without you talking about Bangkok?'

'Did you see that movie too?' Lucy asked.

'Yes. And I don't want to think about it.'

'No, you're right. It was pretty horrible. That was why I started working. To take my mind off Tiffany, you see. So, Al, what do you think?'

'About what?' Al asked, draining his brandy.

'The goldfish. I thought it could be a cartoon.'

'Goldfish?' Al said. 'What made you think about that?'

'Oh, I don't know,' Lucy replied. 'Anyway, the goldfish are swimming in the bowl ...'

'OK,' Al said. 'I'm with you.'

'And one of them says to the other that ... Well, I haven't really finished it yet,' Lucy said. 'It's just an idea, really. You see, I thought they would say the cats were leaving them alone ever since they started eating Purrfect Cat food. I'll think of a punch line later. So, how about it?' she asked Al. 'Pretty cute, don't you think?'

'I think it's a load of crap,' Al said, rising from his chair. He walked distractedly to the window, then turned on his heel and left the room.

Stunned and insulted, Lucy turned to Claire. 'What's wrong with him?'

'I have no idea,' Claire replied. 'How could he possibly not want to think about *goldfish* at a time like this? I mean, let's get a grip here. Tiffany is being grilled by the drug squad down there in that police station, and nobody is interested in Lucy's idea? That *is* strange, I have to say.'

'I'm trying to keep my mind off it,' Lucy said, 'and working is the only way I can do that.'

'OK,' Claire said, sounding contrite. 'I see. Well, I think I'll leave you to it. I wouldn't want to disturb you at this crucial time in your career.'

'What's the matter with everybody?' Lucy said when Claire had left. 'Don't they like cats? Maybe the goldfish were a bad idea. Maybe if they were canaries instead?'

'Or maybe you should just keep your mouth shut?' Patrick suggested, finishing his beer and getting to his feet.

Lucy stared at him. 'What's that supposed to mean?' she asked angrily, getting up to stand in front of the window, her arms folded. 'You have some cheek, you know, to even talk to me after the way you …' She pressed her fingers into her arms. 'I mean I … and the way we … and what you said to me …' She stopped, suddenly out of breath.

'I know,' Patrick said. 'I know, I know, I know.'

'What do you mean?'

'It's all a bloody mess,' he said, 'and I don't know how to fix it. But I can't think about it now.

Tiffany is going through hell and I can't do anything about it. And right now, you're no help at all. So I'll leave you to … to the canaries. I hope you'll all be very happy together.' The door banged as he left the room.

Lucy felt a wave of helplessness wash over her. She turned around and leaned her hot forehead against the cool glass of the window. Why is everything my fault, she thought. Why does everybody always let me down?

*

Later that day Claire was in the kitchen, clutching a mug of tea that was rapidly going cold while looking out at the snowploughs clearing the road to the village and the men digging out the bubble lift. But her mind was not on the scene outside the window. She was thinking about Lucy. It was so hard to accept that you could know someone all your life and still not know what made them tick. And this new Lucy was so different from the girl she had grown up with, or thought she had grown up with. But maybe she was more real? Claire sighed and put the mug on the counter. There was no use dwelling on it. Lucy was the way she was. She jumped as the sound of the phone ringing jolted her back to the present. Oh, my God, the phone is working again. She stared at it as it continued to ring, afraid to pick it up. What will I say? she thought, her heart racing. Will he say it again?

She reached out a hand. I'll just act as if he had said nothing at all. I'll just …

'Hello?' she croaked, clutching the receiver, feeling slightly dizzy.

'Hi!'

'Who's … Oh … Hi.'

'Are you OK? You sound so strange.'

'No, I'm fine. Everything's … fine.'

'Good. I'm sorry to have left you in the lurch like that but there was nothing I could do.'

'I know.'

'Anyway, I'll be back tomorrow so you just have to manage one more night.'

'Great.'

'It wasn't my fault; you know that. I just couldn't get back. I didn't plan it or anything,' Dave babbled nervously, 'and this has never happened before.'

'I know.'

'Right. Good. Was everything OK? Did you go shopping in the village, then?'

'No,' Claire replied. 'We were snowed in. We couldn't even open the front door.' Except for Tiffany, she thought, who managed to do all sorts of things behind our backs.

'Oh shit,' Dave exclaimed. 'That's terrible. How did you manage? Did you …' But Claire hung up, cutting him off in mid-sentence. He'll call as soon as he can, she thought. Better leave the line free. She put her mug in the sink. The phone rang again.

343

'Hello?' Claire gasped.   ... ause how

'Me again,' Dave laughed. 'Just to ... to cope you got the steaks out of the freezer.'

'Steaks?' Claire asked, her voice hol...ing to ...

'Yeah. There are fillet steaks and ... ... of other goodies in the big freezer in the basement. Didn't Emilie tell you?'

'No.'

'What? I don't believe you. She must know about it. It's the back-up freezer, you see. Mr Marchand always stocks that up at the beginning of the season for emergencies like this. Christ, I can't believe you didn't know about it.'

'Well, we didn't.'

'What have you been eating?'

'Porridge,' Claire replied.

Dave laughed. 'How awful. I'm sorry. Anyway, now you can stop eating porridge and have a party. Fillet steak, garlic potatoes, ice cream. How does that sound?'

'Like a dream,' Claire said.

*

'Why didn't you tell us about the food?' Claire asked Emilie.

'What food?' Emilie asked dreamily, her eyes on the picture she was painting.

'The food in the big freezer in the basement. Dave just told me about it.'

'Did he?' Emilie coloured in the sky.

'Yes, he did. He said you knew about it.'

'...' Emilie rinsed the brush in the cup of ... table. 'What colour should I paint ...? This is you here, you see. And this is ... Lucy skiing. I painted Lucy's jacket bla...'

'Emilie! Listen to me.'

'Yes?' Emilie looked up.

'Why did you not say anything about the freezer when we were all trying to survive on porridge?'

'Oh, I ...' Emilie looked at Claire dreamily. 'It was the game you see.'

'What game?'

Emilie looked down at her painting again. 'I was pretending we were starving like in the story. I wanted to see what it would be like.'

'What? You were playing a game? And we were all so hungry. That was very mean.'

'But why?' Emilie dipped her paintbrush into the red paint. 'I think your jacket should be red. Why was it mean?' she asked, filling in the hood of the jacket with red paint. 'It was only one day. And Auntie Penny – she said I could call her that – was so pleased that Uncle Al was eating something healthy like porridge. She said thank you and gave me ten dollars.'

'Oh for God's sake,' Claire snapped. 'Don't you realise that it was wrong? That you made everybody go to bed hungry?'

'Maybe it was good for them? My daddy said once that it would be good for people to feel

hungry just once and then they would re[...]
it felt and know what poor people ha[...]
with.'

'Do you really think it was a good th[...] do
just then? Everybody was cold and tired. That
was *not* a good time to teach people about being
hungry.'

'Why do you sound so cross?' Emilie complained. 'I haven't done *anything*! I was going to
tell you about the freezer right now, because I was
getting hungry. I was going to tell you when I had
finished my painting. But now you're getting to
be so mean and you're shouting.'

'I'm *not* shouting!' Claire exclaimed.

'Yes, you are!' Emilie put her hands over her
ears. 'Stop it! I don't like it when you shout. Leave
me alone! Go away. I hate you!' She burst into
noisy tears. 'I'm going to tell my daddy about
you,' she cried. 'I'm going to tell him how mean
you are!'

'And I'm going to tell him exactly what you
did,' Claire said. 'You told me a lie. I asked you
yesterday if you knew if there was food anywhere
else and you said no. *What* have I said about lies?'

Emilie stopped crying and looked sideways at
Claire. 'You have to make them sound as if
they're true.'

'What?' Claire stared at her. 'Oh no, that was
about something else. That was about paying
somebody a compliment. You see, when you talk
about someone's appearance, or their clothes, it's

346

OK not to tell them what you *really* think in order not to hurt their feelings. That's called a white lie. But, in all other situations, you have to tell the absolute truth. Got that?'

Emilie looked attentively at Claire. 'Can we have chips with our dinner?'

*

'A toast,' Claire said, lifting her wine glass. 'To … Penny.'

'Me?' Penny asked.

'Yes. To Penny,' Claire repeated. 'And Al. To the two of you. I was going to make this toast at the restaurant the other night, but then I had to leave early with little Miss Muffet here.'

'Me?' Emilie giggled, spooning the last of her ice cream into her mouth.

'That's right,' Claire replied, 'so this is the toast you missed.' She peered into her glass. 'Oh. Drank all the wine. Could I have just a bit more for the toast, please?'

'Of course,' Al said, lifting the wine bottle. 'I have to say it was a stroke of genius to find the food *and* the wine cellar as well.'

'I did,' Emilie piped up. 'I found the wine. It's daddy's best wine. He put it there for my wedding, he said.'

'Oh, no,' Penny exclaimed. 'You should have said. We shouldn't have opened that bottle.'

'That's quite all right,' Emilie smiled. 'I hate boys. I'm never even going to talk to a boy. I'm never *ever* getting married and I don't like wine. So you can have it. My daddy won't mind.'

'I'm not so sure,' Penny mumbled.

'Never mind,' Claire said, raising her glass again. 'To Penny and Al.' She took a big gulp and beamed at Al. 'You are probably the happiest couple I have ever met. And I just want to know: what's the secret?'

'The secret?' Penny seemed dazed.

'Yes,' Claire beamed. 'The secret of a successful marriage.'

'Is there a secret?' Penny muttered. 'Maybe we just don't have the guts to split up? Maybe we just stick together out of pure habit?'

'Oh, come on,' Patrick interrupted. 'You two are truly happy. I have to agree with Claire. There aren't many couples like you.'

'You don't know how true that is,' Al said.

'I hope,' Claire declared, 'that one day I will find a man who loves me as much as you love Penny.'

'And Penny,' Patrick filled in, 'you're every man's dream.'

'I am?'

'Because you do what most women probably would love to do but don't dare; you chose to be a wife and mother and didn't give a shit about having a career, or …'

'A life?' Lucy asked.

'What do you know what I give a shit about?' Penny demanded. 'How can you just sit there and decide what I feel? What do you know about what's in *here*?' She struck her chest theatrically.

'Nothing,' Al muttered. 'Absolutely nothing.'

'No, no, no,' Claire interrupted. 'Don't you go all intellectual on me now. To come back to what I said just a minute ago … What did I say just a minute ago?'

'You said that Auntie Penny and Uncle Al are a lovely couple,' Emilie reminded her. 'Is there any more ice cream?'

'Sure, honey,' Al said and took her plate. 'I'll give you the last scoop.'

'That's right,' Claire continued, 'a lovely couple.' She paused. 'I've got it. That word.'

'What word?' Penny asked.

'Not another word,' Al muttered.

'Complicity,' Claire said. 'That's what you have. That's what every happy couple has and that's what I want. Complicity.' She nodded and drained her glass.

'Complicity?' Al said, looking at Penny.

'Well, maybe that isn't *such* a good word just at the moment,' Penny mumbled. She turned away from Al's gaze and looked at the door. 'Talking of complicity,' she said, 'look who's here!'

21

'Tiffany!' Claire squealed. 'Oh, Tiffany, you're back!'

Patrick got up so fast he knocked over his chair. 'Thank God,' he breathed. 'Thank God you're OK.' He wrapped his arms around Tiffany, nearly squeezing the breath out of her.

'Please,' she said, pushing him away, 'there's no need to get all schmaltzy.'

'But what happened?' Penny asked. 'Where have you been all this time? We were so worried, the police …'

'Yeah, that's the first thing I wanted to say.' Tiffany sank down on a chair and poured herself a glass of water. 'Thanks a million for calling the cops. I had such a good time in the clink. It was such fun being interrogated, not to mention the strip search. I'll *never* be able to wear rubber

350

gloves again! And the food was unbelievable. Talking of which …' She looked around the table. 'I see you were far too worried to choke anything down. I suppose the wine and food was to cheer yourselves up?'

'That's right,' Patrick said. 'We were trying to … oh, never mind. What the hell happened? And where were you when the police found you?'

'Wouldn't you love to know?' Tiffany drawled, picking up a French fry and putting it in her mouth. 'Any of this lovely stuff left? I'm starving.'

'I'll get you some,' Lucy said and went into the kitchen.

'I'm still waiting for an answer,' Patrick snapped. 'You disappeared in the middle of the night, without a word. Then you get arrested for possession of drugs. I want to know what that was all about. I also want to know where you were and who you were with. And don't try to be smart.'

'I don't have to try,' Tiffany shot back. 'I'm a lot smarter than you any day.'

'Getting arrested for possession of cocaine is not what I would call intelligent,' Patrick snapped. 'So lose the attitude and answer me.'

'I had nothing to do with the drugs,' Tiffany said, suddenly looking pale. 'you have to believe me, Patrick. I know I've been a bitch sometimes but I would never touch any of that stuff.'

Patrick and Tiffany stared at each other in what seemed like a terrible silent battle. Then

Patrick sighed. 'OK,' he said, 'OK, I believe you. I don't know why, but I do.'

'Good,' said Tiffany.

'But why did you just take off like that?' Patrick asked. 'Without a word to anyone? Have you any idea how worried we were?'

'You didn't seem to care a hell of a lot about me before,' Tiffany mumbled, 'so I thought you wouldn't even notice if I was gone for a little while.'

'But what happened with the police?' Claire cut in. 'What did they say? How did you manage to get away?'

'No, I want to hear everything from the beginning,' Patrick interrupted. 'From the time you left here last night.'

'How did you get down to the village?' Penny asked. 'If that's where you were. We didn't hear you leave. We were sure you were gone to bed.'

'Questions, questions,' Tiffany said. 'So many questions ...'

'How about an answer to mine?' Patrick snapped.

'I just want to say one thing,' Tiffany declared. 'I was so touched by the concern you showed when I was carted off to the police station. I mean, there I was, held for questioning and my brother one of the best lawyers in New York. At least that was what I have been led to believe all these years. I kept expecting you to charge in and tell them you were my lawyer and I didn't have to tell them anything except in a court of law and all

352

that crap, but nobody came. How do you think I felt? Huh? I had to manage on my own. I had to sit there and answer all these questions, wondering where the hell my darling brother was. Or anybody else for that matter.' She looked around the table. 'Some support!'

'But,' Penny said, 'we couldn't get out of here. We couldn't even open the door. And the phones were out of order, you must have known about that. And the police told us not to leave the house, of course.'

'That's a great excuse,' Tiffany snorted.

'Do go on being sarcastic, sweetie,' Patrick said. 'But it won't let you off the hook in the long run, you know. So, cut the crap and answer my question: who were you with? Where did the police find you?'

*

Warren stared at Tiffany as the knocking became more insistent. 'Who can that be?'

'Why don't you find out?'

'Who is it?' Warren shouted. '*Qui'est-ce?*'

'Police!' a voice boomed.

'Shit!' Tiffany whispered. 'What have you done?'

'Me? Nothing. What have *you* done?'

'I don't know. Nothing at all, actually.'

'Let's open the door then and find out what they want.' Warren undid the many locks and the door flew open to admit two uniformed policemen.

'*Bonjour*,' the first one said.

'Hi.' Tiffany smiled.

'Mademoiselle Tiffany Delacy?'

'Yup, that's me,' Tiffany replied. 'How did you know?'

'The description,' the first policeman replied. 'Purple hair, diamond in your nose … Not many young ladies look like this.'

'No, I'm an original,' Tiffany said. Then she looked at the second policeman. 'Look, Warren, it's Jacques from the snowboard team. Hi Jacques.'

'Eh, *bonjour*,' Jacques replied, looking a little sheepish.

'I am Sergeant Fleury,' the first policeman said.

'You speak English,' Tiffany said. 'What a relief. Very good English too.'

'Thank you,' Fleury replied. 'I did a *stage* in Aspen a few years ago.'

'Oh,' Tiffany said, looking at him with big eyes.

'Yes. Never mind. Mademoiselle Delacy, you have been reported missing.'

'Missing?' Tiffany asked. 'But I'm not. I'm here.'

'I can see that.'

'Great. Was that all?'

'No, I'm afraid not. We need to ask you a few questions down at the police station.'

'What?' Warren exclaimed.

'What sort of questions?' Tiffany asked. 'I haven't done anything wrong. I just went dancing

354

at Le Ski Jump bar with a few friends. Don't tell me that's against the law! OK, so I should have told them at the chalet where I was going, but I was in a hurry.'

'That's not what it's about, mademoiselle,' Fleury said gravely. 'I'm afraid I have to ask you to come with us.'

'What do you mean?' Tiffany demanded. 'Are you arresting me?'

'Not yet,' Fleury said. 'We just want to establish your connection with a certain … substance that was found in your chalet.'

Tiffany went pale. 'What?' she whispered. 'What are you talking about?'

'Let's sort it all out at the station,' Fleury insisted. 'If you would come with us, Mademoiselle …'

'I suppose I don't have much of a choice,' Tiffany muttered. 'Warren, will you come with me?'

'Of course,' Warren said and took Tiffany's anorak from the hook by the door. 'Of course I'll come with you.'

'Let's go,' Fleury had said.

*

'Warren?' Lucy asked. 'You were with Warren?'

'Yeah. So?' Tiffany put the last piece of steak into her mouth and pushed the plate away. 'Thanks, that was great.'

'That Australian pansy?' Patrick asked.

355

'What?' Tiffany exclaimed. 'Pansy? Don't talk a load of crap. He's perfectly straight.'

'How do you know?' Patrick demanded. 'Did you … ?'

'That's none of your business.'

'I had no idea you and Warren knew each other,' Lucy said. 'How did you meet?'

'Oh, we just kind of started to talk one day down in the village,' Tiffany replied casually. 'He gave me some snowboard lessons. And then we saw each other from time to time in Le Ski Jump bar.'

'So, last night he came to collect you from here on his snow scooter?' Penny said.

'Yeah. I jumped out the window of your bathroom,' Tiffany nodded. 'The snow was right up to the windowsill on that side.'

'Just like in the story of Rapunzel,' Emilie piped in. 'Except he didn't climb in by your long golden hair.'

'Oh God,' Claire exclaimed, 'Emilie, I didn't realise you were still up. What will your father think? You were so quiet I didn't notice you. Come on, up to bed.'

'But I want to hear the rest of the story,' Emilie protested, 'I want to know what happened in the police station.'

'I'm sure you do,' Claire said grimly, 'but I think the rest of it might not be suitable for such young ears.'

'But Claire …' Emilie complained as she reluctantly walked out of the dining room, 'it was just getting so interesting. And I just know it's going to become even more interesting.'

'I'll tell you all about it tomorrow,' Claire said, taking Emilie firmly by the hand. 'It really is time for you to go to bed.'

'So, go on,' Al urged when the door had closed behind Claire and Emilie. 'What happened when you arrived at the police station? Did they charge you?'

'With what?'

'With possession of …' He stopped again.

'Yes?' Tiffany looked at him. 'Possession of drugs? Is that what you were going to say?'

'Yes, I suppose,' Al muttered.

'Nope,' Tiffany said. 'They didn't charge me with anything.'

'What?' Patrick stared at her. 'But I thought …'

'So did I,' Tiffany said. 'At first. It was really weird. First they took me down to the station and I thought, here we go, fingerprints, mug shots, the whole crime thing, but then they just left us waiting there for hours.'

'Us?' Patrick asked.

'Yeah. Warren and me. He came with me so I wouldn't be there all alone.' Tiffany shot a withering glance at Patrick. 'And he speaks really good French so I thought it was a good idea.'

'OK,' Patrick nodded. 'Go on.'

'Well anyway, there we were waiting. I thought they were kind of letting me sweat so I would be so scared I'd admit to anything. But it turned out they were waiting for this inspector guy, who finally arrived, shouting orders at everyone.'

'Inspector?' Penny asked.

'Something like that.' Tiffany nodded. 'Some kind of big shot. Anyway, to cut a long story short, he asked me a few questions, about where I was staying and everything, and all this time these two plastic bags were lying like time-bombs on the desk. He told the two other cops to leave the room. Then he picks up the phone and starts a long conversation with someone called Marchand ...'

'Bernard Marchand?' Claire, who had just returned from upstairs, went pale.

'Yeah, that's him. You know him?'

'He's Emilie's father,' Claire said.

'And the owner of this chalet,' Al filled in.

'No shit,' Tiffany said. 'Geez, that's amazing.'

'Go on,' Patrick urged.

'Oh, yeah. Where was I? OK, right. The inspector put down the phone. And *then* ...' Tiffany paused.

'Then?' Penny breathed.

'He did something *really* weird. You won't believe this.'

'Try us,' Al said.

'He opened the bag with the coke and tasted it. Then Warren said he muttered something like, "Even if you speak English and get to go to

Aspen, you still come back an idiot." And then he emptied the coke out the window.'

'WHAT?' Penny gasped.

'That's what he did, I swear.'

'What about the grass?' Penny asked. 'I mean the other stuff?'

'He held on to that.'

'What about Ber– I mean Monsieur Marchand?' Claire stammered.

'I couldn't understand what he was saying but Warren told me he said he vouched for everyone in the chalet. We were all personal friends of his. It seems he is a big wheel in the village.'

'But why did the police search the chalet?' Patrick asked.

'Turns out they didn't really suspect me at all,' Tiffany said. 'Seems they're looking for a guy called Michel.'

'Michel,' Claire said, her eyes huge. 'But I thought …'

'Yeah. He has been hanging around the village all week and they have been keeping an eye on him. That's why they searched this place. He was seen around here. Some time last week. And, of course, he was in the bar last night.'

'Do you know him?' Penny asked.

'Slightly. But he's not my type. He's always hitting on women.' Tiffany shuddered. Then she laughed. 'You know, if they were going to book people for smoking pot, it would be pretty crowded in the police station. Most of the snowboard team were passing around joints in the bar last night.'

'But, what did they say about … about this Michel?' Claire asked. 'The police, I mean.'

Tiffany shrugged. 'Nothing much. He's some kind of student. Not seriously into this kind of thing.'

*

'Aren't you coming to bed?' Penny asked.

Al was sitting in the big easy chair by the fire in the living room, staring morosely into his empty brandy glass. He looked up. 'What's that?'

'I said, are you coming to bed?'

'What for?'

'Well, I thought, as it's so late and we've had a tough day, you might be tired.'

'It's been tough, that's for sure,' Al said, looking at her with tired resignation. Penny felt a surge of guilt and sadness as she looked at him, slumped there, all the usual energy and good humour knocked out of him. She sat down on the chair opposite and looked at him without knowing what to say.

'So,' Al said. 'Have you booked your flight?'

'Not yet.'

'Why not? You were in such a hurry earlier. I thought you'd be on the phone to the airline straight away.'

'Well, I thought …' She stopped. 'I thought we might talk first.'

'About what?' He put the brandy glass on the table. 'I thought we had said all there was to say.'

'Oh, but …' She paused.

'What's the matter, honey?' Al's voice was soft.

Penny suddenly began to sob. 'I have nowhere to go,' she cried.

'What do you mean?'

'Think about it,' she wept. 'Where will I go? I can't go back to the apartment. I'll have to book into a hotel. And I *hate* hotels, you know that. And what will I do all day? I can't get a job just like that, not at my age. I have no training. You never wanted me to work, you wanted me to run your home, bring up our child, organise all the corporate entertaining and look *pretty*!' Penny spat out the last words.

'But you did it so well,' Al said.

'That's not the point,' Penny snapped. 'You can't make a career out of choosing the right canapés. Nobody is going to hire me because my daughter was so beautifully potty-trained. I can't put "knows how to accessorise" on my resumé. I can't do anything that really counts.'

'Maybe you could go back to Vegas?' Al suggested. 'You still have the best legs in America.'

'Is that supposed to be some kind of joke?'

'No, I meant that. You do have the best legs. Don't worry,' he continued. 'You're going to be all right. You won't have to work. We didn't sign a prenup, remember? You'll be able to take me to the cleaners.'

'What? Yes, you're right,' Penny said without enthusiasm. She wrapped her arms tightly around herself. 'Oh, God, I don't know what to do.'

'You could go and live in Florida with your mother,' Al said.

'My mother,' Penny snorted, looking back at him. 'She'll never forgive me if we split up. You're the best thing that ever happened to her.'

'I'm sure she'd come round if we tell her she can keep the condo. Maybe she'll like the idea of having you there.'

Penny stared at him. 'Are you trying to get rid of me?' she asked angrily. She was beginning to feel frightened. This row was going a little further than usual and she didn't like it.

Al shook his head and sighed. 'Oh, honey,' he mumbled, 'of course not. I don't want you to leave me. I'll never find a woman like you in a hundred years.'

'What do you mean?'

'Where would I find a woman as beautiful as you? Or as wild? I've always found it so exciting that you are so cool and sophisticated on the surface, then you have that wild streak. I love it that you were a Vegas Babe and that you smoke pot in the bath.'

Penny eyes widened as she looked at him, aghast. 'You knew?' she whispered. 'All this time you knew?'

'Of course. Do you think I'm stupid? Do you think I don't know the difference between a perfumed candle and a reefer? Do you think,' he asked,' that before we met, I didn't have a life?'

They sat and looked at each other in silence for a long time.

'I had no idea.' Penny said.

'I wonder if we really know each other at all,' Al mumbled. 'I thought we had such a great life but it was a bit like something you read in one of those magazines. You know: at home with such and such. Look at their beautiful home, her lovely clothes, their art collection and the view from the living room. But when do they talk to each other?'

'I know,' Penny nodded. 'We have been living side by side, both of us playing our part in this lifestyle, but never really asking each other if we're happy.'

'We're both at fault,' Al said. 'I worked so hard to get my firm off the ground, then, when it did, I forgot you. I just saw you as this very useful partner, who made me look great. My beautiful wife, the best hostess in New York.'

'And I just went along with it,' Penny said. 'My clothes, the apartment, our holidays, the parties … All of that took up my whole life. I didn't give myself a chance to think. I was too busy trying to keep up with the latest trend.'

'But you were a great mother to Jennifer,' Al said.

363

'Was I?' Penny asked. 'Is that why she left home so young? Is that why she has a weight problem?'

'That's not your fault.'

'Who knows?' Penny sighed, feeling totally drained. 'We should have had more children.'

'But we didn't,' Al said. 'You just didn't get pregnant again. Not your fault.'

'But maybe I should have made more of an effort,' Penny mumbled. 'Maybe I should have gone to another doctor, had more tests?'

'Oh, honey, what's the point?' Al asked. 'We had Jennifer and thank God for her. Why cry over something that's in the past and not possible to change? We did what we did. You can't go back, only forward.'

'Mmm,' Penny mumbled. 'Maybe you're right.'

'I know I am.'

'What do we do now?'

Al looked at her. 'Come here,' he said. 'There's plenty of room in this big chair for two.'

Penny joined him in the big chair and they sat with their arms around each other for a long time without speaking, looking into the dying fire.

'You know,' Al said. 'I have nowhere to go either. Without you, I mean.'

'No, you don't,' Penny agreed. 'Can I ask you something?'

'Sure.'

'Would you have married me if I hadn't been pregnant?'

'Would you?'

'Like a shot. But you didn't answer my …'

'Why do you think there was no prenup?'

'I don't know. You tell me.'

'It didn't occur to me to treat us, I mean our marriage, as some kind of business deal. And it didn't occur to me that it would ever come up. I thought we were forever.'

'Nothing is forever,' Penny said.

'No.'

'Let's go to bed and get some sleep. We're both exhausted.'

*

'Good morning,' Patrick said.

'Morning,' Lucy replied, turning her back to him.

'Sleep well?' he asked.

'OK.' Lucy poured boiling water into the kettle. 'Tea?'

'Sure.'

She put two tea bags into the teapot and took butter and milk out of the fridge.

'Nice dressing gown,' he remarked. 'I like the piping around the neckline.'

'Yeah, right.'

'It's kind of cold in here,' Patrick said, sitting down at the kitchen table.

'The heating is going full blast.'

'I wasn't talking about the heating. I was talking about the … atmosphere.'

'What atmosphere?'

'I rest my case.'

Lucy looked up. 'What is this? Some kind of trial?'

'No,' Patrick said. 'Just an attempt at conversation.'

'Isn't it a little late?' Lucy asked.

'No, it's early. Only nine o'clock.'

'Very funny.'

'Sit down!' Patrick ordered. 'Stop walking around fiddling with everything.'

'What's your problem?' Lucy demanded

'What's yours? Can we not sit down and talk to each other? Is it that hard for you to even look at me?' Patrick suddenly got up and walked over to Lucy. He put his hand on her arm. 'Lucy?'

She stopped moving and closed her eyes. 'Don't touch me,' she whispered. 'Please, just don't.'

He removed his hand. 'OK. No touching.'

'Thank you.'

He sat down again. 'I had no idea you loathed me so much.' He shrugged. 'But I don't blame you.'

'You don't?' Lucy sat down opposite Patrick.

'I have been a little unfair to you,' Patrick said.

Lucy lifted one eyebrow. 'A little?'

'Yeah. We've kind of done things back to front, I feel, like eating dessert before the main meal, so to speak. Not that it wasn't lovely. But I thought that if we talked … you know, we could …'

'OK, so talk,' Lucy said, trying her best to look aloof. 'What is it you wanted to discuss?'

'I just wanted to … sort of get to know you.' He poured tea into her cup. 'Milk?'

'Thanks.'

'That's a start. I've just found out you take milk in your tea. How about sugar?'

'No.'

'Milk, no sugar. Like me. Isn't that interesting?'

'Not particularly.'

Lucy looked at him with her cool green eyes. Patrick pressed on. 'What about breakfast? What do you usually eat?'

'A slice of toast and some yoghurt. And then a piece of fruit.'

'What type of yoghurt?'

'Plain.'

'Figures.'

'What?'

'This isn't working, is it?' Patrick said with a sigh. 'You're not cooperating.'

'What do you mean? What do you want me to do?'

'If we were talking about a new brand of washing powder, I suppose you would be a lot more interested? You're consumed by that job of yours; you can't think of anything else.'

'I love my job,' Lucy said. 'I love advertising. What's wrong with that? Why is it OK for you to be completely absorbed by what you do and so wrong for me?'

'I'm not saying it's wrong, I'm just stating a fact. And, in any case, a woman's career is just a substitute for the family life she is really yearning for.'

'Yearning? I'm supposed to be yearning, now?'

'I know you are – all women are.'

'So now you're an expert on women?' Lucy asked, spreading marmalade on a piece of toast.

'I read it in an article in *The New Yorker*.'

'Do you believe everything you read in the papers?' Lucy asked. 'Or only what you want to believe?'

Patrick laughed out loud.

'Go ahead,' Lucy said, 'laugh in that superior way. I don't care what you think, actually.'

'I wasn't laughing because I felt superior. It was a laugh of appreciation, of approval,' he said.

'Can we stop this now? I really don't see the point, to be honest.'

'It's working for me,' Patrick said, still smiling. He leaned forward and gently touched her nose with his finger. 'I see those freckles are back.'

Lucy pulled away. 'Must have forgotten the sun block.'

'You know, I noticed them the first time I met you. I thought you were the most beautiful girl I had ever seen.'

Suddenly furious, Lucy stared at him, her eyes blazing. 'You've got some nerve! How dare you sit here and tell me I'm beautiful? You've treated me like some kind of ... some kind of ...'

'Can't a man pay a girl a compliment?'

'Not if he has ... you know ... her twice and

then pretended it didn't happen. You're acting as if we've just met.'

'Don't you like being told you're beautiful?'

'That's beside the point.'

Patrick looked at her for a moment. 'How about,' he said, 'if we pretended we *had* just met.'

'How about acting your age?'

They stared at each other in silence. 'OK,' Patrick said. 'I get it. And you have every right to hate me. Every right. But I wanted to tell you something.'

'Tell me what?'

'First, that you must know that Tiffany is very important to me. And I am all she has.'

'That's her bad luck,' Lucy snorted.

'Yeah, well … Anyway, I'm responsible for her. I have to look after her and that is not an easy job. And it will be going on for a long time to come, I suspect.'

'So?' The look in Lucy's eyes changed from anger to confusion. 'What does that have to do with me?'

'I'm coming to that.' Patrick cleared his throat. 'If,' he started, feeling as if he was walking on very thin ice, 'if there's is the slightest chance that you … that we … Well, you know.'

'Know what?' Lucy said innocently. 'You're very tongue-tied for a lawyer.'

'And you're a …' He stopped. 'Sorry. I was going to say that if there's any chance at all you could consider having anything to do with me, then you have to know that Tiffany will be very much part of our lives.' He drew breath and looked at her, trying to figure out what she was thinking. 'What's the problem?' he asked when there was no answer. 'Is it Tiffany? Don't you like her?'

'Oh, I have no problem with Tiffany,' Lucy replied. 'I really like her.'

'What's the problem, then?'

'It's you I can't stand.'

*

'What's going on?' Claire asked as she and Emilie were taking off their boots in the garage that afternoon. 'What's the noise?'

'Sounds like the Hoover,' Emilie said. 'Upstairs.'

'It must be the maid,' Claire suggested. 'She must have come back now that the roads are cleared.'

'And, look,' Emilie said, pointing at a pile of bags on the floor. 'Shopping!'

'Dave's back,' Claire said. 'Great. Everything's back to normal. We don't have to do any more housework.'

'Let's go and say hello to him,' Emilie said and started to climb the stairs. 'I bet he'll be glad to see us.'

'Hello, Emilie,' Dave said, turning around from polishing the coffee table. 'Hi, Claire. Nice to see you again.'

'What are you doing?' Claire asked, looking around the immaculate room. 'Have you started spring cleaning early?'

370

'Not really. We just have to have the place looking perfect. My boss is arriving tomorrow.'

'Your boss?' Claire asked. 'Who do you mean?'

'The owner of the chalet, of course,' Dave replied, looking at Claire as if she was a little slow. 'Your boss too, actually.'

'My daddy!' Emilie squealed. 'Is he coming *here*?'

'That's right,' Dave nodded. 'He called about half an hour ago. Wanted to speak to you.'

'To me?' Claire asked, breathing a little faster.

'To both of you. I told him you were on your way home from the ski school so he said he'd call at around six o'clock.'

'But what's that you said,' Clare asked, 'about Mr Marchand arriving tomorrow?'

'That's right. He has a business meeting in Geneva, then he'll take the opportunity to see Emilie. He'll be flying in tomorrow midday. Landing at the *altiport*. You know, the small airstrip at the top of the village. Sorry. I have to go and check upstairs. Mr Marchand is very particular about the state of the chalet. He'll expect everything to be immaculate. I have to get his bedroom organised and tidy up the study. And the kitchen is in a bit of a mess. I don't have a lot of time to get everything ready.'

Suddenly, the phone rang. 'That'll be him,' Dave said. 'Why don't you get it, Claire?'

But Claire stood as if paralysed, staring at the ringing phone.

'I'll answer it,' Emilie exclaimed and ran to the phone. 'Hello? Daddy? It's me!' She listened for a moment. 'It's all right ... the lifts are working and the ski school opened again ... yes ... oh, that's great! We'll go and watch your plane land tomorrow from the terrace of the restaurant ... yes, she's here ... OK, I'll tell her. Love you too, daddy. Bye.' Emilie put down the receiver. 'Daddy said he was looking forward to seeing you again,' she said. 'He said he wants to talk to you about something.'

*

'I didn't know there was anyone here,' Lucy said as she came into the living room early that evening. She felt a little taken aback to find Claire there alone. She had given up on the idea that they could ever be friends again and decided to put Claire and the whole sorry business out of her mind forever once she was back in New York.

'I suppose you were right in a way,' Claire replied. 'There is no one here. No one that counts for you, in any case.'

'But I ...' Lucy started. 'I mean I wasn't going to ...'

Claire got up from the sofa. 'I'm glad you're here. I was looking for you, actually. I wanted to talk to you.'

'About what?' Lucy looked at Claire with suspicion in her eyes. 'I didn't think there was anything for us to talk about. I'm not going to beg for forgiveness again.'

'Well, no, it isn't that …'

'Because I don't want your forgiveness,' Lucy continued. 'I feel that the … the *crime* has been prescribed. I'm going to forget the whole thing, and I'm going to do my best to forget you as well. Because I don't want to have anything to do with someone who carries a grudge about something that happened a million years ago.'

'I see.' Claire sat down again. 'All right, if that's the way you feel …'

Lucy sank down beside her. 'No, it's not. I feel rotten about what happened. Even though I think you could have understood, I see now that I should have discussed it with you, but …'

'But what?'

'I was afraid you would say no. That you would somehow stop me. And I wanted to go and do that degree course. I don't think I have wanted anything in my life as much as that. Ever.'

Claire folded her arms and leaned back against the cushions. 'Go on.'

'That's it. Isn't it enough?' Lucy stared at Claire, willing her to agree. 'Can't you see it was a great chance for me to have a career and make real money, I mean the kind of money that will buy you a fantastic life.'

'So that was what it was all about. Money.'

'No,' Lucy protested. 'You make it sound as if that was all I cared about.'

'Wasn't it?'

'No, I mean, yes, in a way. I wanted what money can give you: independence, security, power. But it's not the actual money, don't you see, it's the challenge too. It's *making* it.' Lucy stared at Claire, her eyes wistful. 'It's hard to explain, but I thought you realised, I thought you knew why I worked so hard all the time.'

Claire shook her head slowly. 'I had no idea you wanted all of this. I had no idea that you were the kind of person who … Well, who was so into money and all that. I feel as if I'm meeting you for the first time. Isn't that strange?'

'You had no idea because you never bothered to find out,' Lucy said.

There was a long silence, during which Claire looked at her hands, clasping and unclasping them, and Lucy clenched her jaw and stared at the grey sky outside the window.

'Shit,' Claire suddenly said. 'Oh, Luce, you're right. I've been so stupid. Stupid and selfish. But, in a way, it was your fault too.'

'Why?'

'Because you let me. You let me have my own way all the time. You always agreed to anything I said and you just let me go on … using you. Why did you?' Claire demanded, her voice shrill. 'Why didn't you put your foot down and tell me where to get off?'

'I don't know,' Lucy said. 'I admired you, I think. I thought the way you were – so pretty and fun and popular – was the right way to be. I thought I was dull and boring and you were, well, the way you were. Everyone loved you. But then, when I decided to go to London, I suppose I felt I had a right to do it. To take that money, I mean. As a payment for all those years ... well, you know.'

'Oh God,' Claire said, hiding her face in her hands. 'Please, stop it. I know what you're saying. I see it all now. I've been such a cow.'

They were silent again. Lucy looked at Claire and thought she had never seen her so sad and she felt, for just a moment, totally drained and unable to utter another word.

'Are you happy?' Claire suddenly asked.

'What?' Lucy looked at Claire, startled.

'I asked you if you were happy. Are you?'

'I don't know. Are you?'

Claire shrugged. 'Don't know either. I don't seem to know anything at all at the moment.'

'I know what you mean.' Lucy sighed. 'Can we be friends again, do you think?' she asked, sounding oddly childish.

Claire shrugged. 'I don't know that either. I think we have to try to get to know each other again. Try and find out who we *really* are.'

'And then see if we like each other?' Lucy filled in, her voice wistful.

'Something like that.'

'What about the past?'

'Why don't we forget that? Doesn't seem to matter anyway. Except that I'm so sorry for ...'

'No,' Lucy cut in, 'don't. No more apologies. I can't stand any more. And that hair shirt doesn't suit you, in any case,' she added with a dry little laugh. 'We are the way we are and we should just accept that. So it doesn't matter any more. I think we should wipe the slate clean.'

'OK.' Claire held out her hand. 'Let's start from the beginning. A new beginning.'

Lucy took her hand. 'Deal,' she said.

22

Penny walked on the newly cleared path to the village. It was getting dark and the lights were coming on in all the buildings. There were several feet of snow on every roof and window sill. The snow crunched under her feet and the black sky was full of stars. She looked into the cosy living room of a chalet, where a fire flickered in the huge fireplace and the soft lamplight shone on polished wood and rugs in warm colours. Next door, in the lounge of a hotel, the chandeliers had been lit in the high ceiling and the leather sofas and mahogany coffee tables gave an air of expensive elegance. Nowhere in the world is there more luxury per square foot than in this small village, Penny thought, looking into the basement of another hotel where a swimming pool glimmered invitingly, with bamboo deck chairs and beautifully coloured towels stacked on shelves around the pool area. Steam rose from the pool, and she could nearly feel how wonderful it would be to sink into the turquoise water, heated to just the right temperature. I'll ask Dave to switch on the hot tub, she thought. Al and I could have a soak later ... But first, I have some shopping to do.

There was a sudden shout and then laughter. Penny looked at a group of young people in worn ski overalls and scuffed boots sitting on a wall eating chips and sandwiches they had bought from the stand nearby. They were pushing and scuffling each other, their faces glowing. They all look so happy, she thought, without a care in the world, least of all that they can't afford a meal in any of the fancy restaurants. They don't even seem to feel the cold.

Penny wrapped her jacket tighter around her as she walked on. That little shop across the street from the *salon de thé*, tucked discreetly between the jewellers and the confectioners, would have what she was looking for. I don't care how much it costs, she thought, it will be worth it.

Al had seem so tired, and sad too. She had never seen him so down. Usually, their rows ended by making up in the most spectacular way. But this time, the fight had been a little too close to the bone. They had both said things that couldn't be taken back so easily. What was I thinking? she asked herself. I couldn't leave him. And it's not his fault I'm growing old. She glanced into yet another beautiful interior and realised this was what she had become used to. She could walk into any of those hotels and book a room, ask for room service, order dinner and champagne. Al would pay for it all as he had paid for everything she had wanted all these years. When did I start taking it all for granted? When did I stop appreciating all Al has done for me? How could I have imagined my life without him? We were so in love, she remembered, we couldn't keep our hands off each other … Here's the shop now. Lovely things in the window. I know I'll find the perfect little item … Tiny bells tinkled as she opened the door and went into the softly lit interior.

*

'Wasn't that what's-her-name?' Warren asked, looking across the street. 'Going into that shop over there.'

'Who?' Tiffany said, looking up from her sandwich.

'The blonde good-looking sheila in your chalet.'

'Penny?' Tiffany looked at the door that had just closed. 'Nah, I doubt it. What would she be doing going into that kind of shop? Wouldn't you think she'd be past it at her age?'

'Don't be so sure. She looks pretty game to me.'

'So, you fancy older women, now?' Tiffany pushed him so hard, he nearly fell off the wall.

'Not that old. She's the kind of woman who'll always be sexy.'

'This is getting serious.' Tiffany looked at Warren and laughed. 'Maybe she'll be booking a private lesson next?'

'I don't think she needs lessons. She's a hell of a skier, you know. I saw her ski the black slope right from the top of the Saulire the other day. Great muscle tone.'

'Don't talk dirty,' Tiffany said and stole one of his French fries. 'God, I'm starving. Who would think snowboarding would make you so hungry?'

'But she was really going fast,' Warren continued, 'taking risks even I wouldn't. It was as if she had some kind of death wish. You know that bit where you have to turn really fast not to fall, that patch that's always icy?'

'Yes?'

'She went straight down.' He shook his head in awe. 'But then she fell. It was a bloody miracle she didn't break her neck. But she picked herself up and got down without any problems. Great skier. And a real lady.'

*

Claire walked out of the living room and up the stairs, following the sound of Dave talking to the cleaning lady. 'Open the window,' she could hear him say. 'Get clean towels for the bathroom, the best ones, you know, the heavy blue ones.' Only the best would be good enough for Bernard Marchand, she thought, and that goes for women too. He wouldn't want a slightly overweight Irish school teacher with no skills whatsoever, who's been around the block a few times more than she'd care to mention. But a girl has her pride. I don't need all this.

'Is this really Bernard Marchand's room?' Claire asked Dave.

Dave turned around from making the bed. 'Well, yes,' he said. 'Why?'

'It's not half as luxurious as the other ones.'

'It has its own bathroom, though. And a lovely view.'

Claire walked around the room, admiring the painting of the Alps over the chest of drawers, touching ornaments, peering at the titles of the books in the small bookcase. 'Balzac,' she muttered, 'Georges Sand. Ed McBain. And, look, John Steinbeck and F. Scott Fitzgerald. Some of my own favourites.'

'Some of them belonged to his late wife, I think,' Dave said.

Claire stared at a small photo in a silver frame of a woman, leaning on her ski poles, her blonde hair framing her face, smiling into the camera. 'Is this her?' she asked, even though she knew it had to be.

'Yes,' Dave replied, looking at it too. 'I believe it is. I never met her. I started working here the year after she died.'

'Oh.' Claire looked at the woman's face and suddenly saw Emilie, or what she would probably look like when she was an adult. The colours of her hair and eyes were that of her father, but her eyes, the shape of her face and her expression were identical to those of her mother. Claire suddenly shivered and turned away.

'Are you all right?' Dave asked. 'You look a little pale.'

'No, I'm fine. I better go and make sure Emilie is changing out of her ski clothes.'

*

Al was working in bed, balancing his laptop on his knees. He glanced up as Penny came into the room. What has she been doing now, he thought tiredly as Penny put her bag on a chair and disappeared into the bathroom. This has been the worst two weeks in a long time, he thought. I was looking forward to a great break with my wife and a few friends. And what did I get? Everyone fighting, the weather awful and then my wife threatening to divorce me. And Patrick has been a right bastard, dragging me into his family affairs with that brat of a sister of his. Bloody lawyers! No use in or out of the courtroom. Always looking for money and trying to fleece you. OK, so he did get me that compensation but there wasn't much left by the time I had paid his bill. And now he's wasting Lucy's time, making her moon when she should be concentrating on that account. Does nobody realise how much effort it takes to bring in the money? At least I'm charging the entire trip to expenses through Marchand's firm. That's some consolation. Those shareholders will be paying. Bastards. Always complaining about the dividends.

'Al, honey?' Penny had emerged from the bathroom.

Al looked up. He stared at her in awe. 'Wow,' he whispered. 'Golly gee.'

'Is that all?' she enquired, sitting on the bed. She was dressed in a black lace negligee, the half-open neckline of which revealed the lace of the nightgown underneath. 'Golly gee? I thought you might try to be just a little more eloquent. This thing cost an arm and a leg, you know, the shirt off your back and a lot more. "Golly gee" just doesn't cut it here. I was hoping for something a bit more romantic.'

'Romantic? What do you mean? I thought you were leaving me. What is this? A farewell performance?'

'No,' Penny said, looking a little embarrassed now. 'I wanted … I thought …'

'What? What do you want now? You've been wanting a hell of a lot lately.'

'Let's not talk,' Penny said, walking over to the CD player. 'Let's just …' She pressed a button, and the room was filled with the throbbing sound of a Brazilian samba. 'Remember this?' Penny asked. She started to dance slowly around the room. She held out her arms to Al. 'Come, dance with me. Like that first time. That's when I fell in love with you. Right on the dance floor of that little nightclub in Soho.'

Al put the laptop on the bedside table and slowly got to his feet.

'Oh, darling,' Penny murmured as he slipped his arms around her waist, feeling her breasts against his chest and the soft silk under his hands. Slowly, they started to dance. 'I found this CD in a shop in the village today,' she said, 'and I just wanted us to listen to it.'

'I know this song.'

'Do you remember what you said to me that first time?' she asked, looking into his eyes.

'No,' he mumbled into her hair. 'I just remember the feel of your skin. I remember your perfume and your mouth.'

'You said I had a lovely body; you said you loved the sound of my voice; you said you liked the way I laughed.'

'I still do. I love all those things about you. I always will.'

'And I remember looking into your eyes and thinking they were nicest, kindest eyes I had ever seen. And you were so strong. A big bear of a man, I thought.'

'You did?' Al said, closing his eyes, swaying to the music, his cheek to hers.

'Yeah.'

'And I took you home …'

'… to my apartment because you were still living with your parents.'

'Yeah,' Al said, sliding his hands onto Penny's bottom, 'and we …'

'No, we didn't. I said never on the first date, and you said how many dates and I said who knows?'

'Oh. Yes. So you did.'

They danced for a while without speaking.

'You know something?' Al said.

'Don't talk.'

'No, there's something I must tell you,' he insisted.

'OK, tell me.'

'I just wanted to say,' he murmured into her ear, 'I would not be where I am today if it wasn't for you.'

'You mean you wouldn't have gone to the Alps?' she teased.

'No, honey, I mean I couldn't have made such a huge success of the firm if you hadn't been there, supporting me and looking after all those little details that were so important. You and I, we made the business work together.'

Penny pulled away from his embrace and looked him in the eyes. 'You mean that?'

'Oh, yes.'

'Oh, darling …' She put her cheek to his again.

'Honey …'

'Mmm.'

He tightened his grip. 'What will happen now?'

'Who knows?' Penny murmured.

*

Claire opened her eyes, not knowing if she had really slept. She seemed to have spent the night waiting to go to sleep. She turned in the bed and looked at the window. Dust particles sparkled in the broad beam of sunlight that came through a slit in the curtains. Claire threw aside the bedclothes, walked to the window and pulled them aside, wincing as the light hit her tired eyes. It was a beautiful day, with a bright blue sky and just one or two small pink clouds over the brilliant white mountain tops. Another bloody stunning day in the Alps, she thought. Another day of struggling with skis and ski lifts, of trying to master the art of staying upright while sliding down those pistes, of falling on my bum a hundred times. Then she remembered; it wasn't really just another day. It was *that* day; the day she would come face to face with Bernard Marchand again. She propped her elbows on the windowsill and stared out without really seeing the lovely view. She could remember every line in his face, that distant look in his eyes, the flecks of grey in his light brown hair and that sad little smile. Claire let her arms fall and sighed as she turned away from the window. Slowly, she went into the bathroom, stripped off her pyjamas and stepped into the shower. She closed her eyes and turned her face to the water.

*

'Bloody mambo,' Lucy groaned, pouring herself some tea.

'What?' Claire asked, looking up from her muesli. 'What's that about mambo?'

'Didn't you hear it?' Lucy said. 'That music. It was playing practically all night. I didn't get a wink of sleep.'

'I know,' Patrick grunted from behind his paper. 'I heard it too. It started early and went on for quite a while. Then it stopped. I thought I would finally get some sleep but just as I was dropping off, it started again.'

'It was that kind of music that throbs,' Lucy said. 'Sort of pulsates, you know?'

'I thought it might be coming from the chalet next door,' Patrick remarked. 'And I even opened the window to hear if they were having a party or something. But that house was completely dark and I remembered it was empty.'

'Weird,' Lucy said. 'Mambo in the middle of the night.'

'It was a samba,' Penny said and took an apple from the fruit bowl, 'and I didn't hear a thing.'

Lucy looked at her. 'Are you feeling all right?'

'I feel fantastic,' Penny beamed,

'Well, I'm off,' Lucy said a little later, getting up from the table. 'I'm not going to miss another minute of this beautiful day.'

'Me too,' Patrick said, putting down his paper. 'I'm going over to the red slopes on the Meribel side of the resort. They won't have groomed the pistes on that side yet.'

'But that's where I'm going,' Lucy said, looking irritated.

'So?' Patrick lifted one eyebrow. 'Do you have some sort of monopoly on that particular side of the mountains?'

'No, but I thought it would be nice to be on my own today, to ski without anyone annoying me.'

'What about your instructor?' Patrick asked. 'Has he the day off?'

'Warren? No, he's giving Tiffany a snowboard lesson. Or that's what he said they were doing. And I don't really need any more lessons.'

Lucy walked to the door with Patrick behind her.

'This I will have to watch,' he said. 'It will be such fun seeing you sliding down the mountain on your ass.'

'Yeah? And I'm going to enjoy watching you twist your other knee and this time I'm not going to as much as lift my little finger to help you. You'll have to wait for some other sucker to listen to you moan.'

'I would be delighted if you left me alone. I don't think I could stand another first-aid lesson from the Girl Guide of the Year.'

Lucy stopped suddenly, making Patrick bump into her. 'Is there any way I can stop you following me around like this?' she asked.

'No.'

'For Christ's sake!' she exclaimed. 'Stop acting like a five-year-old!'

'Would the two of you end this constant bickering,' Penny suddenly snapped. 'It's a pain in the butt to listen to it and, God knows, we have been forced to listen to it since we arrived. You're snapping at each other like two angry dogs. I have no idea what your problem is but go and sort it out somewhere else.' She drew breath.

'What's biting you?' Lucy asked.

'Nothing. I was in a great mood until this silly arguing started,' Penny sighed. 'Please, get out of here, now!'

'Are you coming then?' Patrick asked. 'The lifts are just starting. The snow will still be untouched. Absolutely perfect conditions. Fresh powder like you've never seen before.'

'I suppose I'll have to,' Lucy said.

As the door closed behind them, Penny looked at Claire and sighed again. 'I wish they would just get on with it. We all know what's going on.'

'What *is* going on? I thought they hated each other,' Claire said.

'Exactly. Hate and love. Very similar feelings. And just as strong. And Patrick and Lucy are so alike. Both driven career people, both emotional cripples and both annoying as hell. I hope they will find out very soon how sweet it is to make up after a fight. And the way they have been rowing, their making up should be spectacular.'

'Are you sure they will?'

'No.' Penny shrugged. 'Maybe they'll kill each other instead.'

*

The cable car was just closing its doors as Patrick and Lucy squeezed in.

'What did I tell you?' he said as the big cabin swung into the air. 'We're all alone.'

'I know.' Lucy held on to the rail and looked through the grimy window. 'And the piste machines are just starting on the lower slopes. They won't get up here until at least eleven.'

'You'll have snow up to your tits.'

'Do you have to be so vulgar all the time?'

'I just love them, that's all. What's wrong with that?'

'Everything. What about the avalanche risk?' Lucy asked. 'All that snow that fell ...'

'They were blasting early in the morning. I think it'll be fine.'

'As long as we don't go off-piste.'

'But that's exactly what I was planning to do. The best snow will be off-piste today.'

'I'm staying on the piste,' Lucy declared primly, still looking out the window. 'I'm not going to take silly risks.'

Patrick lifted his hands behind her as if to strangle her.

The cable car silently docked at the lift station at the top of the slopes, the doors slid open and Patrick and Lucy scrambled out. Lucy took a deep breath as she looked down. 'This is ...'

'It is,' Patrick grunted. 'You don't have to describe it. I can see for myself.'

'OK. Let's not talk at all.'

'Good idea.'

They put on their skis in silence.

'What was that?' Lucy asked, straightening up after tightening the fastening of her ski boot.

'What?' Patrick asked, looking innocent.

'You pinched my … my …'

'Ass? The very same little ass you're going to be sliding on down this slope?'

'Yes, I mean … no … Oh just leave me alone.' Lucy put her hands through the straps of her ski poles. 'I'm just going to ignore you. Just look at that slope. Perfect.'

They pushed off down the slope together, up to their knees in the new snow that was lighter than down, finer than icing sugar. Lucy forgot all her bad mood and anger, feeling nearly weightless as she flew down the slope, the snow sparkling, the endless blue sky above her. They skied side by side, breathing fast, concentrating on the skiing, the snow and the steep piste. If there is happiness, this must be it, Lucy thought. She could hear Patrick breathing beside her and suddenly realised how perfectly matched they were. Why is he such a bastard sometimes, she thought, why is he so difficult to understand? And he's so ruthless in his work, how can he have any decency left? He's just like all those other fat cats. Al's not like that though. He is a very clever businessman, but such a sweetie. How come he manages to be so … Cats … ? Fat cats … ? 'My God! I've got it!' Lucy screamed.

'What are you screaming about, you silly woman?' he cried.

'Never you mind,' Lucy shouted back. 'Race you to the bottom!'

*

They arrived at the bottom of the piste in a shower of snow, breathing hard, their faces glowing.

'Wow!' Lucy panted, 'Oh God, that was …'

Patrick looked at her sparkling eyes. 'Was it as good for you as it was for me?' he asked. 'Is that why you screamed?'

'Are you kidding? The earth shook. And it lasted, like, forever.' Lucy looked up at the sky and laughed out loud. 'This was the best ever! Wasn't it?'

Patrick stared at her without speaking. Then he took a deep breath. 'You're some woman,' he said. 'Some bloody woman. An irritating, infuriating, exasperating bitch! Sometimes I just want to take both my hands to your neck and strangle you.'

'What?' The sparkle went out of Lucy's eyes and she felt as if he had punched her.

'Yeah, that's what I feel like,' he continued, 'but most of the time I want to throw you on the floor and screw you. It's that mixture of virgin and tart that gets me.'

'I don't know what you mean.'

'Oh yes, you do.' He put his hands on her shoulders. 'God, you're beautiful. I felt like pushing you over the edge up there to get you out of my hair forever. But then I thought you'd find a way to come back and haunt me.'

'You bet I would, you bastard,' Lucy panted, still out of breath both from the race down the piste and his outburst.

He squeezed her shoulders. 'Want to do it again?'

'Can we?'

'Sure. We'll have time before lunch.'

'You're amazing.'

'I know.'

23

'When are they coming out?' Emilie said. 'They've been in the study for hours and hours, and I haven't even said hello properly to my daddy.'

'I know, sweetheart,' Claire soothed, 'but he had a lot of very important business to discuss with Al.'

'I thought he came here to see *me*, not to have a stupid business meeting.'

'I know how you feel,' Penny said, putting her magazine down on the coffee table. 'I've been there, believe me. But business is very important stuff, you know. And I have the feeling today something really serious is going on.'

'Why?' Emilie asked.

'Because,' Penny explained, 'Al didn't take his cigars with him into the study. When he forgets those, then I know he has a big problem to solve.'

'But couldn't Daddy at least have had lunch with me,' Emilie complained. 'He just *rushed* here from the airport and locked himself in the study with Al. Then Dave had to go in there with sandwiches and we had to eat lunch on our own. I think that was *really* rude.'

Claire silently agreed with Emilie. Her reunion with Bernard Marchand was not at all what she had hoped. He had been rushed and preoccupied, bordering on rude. After giving Emilie a quick peck on her cheek and barely a nod in Claire's direction, he had piled them all into a taxi. He had been on his mobile all through the short trip to the chalet, while Emilie clung to him and Claire secretly studied his profile. He looked exactly like she had remembered him, only younger. But his face was pale and his eyes worried. The minute they arrived at the chalet, he had swept Al into the study with an order to get Patrick in to join them as soon as he came back from skiing. Dave had been dispatched to the kitchen to make sandwiches and coffee and, when Lucy and Patrick, on some kind of high from their recent skiing adventure, finally arrived, they were both immediately called in to join the meeting.

'Couldn't we go in there and just say hello?' Emilie suggested. 'Maybe they would like a break?'

'Yeah, maybe we could ask them to come and have tea with us here in the living room,' Claire added. 'It's four o'clock. They're bound to be a bit tired by now.'

'No,' Penny said. 'It will take as long as it takes. I've known Al to keep going all night, and I'm only talking contract negotiations. This seems to be a lot more serious.' Her face was pale as she looked at Claire over Emilie's head.

*

'Does the deal have to include the chalet?' Al asked, studying the papers.

'It's the only unencumbered asset we have at the moment,' Marchand replied. He pushed his fingers through his hair and sighed tiredly. 'Sorry. I'm a little stressed. The meeting with the bank this morning was a bit of a marathon. And things have been going from bad to worse lately. Advertising is really a tough business at the moment. I thought we were doing all right until I got this call from one of our biggest clients saying they had a cash flow problem and couldn't settle their bill just yet. And we had spent a huge amount on that particular campaign. Then the bank told me they might call in our loan and if that happens ... well, you know what comes next.'

'You'd have to cease trading,' Al said.

'That's right.' Marchand took a sip from the now cold coffee in his cup.

'Well, things are just as tough on our side of the Atlantic,' Al said. 'The economic downturn has been responsible for a lot of businesses going down the toilet.'

'But not yours,' Marchand stated. 'I have the latest report from your company right here. I know you can afford to give me a bit of help right now.'

'Yeah, but do I really want to?' Al muttered. 'Do I need this right now?'

'You wouldn't want to see my firm going down. We have been very successful in marketing American products. We work well together. It'll take you years to build up the same kind of partnership.'

'That's true,' Al said. 'How much are you allowing for the chalet? And the share purchase? Not that these are worth anything.'

Marchand pointed at a column of figures. 'It's all there.'

'I'm wondering how I will show the chalet investment in my books,' Al said.

'What chalet?' Marchand raised a quizzical eyebrow. 'It's in my firm's books as the company's Courchevel conference centre. You're sitting in the main conference room right now.'

'I need to consult with my associates,' Al said and moved over to the window, gesturing to Lucy and Patrick to join him.

Marchand nodded and sat back in the sofa, picking up a sandwich from the plate on the coffee table with a studied air of indifference.

'This might take a while,' Al said.

'Take all the time you need,' Marchand nodded.

'Maybe you'd like to go and have a little chat with Emilie while we look at this,' Al suggested.

'No, I would like to settle the matter now.'

Al glanced at Lucy and Patrick and whispered: 'We have him over a barrel.'

Lucy and Patrick were busy studying the documents.

'It looks like a good deal to me,' Patrick said. 'He's obviously coming in with his best offer straight away. And it's nearly a controlling interest in the company.'

'This payment of ten thousand euros in respect of "sundry expenditure" will need some explanation,' Lucy whispered.

'What's that?' Patrick asked, taking the documents from Lucy. 'I'm the lawyer here.' He studied the text for a moment. 'I'll go and check with Marchand.'

Patrick returned a few minutes later after a murmured conversation with Marchand. 'He says it is actually a contribution to the Courchevel drug rehabilitation programme for young people but it doesn't need to be checked by his lawyers when we do a due diligence.'

'What's that?' Lucy asked.

'It means when we establish that the figures in the presentation correspond with the actual situation on the ground,' Al explained.

There was a pause.

Al was the first to break the silence. 'It's a very admirable charitable gesture, don't you think?'

Patrick and Lucy nodded.

'Is this legal?' Lucy asked.

'Reasonably,' Patrick replied.

Al walked back to Marchand. 'We have a deal, Bernard. Let's join the others. Is it too early for champagne?'

*

'Champagne?' Penny asked. 'You must have struck gold.'

'Not exactly,' Al replied, putting one of his cigars into his mouth. 'Let's just say we … eh, reorganised our business arrangements to everybody's satisfaction.'

'So you're all happy, then?' Penny enquired.

'Very,' Patrick nodded, taking two glasses of champagne from the tray Dave had brought in to the living room. He grinned broadly at Lucy and handed her a glass. 'Now we just have the final details to sort out.'

'That's right,' Lucy said, smiling back at Patrick. 'But that won't be a problem as we know where we stand now.'

'I hope you're not all going to disappear into the study again,' Claire said, looking levelly at Bernard Marchand. 'Emilie would like to have at least ten minutes with her father, if that's not too much trouble.' Her voice was sharper than she had intended and everyone looked at her, startled.

'Of course not,' Bernard Marchand said. 'I intend to spend the evening with you and Emilie

399

and read a story at bedtime as well. To Emilie, I mean. I've finished working now.'

'And, if you hadn't?' Claire asked, unable to stop herself. 'Would you then tell her, sorry darling, but I can't talk to you now. I'll make an appointment to see you at the end of the week unless something more important comes up? What are you? A father or some kind of money-making machine? Some kind of cold, unfeeling ...'

'Let's go upstairs to your room, Emilie,' Lucy interjected, taking Emilie by the hand. 'Let's tidy up your dolls and see if we can find that lovely drawing you made for your father the other day.'

'No, I want to stay here,' Emilie said, pulling away from Lucy.

'But I think you should leave Daddy and Claire to have a little chat,' Penny said, looking at Claire and Marchand, who were staring at each other. 'Uncle Al and I are going to watch TV in the small den upstairs. And Patrick is going too.'

'So, darling, let's go.' Lucy took Emilie's hand again.

Claire was still looking at Bernard Marchand when they had left, her eyes blazing. 'I think it's really shocking to see how you put business before your daughter,' she snapped. And have you forgotten about me? a little voice asked deep inside. Have you totally erased everything we said to each other from your mind, including what you told me the very last time we spoke?

'Look,' he protested, 'it was a life or death

situation. But now it has all been arranged. Everybody is delighted. You have to understand …'

'Oh, I understand all right,' Claire replied. 'I saw you in action. Emilie was so excited today she couldn't eat her breakfast. And when we were waiting for your plane to land, she was nearly jumping out of her skin. And then you just … just … gave her a peck on the cheek and immediately got on the phone. You treated her like some kind of tiresome little dog. She was devastated here this afternoon. How could you disappoint her like that?' She stopped and drew breath, her face hot and her chest heaving.

'Well?' Bernard said, his eyes glittering.

'Well, what?'

'Are you finished?'

'For the moment, yes.' As her anger dissipated, she was suddenly aware of how close he was. She could smell his aftershave and wondered idly again what kind he used. She couldn't quite read the expression in his eyes and she looked away, afraid of what she might find there.

'Good,' he said. 'Do you mind if I say something now?'

'Yes,' Claire replied. 'I mean no. I don't mind. Go ahead.' She backed away, trying to regain her composure, to seem more in control and less hysterical. As she looked at him, she tried to figure out what it was about him she found so attractive. It wasn't any one thing, but a combination of a tall, lean frame, thick, curly greying hair, deep brown eyes and that voice. It was also the way he smiled at her, the warmth in his eyes and a kind of physical force. She didn't know quite why, but she knew she could lean on him and that he would never let her down.

'*Bien*,' he said. 'You were right. I have been a little unfair to Emilie, I have to admit. And I admire the way you stood up for her. And, by the way, I have to say she looks so well.'

'Yes, she does. It must be all the fresh air and sunshine.'

'No, it's the way you have been looking after her, I think. Fresh air and sunshine have done her a lot of good, but your love and attention have made her strong again.' Bernard took Claire's hand. 'Do you remember what I said to you the last time we spoke?'

'Eh, yes?' His hand was warm against her cold one.

'When I said that I …'

'Adored me?'

'Yes,' Bernard said. 'I know this might seem as crazy to you as it does to me, I have to admit, but that's how I feel.' He lifted her hand to his lips and kissed it. 'Marry me,' he said.

'What?' Claire gasped.

'Didn't you hear me? I asked you to marry me.'

'I know. I heard you, but …'

'But what? Maybe you don't feel the way I do? Maybe you don't feel attracted to me at all?'

'No, that's not ... I mean, I am,' Claire said. 'Terribly, awfully and horribly attracted to you.'

'So then ...' He put his hands on her shoulders.

'But marriage,' Claire said, pulling away a little. 'Just like that? Why can't we take it a bit slow, live together for a while, find out if ...'

'There's nothing more to find out,' Bernard said. 'I know how I feel about you and living together is not an option, I'm afraid. I have a child to think of as well. But that's not the point. I'm not afraid to make a commitment and marriage is the ultimate one. That's the deal, darling. Marriage or nothing. If you don't feel ready for it, then ...' He looked at her, waiting for her to answer.

Claire found herself completely tongue-tied. She met his eyes, knowing that what she said next would decide the rest of her life, but the words would not come out.

'Before you say anything,' Bernard added, 'I think I should tell you that most of my money is gone.'

Claire laughed suddenly, feeling the tension disappear. 'Shit,' she said, 'that's a real bummer. I had planned to marry a rich Frenchman, not a poor one.'

'Sorry to upset your plans. I hope you will forgive me.'

'Yes,' Claire said, swallowing hard, her heart beating.

'Yes, you will forgive me, or ...'

403

'Yes, I'll marry you.' The words seemed to come from deep in her gut, and she was unable to stop them.

'*Parfait*.' Bernard threw his arms around Claire.

Finally, she thought as they kissed. I knew it would feel like this: as if I've been waiting for him all my life.

*

'Where's Emilie?' Claire asked. 'We need to talk to her.'

'Watching a movie in the den,' Lucy replied, coming down the stairs. 'I put on *Toy Story*. She loves that.'

'Thanks,' Claire said. 'And Lucy …'

'Yes?'

'Thanks for … you know.'

'Oh. Well, I thought the two of you looked as if you might need a little space.' She squeezed Claire's shoulder and smiled at Bernard.

'That was very nice of you,' Claire said.

'It's the champagne,' Lucy replied. 'It seems to have turned me into a warm and caring human being.'

'Have some more,' Claire said.

'You bet.' Lucy smiled and continued down.

'Wait,' Claire said, stopping in the middle of the stairs.

'What, darling?' Bernard said, taking her hand again. 'Don't tell me you're nervous?'

'I am. I'm very nervous. I've never been as nervous in my life.'

He put his arms around her. 'Darling, we have to tell her.'

'But how are we going to explain? You don't know me at all. Emilie knows me better than you do.'

He looked at her, a smile playing on his lips. 'I know enough about you.'

'But there are some things I have to tell you ...'

He put a finger on her lips. 'No. You don't have to tell me anything. There's nothing you could say that would make me change my mind.'

'But you don't know what I ...'

'You're not going to tell me you lied and you're a chain smoker after all?'

Claire shook her head.

'That's all I want to know. The rest ...' He shrugged. 'Everybody has a past.'

'Yes,' Claire replied. 'And talking about a past ... What about yours?'

'Mine?'

'Yeah, yours and that ... that Annabel.'

Bernard smiled quizzically at her. 'Are we going to drag up every relationship we've had before we met?' he said. 'Isn't that a little childish? We're both adults. We've both been involved with other people. Let's leave it at that and only worry about us and our future together. And Emilie, of course.'

'You're right,' Claire mumbled. 'Of course. But Emilie … she's so … so particular about everything. How is she going to take this? She might not want you to get married.'

'Maybe,' Bernard replied. 'But she has to learn I have the right to a life. It might be very difficult for her to accept this. We're going to have to be very gentle and very careful not to make her feel unwanted or forgotten. I have to make sure she knows she is just as important to me as ever.'

'We'll have to be very diplomatic,' Claire agreed, pulling out of his arms. 'And maybe we shouldn't touch or anything for the moment.'

'You're right. We'll have to get her used to the idea very slowly.'

They crept up the stairs, down the corridor and slowly opened the door. Emilie was sitting on the couch completely absorbed by what was happening on the screen. She turned her head as they entered. 'Hello,' she said. 'Have you finished your chat?'

'Yes, my darling,' Bernard said, sitting down on the couch and slipping an arm around her, 'and we have something to tell you.'

'Oh, look,' Emilie interrupted, 'Woody has just ripped his arm. And do you see that robot over there? The space man? That's Buzz Lightyear. He's very strong and he's going to rescue them all …'

'Yes,' Bernard said, 'I know. Never mind that. Listen, sweetheart. Claire and I … we …'

Emilie turned her head and looked sternly at Claire. 'Did you say yes?'

'What?' Claire stammered. 'How did you know? I mean, yes, I did.'

'Good,' Emilie said, 'I was hoping you would.' She turned back to the TV. 'Can I watch the rest of the movie now? There's only a few minutes left and I don't want to miss the end.'

'You don't mind then?' Claire asked, squeezing Bernard's hand nervously. 'About your father and me? I know we haven't known each other for very long and we have only really met once before but ...'

'Shhh,' Emilie said, 'I can't hear what Buzz Lightyear is saying.'

epilogue

'*Chérie*, are you coming to bed?' Bernard stood in the door of the drawing room, where Claire was sitting on the old velvet sofa in front of the fire, surrounded by cards, envelopes and address lists.

'No, darling, not yet. I have to finish the cards tonight. Especially the overseas ones. The last mailing day is tomorrow.'

'Have you done the family cards? I gave you the list yesterday.'

Claire sighed. 'No, not yet. The French ones can wait. Didn't you tell me last year that French people send cards for the New Year, not Christmas?'

'Yes,' Bernard said, 'but most of my family follow the English tradition.'

'Oh, all right, I'll do them all tonight, then,' Claire snapped. 'Your family are the most important to remember, I suppose. We can forget all about mine and all our friends.'

'Don't be silly,' Bernard said. 'You can't forget anyone, or they'll be offended.'

'Your family will never accept me, no matter how many cards I send,' Claire muttered. 'Stuck-up bloody frogs.'

'Sorry?' Bernard said. 'I didn't catch that.'

'Oh, nothing. Just trying to remember an address.'

'And you know we must not forget Gwen's family. But I've already done those.'

'Good.' Claire nodded.

'Well, I'm going to bed now,' Bernard said. 'God knows how much sleep we'll get before Michel wakes up again.'

'I know. But he's teething now, he can't help waking up, poor darling.' Claire still couldn't get used to their baby's name. She had wanted to call him after her father, or one of her brothers, or the president of France, or the postman, anyone except … But it was Bernard's father's name, so Claire had had to give in. She had been tired after the birth and the move to the apartment in the 17th *arondissement*, where you could still find big old apartments at a fairly reasonable price, had not helped.

'Good night, sweetheart,' Claire murmured as Bernard disappeared into their bedroom. She got up and put a CD with Christmas songs into the CD player and returned to her cards. The sound of Bing Crosby singing 'White Christmas' filled the air. Her mind drifted as she picked up the next card. Lucy and Patrick. Lucy had written frequently since that ski holiday nearly two years ago. First, she had sent a card to Emilie to thank her for helping with that cat-food campaign. The initial idea of marketing the cat food as a low-fat alternative to other brands had been Lucy's, then Emilie had suggested the plot for the video and come up with the suggestion of making a tiny treadmill for cats that lived in apartments. It was amazing to think a six-year-old could be so clued-in to marketing. The TV commercial had become a classic, starring some of the best known cat-stars in Hollywood and making huge profits for both the pet food company and Freeman & Schwartz. Al was so pleased he had made Lucy an executive vice-president of the firm.

Claire and Lucy had started sending each other e-mails, chatting online, the topic of discussion being mainly Lucy's love life. Lucy and Patrick had started dating regularly on their return to New York, and even moved in together, but Lucy moved right out again when she discovered Patrick was a Republican. Claire had given up hope of ever seeing them married, then, suddenly she received an e-mail from Lucy.

You'll never believe this, Lucy had written, *but we got married yesterday. Patrick stormed into my office and switched off my computer, making me lose the whole file of a copy line for a marketing campaign on a new brand of sports shoes, and told me that if I didn't agree to marry him straight away, he would drag me away by my hair. As I had just spent three hours at the hairdresser's, I was forced to agree and he drove us out to this Justice of the Peace in Connecticut and, before I had time to even draw breath, we were married. You would have laughed if you had seen us, me in my old blue suit with a pencil still stuck in my hair and Patrick with his hair sticking up and no tie, laughing his head off. He told me he couldn't stand all the rowing and he knew he would rather be miserable with me than without me. So darling, we're an old married couple. I am still Lucy Mulcahy, though, 'Lucy Delacy' just sounds so silly. Funny how I never thought of that ...*

I better send this to the firm, Claire thought, she spends most of her time there anyway. And she hasn't given me the address of Patrick's loft.

Claire closed the envelope and stuck on the stamps. The fire flickered and a spark landed on the worn rug. The door slowly opened and Claire looked up.

'Emilie!' she chided. 'What are you doing up at this hour?'

'I couldn't sleep.' Emilie sat down beside Claire. 'What are you doing?'

'I'm writing the Christmas cards. Do you want to help me?'

'OK.' Emilie picked up the card to Lucy. 'Can I open it again and write a message?'

'Yes, of course. Here's a pen.'

'I'm glad Lucy and Patrick are married now,' Emilie mumbled as she wrote on the card. 'Do you think they might have a baby soon?'

'I don't know. They have a cat though. A lovely Siamese cat Patrick gave Lucy last Christmas.'

'But that is not the same as a baby.'

'It might be to them,' Claire said.

Emilie picked up the next card. 'Who's this one for?'

'Al and Penny.'

'Are they going to be in New York for Christmas?'

'No, I think they're going to Penny's mother.'

'In Florida? Aunt Penny told me she lives in a condom there.'

'A *condo*, darling. That's an apartment in a big complex.'

They were spending Christmas with Penny's mother in Florida and then they would go on what had become their annual holiday, the carnival in Rio. They wouldn't be skiing this year, as the chalet was being redecorated. It had proved to be a great money spinner for Al, as he let it during the high season to people from all sorts of backgrounds, some Irish, the most recent being a group of TDs, led by some solicitor from Co. Offaly. They were no longer allowing the horsey set, as the last group had trashed the place.

'This one's for Tiffany,' Claire said, giving Emilie a new card. 'Would you like to write the message?'

'What should I write?' Emilie asked. 'The last time I wrote to her, she wrote back and said she could tell from my handwriting that I have a lack of confidence and I'm suffering from "the older child syndrome". What does that mean?'

Claire smiled at her stepdaughter. 'Oh, don't worry about that. Tiffany is just practising. She has a long time to go before she's a qualified psychologist. Or therapist, as they say in the States.'

'But I didn't tell her she could practise on me,' Emilie muttered, writing something on the card. 'Merry Christmas and a Happy New Year,' is that OK?'

'That's fine. Nice and friendly.'

'And nothing for her to analyse,' Emilie added. 'But I liked Tiffany. She's very pretty. Does she have a boyfriend?'

'Yes. I think she and Warren, that's the boy she met when we were at the chalet, are still together. He got a job as a session musician on a television station in New York.'

'Next card,' Emilie ordered. 'Who's that for?'

'That's it. I think we're finished. I'll do the French ones tomorrow.'

'Oh. Good.' Emilie yawned.

'You're getting sleepy. Why don't we go to bed now?'

'No, let's sit here for a while and listen to that Christmas record.' Emilie put her head in Claire's lap. 'I love being here by the fire.'

'So do I.'

'I love Christmas,' Emilie mumbled, as the first bars of 'We Wish You a Merry Christmas' could be heard from the CD player. 'I used to hate it, but now I love it again.'

'You hated Christmas?' Claire asked, stroking Emilie's silky hair.

'Mmm. When Mummy died. It was so lonely and Daddy forgot to buy me presents and we had to go to Aunt Madeleine for Christmas dinner and eat that horrible old goose and oysters and the *bûche de Noel* from Monoprix that tasted so yucky. Then we went home and daddy just sat there with his bottle of brandy and stared at the empty fireplace and sent me to bed.' Emilie sighed. 'It was *awful*.'

'Well, last Christmas was not exactly perfect either,' Claire said. 'Remember the raw turkey? And the plum pudding that was frozen in the middle? And the Brussels sprouts that were like bullets?'

Emilie sat up, suddenly wide awake again. 'And Daddy getting cross at you and asking what kind of Christmas dinner was this and you said you never promised him to be a gourmet chef and he said but I thought you might at least have a little bit of a clue how to cook.' She giggled. 'Then you cried and he hugged you and we all laughed and he ordered Christmas dinner from the caterers.'

'This year, he's cooking the dinner,' Claire said. 'He said he isn't much of a cook either but, at least, he would be sure we would all still be alive the next day.'

'And, this year, we have Annabel,' Emilie added. 'I'm so glad she came to live with us, aren't you?'

'I'm not so sure,' Claire muttered, remembering the row.

'You're not still cross about it, are you?' Emilie asked.

'I found it very hard to forgive your father for deceiving me like that.'

'Ah, but Annabel is so lovely,' Emilie soothed. She looked up as the subject of discussion walked softly into the room. 'Hello, Annabel,' she said. 'We were just talking about you.'

Annabel stopped and looked at them with mournful eyes.

'Don't look so sad,' Emilie said. 'It will be Christmas soon and we'll have lots of fun, won't we?'

'Woof,' Annabel said and wagged her tail.

Acknowledgments

Many thanks to my agent, Áine McCarthy of Font International, for her support, encouragement and enthusiasm. To Ita O'Driscoll, also of Font, for all her help. To my editor, Deirdre Nolan, for her subtle and clever editing. Also to Joseph Hoban and all at New Island.

Many thanks also to Carolyn McGrath for her friendship, chats and emails during the past years. To the Irish Girls: fellow writers who have so warmly welcomed this 'new girl on the block', especially Tracy Culleton for her kindness and generosity and Sarah Webb for the hints and tips about publicity. To Kate Thompson and her husband Malcolm for the very useful advice regarding websites.

I would also like to thank Catherine Daly for setting up www.writeon-irishgirls.com, where writers and readers can meet for discussions and chat. Also to the members of same for their enthusiastic support.

I would like to thank my husband Dennis for 'being there', the cups of tea and general TLC, and my family for bringing me so much joy.

And thank you Elaine, Peter and all the rest of the gang at 'Les Founets' for the thrills and spills of some truly wonderful skiing holidays.